Kiss the Sky

Addicted Series

RECOMMENDED READING ORDER

Kiss the Sky

KRISTA RITCHIE
and
BECCA RITCHIE

BERKLEY ROMANCE
NEW YORK

BERKLEY ROMANCE
Published by Berkley
An imprint of Penguin Random House LLC
penguinrandomhouse.com

Copyright © 2014 by K.B. Ritchie
Excerpt from *Hothouse Flower* copyright © 2014 by K.B. Ritchie
"Extended Epilogue," "Bonus Text Message Thread," and "Bonus Chapter"
copyright © 2023 by Krista & Becca Ritchie
Penguin Random House supports copyright. Copyright fuels creativity,
encourages diverse voices, promotes free speech, and creates a vibrant culture.
Thank you for buying an authorized edition of this book and for complying with
copyright laws by not reproducing, scanning, or distributing any part of it in
any form without permission. You are supporting writers and allowing
Penguin Random House to continue to publish books for every reader.

BERKLEY and the BERKLEY and B colophon are registered trademarks of
Penguin Random House LLC.

Library of Congress Cataloging-in-Publication Data

Names: Ritchie, Krista, author. | Ritchie, Becca, author.
Title: Kiss the sky / Krista and Becca Ritchie.
Description: First Berkley Romance edition. |
New York: Berkley Romance, 2023. | Series: Addicted series
Identifiers: LCCN 2022057974 | ISBN 9780593639627 (trade paperback)
Subjects: LCGFT: Romance fiction. | Novels.
Classification: LCC PS3618.I7675 K57 2023 | DDC 813/.6—dc23/eng/20221206
LC record available at https://lccn.loc.gov/2022057974

Kiss the Sky was originally self-published, in different form, in 2014.

First Berkley Romance Edition: May 2023

Printed in the United States of America
1st Printing

Book design by Kristin del Rosario
Interior art: Broken heart on wall © Valentina Shikina / Shutterstock.com

To you, the reader:

When we originally wrote the Addicted series, we were in college with big, lofty dreams and hopes of Lily and Lo's story finding some people. It became so much more than just one romance between childhood friends, thanks to readers who wanted to see more.

It was about sisters, written by two sisters. It was about friendship, and the family you have and also make along the way. Rose's and Daisy's stories—the Calloway Sisters spin-off series—are woven so intrinsically into Lily's novels because we believe that one life does not stop while another goes on a journey. Every novel impacts every character. So the best way to read Lily's story and not miss a thing is by combining her series with the Calloway Sisters series in a ten-book reading order. It's the order we wrote the novels—all three sisters intertwined together.

This is the Addicted series. Ten books. Six friends. Three couples. One epic saga.

We hope these characters bring you as much happiness as they've brought us throughout the years.

As Lily would say, thankyouthankyouthankyou for choosing them and us. Happy reading!

All the love in every universe,
Krista and Becca

Prologue

Connor Cobalt

Y ou wanna know real life, kid?" a man once told me. "You gotta know yourself first." He drank a bottle of booze from a paper bag, sitting on the backdoor steps of a five-star hotel. I'd wandered outside on my tenth birthday, needing air. Everyone in the convention hall was thirty-five and up. Not a single kid my age.

I wore a suit that squeezed my prepubescent frame too tight, and I tried to ignore the fact that just inside, my mother, with a swelling stomach, pattered around her business partners. Even pregnant, she commanded every single person in that room with a reticence and stoicism that I could easily mimic.

"I know who I am," I told him. I was Connor Cobalt. The kid who always did right. The kid who always knew when to shut up and when to speak. I bit my tongue until it bled.

He eyed my suit and snorted. "You're nothin' but a monkey, kid. You wanna be those men in there." He nodded to the door behind him. And then he leaned in close to me, as though to confess a secret, his vodka stench almost knocking me backwards. And yet, I still anticipated his words. "Then you gotta be better than them."

The advice of an old drunkard stayed with me longer than anything my father ever said. Two years later, my mother sat me

2 · KRISTA RITCHIE and BECCA RITCHIE

in our family parlor to deliver news that I would parallel with that memory. That shaped me in some catalytic way.

You see, a life can be broken down to years, months, memories and undulating moments. *Three* moments defined mine.

One.

I was twelve. I spent holidays at Faust Boarding School for Young Boys, but on one fluke of a weekend, I decided to visit my mother's house outside of Philadelphia.

She chose then to tell me. She didn't set a date, plan the event, make it into something larger than she thought it was. She broke the news like she was firing an employee. Swift and construct.

"Your father and I are divorced."

Divorced. As in past tense. Somewhere along the line, I had missed something dramatic in my own life. It had passed right under my fucking nose because my mother believed it meant very little. She made me believe it too.

Their separation was deemed amicable. They had grown apart. Katarina Cobalt had never let me into her life one hundred percent. She let no one see beyond what she gave them. And it was in this moment that I learned that trick. I learned how to be strong and inhuman all at once.

I lost contact with Jim Elson, my father. I had no desire to rekindle a relationship with him. The truths that I kept close were only painful if I let them be, and I convinced myself fairly well that they were just facts. And I moved on.

Two.

I was sixteen. In the dim Faust study room, smoke clouding the air, two upperclassmen appraised a line of ten guys, stopping in front of each pledge.

Joining a secret society was the equivalent of being accepted to a lacrosse team. Dressed in preparatory slacks, blazers and ties, the lot of us were supposed to grace the halls of Harvard and Yale and repeat the same mistakes all over again.

They asked each guy an identical question and each responded with a simple submissive *yes* and was told to drop to their knees. Then they set their sights on the next boy.

When they stopped in front of me, I stayed relatively composed. I tried mostly to hide a burgeoning, conceited smile. They looked like two apes pounding their chests and asking for a banana. The thing about me—I was not so willing to give just anyone my fucking banana. Every benefit should outweigh the cost.

"Connor Cobalt," the blond said, leering. "Will you suck my cock?"

The question was supposed to show how willing we were to follow orders. And I honestly wasn't sure how far they would go, all to prove this point.

What do I get out of it?

The prize would be a membership into a social clique. I believed I could obtain this a different way. I saw a path that no one else did.

"I think you have it backwards," I told him, my smile peeking through. "You should suck my cock. You would enjoy it more."

The pledges broke into laughter, and the blond stepped forward, his nose nearly touching mine. "What did you just say to me?"

"I thought I was perfectly clear the first time." He was giving me the opportunity to bend down again. But if I wanted to be led by a group of testosterone-poisoned monkeys, I would have joined the football team.

"You weren't."

"Then let me reiterate." I leaned forward, confidence seeping through every pore. My lips brushed his ear. He liked that more than he thought he would. "Suck. My. Cock."

He pushed me back, bright red, and my eyebrow arched.

"Problem?" I asked him.

"Are you gay, Cobalt?"

"I only love myself. In that respect, maybe. And yet, I still won't blow you." With this, I left the secret society behind.

Eight of the ten pledges joined me.

Three.

I was nineteen. At the University of Pennsylvania, an Ivy League.

And I sprinted down the student center, slowing to a brisk walk as I reached the girls' bathroom. I pushed open the door, and a brunette girl with four-inch heels and a conservative blue dress stood by the sink, scrubbing a stain with wet paper towels, her eyes bloodshot with anger and anxiety.

When she saw me enter, she directed all of her pent-up frustration at my incoming body. "This is the *girls'* bathroom, Richard." She used my real first name and tried to fling a paper towel at me. But it fluttered to the ground in defeat.

I wasn't the one who'd spilled a can of Cherry Fizz on her dress. But in Rose Calloway's mind, I might as well have been the offender. We crossed paths every year, my boarding school and her prep school competing at Model UN and honor societies.

I was supposed to be her Student Ambassador today—taking her on tour of campus before her interview with the Dean, which would decide whether or not she'd be in the Honor's Program.

"I'm aware," I told her easily, more concerned by her state. She gripped the sink at one point, like she was about to scream.

"I'm going to kill Caroline. I'm going to rip out her hair one strand at a time and then steal all of her clothes."

Her excessive exaggerations always reminded me of a rumor I'd heard around Faust. That during a health class at Dalton Academy, her prep school, she took her baby doll and stabbed the stuffing with a pair of scissors. Another person said she scribbled over the baby's forehead and handed it to the teacher. The note: *I won't care for an inanimate object unless the boys do it too.*

People thought she was nuts—in a genius *I will devour your soul* kind of way.

I thought she was fucking fascinating.

"Rose—"

She slammed her palms on the counter. "She spilled *soda* on me. I'd rather she punched me in the face. At least I have makeup."

"I have a solution."

She raised a hand to me. "This is an ego-free bathroom."

"Then what the fuck are you doing here?" I asked her with the tilt of my head.

She glared, and I neared her anyway, about to help. She shoved my chest in anger.

I hardly even moved. "That was a little infantile, even for you."

"It's sabotage," she said with blazing eyes, pointing a finger at me. "Academic *gluttony*. I hate cheaters, and she's cheated me out of Penn."

"You've already been accepted," I reminded her.

"Would you go to a college without being admitted to the Honor's Program?"

I said nothing. She knew my answer.

"Exactly."

I tossed the sodden towels in the nearby trash, and my actions started loosening her shoulders as she watched me closely. Then I began to shrug off my red blazer.

"What are you doing?" she asked.

"This is what help looks like."

She shook her head. "I don't want to be indebted to you." She pointed another finger at me and stepped back. "I know how you work. I *get* it. You do things for students and they have to pay you back in some sick way." Opportunity cost. Benefits. Deals. They were the foundation of my life.

"I'm not prostituting people." I held out my blazer. "There's not a string attached to this. I'm not expecting anything in return. Take it."

She just kept shaking her head at me.

My hand fell. "What?"

"Why do you act like that around Caroline?" she suddenly asked.

I read into her question. I heard: *Why do you like her?* Caroline was a typical WASP girl. She always looked at me with predatory gaze, silently asking: *What use will you be to me? Will I marry you some day and take all your fucking money?*

But Rose Calloway was different. She was fashionable. But not a sorority girl. She was a genius on paper. But not a team player. She was quick to loathe others. But not against loving.

She was a complicated equation that didn't need to be solved.

I didn't even have time to respond. That's how fast Rose moved in her state of irritation. She set her hands on her hips and mimicked me from earlier that day. "*You ride well, Caroline. I saw you at the equestrian event last week. How's your mother?*"

"I was being kind."

"You're different around certain people," she told me. "I've known you long enough from academic conferences to see it. You act one way with them and another with me. How do I know who the real Connor Cobalt is?"

You never will. "I'm as real with you as I can be."

"That's complete *bullshit*," she cursed.

"I can't be you," I told her. "You leave a trail of bodies with your glares. People are afraid to approach you, Rose. That's a problem."

"At least I know who I am."

We had somehow drawn towards each other. I towered over her, taller than most men and built like an athlete. I never hunched. Never recoiled. I wore my height with pride.

She raised her chin to combat me. I pushed her to be the best that she could be.

"I know exactly who I am," I said with every ounce of confidence I possessed. "What unsettles you, Rose, is that you have no idea what kind of guy that is." I stepped closer and she stiffened. "If people stare at me and see my problems, then I'm useless to them. So I give them exactly what they want. I am whomever or whatever they need." I held out my blazer again. "And you need a fucking jacket."

She reluctantly took the blazer but hesitated. "I can't be you," she said. "I can't internalize all of my feelings. I don't understand how you can do that."

"Practice."

Our eyes met for an extended moment. There was so much between us that I wasn't ready to uncover right then. I wasn't prepared for the deep conversations that she would force me to have.

Rose Calloway couldn't stand me because of what I was—a guy who wanted to reach the top. The irony was that she wanted the same thing. She just wasn't willing to do what I was to get there.

She slipped on my blazer, which dwarfed her frame. "What part of you do you show me?" she asked.

"The best part."

She rolled her eyes. "If you have nothing real to say, Richard, then why speak at all?"

I couldn't form the words to reply with what she wanted. I'd spent years building barriers and defenses. I could take care of a woman better than any other guy could. But my mother never taught me how to love. She taught me about stocks and history and different languages. She made me intelligent.

She made me logical and factual.

I knew sex. I knew affection. But love? That was an illogical concept, something as fictional as the Bible, Katarina Cobalt would say. When I was a child, I thought love belonged in fantasy with witches and monsters. It couldn't exist in real life, and if it did, it was just like religion—only there to make people feel good.

Love.

That was fake to me.

And I nearly rolled my eyes. *There you go, Connor. That's something fucking real. That's something from the heart.*

"Rose," I began. And she turned to look at me. And her gaze was like the depths of hell. Ice cold. Bitter. Tumultuous and pained. I wanted to bear it all. But I couldn't show her all the cards I held to do so. I couldn't let her in. I'd lose the game first. And it had only just begun. "You're going to do great."

And that was it.

She was gone.

Through a friend of a friend, I learned that Rose Calloway was accepted to the Honor's Program. I learned that she denied the request to attend Penn. For whatever reason, she chose Princeton, our rival college.

Six months later, I started to date Caroline Haverford. Not long after that, she became my girlfriend.

It was a life that I saw coming.

It was one that I was prepared for.

There was nothing spontaneous or alluring about it.

At nineteen, everything was just practical.

Five Years Later

One

Rose Calloway

You know the stories where the strong, brawny man struts into a room with his head high, his chest puffed and his stocky shoulders pulled back—he's the king of the jungle, the big man on campus, the one who quivers girls' knees. He carries an air of unwarranted superiority for the pure fact that he has a dick, and he knows it. He expects the girl to go tongue-tied and agree to his every demand.

Well, I am living that story right now.

The man settles into a seat at the head of the conference table (instead of the chair nearest me) and just stares in my direction.

Maybe he thinks I'm going to be that stupefied girl. That I will cower beneath his deep gray eyes and his combed dishwater-blond hair. He's twenty-eight, stained with Hollywood elitism and self-righteousness. When I first talked to him, he name-dropped actors and producers and directors, waiting for me to go slack-jawed and dopey. "I know so-and-so. I did a project with what's-his-face."

My boyfriend had to grab the phone out of my hand before I cursed at the Hollywood exec for irritating the shit out of me.

He finally speaks. "Do you have the contracts?" His chair screeches as he leans back.

I pull out the stack of papers from my handbag.

"Bring them here." He motions to me with two fingers.

"You could have sat beside me," I retort, standing on two

chunky heels with brass buttons, military-inspired and part of the new Calloway Couture collection.

"But I didn't," he says easily. "Come here."

My heels clink across the hardwood, and I make the perilous catwalk up to Scott Van Wright.

He props one ankle on his thigh, his finger to his cheek as he unabashedly peruses my body. From my slender legs to the hem of my black pleated dress with sheer quarter-sleeves and to the high collar that frames my stiff neck. He traces my dark-glossed lips, my rose-blushed cheeks, and bypasses right over my pissed-off eyes, spending an extra moment fixated on my chest.

I stop by his legs and throw the contracts on the table in front of him. They slide off the polished surface and land on his lap. One stapled stack even slips to the floor. I smile wide since he has to bend down awkwardly to reach them.

"Pick that up," he tells me.

My smile fades. "It's underneath the desk."

He cocks his head, giving me *another* long once-over. "And *you* dropped it."

He cannot be serious. I cross my arms, not responding to his request. He just sits there, waiting for me to comply.

This is a test.

I'm used to them. Sometimes I even dole them out myself, but this one is going to lead me nowhere good.

If I bend down, he'll establish this strange power over me. He'll be able to command me in the same way that Connor Cobalt can force people to do his bidding with simple words.

It's a manipulator's gift.

I'm not even close to possessing it. I think I wear my emotions too much to have that type of influence over other people.

"Grab it," he says, his gaze halting on my breasts again.

I remind myself why I need Scott and why I want the swarm of cameras to document my every move. I inhale. Okay. *You have to do it, Rose. Whatever it takes.* I cringe and drop to my knees. In a dress. This is a job for a personal assistant, not a client.

I hear him click his pen as I scoop up the papers. I'm not wearing a low-cut top where I'll flash him. I don't have huge breasts to really ogle either. The most he can do is slap my ass and try to peek up my dress, the hem perilously rising on my thighs.

When I stand back up and smack the papers to the table, his lips curve upward.

Scott Van Wright (asshole) 1–Rose Calloway (pathetic) 0.

I sit in the nearest chair while Scott stuffs the contracts in his briefcase.

My boyfriend urged me to bring his lawyer to the meeting, but I didn't want Scott to think that I couldn't handle the situation myself. I won't have a lawyer while the cameras follow me, and I'd rather take command now.

Not that I'm doing a terrific job.

If I ordered Scott to do anything, he'd laugh at me. But I attended a few law courses before I graduated from Princeton. I know my rights.

"Just so we have this clear, you work for me," I remind him. "I hired you to produce the show."

"That's cute. But after you signed that contract, you've officially become *my* employee. You're the equivalent of an actress, Rose."

No. "I can fire you. You can't fire me. That doesn't make me your employee, Scott. That makes me your boss."

I expect him to withdraw from this losing battle, but he shakes his head like I'm wrong. I know I'm right . . . Right? "My production company has sole ownership over *anything* the Calloway sisters film on network television. If you fire me, you need just cause and you can't jump to another producer. I'm your only shot at having a reality show, Rose."

I remember that clause, but I never thought it would be an

issue. I figured I'd be around Scott maybe twice during the whole filming process. But these were his first words when he walked into the conference room: "We're going to be seeing a lot of each other." Lovely.

My eyes grow hot. I have to concede on this one. He won. Somehow. I hate it.

"So, now that we have that clear," he says, sitting up and edging closer to me. His knees almost knock into mine. I go utterly rigid. "There are a few details we need to go over in case you misread them in the contract."

"I don't misread things."

"Well *evidently* you weren't using a portion of your brain or else you would have realized that you work for me now. And we wouldn't have wasted . . ." He checks his watch. ". . . five minutes of my time." He flashes me a sardonic smile like I'm a little girl.

"I'm not an idiot," I retort. "I graduated at the top of my class with highest honors—"

"I don't care about your fucking degree," he says sharply. "You're in the real world now, Rose Calloway. No university is going to teach you how to navigate this industry."

Doubt surfaces. I don't know much about reality television, but I've been immersed in the media long enough to know it can help someone as much as it can destroy them.

And I need that help.

I understand exactly why the network would take an interest in the daughters of Fizzle. My father's brand has beat Pepsi for the past two years in sales, and he's working to make Fizzle the soda of choice among southern states. We should be as anonymous as the face behind Coca-Cola, but ever since my family was thrust into the public eye, we've been under intense scrutiny, and it's all because of my younger sister's scandal.

My brand should have exploded from all the media and press, but the name Calloway Couture has been linked with Lily's dirty secrets. And what once was a thriving fashion line in H&M has been destitute in boxes and boxes, piled in my New York office.

I need *good* exposure, the kind that will have women desiring a one-of-a-kind coat, a unique pair of boots, an affordable but chic handbag. And Scott Van Wright is offering me a primetime reality show that will tempt viewers to purchase my pieces.

So that's why I'm agreeing to this.

I want to save my dream.

Scott says, "There will be cameras in your living room and kitchen at all times, even after the three-person crew leaves. You'll only have privacy in your bedrooms and bathrooms."

"I remember this."

"Good." Scott clicks his pen. "Then maybe you'll remember that each week, I expect to have interviews with the cast, which includes you, your three sisters—"

"Not three," I say. "Only Lily and Daisy agreed to the show." My eldest sister, Poppy, wouldn't sign the contract because she didn't want her daughter to be filmed. My little niece has already endured enough paparazzi since Lily's scandal.

"Fine, she would have been a boring addition anyway."

I glower.

"I'm just being honest."

"I'm used to blunt honesty," I tell him. "I just find yours crass."

He eyes me in a new way, as though my words carried a plume of toxic pheromones. I don't understand. I am so mean. I am *glaring* like I want to rip off his penis, and yet, he's *attracted*. There is something seriously wrong with him.

And maybe my boyfriend.

And really, any guy who'd like to be with me. I'm not even sure *I* want to be with me.

"As I was saying . . ." His knee brushes mine.

I roll backwards, and he only grins more. This is not a cat-and-mouse game like he believes. I am not a mouse. And he's not a cat.

Or vice versa. I am the fucking shark, and he's a lame human in my ocean.

And my boyfriend, he's the same species as me.

"Continue," I snap.

"I'll be interviewing you, your two sisters, Lily's boyfriend and his brother." *6 people + 6 months + 3 cameramen + 1 reality show = infinite drama.* I've done the math.

Scott will be conducting the interviews though . . . I internally gag. "You're forgetting my boyfriend," I say. "He's a part of the show too."

"Oh right."

"Don't act like you forgot, Scott. You just said you were practicing honesty, and now, well, you're a bit of a liar."

He ignores my slight. "Every episode will be aired one week after we've filmed. The premiere will be in February, but we're filming ASAP. Like I mentioned over the phone, we're trying to make this show as real-time as possible. It's been six months since it was publicized that your sister is a sex addict. We need to capitalize off that buzz as quickly as we can."

"You and every other person with a camera," I say. There's always at least two chubby males stationed outside my gated house with lenses pointed at us. Lily jokes that they're probably hanging around waiting for her to give them blow jobs. I would be more amused if I didn't see the mail that perverts send her, most accompanied with pictures of their hairy genitals—it's a sick fan club. I sift through her letters before I hand them to her now.

"And lastly," Scott says, "you have no control over how you're edited. That's my call."

I have about as much power over the reality show as I do paparazzi's snap-quick photos.

I can try to act like a non-bitchy, non-argumentative angel on film, and Lily can try to be a virginal saint. But at the end of the day, the cameras will catch *us*. Flaws and all. And there's no forcing something different. That was the stipulation that all my friends and sisters agreed to.

To do the show, we're not pretending to be someone else.

And I would never ask that of them.

We're rolling the dice on this one. People may hate us. They already call Lily a whore on gossip blogs. But in the small chance that people grow to love us—my company may be saved. I just need good publicity so that a retailer has a reason to stock my clothing line again.

And maybe Fizzle won't be so bruised by Lily's impropriety too. Maybe my father's soda company will rise in stocks rather than fall.

That's the hope.

"Are you okay with this?" Scott questions.

"I don't know why you ask. I signed the contract. I have to be okay with it or else you'll take me to court."

He lets out a short laugh and scans my body for the third time. "I can't imagine your boyfriend knows what to do with you."

"Because you've never met him."

"I've spoken to him. He sounds malleable." He taps his pen. "If I told him to drop on his knees and suck my cock, I think he would."

My nostrils flare. I am fuming. "You think that." I stand. "And when he stabs you in the fucking front, I'll be the one smiling by his side."

Scott *grins* at this. "Challenge accepted."

Stupid intellectual pricks.

Funny thing is, I'm dating one.

So while I'm stuck in this moronic cock fight, I know I'm partially to blame.

I knew I should have lowered my standards—dated a guy who rides around on his skateboard with his shirt inside out. I grimace. Just kidding. I'll take my suit-and-tie boyfriend. I'll take the high

IQ and the rapid-fire banter. I just hope Scott's eagerness to unsettle him won't disrupt the reality show.

But if I know anything, it's this:

My boyfriend loves winning.

And he hates to lose even more.

Two

Rose Calloway

I juggle a box of old invoices and a bag of salads and chicken primavera that's hooked on my arm, searching for my keys in my clutch. My phone occupies one palm, and I struggle to maintain perfect balance on my wraparound porch, teetering in a pair of four-inch booties.

I live in a college town: Princeton, New Jersey. And my gated colonial house has acres of sprawling green lands, black shutters and winter flowers. But right now, I can't take pleasure in the serene atmosphere.

A lens gleams to my left, filming. The camera guy is roughly around my age, wiry and lanky. In two days, Ben has talked as much as his other two cohorts, which is not much at all. They just shoot.

His sole presence distracts my juggling act.

And red sauce leaks from the white plastic bag, missing my pea coat and dribbling on my romper. I flail in distress, trying to maintain a morsel of grace, but my box of invoices starts to tilt off me.

And then, all of a sudden, the cardboard is plucked right from my arms, and I am left in an awkward, hunched-over position, avoiding the trickling plastic bag like it's the source of the bubonic plague.

I glance over my shoulder and meet Connor's eyes. And I trace his features quickly: his thick, wavy brown hair, his fair skin and pink lips, striking blue eyes and a conceited smile that somehow never gets him in trouble. He wears confidence like his most expensive suit, with style and dignity and so much charm. I immediately want to combat him, to match him smile for smile, grin for grin, word for word. But right now, that conceited look does not lessen my misery.

Although, I am overly grateful that my invoices weren't scattered along the porch. My profit margin is embarrassing, and I'd rather Connor not catch a glimpse of the numbers.

"Are you auditioning to play Quasimodo?" he quips.

I flash a dry smile. "Very funny."

"Give that here." He gestures with his fingers to pass the food.

"I have it," I say. "The damage is already done." My romper will need to soak in spot-remover for an hour.

Still, he leans over and unlocks the door with his key. I don't know why this rouses me. Maybe the fact that he has a key at all. That he lives with me. I still can't believe our relationship has moved to *that* level. Especially since I have yet to fully comprehend Connor Cobalt, and we've been dating for over a year.

He's the hardest person to understand because he makes it so.

But I would never admit that to Scott Van Wright.

I should be glad that my boyfriend has saved the day by grabbing my things, but the fact that *I* ruined it makes me feel unraveled, as though my hair is frizzy, my lipstick smudged, my dress crooked—oh, well it is stained, so there's that. And my mouth flies open before I can shut it. "You're good at that."

His brow arches, seeing exactly where I'm going. "Of sticking my key into a hole." His hand drifts to the crook of my hip.

"I said nothing about your keyhole," I retort.

"No, I believe you were about to comment on *your* keyhole and my key."

"If you're trying to frazzle me with sexual idioms, it's not going to work."

"I didn't think it would, seeing as how you were the one about to mention keyholes in the first place." It's as though he can read my *mind*. We think alike on too many occasions. "You've been spending too much time around your sister," he adds, smiling as he says it.

I suppose he's right. Lily would have been quick to make that assessment. Keys. Holes. Sex. That's where her mind travels. I would like to say mine doesn't go there on occasion, but I'm only human.

My eyes flicker to the camera, and Ben shakes his head like *you can't look into the lens*. But I'm not embarrassed by our talk. I'm just trying to get used to the third-party presence that lingers like an awkward chaperone on a date.

"The door's open," Connor tells me.

So it is. I pass him my clutch and my phone. Then I sacrifice my hands and dam the hole in the bag, the sauce collecting in a pool but thankfully not streaking a red trail along the hardwood.

I head into the kitchen of my house and spot the second camera guy—Brett, short and stubby and a little plump, the exact opposite of Ben. His eyes grow big as he shoots, a steadicam attached to his chest like Ben.

It takes two point two seconds for me to find the source of his wide-eyed expression. Loren has cornered my sister into a cabinet, his entire body pressed against her so tightly that air can't pass through. They kiss deeply and passionately, as if no one else lives in the same universe as them.

His hands disappear underneath her blouse, but it's quite obvious he's groping her breasts. And then one hand emerges. *Thank God.*

He hikes her leg around his waist. *Or not.*

Lily lets out a sharp gasp, her fingers gripping his brown hair that's thick on top and shorter on the sides. She's tinier than me, and she has lighter hair than I do. I have the bigger ass, the bigger boobs and the fuller hips. She's thin in ways that I'm not.

Connor clears his throat, and Lily detaches from Loren (or Lo, depending on my mood. I usually swap between the two. He prefers the nickname over his full name, but I don't really care).

Lily's whole face reddens.

"Did we disturb you?" Connor asks casually, setting my things on the bar.

Lo wipes his mouth, eyebrows raised. "Actually, yes."

"Don't be crude, Loren," I refute as I set the bag in the sink. Lily tries to hide behind her hands. Connor and I are more comfortable in situations like these.

"Crude?" Loren says with a short laugh. "Last week you told me if you ever saw me with an erection, you'd slam my boner in a doorjamb."

Connor nods to Lo. "In Rose's defense, no one but Lily really wants to see your erection."

"That's not what you said last night," he banters.

Connor's lips rise. "Shh, that's between us, *love*."

I shoot him a look. "You're asking to sleep on the floor tonight." Their friendship, while amusing, is coming at my expense.

Connor eases close to me, and he tilts his head down to whisper in my ear, his eyes full of power. "If you think it's best, I'll convince you to let me back in your bed later."

His voice is deep and sexual, and something that shallows my breath for an instant. I'm about to reply, but Lo tickles Lily's hips and she squeals. They distract me, breaking whatever brief moment was occurring with Connor.

Loren is a recovering alcoholic. Lily is working on her sex addiction. They're at a good stasis, but they can't live alone since isolation is what amplified their addictions in the first place. So they're here. With us.

And it's about as awkward as it seems.

With the cameras around I thought they might be more discreet, but the opposite has happened. Loren has taken PDA to a whole new level.

Some tabloids believe Loren and Lily are only engaged to repair my sister's tarnished image as a sex addict, so Loren sticks his tongue down her throat (on camera), to give the world the middle finger for doubting their love. He really doesn't care what the public thinks at this point.

But I do.

It's why I have the cameras around in the first place.

Before Lily escapes Loren's hold completely, he draws her back to his chest and playfully bites her shoulder. She fidgets with a goofy smile and slaps him on the bicep. His bites turn into kisses.

And both cameras spin off me and zoom in on them.

I don't mind at all. Lily is wearing a signature Calloway Couture piece that viewers at home may like—a plum lacy skirt with a champagne blouse (untucked thanks to Lo's fondling). She's usually in leggings and Loren's baggy shirts without a bra, so she looks slightly uncomfortable in the outfit, but I know she's trying hard to make things right.

I tap on the faucet with my wrist, and Loren tears his gaze from Lily to see the red sauce that washes off my palms.

"Whose heart did you rip out this time?"

Scott Van Wright's. I wish. "Connor's," I say, "but he stopped me before I got that far."

Connor grins. "She has quick hands, but I'm faster."

My eyes narrow. Oh, he wishes.

"When is the psychic coming?" Lily perks up, combing her fingers anxiously through her hair, and she shifts as if her body doesn't fit her quite right. From behind her, Loren tangles his arms around her waist and rests his chin on her shoulder. She immediately relaxes into him.

His presence is a kind of reassurance that brightens her whole being. If she didn't have Loren, I imagine she'd be on street corners, sleeping with random guys to satisfy her sexual compulsions. I'm more grateful that he's here, helping her, than I'll ever let on.

"She should be arriving soon." I use extra hand soap and scrub beneath my nails.

Connor leans against the counter beside me. "A psychic at a dinner party," he says. "Next thing you know, we're going to be pouring salt around the doors and creating spirit circles."

"It's two hours," I remind him, "and you don't have to believe in it to enjoy a reading."

He watches me so intently that my heart starts to pound. My eyes skim his lips and rise back to his intense gaze. "No," he says after a long moment, "I just have to listen to some crock stir up shit between us."

I squirt more soap in my palm. "That won't be happening."

"I can tell the future better than whoever walks through that door—and I bet you a thousand dollars that she's going to make someone cry tonight."

"Fine," I say. "If you want to lose a thousand dollars, then I'll take your bet." Who would cry? Not any of the guys. Not me. That leaves Lily and Daisy, and I do not see my youngest sister shedding a tear. And Lily—she's a wild card. But I would bet on her strength.

"No way," Loren cuts in. He has Lily swaddled in his arms. "That's not a good bet. You need real stakes."

"That's a lot of money," Connor tells him.

"For who?" Loren asks. "You're the heir of a multibillion-dollar company, as is Rose. All of our parents shit gold bricks."

"That's disgusting," I say flatly.

"A lap dance," Loren suddenly says. "If Rose loses, she should give Connor a five-minute lap dance."

My chest constricts, and I glare so hard at Loren that my eyes feel like they're being serrated.

"You don't have to do that," Connor tells me. He studies the way I lock a breath in my lungs.

I am not my sister.

When it comes to intimacy, I am a chicken. I'll fully admit that. I'm more likely to run out of a pair of arms than into them.

And Loren is aware of my hesitance. A part of me wonders if he feels bad for Connor, knowing that I'm not putting out after such a long time together. But maybe Loren's just trying to provoke a reaction out of me.

Which everyone is about to see.

"You don't think I would do it?" I ask Connor. I'm not sure I could grind on Connor. In public. Without being humiliated. I am confident in all areas except these: being sexy, being skilled in bed, being *great* at sex. I believe, wholeheartedly, that sex is not something you can study to ace. No, you have to learn by experience.

And I have none.

So I have a feeling that once I do have sex with Connor, our relationship will be different. Any attraction that pulls between us will be cut with my sloppy moves and my inability to please him.

So far he has never pressured me to have sex, but I wait for the moment when he walks out—when he's had enough of my high-octane personality and my obsessive compulsive behavior.

Hell, I want to walk away from me sometimes. My therapist even hates me. She's prescribed me Alprazolam, Paroxetine, Fluvoxamine and Clomipramine, drugs that I have taken and then disposed of. On them, I feel so high I could be floating through life or I'm so heavy I could be sinking into mortal hell.

I am not the girl you want to sleep with every week. I'm the chase. The one you catch and then release. And once Connor has sex with me, he'll be done. He'll have won the hardest challenge of his life—de-virginizing the biggest virgin.

I know this. It's how all men work with me.

And I never, ever let them win.

But Connor is getting close.

He watches me scrub my skin harder, my whole body tense and unmoving except for the bristle brush in between my fingers.

"Don't answer her," Loren warns him. "It's a trick."

Connor doesn't move his gaze off mine. "I can handle her, Lo." *Yes, he may be the only one.* He edges close and shuts off the faucet.

I turn it back on. "I'm not finished." There's a thin layer of sauce underneath my nails still.

"We both know you won't give me a lap dance. So let's stick to the thousand-dollar bet." His voice is unreadable. If there's disappointment, he won't ever let me hear it.

I feel defeated in some huge way. "I can do it," I retort.

"I'm not trying to use reverse psychology on you, Rose. I really don't think you should." He shuts the faucet off again, and when I go to turn it back on, he slips in front of me, blocking the sink, and he wraps a towel around my hands.

"They're clean," he says.

I glance down at my romper, which is still stained. "I need to change."

Loren cuts in. "So have we established whether or not we'll be seeing a lap dance tonight?"

"Only if I lose," I say.

Connor's jaw muscles twitch, the single sign that I can read. He really doesn't want me to do this, but I don't like the way he's staring at me. Like I'm a scared little bird.

I'm not frightened. Yet. "And if you lose," I say, "what do I get in return?"

Connor gazes at my mouth just as I did him. He brushes his thumb over my bottom lip and says, "What do you want, darling?"

My heart pounds. I want to be great in bed. I want to please him better than he pleases me. I want to beat him.

But I know when it comes to sex, I'm never going to win. I'm at such a disadvantage. So I say, "If you lose, I don't have to give you a lap dance."

"Boo," Lily says.

Loren nods. "Boring."

But the only one who matters says, "Deal." Connor ignores my sister and her boyfriend. He finishes drying my hands. I just now notice how raw and red my skin is. I sometimes get carried away without realizing . . .

"Whose idea was it to hire a fortune teller anyway?" Loren asks.

"Production planned it," I remind him.

Both Brett and Ben give me wild looks at mentioning *production*. We're not live. This isn't *Big Brother*.

"Oh please," I say right at the camera. "Scott, if you're hearing this, *delete* this portion." I glare at Ben. "There you go. He won't spank you for your misbehavior."

And like good cameramen, they stay mute.

Loren watches short, stubby Brett for a long moment. He finally catches his attention. And then he runs his tongue along the nape of Lily's neck, eyes pinned to the camera as if he's seducing the onlookers. Lily practically melts beneath him, her breath hitching into an audible moan. Loren grins wickedly, especially as Brett stumbles back in shock.

And then he sticks his tongue into Lily's ear.

They are toying with the cameramen.

And it's only day two.

Three

Connor Cobalt

A lot has changed since I was nineteen. And then again, things are always the same. I have the girl, but not entirely. If it were that easy—that boring—I wouldn't still be here. Add Scott Van Wright into our lives, a threat on some serious level, and keeping Rose is going to be problematic.

But I'm going to put up one hell of a fucking fight.

He even rescheduled the "magical" party with the psychic, citing some bullshit about time, but really he wants to increase the production value of the entire reality show—I just haven't figured out what he's going to do in order to achieve that.

I rinse shampoo out of my wavy brown hair, the water blanketing me in warmth. I've never lived with a girl. Never shared a space with someone else, not even at my boarding school.

What's mine has always been mine.

Expensive perfumed soaps line the shower ledge. I share the bathroom with Rose. I share the bedroom. We've been at each other's throats for so many years that becoming a team isn't exactly set in the future for us.

We're still very much rivals in bed.

I crank the heat, the steam gathering and beading my chest with water. I lower my hand, picturing Rose as I've never seen her. Undressed. Bare. Wanting. She won't let me in that far.

Not yet.

I place my hands on her bent knees, spreading her open quick and hard. She chokes on a gasp, a pleasured scream locked tight in her chest.

"Please . . ." she cries.

In the shower, I stroke my cock, which tenses with each rhythmic movement, hardening at the flashes of my fantasy. Her body bucking. The fullness of her breasts and hips underneath my strength. She attacks me with the same intensity, but I push her roughly back on the mattress. And her face lights with fire.

I dominate her and give her everything I know she'll adore.

That's the thing about being fucking smart—I understand her better than she understands herself.

My muscles pull tight, and I rub up and down my shaft, an involuntary sound escaping my mouth. I rest a hand on the tiled wall, quickening my movements. *Fuck yes.*

And just as I'm about to come, the bathroom door flies open.

I see her feminine shape through the misted glass, and she can see my form just as easily. A grin overtakes my features, and I watch her turn towards the shower with her hands on her hips. I can practically feel her hot, unbridled anger steaming off her body.

Come to me.

She storms over to the shower and flings open the glass door.

I don't stop.

She stands there, eyes ablaze at the mere idea of me coming in *our* shower. But she stays quiet, not lowering her gaze to catch a glimpse of my erection or opening her mouth to chastise me. She has frozen in silent curiosity, and I gladly take advantage of it.

I watch her, skimming the nape of her neck that peeks from her black silk robe. Her chest rises and falls in deep, physical attraction. But she's too unsure of herself to do something about it. So she stays rooted to the bathroom rug, not even willing to look at my hand that moves with skilled efficiency. She doesn't want to give me that satisfaction or that win.

I grip my cock tighter, a low groan in my throat.

She inhales sharply.

I only grin more. Even though she's confident, brazen and haughty, she's none of these things when it comes to *this*. Sex. Fucking. Affection.

I may be patient, but I'm no longer going easy on her anymore, not with Scott Van Wright in contention. Before I moved in with Rose, I would have placated her. I would have stopped masturbating as soon as she opened the door.

Now, I'm not going to be so nice.

My eyes descend to the curve of her hips, visible with the silk that hugs her waist. I roam her body with my intense gaze, and her legs shift, her knees bending.

I affect her as much as she does me.

I rub faster, and then my body shudders as I release.

She stiffly steps back from the shower before I can meet her eyes, and she plugs in her curling iron at the sink.

I control my breathing, keeping my weight supported with my left hand on the wall. And I let my thoughts realign from hormonal places to more logical ones. I have been with Rose for an entire year, and I've been jacking off for most of it.

Waiting for her—that's not the hard part. Knowing what's best for her but watching her deny it out of stubbornness—that is.

I open the shower door. She caps her toothpaste and places it meticulously back in the organized cabinet. Her body is tense and lit up, and she'll most likely please herself later to alleviate the pulsing between her legs.

She glances at me once, and her eyes immediately flit away. "We have towels, Richard." She points a manicured nail to the rack. "Terrycloth. Soft. Inviting. You might want to try one out."

The corners of my lips rise. "It's just a cock, Rose," I say. "You'd enjoy it inside of you."

She rolls her eyes dramatically, but her neck flushes.

I understand that she's afraid to lose her power. We're equals on many accounts, but when it comes to sex, I am like a god to her mortal standing. And it's driving her crazy. Not that she's ever been completely sane.

I casually walk towards her. "So you've learned politics, philosophy, French, business and fashion at Princeton, but clearly you were a little slow in your dormitory studies. Penn would have served you better."

She glares. "Why? Because your college was filled with juvenile horndogs?"

I ease behind her, and she stares at me questioningly through the mirror. Approaching Rose Calloway is like nearing a sleeping tiger. Every single time there's a chance she'll bite me. "No," I whisper, pulling the collar of her robe to expose more of her neck. "Because I was there." I press my lips lightly to her nape.

And her whole body trembles. Just as my hands fall to the slip of her robe, she spins towards me and places her hands on my chest. Normally I'd back up, but I stand my ground. Right here. Not moving to her demands.

I raise my palms and then clasp my hands behind my back, showing that I won't touch her anymore. But if she wants to curl her hair, she's going to have to do it with me—naked—behind her.

"Back up," she says.

"If I really thought you wanted me to, I would."

"I do." But curiosity glimmers in her yellow-green eyes, and she peers down at my cock for the first time.

She remains stoic, almost unreadable, but the corner of her lip betrays her, rising in a fraction of a smile. When she meets my gaze again, I tilt my head, grinning in satisfaction, the kind that only incites her.

She holds up a warning finger at me. "Don't you dare say *do you like what you see?* I will break up with you right here if you utter those fucking stupid words."

I laugh into a wider grin and say, "I don't have to ask you, Rose. I already know you do."

She pushes me lightly in the chest and tries not to share my smile. "Why am I with you? You're so conceited, arrogant—"

"Narcissistic," I add, "attractive, lovable, brilliant."

"That wasn't an invitation for you to compliment yourself."

"No? My bad, I thought we were listing my best qualities."

Her eyes fall again.

"Yes, my cock is most definitely one of them."

Rose crosses her arms, which shifts her robe, exposing the top of her breast. My body heats at the sight of her smooth skin, her nipple very close to peeking from the black fabric.

"Put your cock away," she tells me.

"You're not with me because I'm a doormat," I remind her. "If you want to walk all over a man, you should have chosen Lewis Jacobson."

She gags. "God, don't even. He stared at every girl's ass when he jogged onto the court." He was a point guard for Princeton—the type of guy who would love to be controlled by Rose.

"Just remember that I'm not going to bend to your will."

"But you're waiting for me to bend to yours?" she snaps.

"And now we're at our five hundredth standstill." I run a hand through my wet hair, pushing the strands back, and her chest rises again at the motion. "Two cooks in the kitchen."

"Two dominants, no submissive," she adds.

I shake my head and try to tone down my grin that is really, really riling her to a bad point. She looks like she's going to slap me. "No," I say.

She gapes. "What do you mean *no*? My metaphor matched yours!"

She doesn't realize it yet, but she's nowhere near dominant in bed. It's a reason why she's slamming on the brakes. She's so in control of her everyday life that she expects the same once she straddles a man. But if she truly wanted that, she'd be attracted to a much different guy than me and she'd already have lost her virginity, riding the fuck out of him.

"I think we both know there's only one dominant here."

Her eyes flare. "Take it back, Richard."

I want to make her feel as confident and strong inside the bedroom as she is outside. It's a goal that Scott Van Wright won't steal from me, even if he tries.

"Take back the truth?" I frown. "That'd make me a liar. And I know how much you hate liars, hun." My hands are still behind my back, but I step towards her.

She grips the sink counter behind her and reaches over to grab a towel. She shoves it at my chest.

I haven't lost yet.

I wrap the cloth around my waist. It hangs low so she has view of my defined muscles. I make time for the gym with Loren and his half brother, but I've always been in good shape. I grew up wanting to reach the peak of physical and mental perfection. It's an unattainable goal. But one I set. One I seek.

People hope to touch the sky.

I dream of kissing it.

Rose spins back towards the sink. She uses the iron to curl loose waves in her straight hair. Most men would be scared of her—gripping a hot weapon. My cock begins to throb as I watch her through the mirror.

She breathes heavily, trying not to pay attention to me, but it's a little difficult. I'm six-foot-four. I'm twice her size. She's small, feminine in comparison to my body that could cloak her easily.

She swallows and says, "Do you think Lily and Loren are having more sex than usual?"

Anytime Lily and Lo's sex life arises, it closes the door to discuss ours. It's a ploy, a simple distraction, but Rose is also truly invested in her sister's recovery. She cares. I do as well, but Rose will always be my number one priority.

"They're touching more than usual," I say. "But I think it's more for the camera's benefit."

"He's teasing her, and she's going to regress . . . after all the progress she's made."

"You have to trust him."

She cringes at the idea of putting faith in Loren Hale. They only tolerate each other for Lily's sake. I'm in a difficult position because I've grown to like Lo as a real friend.

"I need a favor," she suddenly says.

"Favors," I muse with a smile. "It'll cost you."

"I knew being your girlfriend wouldn't have many perks. I still owe you things."

"You have plenty of perks," I tell her. "You just choose not to delight in them." I edge close to her, setting a hand on the counter, my mouth near her neck as I lean in low. She tenses as my hand dips to her thigh. "What favor do you need?" I ask, slipping my palm beneath her robe.

"I'm going to burn you," she says, not as a threat. Fear spikes in her voice. She unplugs the curling iron quickly and sets it aside.

I bite her ear and whisper, "Breathe."

She *barely* exhales. "I need you to give Lo the talk."

I hunch over, resting my chin on her shoulder for a second. My expression stays complacent, composed—the face I carry with me throughout the day, the one Rose calls "fake."

"I think we're past that talk, Rose."

She glowers, her entire body responding to the emotion. Her eyes narrow, her stance closes, her shoulders pull back, forcing me to straighten up.

I almost get hard.

"Don't patronize me," she says. "Lo's going to get my sister pregnant on accident. He's impulsive and careless. So you need to do what you do best and instill some common sense into him."

"I imagine that conversation blowing over as well as a hurricane." I twirl her by the waist so she leans against the counter, facing me. "So it's going to cost you."

She peruses my body with a sharp gaze. "I'm prepared to pay."

My lips slowly rise. "Are you?"

"Yes." But her eyes speak differently, and my smile fades. She's really, truly scared.

"You're safe with me, you know that, Rose?" I ask her. "I won't ever hurt you." I've always treated her like she's an extension of myself.

The more hostile, torrid side, that is.

It's a reason I've become so possessive of her throughout the years, even when we weren't together.

"I know," she says, relaxing her shoulders.

"Then I'll talk with Lo."

"What do I need to do for you?" she asks, too stubborn to back down, even if the unknown frightens her.

"Stop thinking for a minute."

"What—"

I kiss her, my large hand cupping her delicate face, my lips against her soft. Her breath rises to her throat, and her body curves to meet mine. She rouses, clutching my muscular arms with her free hands. The uncertainty still lingers on her lips, hesitating.

I break apart. "Get out of your head," I tell her, my hand lowering to her ass. I push her against me, her pelvis tucked neatly to mine. Her robe slips between her legs, revealing the bareness of her thighs.

A moan pushes through her lips. I pin her against the counter, only the towel separating my cock from her body, and she struggles to gain control with me. Her head dips back in arousal, and she desperately grips my arms, her fingers digging into my biceps. But she looks lost on what to do with her legs, one wanting to wrap around my waist, the other half off the ground with the force of my body.

I hold her left leg up to my side, stretching her, and she lets out a staggered breath. "Wait, wait . . ." she starts, her hands on my chest. She's flushed and warm to the touch, but she plummets right back in her fucking head.

"Rose," I chastise and drop her leg to the ground.

She rests her elbows on the counter, confusion lacing her eyes. *You liked that. It's okay to like that, Rose.* My hand returns to her jaw, caressing her cheek as she processes what happened—my dominant movements that trounced her into a puddle. *My* puddle.

I run my thumb on her bottom lip.

"Je suis passionné de toi," I say. *I am passionate about you.*

Her chest falls, understanding me well.

I slip my thumb into her mouth, and a sharp noise catches in her throat. She blushes at hearing herself. I leave my thumb there and press a soft kiss to her neck, and then I suck sensitive spots, trailing up her collar to her cheek.

She can throw me off at any second.

But surprisingly, she closes her lips over my thumb. She doesn't suck it, doesn't run her tongue against it. I don't think she really knows what to do, but I adore her more for trying. I let her off the hook and quickly replace my hand with my lips, my tongue, trying to lose her with the moment.

Her movements are more assured now, her hands drifting to my hair, tugging, clenching, kneading. Her spine curves again, her body meeting mine once more. *That's it, Rose. I have you.*

You're safe with me.

A full minute passes before that all disappears, before she retreats into her head again, before her kisses shorten, before her lips close and she pulls back altogether.

It was a brief, fleeting moment where I almost had her vulnerable and bare. But if I can put my thumb into her mouth without her biting it off, it's only a matter of time until I'm inside her completely.

Four

Connor Cobalt

Well, I learned what increasing the production value entails.

Here's a new one for me.

Scott Van Wright somehow manipulated *my* girlfriend into moving out of her sanctuary, leaving *our* Princeton house. I really wish I had been there for the conversation and not been stuck in a college lecture hall. I would have rebutted every argument he had that began with "*The Real World*" and ended with "you're *all* living together."

We all lived together in Princeton, New Jersey.

The difference now: Loren Hale's half brother, Ryke Meadows, is moving in for six months. So is Rose's little sister, Daisy. That's six people in one house.

I'm trying to be the encouraging boyfriend, but I can't be at fault for however I act around Scott. I don't like that he convinced Rose to do something that I would have trouble talking her into. It makes me nervous.

Rose stares up at the open ceiling, microphones and wires dangling from the rafters of our new home. Her forehead scrunches at having to live in a Philadelphia townhouse designed especially for production. Three levels. Five bedrooms. One communal bathroom. No yard. A nice hot tub and patio area. And an even larger dining room and kitchen.

"He promised we wouldn't be filmed in the bathroom or the bedrooms," she says with tight lips.

"Promises from anyone other than me mean nothing," I say. "Has he hit you over the head?"

She glares. "It's in the contract."

"Then Lo and I will make sure there aren't any cameras in the rooms."

"And the bathroom," she says quickly.

"That too."

She nods to herself and raises her chin to appear more confident about the matter, but privacy means a great deal to Rose. And this is a lot more intrusive than she anticipated.

"You can always tell him to fuck off," I remind her. "You've said it to men many times before."

"And yet, you're still here."

I smile. True.

She lets out a breath. "No. It has to be done this way."

"And why is that?"

"He said that there'll be more viewers if we all live together. Rich families being filmed in their natural environment has been done before. This hasn't." She pauses. "Except for *The Real World*, but—"

"All I hear is Scott Van Wright in your mouth, and that's really the last place I want another man to be."

She gives me a cold look and says, "I happen to agree with him. I did the research."

"Fine." But what Scott really wants is the most drama possible, the most chaos, and this is the type of setting that'll grant him what he desires. And if Rose is a part of that package, he's going to fucking lose this battle. I just don't want it to be at the cost of Rose's fashion line. If I ruin Calloway Couture, I'll lose her too. Her company is why we're swimming in a fish bowl after all. I'd do almost anything to help her achieve her dreams.

"Plus," she adds, only to provoke me, "our house had poor sound quality. We would've had to move anyway."

"Right, because they couldn't spend a couple thousand dollars to rig better equipment at Princeton. This alternative, moving out, is a hell of a lot more expensive."

"You're turning green. And for your information, you look ugly in that color."

"I'm not jealous," I say. "I hate him for the same reason you do—because he pisses where he eats."

"You haven't even met him yet."

"I already know."

She flattens her black maxi dress with her hands, walking back and forth in the living room space. "You're incorrigible."

"You're pacing. What other things should we point out?"

She hits me with her handbag, and I try hard not to grin.

When she settles down, she says, "After six months, we can go back to Princeton."

She can keep listing off the reasons why the move to Philadelphia is better—that her parents live close by, that Daisy can still attend prep school, that Lo's comic book business is already downtown, that my commute to Penn has been shortened by an hour—but in the end, she wasn't given a choice. Scott *told* her to move. And she did.

Not even that, he chose this townhouse. He didn't let Rose look for a new place that would fit production's ridiculous requirements.

I glance at the purple fringe cloth that covers the coffee table, large white candles lined in a row. Production actually hired people to decorate for the psychic's arrival. As though she's living here too.

"Just don't ask me to be nice to the psychic," I tell her, just now noticing Ben, the skinny cameraman, walk down the stairs. He directs the lens at us.

"I don't care what you do," she says, "as long as you're here."

I try not to look shocked by her declaration. Our tight postures relax, and I draw her to my chest and rub the back of her neck. She melts into me, her normally stiff body finding a moment to slacken. I stare at her fiery eyes that never seem to soften, even if her body does.

"But I thought you could do everything by yourself, darling."

"I can," she says, raising her chin again. "But I like your help . . . sometimes." Her gaze falls to my lips, unsure of herself again. She's waiting for me to make a move.

My lips brush her cheek. "I'm going to spread you so wide, Rose. Your whole body will ache for my hard cock." She tightens against me. "You'll come *before* I fill every inch of you."

A noise catches in her throat, and her hands drop to my waist, hurriedly feeling around for my battery pack to the microphones we wear beneath our clothes.

"Forget about the cameras," I tell her. Ben takes this moment to skirt around us, the camera whipping towards Rose's face. He's another obstacle, a puppet of Scott's. *Just fucking wonderful.* I could shove the camera at the wall, but I resist the violent urge.

I bring my hand to the back of her head, my lips right beside her ear. "You saw how big I am. Imagine that inside of you, all of it, pounding hard until you can't breathe."

"Connor," she warns, her voice weaker than normal.

I grip her hair between my fingers and tug, her chin jutting up. Her mouth opens, and she stifles a sound that wants to come out.

With one hand to the small of her back, I push her body harder against mine, and her cheeks flush.

"Don't be afraid of me," I whisper lowly in her ear. "I may not always be on your side, but I have your best interests at heart."

When I release her, she withdraws, taking two steps back and clearing her throat. She readjusts her handbag on her arm and then says, "I don't think I can forgive him for that bathroom."

She completely drops what just happened. And Scott is the last person I want her to divert to after *I* just talked about fucking her hard.

"To be fair to Scott," I say with a dry smile, "the bathroom has four sinks and two showers. It's not as if it's small. Each shower is even large enough to fit five co-eds."

"It's *communal*. I don't know how they did it at Penn, but I had my own bathroom, shared with *one* other girl."

"Yes, we're all savages at Penn. You should see the football team. They live in caves and eat with their hands."

Her shoulders fall. "I know I'm spoiled and a bitch, but I'm uncomfortable at the idea of someone walking in on me."

"The showers have misted glass. You can't see through them." That's not entirely true. I'd be able to see her body fairly well. "And you walked in on me three days ago." The mention of our moment in the bathroom—where she found me masturbating, where I hiked her leg around my waist—has her whole body tensing in arousal. She crosses her arms to cover the flush that rises on her neck. Only the mention of her sex life (or lack thereof) can make her so flustered.

"This is different."

"I know." Lo, Lily, Daisy and Ryke will be sharing the space too. Adding me was like skipping two stairs at a time for her. With them, it's like trying to stretch over five. "But everyone's uncomfortable, not just you."

She groans in distress. "I didn't want to put them in this situation. The reality show wasn't supposed to uproot their lives like this."

I usually say the right thing. I'm obviously doing a shitty job today. The psychic and Scott have scrambled my head.

I wrap an arm around her shoulder. "Lily wants to help Calloway Couture. She'd do anything for you. And they'll all adapt quickly." To make amends with Rose, Lily even sacrificed being close to her college. She'll be taking online classes so she doesn't fall behind.

Rose stops pacing with my touch. Ben documents her reaction with the zoom of his camera. She stares up into my blue eyes and leans close, her leg pressed against mine.

I comb her glossy hair away from her cheeks, and her arms cling to my waist. I ask, "Are you going to talk about Scott when I kiss you from now on? Or is it only going to be when we have sex?"

She clenches my button-down, fisting the fabric, and tries to throttle me for that comment, but I stay unmoving at her attempt, too strong to be overpowered by her, even if she puts up a good fight. With a huff, she stops trying to shake me. "One day," she says, "I'm going to slap you on impulse, and then I'm going to feel like utter shit." I read her eyes that say: *maybe we should break up before it happens. Maybe we're not good together.*

"You won't feel like shit," I tell her, "because I'll punish you for it."

Her lips slowly part. "You'll punish me?" She chokes on a laugh. "In what way?"

"Just trust me when I tell you that you'll love it."

She swallows hard and shakes her head. "I don't see how I could love a punishment."

"It won't be like detention in prep school, Rose." *Remember, I have your best interests at heart.*

She inhales deeply and she stares at my lips again, silently asking me to come a little closer. Just as I go to kiss her, a jingling sound echoes through the open kitchen that's in sight of the living room. No walls between any of them.

Sadie, my orange tabby cat, pads over to us, the bells on her collar clinking together. Rose spent an hour wrestling my cat just to put the thing on her while I was in class. She wants to know Sadie's location so she can avoid her. My cat scratches women fairly often. She's not fond of the times I locked her up for a date. But just for snapping on a collar, Rose had cuts all along her arms for a week.

I was about to sell Sadie after that, but Rose refused to let the cat leave. I appreciate her for trying to put up with my pet, but I don't want to find her bleeding like that ever again.

Rose lets out a horrified gasp. "We have rats!" She disentangles from my arms completely.

She's not frightened so much as disgusted by the rodent hanging out of Sadie's mouth.

I rub my lips to hide my smile. "Sadie hunts like a champion." I wink.

Rose plants her hands on her hips and stares at me like, *really?* "You just winked at her." Rose's glare turns into a laugh, but when she looks back at Sadie, her face falls again. "It's bleeding . . . oh my God." Sadie drops the rat on the hardwood. "No, no . . ."

"You're fine," I say, setting my hands on her shoulders. "Breathe." Rose is obsessive compulsive—a trait that has gotten out of hand since the paparazzi have clung to the Calloway family.

She blows out a long breath. "I can't cohabitate with rodents." She pauses. "That's a lie. I've lived with Loren for nine months, but I draw the line right *here*."

"So then we'll move back to Princeton." *Win for me. Fuck you, Scott.*

She shakes her head slowly. "No, no . . . I'll just have to deal with this. It'll be okay."

Fine. "Lo, Ryke and I can set rat traps tomorrow." But I add this just to rile her, "The perks of having three men living under one roof."

Contempt crosses her face. "Lily, Daisy and I are more than capable of doing it." But she breathes a little easier at the idea of three guys living here. It's appealing to not be in control all the time. Well, for her, not me.

"By all means," I say, "set them yourself. I fully appreciate female power." I step nearer, closing the space between us. "But you're going to have to put them in dusty, dirty . . ." I wrap my arm around her hip. ". . . places." I slide my hand to her neck and my thumb brushes her lower lip.

She inhales again, remembering where I put my thumb three days ago.

Ben silently films us, but I sense his unwanted presence. My thumb lingers on her soft, wet lip. *Fuck the camera.*

I'm about to push my thumb into her mouth once more, but the front door bursts open.

She pushes off me almost instantly, retreating in her head, realizing who and what surrounds us. I wear my complacent expression, even if I'm highly fucking irritated at whoever ultimately barged through the door.

I see his blond hair first, and my irritation escalates to new volatile levels. I'm already an egotistical ass. I'm afraid I'm about to become the villain of this reality show.

Right now, I don't particularly give a shit.

"Look, another rodent," I say to Rose.

She smacks my chest, but she's smiling.

Scott saunters inside like he owns the townhouse. I'm sure the lease is in his production company's name. Next thing, he'll try to stamp *Van Wright* all over my girlfriend.

"Where is everyone?" he asks, extending his arms. "The psychic will be here in five minutes." I fixate on the duffel bag slung over his shoulder.

I don't like assuming things, but if there are clothes, a toothbrush and a change of underwear in his bag—we're going to have a major fucking problem.

Rose squeezes my arm.

I'm wearing my anger.

That happens—*never.*

"They're all settling into their new bedrooms," Rose tells him. She eyes the duffel. "Traveling somewhere, Scott? Hopefully to California, where you're actually needed."

When he faces my girlfriend, he's not pissed at her insult. No. He *smiles*. His gaze even lingers on her lips—the ones that I just touched. "I'm needed here," he tells her. "It just takes people time to realize what's good for them." He gives Rose a long once-over, and my blood begins to boil. "Nice dress, but you could lower the neckline. Showing your tits would increase the ratings."

"So would shoving my foot up your ass," she retorts.

My lips rise.

So do Scott's.

"Just trying to help," he says smoothly. "I do have a question though. If your sisters are wearing your collection on screen, does this mean they're going to be entering a nunnery too?"

She growls and tries to charge him.

I seize her around the waist, holding her back. I hate that he incenses her like this. That's my fucking role.

My lips find her ear. "You're giving him what he wants."

"He's insulting *my* line."

It's like calling her child stupid. I understand the blow. "Your clothes are perfect, Rose. They're not as modest as he believes. Women will buy them."

My words instantly calm her, and she relaxes against me. I hold her while Scott waves Ben towards us. And then I meet his gaze. "So," I say, "you're moving in."

It's a guess.

But it becomes fact as soon as he tosses the duffel bag onto the floor. "I am."

Rose balks.

"What did production want this time?" I ask. "A misogynist? A natural blond?"

"A love triangle," he deadpans.

Rose's cheeks concave as if she's attempting to suck in all the air from the room. She points her finger at Scott, the red nail polish threatening and incredibly sexy. "If you try to break up Lily and Loren, I will gut you from the inside out."

No, Rose. He wants you.

His arousal practically swims in his eyes as he watches her tell him off. "I'm not here to break up anyone. I'll be introduced in the show as your ex-boyfriend. We dated for a few years in college but decided to amicably break up when your fashion line absorbed all your time. I like my women to be . . . attentive. We're still friends, despite your love of harassing the shit out of me."

I let go of Rose and take a step forward. "We haven't formally met," I say, holding out my hand. "I'm Connor Cobalt. The guy whose girlfriend you want to fuck. And just so you understand, the odds don't look good for you."

He shakes my hand, and I grip him so tight that he struggles to hide a wince. "You're threatened by me," he states, not breaking eye contact. "I'm twenty-eight, and you're—"

I hate ages. "Twenty-four years smarter than you." I tilt my head. "And in ten years I'll be thirty-four years smarter than you. See how this works?"

Rose steps between us, hands outstretched like she's protecting us from each other. But I just want to protect her from him. "All right. Put your cocks away. I've seen enough of them."

We both look down at her with the same desire.

"You haven't even seen mine," Scott says with curved lips.

Is he serious? "I assure you, you've pulled out your cock," I tell him.

"Stop. Both of you," she says, her chest rising in her dress, her breasts more apparent, even with the high neckline. *This*, interjecting herself in the middle of a fight, even tame, causes my dick to throb. I struggle not to pull her into my chest, away from Scott and his lingering gaze. She wouldn't appreciate me claiming her. But if he's going to try to take her from me—there's only so long I can withhold from doing so.

Anyway, I don't think *she'd* appreciate another girl hitting on me this way. In fact, I'm almost certain she'd rip her to shreds and grab me.

Rose spins towards Scott. "You're the executive producer."

"Yes?"

"So you're in charge of production. You make the rules. So you can leave."

"Yes, but I also have the network breathing down my neck. GBA expects certain things from *Princesses of Philly* when I pitched the show to them. My placement in the house was a promise I made."

He's planned this for that long?

Maybe he's smarter than I thought.

Rose fumes. "If the network wants you here, then fine. But the moment I think you're fucking with my friends and their relationships, even mine, you're *gone*. My company isn't worth hurting everyone I care about."

"Okay," Scott says evenly. "But I can't be held accountable for your feelings, Rose. If you end up liking me, that's completely out of my control."

Well, he's still the douchebag I thought he was.

Rose snorts and backs up into my chest. It's intentional. And I could kiss her for it. Instead, I wrap my arm protectively around her collar, and she clutches on to me.

"I'd rather burn," she tells him.

Scott just smiles and motions to Ben, who's filmed the entire scene. "Get everyone in this fucking living room. We have a psychic segment to shoot."

Game on.

Five

Rose Calloway

He's cute," Daisy says, appraising Scott from the kitchen. The main level of the townhouse is all one open space, so we have a direct view of the four guys in the living room, sitting on various pieces of leather furniture. The frizzy-haired psychic is on the ottoman, shuffling her Tarot cards.

Lily and I give our youngest sister a long stare. Mine contains a strong warning, but Lily looks more confused, like a puppy wandering the side of a road. I'd only stop to help a sad dog if they shared my genetics. Cruel, maybe. But survival of the fucking fittest. Blood is thicker than water. Choke on all of those clichés. They're true.

Daisy adds, "I mean, if you're into the whole blond, scruffy alpha-male vibe." She bites into a carrot with a crooked grin.

"You mean if you're into the whole domineering, jackass vibe," I refute.

"Or that," she says. "But no offense, Ryke is more of the jackass." She says it with an even larger smile. Yes, she's friends with Loren's brother, who happens to be twenty-three. It'd be stranger if she didn't hang around high fashion models older than even him.

My two sisters and I have excused ourselves from the palm reading to replenish on pizza and drinks. But really, I wanted to leave the guys to grill the producer . . . or rather—my fake ex-boyfriend. I internally gag every time I think of "Scott" and "boyfriend" in the same sentence. He's put this disgusting chili pepper and pickle taste in my mouth. And for anyone who finds that combination pleasant, I'll give you Scott's number. He's all yours.

I watch Connor and Scott's tense conversation as they share the same couch. They both sit tall, silently establishing their dominance, but a good amount of space separates them.

On a plush chair, Ryke observes our producer with a dark scowl but is smart to stay quiet.

However, Lo constantly interjects, sitting on the loveseat. And while the other guys keep their voices low, I can *hear* his heated retorts from the kitchen. He gesticulates with his hands, pointing at Scott more than once.

"I think they're all assholes," I say matter-of-factly. "Some just have more redeeming qualities than others." Kind of like us. I'm not the most likable girl in the world.

Savannah, the redheaded camerawoman, stands beside the oven. She's around our age and wears a skull and crossbones bandana over her braids. She focuses the camera on Lily, which is not good. My twenty-one-year-old sister is the only person who has trouble *not* looking into the lens.

"I don't like Scott," Lily says, her eyes flickering to the camera with each word. She nears Daisy and cups her hand around her mouth to whisper. "He stared at your boobs for like a whole minute."

Daisy shrugs and climbs on the counter, swinging her long legs. Her dyed blonde hair drapes to her waist. She'd cut it if her new modeling agency would let her. "There are photographs of me in my underwear," she says (too casually). She pops a piece of broccoli in her mouth from a vegetable tray. "When guys read the magazines, they could be doing more than staring at my boobs."

Lily flushes red in embarrassment.

Daisy frowns in confusion and then she laughs lightly. "You used to jack off to mags? That's fucking awesome, Lil."

I suck in a sharp breath, worried by my little sister's lack of filter in front of the cameras. But I don't scold Daisy for her bluntness. I don't want to make it seem like female masturbation is a bad thing. I wholeheartedly approve, but Lily is a recovering sex addict who has been known to compulsively delve into self-love and porn, abusing both. Those days are over for her. They have been for months.

"I don't think girls can jack off," Lily tells her, collecting her bearings. She tries to act more confident, straightening up.

Daisy swings her legs, hitting the cabinets below with her high laced boots. I would care more about scratching the wood if this was my house. But it's practically Scott's. *So scuff away, Daisy.* "You're totally right." She nods. "I guess it would be like rubbing one out?"

"Girls can jill off," Lily says.

"What?" Daisy and I say in unison.

"You know . . ." Lily turns bright red again, only her flush looks like an allergic reaction. Red splotches her arms and neck. Her eyes flit to the camera and then back to us. "Jack and Jill went up the hill. Guys can jack off. Girls can jill off."

Daisy cracks up laughing, hitting her leg with each full-bellied sound. "Holy shit . . . That's awesome."

I smile too. I love my sisters for so many different reasons.

I slide a piece of pizza out of the box with a napkin. "You're sixteen," I say to Daisy. "Men shouldn't be thinking about screwing you while they look at your photos. They should know better."

"I'll be seventeen in a month," she says. "And it probably happened to Brooke Shields, so . . ." She shrugs like that makes it okay. It doesn't. No one likes that they're calling Daisy a sex symbol in the media just because Lily is a sex addict. Daisy was only a high fashion model before all the publicity, in background shots, a few small campaigns. Nothing big. Now she's a supermodel, posing more suggestively, wearing less and less clothes.

I don't even want to think about what will happen when she turns eighteen.

When she can legally pose nude.

I wish she would care more, but she entered the modeling industry at such a young age that I'm not sure she'll ever see her body as something other than an object to the male gaze.

"Girls!" Scott calls. "We only have the psychic for another half hour. You need to come back."

We shuffle out of the kitchen and into the living room, pizza and drinks in hand. I pass Connor the plate he requested and sit beside him, which happens to *also* be next to Scott. I'd kick Scott somewhere else but I don't want to put him next to Lily (a sex addict with a stable boyfriend) or Daisy (a sixteen-year-old high fashion model with impulse issues). Seriously, my little sister dove off a forty-foot cliff in Mexico.

I wish I was exaggerating.

Lily slumps beside Loren on the loveseat, and he pulls her a lot closer so her legs are over his lap, splayed across him. She leans into his chest as she picks the pepperoni off her pizza.

"Do me next," Daisy says with a roguish grin, plopping on the floor. She leans against the legs of Ryke's chair and holds out her hand to Madame Charmaine. The psychic's peppered hair is so thick and frizzy, like she brushed her curls. Sun spots mar her skin.

Ryke has kicked up his feet on *my* cedar coffee table that was transported from the Princeton house. *At least there's that ugly purple tablecloth on top.*

But I can't restrain myself from saying something. "Ryke, I can see the mud on your boots."

His brows rise and he runs a hand through his brown hair. His features are harder and more brooding than Loren's, but he has the same lean and muscular build. Not bulky but incredibly fit. He nods to his brother. "Please tell me this isn't a regular fucking thing with her."

"Oh yeah." Loren steals the pepperoni off Lily's plate and pops one in his mouth. "Don't leave the toilet seat up unless you want a ten-minute lecture."

"It's called respect," I retort.

Lily raises her hand. "I agree with Rose."

Ha! Take that, Loren.

But he ignores me and playfully bites Lily's neck. Her face lights up in a giddy smile.

My achievement is popped in an instant. I just feel . . . strange at being thwarted by Lily and Lo's constant *blinding* love. Instead of being agitated by their in-the-face groping, I'm a little more aware of what I have. I turn to Connor, and for some reason, I can tell he's been watching me, studying me, understanding everything. I trace his features: the smoothness of his unblemished skin, the waviness of his brown hair and the curve of his muscles in his arms and chest, beneath a sophisticated button-down and behind those all-knowing blue eyes.

He is power and perfection in so many ways that I will never admit aloud. His head would be humongous by the fact. But when I was younger, I often thought about what it would be like to be with him, physically.

I was sixteen when I first pictured Connor inside of me, and the most contact I had with him was verbally fighting at Model UN Conferences. Literally, we'd stand in the hallways of a fancy hotel and argue about Epicurus and his philosophy on intangible things like love, happiness and God. Once Connor went off on a tangent in *French*, I tried to keep up. I vowed to be better than him. And so I studied harder. I opened more books. I made sure I was fluent enough to understand him and then more—to stump him. I never did, but I also never fell behind.

I am smart only because I spent hours reading. Connor is smart because he's naturally gifted, but he does study harder than even the average person. I envy him—that he can carry all of these talents and never be weighed down by setbacks and hardships. He just keeps moving forward.

He makes me believe that anything is possible. I don't think I'll ever find someone quite like Connor Cobalt.

He places a hand on my neck and his thumb rubs a sensitive place that sends chills down my spine.

I'm glad to have him, even if I was fine with being alone and single beforehand. How we came to this place still feels like a cosmic alignment. Out of the blue, I learned he was Lily's economics tutor at the University of Pennsylvania. It wasn't a ruse to get closer to me. He had no idea she was my sister at first, and Lily chose him at random. At the time, Connor and I only saw each other once a year when Princeton and Penn competed in a Quiz Bowl Tournament, and this was a chance for him to meet me more often. For us to reunite.

And Connor's never been one to squander an opportunity.

So when he saw me at Lily's old apartment, he asked me on a date. I said yes because he was challenging me to step out of my comfort zone, as he's done all these years. I wonder if having sex will be the day where everything ends, where our journey of losing and finding each other will finally come to a close.

I turn back to Ryke, who has *not* moved his boots. I make sure that he meets my glare.

He holds up his hands in surrender. "Look, if we're going to live together then we need to establish some fucking rules."

Madame Charmaine cuts into our discussion. "You're single now but you will find someone very soon," she tells Daisy.

"Well that's not right," Daisy says, the cameras rotating to her. "I already have a boyfriend."

Ryke's boots finally fall to the floor. "Since when?"

"Since last week."

Madame Charmaine holds up a finger. "Aha!" she exclaims. "*Soon.* Very soon."

"So soon that the events have already happened," Connor says. "Are we changing the definition of precognition today? Shall I call Merriam-Webster?"

Lo breaks into a grin. "You're nasty today, Connor."

"I have a limit on bullshit. Magic tips the scale."

"It's not magic," Madame Charmaine rebuts with ease. "I have the *sight*."

Connor pauses. ". . . like I was saying."

"Why haven't any of us met your boyfriend?" I ask Daisy, trying to steer this to a better direction, one that doesn't make Connor look like a bigger prick than he really is. But I have a feeling Scott will edit him in the worst light no matter what.

Before she answers, Ryke whispers in her ear, and they both suddenly stand at the same time. We're all on edge until Ryke sits on the floor, taking her spot, and she settles in his chair, her legs crossed underneath her.

Ryke has his nice moments. I'll admit that.

"Daisy," I say. "Did you hear me?"

"Yeah . . . um." She swats her hair out of her face. "He's not really the meet-and-greet kind of boyfriend."

"So basically you're just fucking him," Ryke blurts out.

Oh look, his nice moment just passed.

At least I can forecast that he won't make a move on Daisy because of her age. I think he's more likely to run into traffic than hook up with her.

"Not in front of the cameras," Connor advises.

Ryke shoots him the middle finger with an added glare.

I can feel Connor's chest rising in irritation. "I don't know why I care," Connor says. "It's not like anyone will understand you anyway. You curse every other word. They're going to literally bleep you out of the show."

"And that'd make you so fucking happy."

"I'd be happier if I could tie you up to the front porch and leave you there. I'd even be kind enough to toss you a steak bone to gnaw on."

Lo can't stop laughing.

Ryke's eyes darken at his brother. "Where's the fucking loyalty?"

His laughter dies down and his lips fall. "Did you hear what you said to Daisy? Honestly, how about *never* bringing up her sex life. And then *maybe* I'll consider siding with you."

"You guys." Daisy waves her hand to regain focus. "I'm not screwing my boyfriend. I just don't want any of you to meet him. He's kind of dumb."

Ryke's jaw hardens. "He's dumb? Then why the fuck are you with him?"

Daisy shrugs and avoids his dark eyes. "He's nice."

Scott suddenly scoots closer to me, his hip pressing against mine. I want to edge towards Connor, but I *don't* want to look frightened of Scott. So I stand my ground and feel his warm breath on my ear.

"You should go next. See what your future holds."

I bristle at the thought of being told something like *someone you love will die soon* or *you'll marry a stupid man*. Connor may not take stock in psychics, but a part of me will always be a little superstitious.

"Madame," Scott calls before I can stop him. "Rose would like to go next."

"And then you?" Connor asks. "We'd all love to know when you'll die."

The muscles in Scott's jaw twitch.

Madame Charmaine sidles over to our couch and kneels in front of me. She snatches my hand and scans the lines on my palm wildly. "Mmm."

I don't like *mmm*s. They sound like unintelligible baby muttering, which is the equivalent of sticking a sharp needle in my ear.

"I think . . . that I will have a better reading with cards." She pulls the shuffled deck from her pocket. "Split this in half. Do not flip them over."

I do as she says, randomly picking from the pile, purple crescent moons printed on the back of each card.

She returns to her ottoman beside the coffee table and starts flipping the cards right side up. I can't see any of the designs, but I think I spot a white unicorn on one, which has Connor rolling his eyes.

Even so, he intertwines his fingers in mine and kisses my knuckles, as though I need extra reassurance before she exposes my future.

She overturns the last card. "I see," she says and nods. "You're very fertile. I sense two strong male spirits in your life, possibly twin boys in the future." She has to be joking.

A crying baby—that's a personal circle of hell for me. When my older sister, Poppy, had her child, I didn't acknowledge my niece until she could form intelligible sentences. I have nothing in common with kids. And no one needs to tell me I would make a horrible mother. I know it's true. Which is why I plan to *never* have children.

"Take it back," I snap.

"I can't return a reading."

"It's not a purse, Rose," Connor chimes in, his lips rising. "It's your future." His amusement is palpable.

I point a finger at him. "Shut. Up."

Connor grabs my hand and says, "I won't believe in it if you won't."

He doesn't seem that upset by my declaration (technically I've voiced my baby-disdain before so it shouldn't come as a surprise) but I strangely ache for a true answer. For his honesty. I know he's not going to share it now, not when the cameras are rolling and with Scott sitting right beside me.

"Deal," I say.

The psychic clicks her tongue. "I think I'm picking up someone else's energy. It's very black, very dark, not good at all."

"Definitely Connor," Loren says with a wink.

Connor actually cracks a smile, and as far as I can tell, it's genuine.

"No," Madame Charmaine says. "It's from her." She stares right at Lily. *No, no, no.*

"You're going to be married soon, are you not?"

Lily slides lower on the loveseat, uncomfortable with the attention, especially as Brett and Ben direct both of their lenses at her. "Yes," she says in a small, feeble voice. Lo sets their paper plates on the coffee table.

"All right," Connor says, standing and nearing the psychic. "I think that's enough magic for one night." He puts a hand on Madame Charmaine's elbow, and she rises with the pressure. "It was really nice to meet someone who's dabbled in the dramatic arts, but I think it's time for you to go."

Loren mouths *thank you* to Connor, and then he rubs Lily's back.

But Scott has to ruin it as he stands. "I'm in charge of production, Connor. I say when these events end." He looks to the clock. "And we have ten more minutes."

On cue, Madame Charmaine directs her next question to Lily. "This wedding, you don't want to go through with it, do you?"

"What?" Lily's eyes grow wide. "No . . ." She looks to Loren. "I mean, yes. Yes, I do want it. Why wouldn't I?" She glances at the camera in alarm. "I . . . I love Lo so much. He's my best friend . . ."

"Hey," Lo says, tugging her to his chest, now settled on his lap. "You don't have to tell that old hag anything."

Ryke shakes his head and mutters under his breath, "Did he just fucking call her an old hag?"

"Yep," Daisy says.

"Fucking fantastic."

Lily doesn't look well. Her shoulders curve forward like she's a shivering puppy caught in the rain. I stand next to Connor. "Okay, Madame . . ." I can't even say her name without rolling my eyes too. ". . . either you leave early . . ." I give Scott a glower before he can refute. "Or stop badgering my sister."

But her lips fly open again. "Why would you get married if you're full of apprehension?" she asks Lily.

I am going to kill Scott! If he planted these questions at all . . . I actually let out a little growl, and Connor puts a hand on my shoulder. I want to pluck out Scott's eyeballs with my nails. And then stomp on them with the sharp point of my heel.

I spin towards him, my eyes growing hot. "Did you tell her to ask these questions?"

Scott feigns confusion. "Now why would I do that?"

Lily stammers. "I-I'm not apprehensive." *But she is.*

After her sex addiction became public, Fizzle's publicists suggested the best options for damage control. At the top of the list—a marriage. It would show that Lily's in a committed relationship. That she's not as deviant as the world believes.

So our mother and father have cut Lily off financially until she legally marries Loren. And our parents wanted them to wait a full year, so it wouldn't seem like a shotgun wedding. Not very many people know that this is a scheme. But even so, the marriage will be real. In six more months, she'll no longer be a Calloway.

This is not a wedding out of love (even though they'd most likely marry in five, six years regardless). Our parents decided this for them, and so the wedding is just one based on money and appearance. Nothing more.

Lily *and* Loren both have reservations and doubts. I've talked to Lily about it, and she's told me point-blank that she hates the idea of looking back at her wedding pictures and just seeing something fake and cold. I want their marriage to start out on good terms too, but I can't see a way out of this.

And I do agree with my mother on some level. I do think this will help Fizzle because it will repair Lily's image in the media. Do I believe it's worth it? That's only Lily's call. I know she's complying with the wedding more out of guilt for hurting Fizzle, our father's company, than regaining her inheritance.

Madame Charmaine holds up her hands. "There are so many emotions." She presses her fingers to her forehead.

Connor's composed, unreadable face is slowly breaking in annoyance.

"It's not me!" Lily shouts all of a sudden. She springs from the couch. "I love Loren. Look." She kisses Lo on the cheek and then the lips.

He recoils, the exact wrong thing to do to her right now. But he's trying to understand her mental state, which is gradually going sideways. My sister is like a ball of twine that can unravel slowly or quickly, depending on the person tugging at the other end.

Lily flinches back, not expecting Lo to stop kissing her. She bumps into the table and knocks over a lit candle. *Oh my God.*

"Oh, I didn't mean . . ." Tears flood her eyes, thinking she's ruined everything. She tries to lift the candle back up, but Loren catches her around the waist, pulling her to his chest before she burns herself.

The flame ignites a paper napkin and a paper plate. Daisy picks up the napkin like it's a dirty diaper, not a ball of fire. "Whoa, guys, this is pretty warm."

"Really?" Ryke says, grabbing her wrist and trying to relinquish the burning napkin from her.

"Yeah, really, really. Want to feel?" She smiles playfully, waving the thing towards him. He doesn't even jerk back.

"You're hilarious."

"I thought I was just smoking hot."

I'd like to say that I am the normal one out of my sisters, but I am frantically trying to grab the pitcher of water that sits on the edge of the coffee table. So much so that I knock over another candle.

Just lovely.

The cameras are swinging behind us, as wild as the flames.

Daisy has to toss the napkin back down on the table before it burns her hand. And the psychic yells something about her cards, gathering them in a messy stack.

And then a pair of hands peel me away from the growing flames that have eaten our napkins and started for the purple tablecloth. "The water," I start, but Connor places me by the wall and then brings out a fire extinguisher.

In seconds, my boyfriend has snuffed out the fire. And the psychic has bolted from my house with her purple bag in tow.

The quiet lingers, and all we hear is a muffled, "ImsorryImsorry-Imsorry."

My heart constricts, and I find Lily mumbling the string of apologies into Loren's shirt. He has his hand on the back of her head, his features sharpened. When he looks up at me, he says, "Thank God for Connor, right?" He tries to play off the pain that contorts his face.

"God always has a way of stealing my credit," Connor says.

Loren's lips curve in a small smile.

I think, in this moment, I love Connor more for lightening the mood than for saving my cedar coffee table. But I am glad this table isn't burned.

It's an antique.

Loren lifts Lily in a front piggy-back so she doesn't have to meet the camera's concentrated gaze.

Scott turns to me. "Looks like we'll be seeing that lap dance after all."

"Excuse me?" I sneer.

The room blankets in tense silence. Scott grins. "You made a bet a few days ago. I saw the footage. If someone cried during the psychic segment, you'd have to give your boyfriend a lap dance."

Shit. Fuck. Shit . . .

"Lily didn't really cry," I say instantly.

Loren shifts her a little, and I see his T-shirt, wet with her tears. She wipes her cheeks quickly, trying to hide her sadness, but it's there. I forget that Loren's not on my side for the bet. Hell, he's the one who proposed the wager.

I snap at Lo, "You should feel awful for profiting off of her emotions."

"She was there when you made the bet," he reminds me. "Lap dance rain check? Lily and I want a front-row seat."

Lily mutters something that sounds like *only if she wants to.*

"Fine," I say as Connor's hand skims my waist. I step out of his touch, anxiety heating my neck more than the small fire ever did. *I am going to have to gyrate on him. In public. With millions of people watching later on television. Oh. Shit . . .*

The only upside: the first episode is airing in February, a month from now. So I have some time before people witness my inability to grind.

"I think we missed something," Daisy says to Ryke.

He stares down at her. "Apparently I've been missing a lot of fucking things lately."

She looks away from him, and when she notices I'm watching her, she just smiles at me. I think Ryke is worried about her. We all are. There's a small fear she's going to end up like Lily—sex crazed and compulsive. All this media attention is affecting her at school in ways that no one knows. Daisy won't talk to us about it. And she could very well blow off steam in a bad manner.

Loren carries Lily out of the living room and up the stairs, her legs wrapped around him. Wiry Ben follows close behind.

I turn slightly, and my arm hits a camera. Pudgy Brett has a big smug grin on his face, as if he won the bet too. Well I guess everyone fucking won but me. "Put that smile away, Brett, before I make it a permanent frown." My threat does sound serious (it's really not), but I'm edgy enough that I feel like I could truly cause astronomical damage.

I glance around at the coffee table. White foam. Charred napkins. Burnt food. Dirtied plates. An overturned ottoman. Is that a stain on the rug? Oh . . .

"I'll clean it up," Connor tells me.

"I'll help," Scott adds.

Connor gives him a look.

"What?" Scott smiles. "I live here now. Might as well lend a helping hand."

I have a feeling that a "helping hand" is more than I'll get from Scott.

Six months. Six months.

If I repeat it, maybe it won't feel so long.

Six

Connor Cobalt

This is a shit waste of an afternoon.

The thought runs on repeat as I listen to another Cobalt Inc. board member drone on about advertising and angel investors. I have the urge to stand up and let everyone know that they have successfully battered the conversation.

But I don't.

These are the highest-ranked employees in the company. If there's any hope of taking the reins to Cobalt Inc. without looking like I undeservingly inherited it, I have to bite my tongue. The company owns brands like MagNetic, Smith & Keller paints and other profitable subsidiaries—things that have lined my pockets since birth.

I feign interest as best I can, but I'm sitting at the head of a long conference table filled with twenty middle-aged men. During these meetings, I'm my mother's interim—a position she granted me two years ago. It means nothing really.

On paper, I'm still just her son. This is merely a test.

My mother has never been quick to let go of the empire she built from the ground up. In order to be a board member, become the CEO and acquire her shares, I have to prove myself. Like these meetings or certain tasks she gives me at the least opportune moments. My cell phone is always in my pocket, threatening to go off.

I keep waiting for the sudden demand to entertain her business partners or a family friend. And I'm always grateful when she's decided to leave me alone for the night.

I type "notes" onto the small tablet in my lap. Really, I'm outlining an assignment I have to complete tonight for one of my business courses at Wharton. I may have graduated from Penn last year, but now I'm in the big leagues. Grad school. I want an MBA. I don't need it. Not really.

I'll be CEO of Cobalt Inc. with or without the degree. But the respect I crave won't be handed to me so easily.

My phone buzzes in my pants, loud enough for Steve Balm, the COO and my mother's most respected board member, to pause his discussion on finger paints. Steve has been ranting about primary colors and the hearts of children everywhere. He wants to fuck over Crayola. Not his words, but I read between the lines.

"Are we interrupting you, Connor?" Steve asks, his gray brows furrowing critically. Steve and I have a long history. I suppose it began at birth—when he was dubbed my godfather.

I don't make a move for my phone. "Did I say anything?" I refute. I hit the mute button before it can vibrate again.

"Aren't you going to answer that?" Gary Holmes, a stocky-built board member asks a few chairs down. "Could be Hollywood. You're a movie star now, aren't you?"

Light chuckling filters across the room. They jest because they knew me when I was seven years old, when my mother carted me through the hallways.

I am a boy in their eyes.

I won't win them over by arguing, by pounding my fists against my chest and demanding to be taken seriously. So I turn to Steve. "If you'd like to drive this company into the ground, by all means choose to spend millions of our research fund into finding an un-patented health-friendly finger paint."

Steve doesn't reveal whether he agrees or not, his face as blank as mine.

"Katarina wants to expand." Steve directs the statement to the boardroom. "She's giving us a week to propose *viable* options to take Colbalt Inc. to the next level."

"We could just get in bed with Fizzle," Gary says. "Connor's already a quarter of the way there."

Before the room can erupt in another wave of laughter, I ask, "And what would we do with Fizzle? We're a paint and magnet company. Should we poison consumers with our magnetic soda cans?" Everyone remains quiet, eyes flitting between one another. I keep my gaze pinned on Gary as he reddens and sinks lower into his chair.

I straighten, silently reminding everyone who's *not* a child in the room.

"It was a joke," Gary says in defense. He looks to Steve for support, but my godfather never offers him a life vest. If you're drowning, you fucking drown.

"Unless they involve productive opinions, keep your jokes to yourself," I say sharply. *Now* I slip my phone out of my pocket. It was a text . . .

Virginia Woolf, Jane Austen, Anne Brontë—Rose

My lips threaten to rise, and it takes all my strength not to smile. I begin typing and speaking at the same time. "Katarina just notified me that she's on her way," I lie. Though after reading a quick email this morning, I do know she's coming later.

Fuck. Kill. Marry. I type back and hit send before pocketing my phone.

"Any other fabulous ideas, Gary?" Steve asks. And *there* it is. His opinion. I meet his eyes and he gives me a small nod, letting me know he agrees with me. I don't let out a breath of relief. This is just one meeting of many.

Katarina arrives only five minutes later, and after Steve offers her a brief update, the board members clear out of the conference room. Leaving me alone with my mother.

Her deep, dyed red hair cascades in waves over her shoulders. She takes a seat in Steve's open chair at my right-hand side. This won't be a quick conversation then, but I've already spoken to her about the reality show.

I laid out the pros and cons in a spreadsheet, outlining all the reasons why I should be in the show. Mostly for Cobalt Inc.'s benefit. Exposure. Putting a face to our brand. It's something that my mother wants but has never been able to do.

The only risk is bad press. Fizzle and Hale Co. stocks dropped considerably after Lily's sex addiction was publicized. I was distanced enough from Rose's sister that Cobalt Inc. didn't suffer, but I'm edging myself closer to the Calloways. My mother has voiced her mild disapproval. She doesn't like taking risks or getting her hands dirty. But that's why she has me.

"Where are the cameras?" she asks, diving right in.

"There are only three cameramen," I explain again. "They won't follow me if I'm not with someone else. So if you're worried about them coming into this building—"

"I'm not." She pulls out her smartphone and simultaneously types an email while she speaks to me. "I'm worried that this girl is going to ruin you."

"Her name is Rose, and she's not going to *ruin* me." She's never met her, but they've both been pressuring me about letting them have coffee together or brunch. I just don't see what good will come of it. And so I make excuses about my mother never having time to see Rose. And Rose never having time to see my mother. It's a shit thing to do, but I'm certain they'll hate each other. I also believe Katarina will try to run Rose out of my life, and I want her firmly by my side.

My mother pockets her phone and her eyes darken with displeasure. "She's a powerful girl who started her own business as a teenager. She's driven, independent and passionate."

All the things I admire, and yet, I know she's about to turn every quality into something sinister and wrong.

"Working women don't have men. We can't keep relationships. We are married to our careers." She announces each sentence like a nail in a coffin, pounding down the reality around me. "The children we do have are sent to boarding schools or are raised by nannies. It's the life I wanted, even at the sacrifice of my husband and my child. You don't want to walk into that, Connor. You're smarter than that."

I refuse to stare at the table, to look away from her dark blue eyes. I meet her powerful gaze with one of my own. Her words may affect me to some degree, but I won't ever show it.

I don't talk to my mother about my relationships very often, and any mention of Rose usually accompanies some sort of disparaging snort and blasé brush off. When I told her that I was moving in with Rose, she wouldn't speak to me for weeks. She'd prefer that my girlfriend moved in with *me*. Not the other way around. I was willing to uproot my life for Rose, and according to Katarina Cobalt, other girls would have gladly walked into my home. In her eyes, I chose a path that doesn't benefit me.

I had to use Steve Balm as an intermediary just to talk to her during that time.

Our communication reopened only after I explained the reality show and how it can help Cobalt Inc. if I take the right steps.

"You need to set your sights on a girl like Caroline Haverford," she tells me. I internally grimace, but I don't let on that her name sends knives into my spine. I dated Caroline. I fucked Caroline. But it was business. Like my relationship with my mother. Like my life.

Is it so bad to want something real?

"I'm with Rose," I say sternly. "That's not going to change."

Her nails rap on the table, frustrated. Katarina Cobalt always gets what she wants, and this is the first time I've put on the brakes, unwilling to give in to her requests.

"Caroline will be there for you. She'll have time for you. Rose won't. You'll grow resentful and bitter of each other. And as years pass, you'll realize you're sleeping next to a stranger."

"Are we still talking about *my* relationship?" I ask her with an arched brow.

Her lips press in a tight line. "Do you love her?"

"Love is an irrational feeling," I say. I hate that I actually believe these words. "It makes smart people do stupid things. My relationship with Rose is . . . stimulating." I think I'm a sociopath. *Fuck*. I need to see Frederick.

"Good," my mother says with a nod. "No need to make this into some tragic Shakespearean tale. At least she hasn't corrupted your mind yet."

My mother rises from her chair and straightens her pencil skirt.

"I'd like to meet her," she tells me for the thousandth time. "Schedule an appointment with Marci, and if you don't, I'll call Rose myself. We don't need you to lie for us anymore."

Her heels click away, leaving me to picture the impending meeting of Katarina Cobalt and Rose Calloway.

There will be screaming. Yelling. Possible bloodshed.

Though she's resilient, I'm not so sure Rose will come out victorious this time.

My cell phone chimes and I see the name flash across the screen. *Scott Van Wright*. Wonderful.

When I answer the phone, I make sure I have the first words. "Scott, how sweet of you to call, I was beginning to suspect you didn't like me very much."

"Why would you get that idea?" *You want to fuck my girlfriend*.

"You like Rose better." I throw out the bait, testing his response.

"I do like her better," he tells me. "She's prettier." I wait for him to add something crude like "and she has a pussy" but he doesn't. Either I've been hanging around vulgar people for too long or he's censoring himself.

"Many men would disagree," I say casually. "So why the sudden call?"

"I'm picking up food from the grocery store. I thought I'd get some of Rose's favorite things. What does she like?"

"Me."

He lets out a laugh. "This phone call is being filmed, you know. I have you on speaker." He says it like he caught me in a spider's web.

"She also loves my cock, my hair, my brain, my body—"

"Yeah, she loves you so much that she's *still* a virgin." He must have discovered that from an interview. Or maybe footage of someone mentioning it. Rose isn't ashamed of being a virgin at all, so I could see her admitting it to the cameras.

"And you're her ex-boyfriend," I say blankly. "She has intimacy issues, and it's not a far reach to conclude it's from your impotence." None of it is true, but I hope he airs this.

Doubtful.

He snorts.

"Oh, and she loves dark chocolate," I say.

"I'll just grab the condoms. How's that?"

I clutch the phone tighter. "You're asking for my permission to have sex? That's kind. And the answer is no. I'm already taken."

He laughs dryly. "You're a fucking prick."

"I've been called worse," I say, my voice casual still. "But I'm the prick with the girl. And she's not inflatable."

"I'll see you at the townhouse," he says, ignoring my comment. "You'll be back really late, right? You've got work, college. All that shit. Don't worry, buddy. I'll keep the girls company."

He hangs up, and I replay the conversation in my head. He unnerves me more than any other human being, and the fact that I don't have to impress him makes my lips unnaturally loose.

He called me. To fuck with me.

It's working.

Seven

Rose Calloway

You're not supposed to look at the cameras," I remind Lily for the umpteenth time. She's trying to ignore Ben and Brett as they film us from two different angles, but I can tell they make her uneasy.

At least without Loren around.

Her boyfriend seems to take her mind off of everything else, melting her nerves to a placated pool.

Lily tags along by my side as I bustle around the kitchen and make a Cobb salad to bring with me to the Calloway Couture offices. I try not to overanalyze why she's become glued to my hip.

She leans in to whisper, "What if I have a booger or something in my nose?" Her eyes flit anxiously to the lens again. "Or what if I get sauce or cheese or peanut butter all over my face? I'm a messy eater. Are they going to use the footage?"

I set the carrots on the counter and when I turn around, I almost bump into her again. She steps back and I place my hands on her shoulders.

"I don't have any control over editing," I tell her for *another* umpteenth time. I also want to tell her that she doesn't have to do this. That if she wants out of the show, I'll be okay. I'll be happy.

But that's not the complete truth.

The success of Calloway Couture relies on this show, and the success of the show relies on Lily and Loren.

"I'm going to get over it," she tells me, reading my expression well. "It's just new. New things are always kind of scary, you know? Well, you probably don't know." She laughs nervously. "You're not scared of anything."

That's not true either. I was scared not long ago. Terrified. Someone—who I will not name—put his thumb in my mouth. And I think I liked it.

My phone buzzes on the counter, and I wipe my hands on a towel before I swipe the screen. I have two new texts.

The first: 5 months and 20 days until the wedding—Mom

I'm not even surprised at this point. I receive a daily countdown from her, reminding me that I've taken responsibility of planning Lily's wedding.

I open the second text to distract me from all the things I still have to do.

Prince Charming, Robin Hood, Beast—Connor

Really? I texted him three brilliant female authors and he gives me Disney characters to choose from? Oh, he's starting a war.

I type quickly, not even having to think twice about my choices. Kill. Marry. Fuck.

Less than a minute after I hit send, I receive another message.

You would fuck the Beast over Robin Hood? Explain.

You're not even going to mention me killing Prince Charming? Deflection in a text is my specialty.

Not surprising. I would kill Prince Charming as well. Always believing every girl needs to be rescued from a tower. He's an asshat.

I smile, my stomach fluttering at his words.

"Is that Connor?" Lily asks, eyeing my smile suspiciously.

My lips level and she peers over my shoulder to try and read the text. I hold it close to my chest, and her eyes twinkle in amusement.

"Are you texting naughty things?" she asks with glee.

Should I be? What couple texts about killing off Prince Charming? If I seriously evaluate my relationship with Connor, it will rank somewhere closer to strange than normal.

My phone buzzes again, but I don't pull it away from the security of my blouse. "What do you and Lo text about?"

Her face wrinkles in thought. "Well, *I* text him things I'd like to do. And he usually replies with a generic *okay* even if at times he's a big fat liar and we don't do it anyway." She shrugs. "He's a brief texter." Her smile brightens at another thought. "But *sometimes* he'll randomly send me messages like this . . ." She holds up a finger for me to wait while she opens her flip phone with her other hand. The old device doesn't have internet or apps. The less temptations for her to look at porn, the better. "This is what he texted me last week."

She raises the phone to my face. Brett's and Ben's cameras try to zoom in on the screen. Lily cups her hand around it protectively.

I read the text quickly. I miss your pussy.—Lo

How eloquent. Lily practically beams. "He doesn't do foreplay texting," she explains. "So whenever he sends something dirty, it's like Christmas."

She motions to my phone. "What does yours say?"

"Just work stuff," I answer evasively.

I type back: Robin Hood is a manwhore. I'd want to join the Merry Men, not join a notch on his bedpost. The Beast is probably a virgin.

As soon as I hit send, my stomach falls. What the fuck did I do? I blame Lily, who peers over my shoulder as I type, distracting me from rereading the message.

I basically just admitted to wanting to have sex with a virgin.

Connor is *not* a virgin.

I don't have time to think. The doorbell rings. I pad across the kitchen and living room to answer it, leaving Lily by the refrigerator. I glance back for a quick second to make sure she doesn't crumble without my presence. I relax when I see her focused on my salad, slicing cucumber.

Ben follows me with his steadicam contraption, and without Lily constantly eyeing the lens, I have an easier time pretending he's invisible.

When I open the door, my entire mood shifts. I hope I'm giving off the *I'd rather murder an entire bale of sea turtles than be near you* look. Scott Van Wright's lips upturn into a cocky, holier-than-thou smile.

I must be doing something wrong.

"Most girls answer the door with a *hello*," he tells me.

"Don't you have work?"

"You are my work, Rose."

Great. I still haven't fully wrapped my head around the fact that Scott lives with us. I woke up at five in the morning with Connor just to use the showers when no one else (mainly Scott) was up to view the outline of my naked body. I *know* you can see shadows through the misted glass doors. I'm not an idiot.

And now he's here.

He will always be around, I realize. I just have to fucking deal with it.

He holds up plastic grocery bags. "I come in peace." His eyes dip down to my dark blue blouse with gold buttons on the shoulders. The cut is just slightly lower than the one I wore for the psychic party, but a gold necklace disappears between my breasts, the chain accentuating my small C cups more than usual.

"I see you changed your wardrobe. We're out of the nunnery and now in grade school. Not perfect but we're getting closer."

I try to slam the door back on him. His hands are filled with groceries so he has to use his hip to keep it open.

"Talk about my clothes again," I seethe, "and we'll just see how close my foot is to your ass."

"Fair enough," he says easily, no snarky retort. I think he's just trying to buy time to avoid spilling milk on the floor.

I let out a strained breath and open the door wider, leading him into the kitchen.

Lily looks up from the salad bowl, eyes big with questioning. She hasn't been alone with Scott without Loren present. But it was only a matter of time before it happened. Everyone has places to be during the day.

Me: Calloway Couture in New York. The commute is killing me, so I rented an office in Philly. But I drop by the main office once a week to check in.

Connor: Penn or Cobalt Inc. in Philly.

Loren: His comic book business in Philly.

Daisy: Prep school in Philly.

Ryke: Well, I'm not quite sure where the hell he is. Maybe indoor rock climbing at the gym. He graduated last year like me but has made no move to do anything with his journalism degree. He even stopped working for *The Philadelphia Chronicle*.

And then there's Lily.

Now that she takes online classes from Princeton, she's the only one home. I'm nervous about Lily spending so much time with Scott. Maybe I can convince her to come to the Calloway Couture offices with me.

Scott sets the plastic bags on the kitchen counter, and Lily scoots out of his way, avoiding his eyes, his body, anything that belongs to him.

"I don't bite," Scott tells her.

"I know, I just . . ." Her gaze stays firmly planted on the ground.

Frown lines crease his forehead.

I'm sure he imagined my sex addict sister to be this confident, unabashed girl who falls on her knees at the presence of a cock. Most people do. All it takes is a five-minute conversation to understand that my sister is none of those things. She is shy, nervous and plagued with social anxiety. Her confidence is only in sex.

Sometimes, I believe we're opposites.

"She's shy," I say for her. "Don't take it personally."

"A shy sex addict?" He stares at Lily like she can't possibly exist. "Are you fucking with me?"

She flushes almost instantly, and I glower. "Leave her alone."

Lily raises her hands. "No, it's okay. I want to explain myself . . ." Her eyes flit to the cameras.

"Don't look at the lens," Scott scolds like she's a child. "It's not a hard concept, honey."

"Can you say anything without sounding like a pig?" I ask.

He grins like I offered to blow him. *Ughhh.* I am a challenge, I get that. I am the bitch he wants to ensnare. But my insults really, really shouldn't turn anyone on this much. If I started complimenting him, would he suddenly be disinterested?

Lily gives Scott her attention. "I want the viewers to have a real, honest portrayal of sex addiction. At least one story. My story. So maybe if there's another girl who's like me, she won't feel so alone."

"All right," Scott says with a nod. "I'll bite. Why the hell do you look scared around me? Shouldn't you want to get on your knees about now?" He opens the refrigerator and shelves the sour cream and milk.

"I'm in recovery," Lily refutes. "I have a boyfriend. I don't want to have sex with anyone but him. So, no, I don't have any desire to drop on my knees. And I've always been shy. Just not . . . during . . . *it.*"

She's told me that she feels like a completely different person during sex: empowered, strong. It's the only thing she believes she's good at, and she's taken the knowledge to heart. After sex, she's flooded with shame, thinking she'll never amount to anything more—that she's truly just a slut, that her one talent in life is fucking. And she's compulsive with the act to the point of being unhealthy. A female who's great at sex—who has it five times more than the average male—is not something she can gloat about. Not in a society that easily labels her as a whore.

Lily's lifestyle is filled with humiliation. There's no triumph in that.

And I wish I could protect her, but you can't shield a girl from the world without taking her out of it.

"You can't even say the word *sex*?" Scott says with a laugh. "Jesus Christ."

She tucks a piece of hair behind her ear and turns to me, trying to ignore him but I see the hurt shadowing her face. "I'm going to start some homework," she says in a small voice.

"Hey . . ." I wipe my hands on a towel and touch her shoulder before she leaves. "Don't listen to him," I whisper. "He's disgusting."

"I know. Connor told me the same thing this morning."

I frown. "He did?"

"Yeah, he said that Scott would make fun of me and I just had to remember that everyone hates Scott and loves me." She laughs but her eyes brim with tears. She wipes them before they fall. "I don't mean to cry so much this week, honest. I think I'm on my period. I can use that excuse, right?"

I give her a hug, even if mine are the rigid kind. My heart breaks for her every time someone condemns her addiction. As if it's a stupid joke. It's not. And she's not gross or weird or pathetic for how she feels. If the world slandered my name every day on social media sites, I'd be worse off than some tears now and then.

"Will you call Lo?" I ask. Even though he irritates me, he always seems to say the right things to brighten her mood.

"Yeah, I think I might." She gives me another hug before leaving to her room. And leaving me alone with Scott.

My anger boils inside of me, and I have the impulse to slam open drawers and find a serrated knife to wave at his dick. I spin back towards the double-door refrigerator and notice that Scott has almost emptied all of the grocery bags.

"You're a vile human being," I tell him coldly, "and I could rip you apart right now, but I actually pity you."

"Why is that?" He narrows his eyes and shuts the pantry door.

"Because you just insulted the only girl you should have never picked on. Once you're on Loren Hale's shit list, you generally don't ever get off."

"The guy with the sharp cheekbones, right?" Scott muses, as if he doesn't know the twenty-two-year-old guy all over the news, who he's *met* and lives with. "He doesn't look that threatening."

"He's going to make your life hell," I say with a smile, "for six *long* months."

"Well, while you're celebrating my demise . . ." He reaches into the last bag and then hands me a chocolate bar. "I bought you this. I heard it's your favorite."

My smile only widens as I turn the dark chocolate over in my hands. *Connor.* My eyes rise to Scott. "I despise dark chocolate. But nice try."

He clenches his jaw as I shove the chocolate bar back in his chest.

I head to the staircase, and I can feel his hot gaze plastered to my ass during my short trek there.

I don't dare look over my shoulder to verify.

No way is he stealing my win.

Eight

Connor Cobalt

The crew is on a lunch break, so the only cameras that film us are attached to the walls and ceilings. It's a slight relief not having to ignore someone in the room.

Ryke, Lo and I are on the lowest level of the townhouse. A few days ago, Daisy found two rats squeaking in her closet, feces inside her boots. If that had been Rose, the house would have been flipped upside down. But Daisy was quiet about the whole ordeal and just mentioned it to Ryke. She wanted us to handle the issue without alarming her sisters.

So I lean against the wall while Lo squats in front of the crawl space with a trash bag. Ryke has disappeared inside the three-foot tall basement, the surface a brown soil, and the strong stench of mold and mildew permeates from the small square door.

We wait for Ryke to check the rat traps that we set.

"You look like shit," Loren so eloquently tells me.

He's right. Dark circles shadow my eyes, and if it wasn't for the wall supporting my body weight, I'd be on the ground. I'm fueled by two hours of sleep. Being Saturday, I planned to catch up this morning, but I received an impromptu text from my mother. I had to take Cobalt Inc.'s senior advertising team to breakfast and talk about product placement.

I suppose I could take a nap now, but I sip my coffee instead. I'd rather not miss *this*.

Watching Ryke inch around a cobwebbed space in search of a dead rat. I smile. *Fuck sleep.* It's the little things in life that matter most.

"I'm a grad student trying to take over a multibillion-dollar company," I say to Lo. "If I didn't look like shit I'd be on drugs."

I hear Ryke bang his head against a pipe. "*Fuck me,*" he curses.

"Fornicating with the rats already?" I ask, cupping the warm mug.

"Fuck you, Cobalt," he says with a grunt as he moves slowly. "The shortest one of us should have crawled through here."

Lo immediately takes offense. "If I knew you were going to bitch, I would have done it myself, and I'm only one inch shorter than you, *bro.*"

Ryke hits his head again and lets out a frustrated growl. "I'm still six fucking three."

Lo rests his forearms on his thighs as he squats and watches his brother through the door. "Besides being a giant, what's taking you so long? You set the trap. You should know where it is."

"It must have carried the trap with it."

"Just use your nose," I suggest. "Dogs have the best sense of smell."

Lo laughs while I casually take another sip from my coffee.

"Fuck off," Ryke curses, which sounds really less threatening through the wall.

My phone vibrates in my pocket. I take it out and read the text quickly.

Have you given *the* talk to Loren yet?—Rose

I'm not surprised Rose has reverted back to fixating on Lily and Loren's problems. She likes caring for her sisters, but I think focusing on Lily and Lo distracts her from dealing with her own issues.

I text back: I'll do it right now.

One less problem that she obsesses over, one less stress in her life. I pocket my phone, and as I turn to Lo, I frame Rose's question as my own. "Is Lily having more sex than usual?"

Rose doesn't know this, but Lo is surprisingly forthcoming about sex with Lily. He's motivated by the fear of enabling her again, and it helps that he trusts my sage advice.

"She's not having it, but she wants it." He stands up, the trash bag still in hand. "This whole fucking reality show puts her on edge. And she medicates her anxiety with sex, which means I'm not getting laid for the next week, and she only gets my fingers." He looks at the camera attached to the corner of the ceiling and wall, and he waves his fingers at the lens. Then he winks.

And *that* is why this show is going to be popular. The unfiltered narrative is exactly what makes good television.

"So you're not having sex?" I say, not adding any disbelief to my tone, even though it rings in my head. They're almost always fucking at night and in the morning. It's easy enough to hear through the walls.

Loren rubs the back of his neck, probably trying to decide if he's going to lie or not. When he drops his hand, he says, "No, I mean . . ." He takes a breath, and I wait it out patiently. "We fucked the other day. She was a little compulsive afterwards, so I want her to abstain for three or four days and see how she does with that."

"And you used condoms?" I ask.

He goes quiet for a second and then bangs on the wall with his fist. "Ryke, hurry the fuck up."

"Lo," I say.

He turns on me with heated eyes. "This conversation is over."

"I'm trying to imagine what Lily will look like pregnant," I say casually. "Would her entire body swell or just her belly?"

"At least I'm getting laid," Lo refutes, pure malice edged in his voice. "How long have you been *fucking* your hand?"

He clenches his jaw after he says the words, holding back a grimace. Lo has a way of cutting people up with words, and he's improved from the first time I met him. He was a drunk asshole. Plain and simple. Now he's a sober asshole who regrets when his filter doesn't work properly.

Lucky for him, I'm difficult to piss off.

"My hand and I go way back," I say nonchalantly and even produce a smile.

He seems to relax when he knows he hasn't pushed me away.

"I'm not your brother." I motion towards the crawl space where Ryke has effectively disappeared. "I'm not going to curse you out for doing something stupid. But I am dating your girlfriend's older sister, so my own balls are on the line here."

He nods like he understands. "The repercussions of getting into bed with a she-devil."

"And I fucking like her," I refute, "so make my life easier and use a condom."

I don't tell him that he's not ready to be a father, that the idea (for anyone) of Lily becoming pregnant is frightening. I don't tell him that alcoholism is hereditary or that he's too busy to raise a kid right now. He knows all of this. He's heard it a thousand times from Rose and his own brother.

What Rose and Ryke don't understand is that if you say something over and over again, you can become desensitized to it. Andy Warhol used the theory in his painting of the electric chair. He repeated the image until you could no longer see it as something heinous.

It lost its meaning.

I don't repeat what's already been said. I want my words to mean something.

So I gave him my selfish reason.

I'm the asshat who only cares about himself.

I am what he needs me to be.

He stares at the ground for a long moment, processing. "I'll be better about it," he mutters under his breath.

Noise from the crawl space ends our conversation. Ryke must knock into three pipes at once. He coughs and says, "There's so much fucking mold down here. No one should be fucking living on this floor until we hire someone to clean it."

Lo bends down to the door again. "If this is your way of getting Daisy to room with you, you can *forget* it. I'm just barely tolerating your friendship."

"Are you fucking kidding me?" Ryke retorts. "There were rats in *her* room, she's living near mold, and your first assumption is that I want to fuck her?"

Loren's eyes narrow. "I didn't say anything about fucking her."

Ryke groans.

Daisy is a sore subject between them, clearly. Since Ryke and Loren have a new relationship—just meeting a year and a half ago—there's tension involving the Calloway girls. Loren grew up with them. Ryke did not. Naturally, Lo would be protective of Daisy, but the problem I have is that he's constantly consumed by Lily, always taking care of her, that he has no room to do so for another girl, not even one he sees as a little sister.

So while Lo believes he's protecting Daisy from his half brother, he's really creating a barrier between Daisy and the only person here who'll look out for her first rather than last.

And yet, I can't say a word about it. I have to let these things play naturally. My interference won't do any good. My words wouldn't resonate with Lo the way I'd want them to. So I stay silent on the matter.

"I'll fucking room with Scott," Ryke says, speaking loudly so we can hear him from the hallway. "Daisy can take my room. Or I'll stay down here and switch with her. I don't give a shit. None of the girls should be around this."

"And what if she hears Lily and me fucking through the walls? There's a reason she's on the lowest level."

Ryke says nothing, but I can practically feel him fume from far away. Lo looks over his shoulder at me, asking with hard eyes whether he's right or wrong.

"You can't censor a girl who's nearly seventeen, especially not a high fashion model," I tell him, my words not harsh like his or rough like his brother's. I'm one hundred percent even-tempered, calm. At ease. It gets him off the defensive. "She's heard and seen everything you have, if not more. I'll call someone to look at the crawl space, but until it happens, Rose would want her sister somewhere clean."

After a minute digesting my words, Lo sighs and lets go of the argument. "Ryke, you'll room with Scott?"

"I said I would."

"Fine. More eyes on that prick, the better, right?"

Ryke says something in affirmation, but I can't quite hear. He thumps around too much. "Fucking A," he curses, his voice much louder. He tries to pull his body out of the tiny space.

Lo grabs Ryke underneath his arm as he squeezes through the door.

When he's on his feet, he holds up the trap with the dead rat, the tail mangled like it dragged the weight from its back end.

"Have we found you a new profession?" I ask, my lips rising.

"At least I can get my hands dirty, princess." He waves the trap (and dangling rat) at my face.

I don't even flinch.

Ryke rolls his eyes and goes to toss it into the garbage bag.

"Wait," Lo calls. "Maybe we can do something with this thing."

"No," Ryke and I say together. I contain my grimace. Even though Ryke may be one of the smarter people living in the apartment, I don't enjoy agreeing with him. It's like siding with a guard dog instead of a human.

"You didn't even let me finish," Loren says angrily.

"You want to use it against Scott," I reply.

"He's the fucking producer," Ryke reminds him. "You start a war with Scott and he could turn you into a psycho on the show. Just fucking relax."

"He made Lily bawl!" Lo yells. "I'm not going to sit here for six months and ignore all the shit he says. This is different than social media and gossip blogs. We're living with this bastard."

Footsteps sound on the staircase, and all of us go suspiciously quiet. When the body rounds the corner, Brett emerges, breathing heavily with the steadicam attached to his chest, and he only sprinted down one flight of stairs.

"Scott wants . . . you all in the living room . . . for the lap dance," he pants.

Scott Van Wright is dictating everything. When. How. Where.

I fucking *hate* him.

Lo looks to me, waiting for me to nod in approval of his methods to fuck with Scott.

I may hate Scott, but I'm not to that point yet. I won't do something malicious or cruel that'll have him checking into a psychiatric hospital, mentally torn to shreds.

I fight my battles much differently than Loren Hale. And while it may not be as quick or effective—I have to trust that I have the power to keep my friends from falling tragically apart.

Nine

Connor Cobalt

When we climb up the stairs to the main level, I find Rose and Daisy talking in hushed tones near the fireplace mantel. Daisy shifts her body to block the camera, sidestepping every single time Ben tries to get a shot of Rose.

I rub my lips as I study my girlfriend. She holds in a breath, her neck stiff as she listens to her sister.

And she actually wears pants, dressed in a Calloway Couture black sweater and a different brand's skinny jeans. She's afraid of flashing the cameras, and she's expressed, more than once, that the only dances she knows are from cotillion. The waltz and foxtrot.

Grinding is out of her repertoire.

Lily suddenly appears and slams her fist into Lo's shoulder.

He mock cringes. "Ow, what the hell was that for?"

"For making this stupid bet," Lily hisses, lowering her voice as Brett zooms in on her, a boom mic attached to his steadicam. But it doesn't matter if he captures her words or not. We're all wearing microphones that'll pick up her voice. And the house is littered with sound equipment.

Scott sits on the leather couch. His eyes meet mine, and he plasters on a smug smile.

I hide everything in my features—especially the anger that threatens to surface.

"What is Daisy doing?" Ryke asks.

Lily holds on to Loren's hand. "Giving Rose advice."

Ryke's brows furrow. "You're the fucking sex addict. Shouldn't you be giving the advice?"

"Hey," Lo warns with a glare.

He extends his arms. "It's an honest question."

"It's also rude."

"I'll ask nicely then." He looks back at Lily. "You're clearly more experienced than your little sister. So why the fuck aren't you instructing Rose?"

Lo shakes his head. "Pathetic."

"That's the best I have."

Lily touches her chest. "I like club dancing, but I've never personally given a lap dance."

"And Daisy has?" Ryke asks in disbelief.

"She said she did it once." Lily relaxes against Lo's chest, and he holds her close.

Ryke lets out an angry breath. "You do realize that ninety-percent of a lap dance is basically the same thing as when a girl fucks on top? You know, *riding* the guy."

"I don't think Rose wants to take the lap dance to that level on camera."

Our talk is cut off by a scraping noise. I watch Scott drag a dining chair into the living room, the legs scratching the hardwood.

When he places it in the center, he taps the frame of the chair. "Take a seat, Connor."

I don't take kindly to orders unless there's a greater benefit for me. And in this instance, there's none.

All eyes and cameras hit me, waiting for my reaction, wondering, quietly, if I'll adhere to Scott Van Wright's simple request. Rose stands impeccably straight, her bones hardened and stiff. All I see is fear, something that I desperately want to take away.

I stare right at Scott and break the strained silence with a few words. "Take a seat, Rose." My gaze never leaves Scott, not even as the humor abandons his eyes.

"That wasn't the bet," Scott says.

"I'm amending the terms."

Rose's heels clap against the hardwood as she struts to the chair. She sits down with her shoulders pulled back and her ankles crossed as if she just took her fucking throne.

My body heats just watching her.

I redirect my attention to Lo, who has his arms splayed over Lily's shoulders. "You're still going to see a lap dance. You okay with that?"

"That's all I want."

"Wait." Daisy holds up her hands and then points at me. "*You're* giving Rose a lap dance?"

"Yes." I untuck my black button-down from my slacks.

She smiles brightly. "Okay, we have to record this." She turns as if she's going to get a camera, and her elbow knocks into Savannah's Canon Rebel. "Oh . . . right . . . never mind." Only Daisy, a girl who's swarmed by photographers for her job, would momentarily forget that we're all being filmed.

"This I have to fucking see," Ryke says, settling on the couch next to Scott. Everyone takes seats, ready for the show.

But I lock eyes only with Rose as I approach her. She white-knuckles the side of the wooden chair, afraid and anxious and aroused.

She trails my body as I unbutton my shirt, and her breathing deepens.

The unknown is frightening for her.

But it can be the wildest, most tempestuous out-of-body experience she'll ever have.

Get ready, darling. This may spin your head.

Ten

Rose Calloway

Oh.

    My.

    God.

Connor slowly pushes the last button through his black shirt, club music blaring in the background from a pair of speakers. He stands confident, tall and domineering, like a perfect marbled statue, never once looking away from me.

I refuse to cower and crumple into a frightened ball. So I sit stiffly, waiting for him to near me. Waiting for—I don't know what. I have no idea what Connor Cobalt plans to do after that.

"Shake your ass, sweetheart!" Loren yells over the bass.

Connor doesn't give in to Lo's wish, and I feel Scott's penetrative gaze on me as he watches from the couch.

The moment Connor's legs brush against my knees, all the air tightens in my chest, chained deep inside my ribcage. He places his feet on either side of my chair, still standing and towering above me. I absorb his position, and my heart has decided to dance on its own, clenching and flipping and fluttering. Basically spasming. My heart is doing an idiot dance, the equivalent of shaking stupidly on the floor.

And then he tilts my chin so I look into his bottomless blue eyes. Power radiates in his motionless stance.

My neck grows hot, and he pries my hands off the chair, guiding them to his ripped abs. I feel him in ways I haven't before, the lines and hardness of his muscles. I warm the longer I run my hands along his body. I've thought about this so much. About what it would be like to be beneath someone as strong as him. I just never allowed myself to give him that victory, in fear that he'd run off with it and leave me behind.

I realize I'm practically eye level with his crotch. My ankles hurt as I cross them tighter together, forcing my legs shut.

My panties are soaked. That's all it took—him standing above me. *Really, Rose?*

I wait for him to shake his ass in my face or do some silly dance moves on my lap. But he doesn't perform either.

Scott clears his throat and lets out a laugh. "Connor, are you sure you know what you're doing?"

Connor stares right into my eyes and says, "Je sais toujours ce que je fais." *I always know what I'm doing.*

He unbuckles the belt to his slacks. And my heart pitches wildly. Really, my heart needs to go sit on the bleachers and take a serious time-out.

"You're not going to like me very much if you move. So stay fucking still."

It's not possible to move anyway. I am frozen to this chair.

He slips off his leather belt, and I fixate on it as he lowers to me. But instead of sitting on my lap, he rests his hands on my knees, breaking them apart, spreading my legs open. It allows him room to sit on the seat with me. The music still thumps loudly in the background, unraveling my senses.

My eyes widen in alarm, and I clutch his biceps. I try to breathe normally, but my lips are sealed shut, afraid, mostly, of any noises escaping. Pleasurable, fearful—all of the above.

He suddenly grips me by the waist, the belt wrapped around his hand. And he slides my back halfway down to a slumped position. One of his hands grips the top of the chair. He now shrouds my face from the cameras, but in the same instance, he dominates me completely.

He unwinds the belt and brings my wrists behind my back. He binds them together, the leather snug on my skin. Connor knots the belt and then cups my face. He begins rocking to the beat of the music.

He grinds his pelvis into mine, following the rhythm and tempo so it's not just dry humping. He's giving me a lap dance, and it's more sensual than anything I could have accomplished.

I struggle to keep my eyes on his. I am so aware of the people in the room, of the cameras, of the fact that he's on *top* of me, my legs hanging with uncertainty around him.

As his hardness digs into me, my nerves prickle, and my toes constrict in my high heels. *Oh my God . . .*

Is this really happening? In front of everyone? And soon-to-be nationally televised.

What did I get myself into?

His parted lips reach my ear. "Ne pense pas." *Don't think.*

That's a little difficult, Richard. But I can't open my mouth to form the words. His movements quicken with the music, rougher, and I grit my teeth hard to hold in a sound that tickles my throat. *Oh . . . God . . .* This shouldn't arouse me this much. Not with everyone watching.

I shut my eyes for a second, my head tilting back. He still holds my face in a strong, controlling hand. His mouth is so close to my cheek as he moves. I don't have to look to feel him studying me, watching me, a keen eye on all my needs. He knows me too well.

He grinds hard, and a sharp noise jumps out of my mouth. *Shit.* Before I can dwell on what just happened, he takes his hand off the chair and slides it to my thigh and up towards my bottom. My eyes shoot open, and I jerk my hands, but they're caught in his belt restraint.

I glare, and his smile grows, filled with that familiar arrogance.

I am much more aware of what's going on. I peek behind his arm and spot my sisters. Lily's mouth is permanently hung open, but Lo covers her eyes with his hand. So it's safe to presume she caught Connor being wicked in public, which is a rare sight to behold. He's usually only so uncouth in private.

Daisy sits on the armrest of a couch, and she wears a big grin. Ryke and Lo just watch in curiosity. And Scott . . . as soon as I turn my head to look at the producer, Connor grabs my chin and forces me back to him.

"Lui donneriez-vous ce qu'il veut?" *You would give him what he wants?* His eyebrow arches, and then his lips press to my jaw, kissing gently before sucking deeply.

The breath rushes out of me. The moment his eyes meet mine again, I say, "Il ne peut pas m'avoir." *He can't have me.* I should stop there. I shouldn't add anything else. But I don't want to lose this battle. I don't make this easy for Connor. I give him the challenge he craves. "Aucun homme ne peut." *No man can.*

His lips find my ear again. "We'll see." And then he wraps an arm around the small of my back, melding my body to his, and his other hand slips into my hair.

Before I can think about anything, he kisses me on the lips, his tongue parting mine, his whole body pushing against me. The place between my legs pulses for a heavy force, and my limbs tighten in rebut. *Good God . . .*

The music cuts off. And I realize that Connor has stopped rocking against me as soon as the song ended. We're kissing more passionately than I can ever remember, his fingers grasping my hair, my wrists digging against the leather as I want, so desperately, to touch him back.

"All right," Scott says. "That's enough."

His voice yanks me back into my head. I withdraw from Connor and turn my face before he can kiss me again. My body is flushed and sweaty, and my heart can't stop pounding.

"Wow," Daisy says, clapping, "that was hot. Solid ten."

"How much did I miss?!" Lily cries out, trying to pry Lo's fingers off.

"It was way too scandalous for your pretty eyes, love," Lo says with a grin. He drops his hand and kisses her on the temple.

I still try to catch my breath. Connor watches me carefully as he unties the belt. I keep my eyes narrowed at the wall. *What just happened?*

When Connor stands, I straighten up on the chair, but my muscles won't cooperate to do more than that.

"We were supposed to see a lap dance," Scott says. "Not a porno."

"Did I make you uncomfortable?" Connor asks in his usual impassive voice. He tucks his shirt back in his slacks and begins buttoning it. But he stays close to me.

Scott says nothing in reply.

"Allow me to accommodate your feelings then," Connor tells him. "There's the door. You'll be much happier on the other side of it."

Loren almost breaks into a giant grin at the diss, but his hot-tempered glare pins to the producer instead.

Scott scratches his scruffy jaw and just nods. Then he heads into the kitchen. On television, I wonder who's going to come across as the bigger asshole in this scenario.

Ryke stands and says, "Cobalt, were you or have you ever been a stripper?"

"No one would be able to afford me."

"It was *Magic Mike*, wasn't it?" Lily asks. "You had to have seen that movie." She turns to Lo and gives him round pleading eyes. "Let's see it just *one* time. It's not porn."

"Channing Tatum's abs might as well be porn," Daisy interjects.

Lo just kisses the top of Lily's head in reply.

She lets out a resigned sigh, and her eyes trail off in thought. "I do need a shower after watching that." Her cheeks immediately redden at the slip and her eyes bug. I can practically hear her thoughts: *Did I say that out loud?* Yes. Yes you did, Lily.

Daisy nudges her arm with a smile. "I totally call it after you."

Ryke and Lo groan, but Lily relaxes at the idea that she's not the only one aroused. Hell, I can't move because I know just how wet I am. Connor basically just electrocuted me with his pants *on*.

Ryke stands up from the couch. "I'm going to the gym. Anyone want to come?"

Daisy gasps. "You masturbate at the gym?"

He chucks a pillow at her face, and she catches it with a playful smile.

Loren turns to Lily. "You're really going to take a shower?" His voice is full of disbelief. I've heard them arguing about the bathroom situation since we moved in. Lily has yet to bathe, mostly out of fear of Scott walking in. I would coax those fears if I didn't have the same ones, hence why I shower at five in the morning.

She goes quiet, and Loren drops his voice. "You smell like sex," he whispers, but I'm still close enough to hear. "You've got to take one soon."

She stares at her hands. "Can we take them together? I won't do anything, I promise. I'll feel . . . safer."

There's a long pause before he says, "Only if we wear bathing suits. I just don't want to tempt you for six months, Lil."

Her face brightens and she throws her arms around his neck.

I rub my sore wrists, unsure of everything for a moment. Connor suddenly grabs my hand and effortlessly lifts me to my feet.

He stares down at me, and I realize what could have happened today. I could have awkwardly fumbled around him. I could have embarrassed myself on national television. Instead, he made me feel desired and hot instead of mortified and cold.

My eyes blanket in gratitude, the *thank you* on the tip of my tongue.

But his thumb brushes against my cheek and he says, very softly, "You're welcome, darling."

I exhale, glad that I don't have to struggle to produce the words anymore. The kitchen cupboards clatter loudly as Scott lumbers around.

"You fucked with his plans," I whisper.

"He'll wipe his tears and get over it later."

I'm not as optimistic. "Or he's going to find something that you can't screw up."

Eleven

Rose Calloway

t's still dark outside when my phone buzzes on the nightstand. I rub my drowsy eyes and check the clock. *4:30 a.m.* I reach perilously for my phone in the dark and knock off a bottle of aspirin. It clatters to the floor, and I look over my shoulder to make sure Connor hasn't woken up.

He remains unmoving on his side of the bed.

We didn't have sex. We've been amicably sleeping together without doing more than I want—which isn't quite right. I'm not exactly sure what I want when it comes to sex anymore. But I hesitate to give him that part of me—the part that he may take in triumph and then disappear with.

Carefully, I turn on the phone and cup my hand around the screen, blocking the glow.

5 months and 12 days until the wedding—Mom

Thanks, Mom, I text back, knowing she won't catch the thick sarcasm.

Yesterday, when she sent me the *5 months and 13 days* update, Lily opened the text on my phone. She almost needed a paper bag to hyperventilate into. She wants to be married about as much as a dog wants to be hit by a car. Planning the wedding is like shoving her into traffic, which is why I offered my services.

Planning. Organizing. Preparing. These are things I excel in. I even mediate between my mother's requests and Lily's wishes. As far as our parents go, Lily has tried to have little contact with them. The guilt of hurting Fizzle is a wound she doesn't like to reopen often. So I have become Lily Calloway's middleman—always reassuring our parents that she's not bingeing on cock.

Although if I said such a thing to my mother, she'd have a coronary.

But every time I ask my sister about invitations or music, she turns pale and mumbles something like *you choose*. So I'm no closer to planning the wedding than Lily is to wanting to get married. Which infuriates our mother. I'm sure I'll receive a phone call and lecture about time management later this afternoon.

"Everything okay, hun?"

My heart jumps at Connor's voice. I roll over to see him wide awake, head propped up by his hand.

"It's just my mother," I say in a whisper. "Sorry I woke you." I'm about to roll back to the far end of the mattress when my phone buzzes again.

Send me the Calloway Couture sales reports from last week. I'd like to have a financial advisor look over them.—Mom

I let out an aggravated growl. "She knows I don't want her involved in my company anymore," I say more to myself than Connor. "Why can't she just back off?"

I don't reply to her in text again. From experience, I know it's best not to start an argument over the phone. Especially one at four thirty in the morning.

"So you do want to talk," Connor says with the raise of his eyebrows.

"No." I blink and shake my head. "Sorry. It's too early . . ." I go to turn and Connor catches my arm.

"I have time for you," he says. I watch him sit up, fluff his pillow and lean against the headboard. He waves me on. "Let's hear it."

I rise a little, my legs tucked in front of me, and I tug the hem of my royal-blue silk nightgown. "When I told her I wanted to do a reality show to help Fizzle and Calloway Couture, the first thing she said was, *it'd better work, and if it doesn't, then I have two daughters that have ruined the Calloway name.*" I stare at the sheets and shake my head. "Who says that to their own daughter?"

Connor is quiet as he patiently lets me vent. Usually, I wait until therapy to unleash my aggravation. But at the end of those sessions, I'm always prescribed anti-anxieties, whereas Connor usually ends our conversations by calming most of my worries.

I continue as I think about her texts. "And even though I've reminded her a hundred times that I have Lily's wedding under control, she insists on butting in. *You can't have red velvet cake, Rose. Make the color scheme gold, like Fizzle, Rose. That venue is too small, Rose. Oh, but that one is too large.*" I throw up my hands after imitating her. "I can't do anything right."

"Have you tried ignoring her?" Connor asks.

He knows I haven't. I crumble at my mother's persistence. And even if she becomes overbearing and a little too much to handle, there is a part of me that loves that she cares. That she'd rather spend her time thinking about her daughters than worrying about mindless matters.

"I love her even if I hate her," I say, not entirely responding to his question.

"A paradox," Connor muses. "I like those. They make life interesting."

My eyes flit to his. We don't have these heart-to-hearts often. It's much more fun to debate over Freud's misogynistic theories. But we've spoken about Connor's relationship with his own mother a couple times. She's not cold or maternal. She just *is*. At least that's how he's always described Katarina Cobalt. As if she's nothing more than his boss.

I'd love to meet her, but Connor has lied to me about her being busy for over a year. He doesn't want me to see her for whatever asinine reason, and even if he won't tell me why, I respect his opinion. So when she called me a couple days ago, I brushed her off with the same excuse Connor has been using. *I'm* too busy for coffee and definitely too busy for brunch. It was rude, but if she listens to gossip and socialite mutterings, she'd know I'm a bit of a bitch.

"Mothers are all slightly insane," Connor says with a small smile. He just quoted J.D. Salinger, and he waits for me to say so. But I keep my lips tight like I lost him somewhere. His smile fades. "J.D. Salinger."

"Really? Most mothers are instinctive philosophers," I shoot back.

He grins again. "Harriet Beecher Stowe. And I couldn't agree more."

"I wasn't trying to stump you, so don't gloat." I want to hear the truth, not someone else's words. "Tell me something real."

And in one swift motion, he tugs my ankle, pulling me flat on the mattress. My nightgown rises to my belly, revealing my black cotton panties. Before I can fix it, he startles me by placing his hands on either side of my body, hovering above me. There's challenge in his eyes. To stay still. To not be afraid of him.

I inhale, fire brewing inside of me. I don't shift my nightgown, and my eyes narrow, finding my combative side. "You didn't answer me."

His eyes dance over my features. "You're not going to like what I have to say."

"I don't care. Just tell me anything."

"As long as it's real?"

"Yes."

He smiles. "Where do I even start?" His hand skims the bareness of my knee, up towards my thigh. "Besides what I'd love to do to you right now and tomorrow and for the rest of my life, I hope that someday, I'll watch you grow big and round . . ." He kisses my belly, and his mouth trails a line to my hipbone, dangerously close to my panties. ". . . and I'll hold you in my arms . . . every . . ." He traces the skin above the fabric. ". . . single . . . night."

I become so absorbed by his words, and I react how he probably predicted. I put two firm hands on his chest and push him to a sitting position.

His eyebrow arches. "Yes?"

"You want children?" I gape. I wasn't sure what he really wanted. But the fact that he's not on board with me—that we have *diverged* somewhere—has my heart rate at a hundred and five. I thought Connor was the male version of me. But I realize I'm not dating myself. I'm dating someone much different. Whether that's *better* is to be seen.

"I told you, you weren't going to like my answer. You said you weren't going to care. One of us lied."

I glower. "You want children."

"Does saying it twice make it more real?" he asks, his fingers touching his jaw. He's smiling, loving this way too much.

"Why would you want children? You're . . . you."

"You're right. I am me. And *me* wants eight screaming kids, who will bounce on our bed in the morning, who will beg you to braid their hair, who have your beautiful eyes and your brilliant mind. I want it all, Rose. And one day, our children will have it all too."

"*Eight* kids?!" I fixate on this. "I can't even stomach having *one* kid and you want me to birth a lineage? I'm not the Queen of England procreating to secure our empire with an heir."

He grins into a bright laugh, his teeth almost too gorgeous to stare at. He wrestles me back to the mattress, and he kisses my cheek. "But don't you want a son and daughter to succeed you," he asks, "to raise them as your own, to know that your legacy will still remain long, long after you're gone?"

"It's still all about you," I say, understanding completely now. "Could you even love your children?"

His smile fades again, and he becomes impassive, poker-faced. "I'd love them."

I wish, more than anything, he wouldn't *try* to lie to me. That angers me more than hearing the truth. "You only love yourself."

"I love you." He's practically mocking me.

I push him up again, and I rise to my knees. My lips find his ear, my voice hot and cold all at once. "I *don't* believe you." I scoot to the edge of the bed, to climb off. He catches my arm again.

"I meant what I said," he tells me seriously, "before you brought love into the equation."

"That's the thing, Connor." I untangle from him. "Love should always be in the equation when children are involved. You're just lucky I don't hold that stipulation." I step off the bed and straighten my nightgown.

"Where are you going?" he asks, worry creasing his brows. We fight often. And we make up even more. It's not as though my storming off is out of the ordinary.

"To take a shower."

"It's five in the morning. Come back to bed."

"No," I say. "I want to shower before anyone comes into the bathroom." I head towards the door.

"Rose . . ." He starts but he stops himself before he gets that far. I feel like I'm eighteen again.

And Connor's that nineteen-year-old boy who lent me his college blazer.

I wait for him to speak, but like back then, he just stares at me with those deep austere eyes, with shadows of the truth hidden behind pools of blue.

So I say, "I don't mind that you don't love me the way I do you." I tuck my hair behind my ear. "Thank you for at least trying."

And I leave.

But he knows I'll be back.

In nearly ten years of knowing Connor, we always seem to return to each other—even when we were thousands of miles apart, on two separate planes of existence—even when it seemed like our futures had strayed.

He may not believe in fate, but I do.

And I know I'm fated to be with him.

Twelve

Rose Calloway

5 months and 10 days—Mom

I slip my cell in my purse, about to head to the Calloway Couture offices. Savannah stays close by my side with the camera hovering. As soon as I head towards the door, it whips open and Daisy walks in with her white motorcycle helmet beneath her arm.

"Hey, Rose." She sets the helmet on the leather couch and twists her long blonde hair in a loose bun atop her head.

But she's not alone. Brett enters with his steadicam, and Ryke shuts the door behind them, his black helmet dangling in his hand. Ryke slumps down on the couch and runs his fingers through his thick tousled hair.

"Good, I caught you," I tell Daisy, deserting my plans for a second. "I want to give you something before I forget." I should really get Lily in the living room too. But she's much harder to wrangle. "Stay here." I head to the hall closet and return with a shopping bag.

Before I pass her the bag, I notice the way Ryke and Daisy share furtive glances. She shakes her head at him, and he grits his teeth, his jaw locking into hard-cut lines.

"Is everything okay?" I ask with a little edge. I don't like being out of the loop. If it involves my sisters, I want to be in the center fucking circle.

"Perfect," Daisy says with a bright smile. I don't believe her, and I have a suspicion Ryke wants to come clean since he shakes his head now. She grabs the bag out of my hand to distract me.

I let the issue go, only because I can't prod today. I need to get work done at my office, and if I dwell on my little sister, I'll worry until someone spills the truth. It's probably not that bad anyway. I'm sure she just sped down the highway on her Ducati and almost got herself killed. In Daisy Calloway's adrenaline-fueled world, that situation is like the sun rising and setting.

"Ooh," she says. "Which one is mine, the tie-dye or the leopard-print?"

Ryke frowns. "What the fuck did you get her?"

I shoot him a glare. "Not whatever you're thinking."

"Panties," Daisy tells him.

"That's exactly what I was fucking thinking."

She smiles. "I know." And she pulls out a plastic package that does *not* contain panties. "Pepper spray." She glances at me. "I think I'll take this one." She holds the tie-dye package.

"Since you and Lily have given up your bodyguards for the show, I thought it would be a good idea to have some sort of protection." In order to film, Scott had a proviso that Daisy and Lily ditch their bodyguards, who had been keeping them safe from paparazzi after we went from anonymity to celebrity. "I also signed us up for a self-defense class."

"Didn't you used to take those classes all the time in Princeton? Why would you want to go to another one?"

"Because you girls should learn."

"I don't know if I have the time," Daisy says honestly. "I'm booked for shoots a lot this week."

"I think it's a good idea," Ryke chimes in from the couch.

My brows jump. "Really?"

"Sure," he says, his eyes not softening like mine. "And if Daisy doesn't have the fucking time, then Lo, Connor and I can help out here. We can push the furniture to the walls for space." I would love to beat the shit out of Loren. But what's more appealing is trying to pin Connor to the floor. I'd revel in that win for months.

"You want to help?" I ask Ryke.

"Why does everyone find that so fucking hard to believe?"

"I don't," I say. "I'm just wondering why you're so concerned all of a sudden."

"I'm always concerned. I just don't voice my opinion every five seconds like you."

"You're a jackass," I tell him casually.

"You're a bitch."

"Thank you." I grab my phone out of my purse. "And I accept your help by the way. Lily really needs to learn how to protect herself without running behind Lo's back."

"Yeah," Ryke says, "but you girls need to fucking admit that you can't protect yourself against a hoard of angry guys with a mini bottle of pepper spray and a kick to the nuts. It's better if we're there too."

I dial Lily's number. "I disagree," I say. "The tip of my heel to your ball sac would cripple you."

"*A hoard* of fucking guys," Ryke emphasizes. He purposefully rests his dirty boots on my coffee table.

I choose not to break his neck. This time.

Daisy pries the plastic open and pops out the canister from the packaging.

I press my phone to my ear, the ringing incessant.

Daisy shakes the pepper spray. "Should I test it out?" She grins and points the nozzle at Ryke. "Stay away, you pervert!"

Ryke's face darkens, not amused.

She drops her hand and walks over to the couch, plopping down beside him. They have an intense whisper-conversation that Brett tries to catch by edging close to Daisy. Ryke physically plants his hand on the camera lens and drives Brett back, putting space between them.

Brett glares. "You can't touch the cameras, Ryke. How many times do we have to tell you that?"

"Back up and I won't."

Brett shakes his head, but he shuffles backwards.

I concentrate on my phone call, and the dial tone sounds after the last ring. I groan and click the "off" button. "LILY!" I shout. I know she's upstairs, and I want to give her a bottle of pepper spray before I leave.

When I glance back at my little sister, I scrutinize the way she leans into Ryke as she whispers something to him. Her eyes drift over his features in a curious, impulsive manner, and my heart quickens.

She's going to kiss him.

And then when her lips stop moving, Ryke puts a hand to Daisy's cheek. And he forces her face away from his. It's a gentle push that has her trying to tackle him on the couch with a laugh. They're verging on flirting, even when his brooding features say that he's pissed at her.

He struggles to hold her still as she slides beneath his arm and snatches his helmet. She swiftly fits it over her head, and he tries to pull it off her, his lips slowly upturning. But she wiggles out of his hold, and in seconds, she's suddenly straddling his lap. He flips up the visor to his helmet and stares harshly at her, hiding his partial smile.

I worry that the cameras will pick up *any* chemistry between them. My mother will not approve of a Ryke Meadows and Daisy Calloway coupling. For multiple reasons.

"Both of you, stop it."

Ryke snaps awake, and he shoves her completely off his body. Her back hits the cushions.

His eyes flit from me to the staircase. "Lo!" he yells. "Lily! Get your asses down here!" His voice is a lot louder than mine.

From upstairs, feet patter but then they stop and go quiet, hesitating to join the land of people and real, adult things. Lo and Lily keep to themselves, living in their own hazy, addicted world. Here, it's a bit scary.

"Loren fucking Hale!" Ryke calls.

Nothing.

Daisy rises to her knees and grips the back of the couch. She peers up at the staircase behind me. "Lo! Lily! A comic book came in the mail for you!" She pulls off the motorcycle helmet.

Enticing Lo with something that's *not here* will put him in a worse mood.

But it works.

Lo and Lily stampede down the stairs. "It's mine!" Lily shouts at him. "I ordered the new *X-Men* comic." She tries to shove him into the wall, and they block each other mid-stair.

"And I ordered the last issue of *New Mutants*." He steps forward and she jumps in front of him, gaping.

"You've already read that! Mine is more important." She spins to race to the door.

Daisy crouches behind the couch.

Before Lily reaches the bottom stair, Lo snatches her by the waist and throws her across his shoulder.

"Not fair!" she retorts, trying to squirm from his strong grasp.

He carries her to the door without so much as glancing at us in the living room. When it comes to comics, sex and booze, they have a one-track mind.

Ben creeps down the stairs, the camera positioned under his arm. He looks slightly petrified from being alone with them, his eyes bugged and his legs shaking.

They must have been in the study room and not a bedroom, or else he wouldn't have been able to film them. And I'm sure they were making out with more heat than a horny cat—just to say *fuck you* to the cameras. They've been at it all week. It's only getting worse the longer Lo has to put up with Scott.

Lily said she's been purposefully trying to distance Lo from the producer and finding ways to keep them apart for as long as possible. I think it's a brilliant idea.

Ben almost drops his camera.

"Steady hands," Savannah says to him.

Brett rolls his eyes. (I'm not a big Brett fan.)

Ben lets out a nervous laugh. Documenting Lily and Loren is like being an extreme voyeur, peeping in on their intimate affairs. I bet he feels a bit gross and wrong afterwards. Even reading about Lily's sex life online leaves me feeling violated. I imagine it's ten times worse for Lily.

"Wait . . ." Lily says from the door. "There's nothing here."

I grab the shopping bag and head over to the two of them. "This is for you," I tell Lily. She brightens when she thinks it's the comic. But as she sifts through the bag's contents, her face falls for the second time. "Pepper spray?"

"For protection."

"No, she thought it was for greasing pans," Loren retorts.

I glare.

"You're going to treat us like idiots," he says, "you're going to get an idiot response back."

Touché. "I'll be leaving."

"Look at that, Lil. The queen has announced her departure. Should we bow?"

"Lo," Lily warns and gives him a sharp look, and for Lily, those don't come often.

He shuts his mouth, which must take a great, great deal of effort.

"Go sit with your jackass brother on the couch," I tell him. "And just so you know, I like that jackass better than you, and I've known him fifteen years less." I flash Loren a dry smile. "See you tomorrow."

Loren usually has the last word, but I slam the door behind me before he gets it. Bickering with Lo solidifies my day as a normal one. The bad days are the ones where everything is a little off. So far, so good.

I jinxed myself.

I know Connor does not believe in such things, but *I know* I fucking did something wrong. I said, *so far, so good*. And OF COURSE something decided to blow back in my face.

Scott is here.

At my office.

He just showed up while I was in the middle of rearranging my inventory into plastic tubs. I was separating them according to seasons, trying to unearth the spring and summer collections that we'll need to wear soon for the show. I've been letting my sisters wear their own clothes at certain times, just because I don't have enough pieces for six full months, even if we wear an outfit twice. Hopefully Scott airs the footage where we're all dressed in Calloway Couture and not Old Navy, which Lily gravitates towards.

"You work too hard," Scott tells me, setting down a plastic bag on my white desk. Boxes and tubs line the large loft space. Besides that and my desk and a pig, there's not much else in here. Oh, wait, there is Brett who films us.

Scott's kindness must be a result of the camera in his face, trying to capture some footage of him being nice. Must be painful for him.

"I don't," I say. "The people who work hard are the ones dedicated to protecting our country, who do better by it. I just design clothes." I snap the lid onto one of the tubs and wipe my hands on my black pleated dress, the seam touching my thighs (not good) and my collarbones (thank God). At least I have on sheer black tights.

"I brought you dinner."

I watch him pull out *two* Styrofoam to-go containers, vaguely interested. I ignore my stomach, which threatens to grumble on the spot.

He opens the containers, and I see the lines of sushi, the little dab of wasabi and bundle of ginger. I barely hear him say the name of my favorite sushi restaurant in New York. I'm too slack-jawed that he got something right. Maybe I've been too harsh, too bitchy and judgmental just because he's from California and says a few sleazy things.

I grimace as I try to come to terms with being *nice* too. I clear my throat and straighten my spine. "I only have one chair." I near my desk and peer into the plastic bag, taking out chopsticks and soy sauce.

"That's okay. You can sit on my lap."

I glare.

"Just kidding," he laughs. "I'll sit on your desk."

Fine. I settle in my rolling chair and pick the to-go box with the rainbow roll, also my favorite. Connor usually brings me dinner in the city, and the fact that he's been replaced by Scott agitates me. "So who told you I liked sushi?" I ask him.

As promised, he sits on half of my desk, his legs hanging close to me. "I've always known it's your favorite, babe."

I pause, my chopsticks frozen above the ginger. So he's definitely playing into our *fake* old relationship. Two can play this game. "I never ate sushi with you," I retort. "You said you hated it, and you always made me eat alone."

His lips twitch in a cringe, which he hides very well. He sets his to-go box on his lap. "Things have changed."

"You like sushi now?"

He eats a piece, chews and swallows. "I *love* sushi now." He smiles, and I absorb his features, the dishwater-blond hair that's styled in a messy, dysfunctional way. And the light layer of scruff along his jaw that makes him look a little older than his age.

I hate that he's not ugly. I wish he had a thousand warts and a hairy nose. Instead, he could be an actor on a daytime soap, not a producer.

"You miss me," he suddenly says.

My eyes tighten. "Not for a second." My phone buzzes on the desk.

Scott snatches it before I can.

"That's incredibly rude," I tell him as he opens my text.

He lets out a laugh. "*Marilyn Monroe, Paul Newman, James Dean.* Your boyfriend is so fucking weird." He tosses the phone back to me, and I just barely catch it without dropping my chopsticks.

"Sometimes weird is better than normal," I say. "Normal can be boring."

He touches his chest. "I'm not boring, honey."

Why does he have to say everything so condescendingly? "I fell asleep every time you wanted to have sex. What do you call that?"

"A personal problem."

I roll my eyes and quickly text Connor back. Fuck. Marry. Kill. I'm more comfortable with the idea of having sex with a woman than I am with a man, as strange as that may seem. Connor will most likely pick up on this, but I don't care. I hit send and set my phone back safely on the desk, away from Scott's grabby fucking hands.

"I saw your mother yesterday," he says.

"You did?" I try not to act surprised, but my heart has lodged in my throat for a second. Why would he visit my mother?

"We ate lunch and caught up. It was like old times." He passes me a water bottle and then takes a swig of his Cherry Fizz. "She said she wished Daisy was around, that the house was too quiet without all of you girls there."

"Stop," I tell him, standing up and setting the sushi on the desk. It feels like fool's food, a trap, something you give a three-headed dog before sneaking into a treasure cove.

He frowns. And I can't tell whether it's real or fake. Honest or deceitful. "What's wrong?"

"You don't know me," I refute. I return to my tubs of clothes, but I don't want to squat down in front of him.

"I do know you," he lies.

I spin around and realize he's casually leaning against the front of my desk. "Can you please leave?"

"I don't get it. I say one thing about your mother and you throw a tantrum."

I glance at the camera. I don't want to vilify my mother to the nation. I don't want to cause her that pain. She's a good woman even if she does bad things sometimes. But the more he pokes me, the more these thoughts and feelings resurface, the more I can't bite my tongue. That's Connor's specialty. He's the river that idly passes between mountains. I'm the volcano that destroys a village.

"What is it?" he taunts, his voice anything but kind. He wears an antagonistic smile. "She didn't buy you a diamond necklace? She forgot your eighteenth birthday?"

"My mother would never forget my birthday," I tell him. "She's always been there for me."

Scott shrugs like I'm insane. Maybe I am. Maybe my feelings are irrational. Maybe I'm losing my mind with all the stresses in my life. "She was upset that she was an empty-nester. It's normal, Rose."

"I don't want her to take Daisy back," I suddenly blurt out.

Scott frowns again. "Why not? Do you have some perverse fantasy about raising her, becoming a mother because Connor won't have kids with you?"

"Fuck you," I curse. I grab my handbag and lift one of the tubs awkwardly in my arms. Scott doesn't offer to carry it for me (not that I would let him). "You can see yourself out."

"My pleasure."

I struggle to open the door with one hand. This time, I don't have Connor behind me to scoop up the box and help. I manage fine at first. I breeze through the door and head down the hall, breathing sporadic breaths that slide down my throat like brittle knives.

The tub drops out of my hands by the elevator. The lid cracks, and I hurriedly fold each article of clothing before placing them back inside.

I don't want to float inside my head, but the longer I take, the more I feel the past whisper against my neck like a cold, familiar ghost. I see my oldest sister, Poppy, who grew tall before the rest of us, who was out the door, married and pregnant in practically no time at all.

When she left, my mother focused her excess attention on me, pressuring me to continue ballet, attending every practice and recital, filling my schedule with dinner dates and functions. And I wanted to make her proud. How else can you give thanks to someone who gives you *everything* you desire? Who showers you with things that glitter? You become someone they can gloat over; you become their greatest prize.

Connor is right. He talks of monetary values. Of benefits. Opportunity cost. There is a price that you pay growing up in luxury. You feel so undeserving of everything around you. So you find a way to *be* deserving of it—by being smart, by being talented and successful.

By building your own company.

With Calloway Couture, I could make my father proud—to show him that I could follow his entrepreneurial footsteps. The failure of my company feels not only like a failure of my dream, but a failure of my place in the family. Of my right to have these beautiful things.

But I have to remember what else my company means to me.

What it has been. How it's saved me. It was an outlet where I could be creative despite my mother's constant nagging. I used to come home, rub my abused toes from pointe shoes, and sketch on my bed, in private. I was twelve. I was thirteen. Fourteen. I found solace in fashion. I found peace and happiness.

It was something for *me*. My mother couldn't take my designs. She couldn't make them hers. I created each dress, each blouse and skirt. They were the clay that I could mold, even if she continued to try and mold me.

And then I left for Princeton when I turned eighteen. My mother lost me, the daughter who she fought the most with, but only because I was the daughter she turned to, the one she talked to, the one who spent nights listening to her prattle, who heard her advice, even if I chose not to take it. I love that she loves me. I just wish she let me breathe for a moment in my life.

My mother still had Lily after I left. But she brushed over her, believing she was set for life with Loren Hale, the heir of a multibillion-dollar company almost as lucrative as Fizzle.

So that left Daisy.

I knew exactly what would happen to her the moment I went to college. I knew she'd take my place as consummate daughter, ready to say yes to my mother the moment I shut the door. But as a teenager, I fought my mom each step of the way. I was bitchy and obstinate.

My sister is none of those things.

I cried when I finished unpacking my dorm room. I was smart enough to see what would happen. And I couldn't do anything about it. Daisy would bend to my mother's desires, to her selfish ways. She would sign Daisy up for so many classes to where she couldn't see straight. She would make her date whoever she chose. She would dress her in fancy ball gowns with too much frill and lace. And she'd parade her around like a toy doll with no voice and no brain. No matter how much I called Daisy to check in, to listen to her words crack before she layered on the false optimism, I couldn't change the course of things.

I thought for sure Daisy would turn to drugs.

I thought for sure she'd party too hard to try to reach the air that my mother always sucked dry.

I coped by scribbling in a sketch book at that house. I couldn't see that as a path for Daisy. I only saw blackness. And I'll never forgive myself for what happened, how blind I was.

I was focusing on the wrong sister.

Lily was heading down that dark road, feeding an addiction that not many people understand.

Daisy wasn't even close to that yet.

But I fear making the same mistake—not helping Daisy like I was too late for Lily. I don't want my mom to exploit Daisy with her modeling career just so she can brag to her tennis club friends. I want my sister to watch late-night movie marathons, have slumber parties and eat too much ice cream. But her childhood already consists of stumbling home with tired eyes from a midnight photo shoot, from going on go-see after go-see where people pinch her waist and call her fat.

This is my price I pay for my wealth.

I'm sure of it.

No matter how much I want to save my sisters and just keep them close, I feel as if I'm destined to watch them fall.

Thirteen

Connor Cobalt

I check my watch. 4 a.m. The stationary cameras in the kitchen rafters film me, but there's no possibility anyone would want to watch me, alone, right now. I just take pleasure in the idea that Scott will have to sift through hours of footage of me doing monotonous tasks, like studying. I find time to give the cameras the finger too, even if it's childish.

Ryke would definitely do it.

And if I can tell Scott to fuck off at four in the morning, then I'll gladly take the opportunity. The benefit is just too fucking good.

I pour black coffee into a larger mug and fit the pot back. As soon as I turn around, I flinch and almost spill the hot liquid on my button-down and slacks. "Dammit, Rose."

She wears her black silk robe, but I focus on her hands that fix firmly on her hips. "You never came to bed."

I take a sip of my coffee and pass her easily, heading to the kitchen table, papers spread around my open laptop. "I have business reports due tomorrow. I don't have time to sleep." She follows me, and just as I near my chair, she kicks the legs, and it overturns and clatters to the floor.

My brows jump as I look from Rose, her arms crossed, and the chair on the floor. "Are you trying to start something?" I would smile if my eyes didn't feel like lead. My temples pound as though someone repeatedly swung a bat at my face. She has more leverage on me when I'm this exhausted.

"Let me help you with the report," she says.

"No." I set my mug down on the table so I don't burn her or me. Her vexed stance and piercing yellow-green eyes tell me what she may do next. And it's not going to be delicate.

"Richard, you can't live off two hours of sleep a day. So either I help you or you're going to turn your report in late and try to get an extension."

The latter is not an option, and while I think Rose is fully capable of helping me, she needs the sleep as much as I do. There's no point in both of us suffering while I try to get my MBA.

"Go back to bed," I say flatly.

"You're stubborn."

"I'm determined," I refute. I layer on a complacent smile, which causes her chest to rise in irritation.

She shoves me hard, and I sway at the force, already predicting it enough to brace myself. But she catches me off guard, darting to the table and gathering my papers. She scans the words quickly.

"Rose," I warn. "You're not helping me." I try to collect the papers from her, but she holds them above her head, as though that'll work. I easily snatch a couple, having the height advantage.

"I can calculate these numbers," she says, glancing at the computer screen.

"I have no doubt that you can. But you're not going to." She tries to reach for my laptop, but there's no way I'm letting her touch it—tired or not, I block her with my body and shove her back with enough force that she stumbles into the wall.

She gapes and then her lips tighten. "You always talk about how I need to accept help once in a while. You're becoming a—"

"Think hard before you finish that sentence, darling."

Her eyes brighten at the challenge. "A hypocrite."

That's it. I grab her around the waist, and she starts hitting my chest with closed fists. "Set me down right now, Richard!"

I carry her towards the kitchen sink, my hand gripping her ass, while she thrashes against me. When she bites my arm, I grimace into a laugh. "You want to play rough?" I set her feet on the ground, and before she can orient herself, I push her hard against the kitchen island.

I lose my hand in her hair and yank forcefully. She gasps, but she blinks quickly. "Let me help you."

"No."

Her nose flares. And she slams the heels of her palms into my chest, forcing me back. "*I'm* doing half of your report." She's about to storm over to the kitchen table, but I seize her again. My lips find her ear as I draw her ass towards my cock.

"No," I force, "the only thing you're going to do is sleep." My hot breath hits her skin as I lower my head. Her perfume smells like white roses and ivy—a scent that dizzies me in an intoxicating lull. I love every inhale. My lips skim her neck before I suck deeply.

She lets out an audible noise of pleasure before spinning on me again, her gaze flickering to my laptop.

"No," I tell her.

"Yes."

When we disagree, we usually don't speak for a couple days until one of us concedes. I don't want that to happen tonight, not with Scott upstairs trying to encroach on my territory. I watch her shift in anger, her black robe stopping mid-thigh. Adrenaline pumps into my veins as her blazing eyes dance over me.

I rub my sensitive lips, and I make a calculated decision. I shove her into the island again, and she lets out a sharp noise. She tries to fight me at first, but I pin her to this place with my pelvis, her spine curving against the counter.

I squeeze her chin and glare as though she's been a bad fucking girl, a look she rarely sees from me. Her whole body shudders. I feel every quake against my chest, my legs, my arms and groin. Her lips part and a high-pitched moan staggers upon release. The noise grips my cock so tightly that I choke on a groan. I want to be so far inside of her. I want to pound between her legs until her eyes flutter, until her limbs slacken in exhausted defeat.

She breathes heavily, as do I, and I trace her lips, her flushed cheeks, her narrowed eyes.

"I'm helping you," she says with a raspy voice.

"No," I say before I bite her lip. She moans again, and I slip my tongue into her mouth, kissing her forcefully. She returns it with just as much power, her hands clenching my hair with a desperation that I haven't seen from her in a while.

I lift her up onto the counter and pull her legs towards me. I wrap them around my waist, not giving her time to be uncertain. My hands drift underneath her robe, relaxing on the bareness of her thighs. I kiss her while guiding her shoulders onto the cool counter. My lips break from hers, sucking a line from her collar towards her breasts. With one hand, I slowly untie her robe, and then her eyes meet the cameras overhead.

She shoots up and places two hands on my chest. "Wait . . ." Her eyes flicker to the rafters again. I don't want Scott to see Rose naked any more than she does, but I knew this would be the easiest way to get her to forfeit.

I'm not really a winner in this scenario. My cock hates me, dying to slip between her legs and thrust for as long as we both can last.

"Let me help."

"I'm either fucking you right now. Or you're going to bed."

She realizes there's no alternative. Really, I wouldn't deflower her in the middle of the kitchen with cameras pointed on us. I may be horny, but I have an idea of how I want to take her virginity. And this isn't it.

"Fine," she concedes. "I'll go to bed this once, but if I catch you up again like this, *I'm helping.* Or you're going to wake up with bruises."

"Such threats." I kiss her cheek, my lips lingering.

She holds my arms and swallows hard. I put a little space between us, but I keep my hand on her knee as she stays seated on the counter. A sudden thought sweeps my brain. It's one I've meant to ask before. "Where do I rank in your life?"

She frowns and shakes her head in confusion. "You want me to rank you?"

I nod. I want to know how far I have to climb to be her first importance. I'm willing to work hard to get there, but I need to know who fills her heart before me and if I'll ever be able to surpass them.

"I have siblings," she says.

Her sisters outrank me. All three of them. That's what I thought. "I almost had brothers," I tell her honestly.

Her face falls. "What?"

"Twins. They would have been fourteen by now." I skim her knee with my finger.

"How can you say it like that?" she asks.

"Like what?"

"Detached."

"I'm not the one who carried them for nine months."

She slaps my arm. "Stop being an ass. This is serious."

"I know. That's why I'm telling you. I'm not sure if having brothers would have made me a different person." I've often thought about this event and how it could have reshaped my life, but it's too foggy to see a clear outcome. They would have been ten years younger than me. They would have gone to boarding school, been distanced from my life at Penn. Would I have been as fiercely protective of them as Rose is to her sisters? I don't know. I was never given the chance to see. "My mother had complications during their birth. They both passed, and I have no idea how she coped afterwards. She seemed . . . fine. She could have been as cold as she appeared to be, or she could have just hid her grief. I wouldn't know."

"Didn't your parents separate two years later?"

I nod. "But I think their marriage was already strained when she was pregnant. I rarely saw them together."

"Do you think . . . ?" She trails off, not able to say the words.

"That she cheated on him? That those weren't his kids?" I shrug. "Maybe. But all of it is neither here nor there. It's all just . . . gone."

She exhales loudly. "That's a lot to take in, Richard."

"No one knows that except Frederick. I didn't think it was important."

"It is," she says.

I still don't see how, but somewhere in the recesses of my mind, I must have believed it was significant too or else I wouldn't have shared it. "So you love your sisters the most?"

She runs her fingers through her shiny brown hair. "I can't imagine loving anyone more than them."

"You do realize that Lily loves Loren more than anyone else on the planet? If they were both given the ultimatum of oxygen or each other, I'm fairly certain they'd choose to suffocate."

She contemplates this for a second, her brows scrunching in thought.

"I'm not asking you to love me," I tell her. "I think we're both smart enough to choose oxygen." *I don't see how love could benefit me.*

Her eyes fall and her lips downturn. After a full minute of silence, she says, "I'd choose to die if it meant my sisters could live. You think it's stupid, but sometimes love is worth every foolish choice you make." She hops off the counter. "Oh, and you're my number three."

"I beat Poppy already?" I fight a burgeoning smile.

"I see her less than I do you."

I fit my arms around her waist. "Don't ruin it," I breathe, kissing her neck lightly. My hand lowers to the small of her back, and I leave her with one last kiss to the forehead that feels more genuine than all the others. "You've bewitched me, body and soul."

She glares. "And *you* ruined it with a quote from *Pride and Prejudice*."

I grin. "What? I thought we were purposefully being cliché."

"Maybe next time, quote the book and not the film."

My eyebrow arches and I recite theatrically, "You pierce my soul. I am half agony, half hope." I shake my head. "Doesn't have the same ring to it, darling."

A laugh escapes her lips. "Go back to work. I'll see you in the morning. Oh wait"—she feigns surprise—"it is the morning. I'll see you when we cross paths again." I watch her walk to the staircase, her lovely round ass bouncing against her silk robe.

"How can you be sure we will?" I ask before I return to my computer. She hypnotizes me, gluing me to this very spot.

She glances over her shoulder, her silky hair molding her beautiful face. "Because," she says, "we always do."

Fourteen

Rose Calloway

I don't go back to sleep. I decide to take a shower before the rest of the house wakes up. The bathroom is my hell. I think it's the third or second circle. Scott Van Wright, a devil in disguise, stands firmly in the first.

A chest-high tiled wall *barely* separates one shower from the other. As though we need to high-five while we're shampooing our hair.

I wash quickly, but I have a particular routine: scrub beneath my nails at least twice, rinse, shampoo, wash, condition, repeat. I've already finished with those steps. But I still have others to do.

I prop my foot near the hot-and-cold knob and shave my leg. I slow down to avoid cutting my ankle or knee.

And then the door swings open.

I drop my leg, warm water dousing me from the showerhead. *Please be Connor.*

I process that sudden realization—that I'd want it to be him, out of everyone, that'd I'd hope for it. Even if it would pull him away from his business project.

I hate that I'm attracted to a man who thinks love is nothing but a weakness. But I also adore that there's no one else remotely like Connor Cobalt in the world.

And I'm the one who has him.

When I look back up, *Scott* is already halfway inside, heading to one of the sinks in the center. He barely acknowledges me, just turns on the faucet and starts brushing his teeth. I solidify to stone. And I only move to cover my chest with my arms, standing underneath the showerhead, as though the downpour of water will clothe me.

I should ignore him and just go back to shaving, but I can't reawaken my taut muscles.

I shouldn't watch him either, but I find myself scanning his features quickly. Messy dishwater-blond hair, scruffy jaw and reddened eyes from the early morning.

He spits into the sink, and his gaze meets mine as he wipes his mouth with a towel. "Yes?"

"I didn't say anything." My voice is not even a little kind. I don't know how to defrost the ice that clings to each syllable, even if I wanted to.

"You're staring." This fact gives him permission to lower his gaze to the misted shower glass.

I don't look away. I will not come across as a frightened bird.

"I wondered if you were a bush kind of girl. Now I know." He tops it off with a half smile.

I purse my lips. He can't see *that* much detail through the glass. "You're a pig."

He tosses his toothbrush back in a cabinet underneath the sink and leans against the porcelain rim. "And Lo calls me Mr. Hollywood. Do you all have a thing with nicknames?"

"Loren also told you to eat shit in the same breath, so I wouldn't gloat."

His grin never falters, in fact it widens. "You forget that every curse word, every *pig* and insult is another notch for ratings. So keep 'em coming, honey."

He prefers to provoke Loren since he's fishing for drama. He'd like for me to curse him out too. Maybe I should seal my lips shut and let him deal with the silence. We could still have great ratings without being nasty. But it's harder for me to be nice than mean. However awful that seems.

Scott steps closer to the showers, and my eyes tighten as I glare so hard. I continue to hide my breasts with my arm, but everything else is exposed. I could reach for the towel, but surrendering is not an avenue I'll take. I'll look foolish and scared, which'll sit like deadweight in my stomach.

He *slowly* steps out of his pants.

"What are you doing?" I ask.

He cocks his head. "Taking a shower, Rose." He motions to the available "stall" beside mine—the one so close that we could practically high-five. "Do I need your permission?"

"Yes." I straighten my shoulders. "And you're *not* getting it."

He laughs. "I was just being a dick when I asked. I don't really care about your permission."

I don't really care about your permission. His words gnaw a hole in my brain. I hated him before. I think I *loathe* him now.

He removes his white shirt, and my eyes linger on his abs for point-two seconds. They're okay . . . Defined, but more *I lift too many weights and drink a shit ton of protein shakes* sculpted than the natural *this is my body. I'm just fucking hot* look. Which all three guys in the house possess in spades (even if they all *do* work out together).

My loyalties lie far, far away from Scott Van Wright—and even a simple compliment about his body feels like kissing a pig who shit in my yard.

I catch a glimpse of his red briefs.

This is not okay.

Fuck it. Where's my towel?

I go to reach over the glass door to retrieve the cloth off the hook, but Scott snatches it—and it slings right out of my grip.

You have got to be—"That's *my* towel." This is *not* okay.

"Now it's mine." Scott acts modest all of a sudden, tying it around his waist so he can shed his underwear.

I fume. Outwardly. Steam may as well be blowing out of my ears. "What, no peep show this morning?"

"We'll save that for the bedroom," he says. And winks. He *winks* at me. My insides shrivel in repulsion. I think he just poisoned my uterus.

He takes off his briefs, all while keeping the towel snug around his waist, and then he kicks his underwear to the side. His eyes pin to me, a smile playing at his lips. Yes, he is naked underneath that towel.

And yes, I am very much naked in the shower right now.

I'm not quite sure things could get much worse.

"Sorry that phone call took so long, darling." Connor's voice emanates from the doorway. "The partners wouldn't stop talking about finger paints."

A sudden wave of relief crashes into me. My teammate has arrived to tag me out of this disaster. Somehow he saw or heard Scott in the bathroom and came to retrieve me. Maybe he finally realized that I can finish his project *for* him.

Thank you. I'm out of here.

And then Connor says, "My shampoo, is it in there?"

That relief is squashed by anxiety. I understand now. He wants to come into the shower. He plans to beat Scott this round and push our relationship to a place where it should already be. I try to pump my chest with more confidence, but he still wants to hop in here with me. And in order for Connor to win, I can't be shocked by his arrival. I can't push him away like he's less than my boyfriend. I need to be as comfortable around him as I should be. I can't say *wait* like I did downstairs. I have to let him keep going. Full speed ahead. No fucking brakes. *Grow some bigger balls, Rose Calloway.*

Yes, I think I can do this.

I scan the shelf with an arrangement of female and male hair products. I find his black bottle that costs more than my conditioner and body wash put together. "Your precious shampoo is here," I say in my usual biting tone.

"You shouldn't insult my shampoo. I've been told my hair is my second best feature." He ignores the fact that Scott still stands outside the second shower, his hand on the glass door, frozen as he watches.

I only notice Scott from the corner of my eye. He waits for one of us to acknowledge his presence. And I refuse to entertain his snide comments.

Even though, really, it's more than rude to be bathing in a communal shower together. I know Lily has already done it . . . though in her bathing suit. And I wouldn't be surprised if Daisy has too with her new boyfriend (that no one has met yet).

I want to not care and just "go with the flow"—I've never really been like that.

Connor quickly unbuttons his shirt and tosses it aside, now only in black slacks. As he nears my shower, he's *clearly* taller than Scott.

Connor combs his hand through his hair. "It's thick, full— something to grab on to."

Is he still talking about his hair? My eyebrows rise at him in question, and he shows off a million-dollar grin. I stare at his crotch, unabashed about looking now.

"And what's your first best feature?" I challenge. *Your cock, most definitely.*

"My ass." His smile widens. And with this, he steps right out of his pants and boxer briefs. Completely fucking naked.

The glass door still separates our bodies, but Connor has just shed his clothes *right* in front of Scott. And he doesn't even care.

He acts like the producer deserves none of his attention, as though he's as low as weeds in cracked pavement.

Connor is the sexiest he's ever been.

He opens the shower door confidently, and I try not to shy away. No man has ever seen me *this* naked and that's all about to change.

And in order to give Scott the middle finger, I can't be alarmed when Connor's naked body comes into contact with my naked body.

There's just a whole lot of naked in this scenario.

With no room for fear.

Fearless nudity. I do like the sound of that.

I pull my shoulders back and drop my arm as Connor steps inside, careful to block my exposed body from Scott. He closes the door behind him.

His tactic to neglect the third party works for the most part. Scott stands outside of his shower stall, just *watching* us in curiosity, as though he's considering grabbing a video camera. If he does, I will snip his fucking . . .

My thoughts trail off as soon as Connor nears me. His eyes drop, climbing from my bare legs and rising higher and higher. His gaze momentarily pauses on the spot between my thighs, and I swear he smiles ever so slightly. Places that no man has ever touched ache for hard pressure. All because of his stupid smile. And those eyes, I suppose.

They heat me as much as the shower steam, his blue irises ascending once more from my feet to my breasts, where he lingers. I check the state of my nipples. Erect. *Of course.* My pulse speeds crazily, and each bead of water scorches my skin.

And yet, I don't want to move. I want to stand right here and burn with this fire.

Connor closes in, and his hardness brushes against my belly. I feel so short without high heels on. I look up. The water rains down on his body, where his muscles curve in hard, defined lines, leading to his cock. Just seeing *that* stirs something deep inside of me, the heat and his body numbing my brain.

A strong *need* heightens, the kind that would like a real dick and not a rubber one—the kind that I've snubbed for a long, long time. This is something I would have fantasized about at sixteen in my bedroom. Connor Cobalt entering my shower like a dominant god, his intelligence trouncing mine for a long, stimulating moment.

He reaches over me, grabbing his expensive shampoo, and his arm rubs against my shoulder. My chest collapses. Just like that.

I don't breathe.

I can't move.

I'm surprised my brain hasn't *completely* shut off. But then I would really be pissed. My brain has never ditched me before, and like hell the first time would be because of a penis.

Fearless nudity. Right. I suck in a breath and command my confidence to return.

"Your project," I whisper to Connor. He needs this time to work, not guard me from the sleazy producer. Normally I would protest against the backup, but I wish, more than anything, he'd stay right here.

"I finished it," he says, his face naturally unreadable. It could very well be a lie, but I'd rather not reignite that argument.

The other shower turns on, and I hear the water splash against the tiles. Scott decided to make this situation more awkward. I'm about to look over and shoot him one of my signature death glares. But Connor rests a hand on my bare hip and maintains my position here in front of him. He stands between me and Scott, the chest-high wall also adding a bit of a barrier between us and the producer. I pull a wet strand of hair off my lip. Despite being shielded by a six-foot-four muscular man, my fury ejects. "Nice of you to wait ten minutes, Scott. If my shower ends up being cold, I'm going to—"

"What? What are you going to do?" Scott says in amusement, most likely *smirking*. "Assault me with your nails? Claw me? Please do. And be sure to forget the towel when you come into my shower."

Uh . . . *fuck*. I suddenly realize that giving Scott attention is the equivalent of kicking Connor to the ground.

My boyfriend can be the bigger person in most situations. I tend to take the low road.

Connor lets his annoyance pass through his features. His jaw sets tight and his eyes flash hot at *me*. Just when I wonder if he's going to punish me, as he once said he'd do, he returns to his shampoo, actually washing his hair.

Disappointment floods me. Is it bad that I wished he punished me somehow? I guess I should go back to my routine then . . . I bite my gums, trying not to be distracted as I grab my razor. But he's much larger than anything I've put inside me, and he's only semi-hard.

"So what's your job title at Cobalt Inc.?" Scott asks Connor.

"Interim CEO," he replies civilly. I think Scott's just trying to provoke Connor.

"So it's temporary?"

"Provisional, momentary, brief," Connor lists with a casual tone. "More synonyms for 'interim' in case you need them."

Scott snorts but has nothing to fling back in my boyfriend's face.

I concentrate on bathing. I still have to shave my leg. And that means bending over *in front* of Connor. He continues to hide me from Scott, so I have no clear view of him—thankfully. I don't want Scott to see my ass. He can look at Connor's all day—you know, since it's his *best feature*.

Maybe I can skip shaving.

I shudder.

Fuck it. I've come this far. I'm naked in a shower with a naked man. I can bend over a little. I lather soap on my leg, and then I lean over to finish shaving. My bottom rubs against his dick, and I go to stand up and scoot forward, away from him, but Connor puts a hand on my back, forcing me to stay down.

His other palm caresses the soft flesh of my ass. And then he squeezes me hard, and I hear the warning in his grip: *don't give Scott anything of yours.*

I wince and can't help but smile, loving that he cares. He alternates between a forceful grip and a soft one, rubbing and clenching, nearing the spot between my legs. Not yet entering. My arms shake as I attempt to shave, especially when he massages my bottom and then slaps it. *Ahh . . . fuck me . . .*

Why does that feel so good?

He releases his hand on my back, allowing me the option to stand, but his fingers perilously dip to the crease of my ass.

He lowers them. And I yelp, a sound that has *never* left my mouth before. I've just been startled out of my fucking *mind.* Holy . . . I knick my kneecap, drawing blood, and stand up straight, causing Connor's hands to fall from me.

Scott laughs. He's fucking *laughing,* which only pummels me with more guilt and shock. I just rejected Connor right in front of Scott—is that what it looks like? I slowly turn around and meet Connor's complacent, composed and most importantly *unreadable* expression. I channel so many apologies through my face. I'm using facial muscles that have been static for the past twenty-three years.

Scott's chortles still scald my eardrums. Out of haste, I try to turn on the producer and curse him out, to ineloquently explain how it wasn't just Connor. If any man tried to do that with me, they would have been met with the same alarmed response.

But Connor pinches my chin and forces my gaze on him. Our eyes connect on a different level. The world becomes small.

No Scott.

No shower.

No rush of water or nakedness.

Just me. Just him. Just us.

Together again.

Desire blankets and pulses and shrouds me in its heady web. Wants and urges bubble, feelings that have been caged since we moved to the townhouse. It all springs to life, and I see the longing swim in his deep blues.

We haven't gotten off in a while. I haven't masturbated in our bed, fearful of the noises catching on microphones outside the walls. And Connor used to masturbate in our shower, which has become complicated with the communal style here.

We're both horny as hell. *Especially* after arousing each other downstairs.

And then his thumb brushes my jaw, my lower lip, and slides into my mouth.

An audible noise of consent, of yearning and delight escapes.

It's a moan that I am not so quick to catch this time.

Fifteen

Connor Cobalt

She closes her lips around my thumb. Her pleasure flushes her cheeks and causes her to shift towards me, my cock throbbing for her tightness, for the place that she's let no man into.

I want to remind Rose that *I'm* the one who causes her body to tremble—not the fucking moron one shower over. Her anger towards Scott only fuels him and lets him believe he has power over her. Biting comments, insults, that love-hate relationship is *our* dynamic.

He can't have it.

But as soon as she makes a noise, he shuts off his shower. I watch him wrap a towel around his waist, and he glances at me once with cold, pissed eyes before he shoves through the door. I'm not uncomfortable by the situation, but hearing my girlfriend moan from *my* touch must have been his limit.

My free hand slides to the back of Rose's neck, holding her very close to me. I lower my head and whisper, "I'm going to put something else in your mouth, Rose."

Her eyes meet mine with questions. I say only one thing with my gaze.

You're safe with me.

She can leave. She has full capability to knock me back in the chest and chastise me about commanding her to drop to her knees.

Rose is not shy. She is not weak or insecure. If she doesn't want something, she'll let me know.

She's a virgin, I remind myself. Giving her what she craves, what she'll love but denies—it's going to take time, no matter how much my body protests the long wait. But if she can accept this, to begin to submit in bed, then we can finally move forward.

As she processes my words, her body responds by curving towards mine. She wants to let go for once. I know this. She knows this. She just has to decide if she's going to allow herself that pleasure or refuse it on some higher, ridiculous moral ground.

Her fingers skim my wrist, and I remove my thumb from her mouth. Quite slowly and effortlessly, she sinks onto her knees, eye level with my dick. I want to drive it into her mouth, to fuck her the way I want to fuck her pussy. *She's a virgin.*

Patience, Connor.

I grab a fistful of her wet hair, the shower pelting her beautiful body in waves. Her breath deepens as she looks from me to my partially hardened cock. I rest a hand on the tiled wall.

Rose seizes my shaft with light, tender hands, so unsure of how to hold it.

"Put it in your mouth," I urge with a deep, possessive voice.

She gives me a sharp look, one that's ten times harder than her grip. My whole body reacts to her gaze, thrumming in pure fucking want. I enjoy how difficult she is. I stare down at her, watching as she opens her mouth wide enough to put me between her lips.

I'm not even halfway in before she stops. Her hands fall to her thighs, so uncertain again.

She tries to withdraw, and I immediately clench her hair. Her gaze is all fire, all tumultuous and hot. But it's not a look that says *stop*. It's one full of passionate, ugly, beautiful words and curses. *Fuck me*s mixed with *asshole*s and *cocksucker*s and *hell fucking yes*es.

She's complicated. Just the way I like.

"I'm going to fuck your mouth, darling," I say bluntly. I grip her hair harder, and her hands shoot out to my wrist.

A moan garbles in her throat, my cock only barely inside her mouth. She meant to threaten me, and the surprise coats her eyes at the sudden revelation. That she's more turned on than anything.

I ease out of Rose, my cock popping from her lips. I keep one hand on the tiled wall but the other falls from her hair to her neck.

"I'm doing this wrong," she says. "I knew I would be awful."

"You haven't done anything yet," I tell her with a smile. "You can't be awful at nothing."

"Don't baby me," she snaps. "If you're going to teach me, I want you to do it right. I want to be the best." She waves me on, her eyes pinned below my waist with challenge and more delight.

If that doesn't get me hard . . . *fuck*. I grow, and her eyes begin to widen, probably wondering how she's going to fit it into her mouth now.

"You will be the best, darling," I say. "Hold on to it." I want to start this way for her. And then I want to do it *my* way.

She grips the base in that same delicate manner.

"That's strange," I say.

"What?" She frowns.

"You threaten to castrate men ten times a day but yet you hold my cock like you want to tuck it into bed."

Her grip immediately tightens, and my lips part from the sudden sensation. I laugh into my next words. "You're an excellent pupil so far."

"I graduated with highest honors," she says. *Yes, I know.* I attended her graduation. I saw her walk across the stage and accept her diploma. I was able to witness the look of accomplishment and freedom from four years of hard work and educational slavery. Those memories I hold close.

"You're a conceited little honor graduate."

"Little?" She raises her eyes.

"You are shorter than me," I remind her. "It's time for you to shut the fuck up and put my cock back in your mouth."

Her eyes grow hot at my words, but the rest of her body reacts differently. She presses her thighs together. Wanting. Ready.

To make me come.

She takes me inside her mouth again, slowly, not yet halfway before she nearly chokes. With one hand on her head, I readjust Rose and shift my hips so the position is more comfortable for her. This angle works better, and she shuts her eyes while she eases me in a little further. She's not horrible, but she's not fantastic either.

She stares off, hesitating.

She's drowning in her beautiful fucking mind. I don't want her to think about whether she's doing something wrong or right. I just want her to feel.

"Take your hands off."

She glares and tries to pull back to yell. I know she wants to try—to prove to me that she can do it, but that's not what needs to happen. I hold the back of her head tightly, keeping her here.

"You want to please me? Then do as I say."

Her eyes narrow, but she releases me. And I use one hand and my hips to guide myself further into her mouth. *Fuck.* That feels good.

She gags once, and her hands fly to my ass, gripping me hard.

"Rose," I groan. My strokes are shallow and then they become deeper . . . deeper until tears seep from the corners of her eyes, her body shaking.

Her legs slowly give out, and her back rests against the warm tiles, the water showering our bodies. I drive into her, my pelvis rocking, having complete control on how much of me she takes between her lips.

Her legs squirm, her toes curling and her chest lifting as I quicken my pace.

"That's it, darling," I say with a tight breath. "You're safe with me."

After a few minutes, I come and slide out of her quickly.

"Spit," I tell her, sitting on my knees.

She turns her head and does as I say. She wipes her lips, her breathing heavy. I collect her in my arms, holding her while she digests what happened.

Her own arms wrap around my neck, and she presses her forehead to my collar.

I rub her back, the water slowly turning lukewarm. As she rests on my lap, something strong grips my heart. I've never been so possessed by another person before. She consumes my body and mind in ways that I can't articulate.

I comb her wet hair away from her face.

Right now, I want to kiss the place between her legs more than she can possibly understand. I want to taste her and watch her back arch. To see her reach a peak like I just did. After a couple minutes, I begin to readjust her, spreading her legs on either side of me.

She puts a hand to my chest almost as soon as her ass hits the tiles. "No," she says, disentangling from me. She stands.

I stay on my knees and frown at her change of heart. I'm confused—and that doesn't happen often. "You can't deny what your body responds to. You liked it, and that's all right, Rose."

"I know." She nods with more assurance. "I just don't need you to give me anything in return. That was for you."

"I want to make you come." *And I'm going to fucking do it*. I hold her ankle and kiss her knee. "You'll love it. Trust me."

"I don't care." She pries my hand off her leg.

I stand up now, my gaze harsh on hers. "*I* fucking care."

"This wasn't quid pro quo. I wasn't going to blow you so you could get me off."

She's jumped on a new page of our book, and she's left me to find which one that is. "You're aroused," I tell her. "Lie to me and tell me you aren't going to go back to our room and touch yourself."

She raises her chin, not backing down.

I could shove her against the wall, watch the breath leave her lips, watch her body respond in vicious hunger. She'd let me please her. But I don't want to push her to that place without understanding her sudden reservations.

She takes one step towards me and says, "I don't need you to make me come." Fear swims to the surface of her piercing eyes.

And it clicks. Just like that. I see the ocean beneath her words, the deeper meaning to everything. I bring her into my arms. I don't care that her limbs are stiff.

She tries to push me away, and I hold her to my chest in a tight hug. My lips skim her ear as I say forcefully, "Vous avez tort." *You're wrong.*

Her body flushes, and I abruptly release her, shut off the water and find a towel nearby. I wrap her in the soft cotton while she stares at me, questioningly, wondering if I'm going to elaborate.

She finally says, "I'm not wrong."

"You think your virginity is a prize that I want to win and run away with. Am I right?"

"Don't manipulate me." She shakes her head. "I don't need you to tell me what I want to hear just so you can win that much easier."

She's crazy to believe such a horrible fucking thing. I want to hold her longer, tighter, to calm her with my words. "I'm not manipulating you, Rose. You're smart enough to understand me. And if you truly believe I'd manipulate a woman just to fuck her, then you don't know me very well."

"Don't *lie* to me." She points to her chest, her eyes wild. "I'm a pit stop to you. I'm the halfway mark until you find a woman who will kneel in and out of the bedroom."

"If I wanted a wallflower out of the fucking bedroom, then I'd never even talk to you, Rose." What gets me off is the way a strong woman can give herself to me the moment she passes through a door, the minute I can overpower a girl during a fit of passion. And then we can go back to matching each other once again. Why would I want someone who can't keep up with me? What enjoyment is there in that?

She shakes her head, not believing me. Why can't she *fucking* believe me? It's the goddamn truth!

"You need someone who will be by your side twenty-four-seven," she says. "Who has no greater obligations that will divide her attention from yours. I have been a ten-year-long chase for you, Richard. Nothing more."

I try not to expose my hurt, but it literally tears at my face, too livid to conceal. She's driven something hard and cold inside of me. "No," I force. "No, Rose. You're so fucking wrong."

She breathes heavily, clutching the towel with a firm grip.

I near her, cupping her face with large rough hands. I stare down into her yellow-green eyes. "You're not a pit stop. You're my *finish line*. There's no one after you." I kiss her powerfully, my tongue parting her lips, and she responds. But not as much as I hoped. So I break apart and add, "I want you for eternity, not for a brief moment in time."

I don't understand why every time I speak it sounds like an empty pickup line.

I can't lose her.

Not because of *this*.

I try to imagine a life without Rose and I see something gray, something motionless—a world without time and a place without color. I see mundane and dreary and lackluster.

I can't lose her.

Not for anything.

She places a kiss on my cheek. "I want to believe you, and I'm going to trust you, but just as a forewarning, it may take more than words in the future." With this, she opens the shower door and she leaves me with a new challenge. But I'd be with her without all the tests—all the hoops she makes me jump. I do enjoy them.

But I enjoy her more.

Sixteen

Connor Cobalt

'm late.

I fucking hate that I'm late. Even with my legitimate excuse—five hours of Wharton lectures and another two-hour business meeting at a New York City restaurant—I'm still unnerved. Time is obstinate, constant and undeniably aggravating. No matter how hard I try, time will not bend to my will.

The traffic on my commute from New York to Philly resurfaces my frustration. A man in a green truck lays on his horn to my left, as if noise will magically part the congested freeway. I hold back the urge to roll down my window and remind him that he's not Moses and magic does not exist.

I pinch the bridge of my nose as I reread the last text from Rose.

It's on soon. I'll tape it just in case.—Rose

The first commercial for the reality show airs tonight. And Rose is already preparing for me to miss it. For most, being late for some stupid thirty-second television promo spot wouldn't be a big deal. They'd shrug it off.

But it's not okay.

All it takes is one time. One single moment where I walk through the door ten minutes late and everything could change. The *what if*s in life aren't impossibilities. *What if*s are parallel paths that could happen—that could be. In one moment, a *what if* can be fact.

Scott Van Wright is a what if.

If I hadn't heard the shower turn on, the pipes rumbling through the walls and ceiling, then I would have never gone upstairs. If I had no desire to tell Rose to go back to bed, to take a shower later, then I would have never heard Scott's voice through the door, tangled with hers.

What if I never entered the bathroom to break apart what could have been?

Scott forcing himself on Rose is an image that cripples all the others in my head—it's what makes my spot in this car and not with her so painful.

Another honk fractures my thoughts. I accelerate and close the small gap to appease the asshole behind me. My eyes shift to the exit signs and the words blur together, almost unreadable. I blink and try to focus, but it barely helps.

Don't worry. Do not fucking worry, Connor.

I'm starting to feel the effects of thirty-six hours without sleep. The night is my graveyard shift. Proposals for class. Business emails for Cobalt Inc. Everything and anything that needs my attention. I've pulled all-nighters before, sure, but I have a rule to never exceed the thirty-six-hour mark. Sleep deprivation promotes brain inefficiency.

This is what I get for ditching my limo. I could have taken a nap in the back seat while Gilligan drove me to Philadelphia. But as soon as filming began, I opted to drive myself in a silver sedan. I may have been granted luxury, but I work hard. And if I'm videotaped being carted around in my limousine, all anyone will see is a lazy son of a bitch.

My eyes sag, and I feel the exhaustion weighing on my muscles. I make the conscious decision to carefully pull off the next exit and park in front of a drug store.

I take out my cell phone and walk inside.

"I need you to prescribe me Adderall," I say into the receiver. My loafers clap against the tiled floor and the attendant gives me a narrowed look. With my black slacks and white button-down, I look better suited for Wall Street than some drug store off a freeway.

"No." Frederick doesn't even hesitate. "And next time you call, you can lead with *hello*."

I grind my teeth as I stop in front of the boxes of decongestants. Frederick has been my therapist since my parents' divorce. My mother's words: *I can hire someone if you need to talk.* So I spent weeks combing through potential psychiatrists to give the whole "talking" thing a go.

Frederick was on the college fast track, and I met him when he graduated med school at just twenty-four. He had this air about him. He was hungry for knowledge, and that kind of passion was lost in the other thirty- and forty-year-old shrinks that I had interviewed. So I chose him.

He's been my psychiatrist for twelve years. I would call him my best friend, but he constantly reminds me that friends can't be bought. He earns a staggering sum from me every year, and I overpay for these moments—the ones where I call him up at any hour of the day and he gives me his full undivided attention.

Our last session, we discussed Scott Van Wright, and I tried (rather poorly) not to call the producer names like I was seven and spitting on a bully. But I think I may have used the words "fallible, conceited human bacteria" when Frederick asked me what I thought of him.

Thankfully psychiatrists have an ethical duty to keep secrets.

"*Hello*, Frederick," I say, trying to keep my tone even. He's the only person who has seen me at my worst. Broken. Unusable. But I like to keep those moments as infrequent as possible. "You can call the nearest pharmacy in Philadelphia. I'll pick it up there."

"I can, but I won't."

I let out a long breath as I scan the shelves. "This is not the time to be obdurate. I'm late as it is."

"First, calm down," he says, and I hear rustling on the other end. Papers shuffling around maybe. He likes to take notes.

"I am calm," I say, layering on the complacency in my voice for further effect.

"You just used the word 'obdurate,'" Frederick refutes. "Usually you just refer to me as a stubborn swine. Do you see the difference?"

"Don't patronize me."

"Then don't patronize me," he rebuts. Normal therapists shouldn't be this argumentative, but I'm not a normal patient either. "You remember our conversation right before your freshman year at Penn?"

"We've had many conversations, Rick," I say casually. My fingers skim over two different brands of nasal decongestants. I check the labels for the ingredients.

"The conversation about Adderall, Connor."

I clench my teeth harder, my back molars aching. Before college, I told Frederick that if I ever came to him for Adderall to deny me the prescription. No matter what. I wanted to succeed in college on my own merits. Without stimulants or enhancers. I wanted to prove to myself that I was better than everyone else and that I didn't need a goddamn pill to do it.

"Things have changed."

"Yeah, they have," he agrees. "You're in your first year at grad school. You have a long-term relationship with a girl, and your mother is preparing to hand over Cobalt Inc. to you. And now you have to deal with a reality show. I fully admit, Connor, you're able to juggle work and stress better than ninety-nine percent of people on this planet. But this might be humanly impossible, even for you."

This isn't the first time he's told me that I'm taking on too much, but I don't have a choice. I want *everything*. And if I work hard enough, I can have it all. That's always been how my life runs; I refuse to believe this is any different.

I grab the decongestant with the highest milligram dosage of pseudoephedrine and then walk further down the aisle towards the caffeine supplements.

"I agree, it's not humanly possible. At least not without losing some sleep. And going through my day, like a body without a brain, half-coherent and lazy-eyed, is not an option for me. I need stimulants."

"What happened to never succumbing to frat boy tricks?"

"Guilting me? Really, Rick? Isn't that a little low for you?"

"You're the one that told me to use whatever means necessary to talk you out of it," he says. "There was a time in your life where you'd rather jump off a bridge than take Adderall. I know things have changed, but just think about that for me, okay?"

I stare at the caffeine supplements, trying to unbury an alternate path. But I see none. To have it all, I must sacrifice something. That *something* begins with sleep.

"If you don't prescribe me Adderall, then I'll be purchasing pure ephedrine on the internet," I threaten. Buying pills on the internet is dangerous. I can imagine all the other unknown, untested ingredients accidentally laced in them.

I'm smarter than Frederick, and he's aware of this fact. A long time ago, he made me agree to be honest to a fault. To never manipulate him.

I won't. Which is why this isn't a bluff.

"What are you taking right now?" The tone in his voice has changed considerably. It's tempered like his syllables are carefully placed. He's concerned, and I don't ask how he knows I'm grabbing medicine off a shelf.

He's had twelve years inside my head.

"Decongestants and 5-Hour Energy." I bring the items to the counter and the attendant rings me up at a sluggish pace. I have to show my ID for the decongestants, and she gives me a long, harsh stare. Yes, it's a little suspicious buying these items together. But I'm twenty-fucking-four. Not a child.

"That's a trick that teenagers use to get high, you do realize this?" Frederick says over the phone, still trying to convince me to stop.

I take the paper bag from the attendant and leave the store, the bells on the door clinking together on my way out.

"I'm driving," I refute. "I can either take stimulants or cause an accident. Would you like a four-car pileup on your conscience?"

"How long have you been awake?" he asks.

"Isn't that the question you should have started with?" I uncap the pill bottle and toss a couple into my mouth and wash them down with a swig of the 5-Hour Energy.

"Start answering me straight or I'm hanging up on you," he says sternly. I roll my eyes. Frederick has his limits, even with me. I lean back in the car seat, waiting for the pills to kick in to where my eyelids don't feel like lead.

"Thirty-seven hours."

"So you broke two of your rules tonight."

"I haven't taken Adderall yet."

"No, but you took *something*."

I don't say anything. I wait for Frederick's obligatory advice, which arrives about now.

"You have to give something up," he tells me. "And it shouldn't affect your health. So start looking at things in your life that aren't necessary."

What would that be? Cobalt Inc. is my birthright. And the only aspiration I ever had was to get an MBA from Wharton. Is my dream not necessary?

So that leaves Rose and the reality show. They're intertwined. To have one, I must have the other. Rose's necessity may be called into question. One doesn't need a partner to live. To succeed. But

Rose is not something I'm ever willing to let go. Necessary or not. She's mine.

"My life is filled with essentials," I tell Frederick.

There's a long, strained silence that pulls over the phone. I wait it out.

When Frederick finally speaks, he sounds a little defeated but otherwise as calm as me. "I'll order the Adderall, but the prescription won't be filled until tomorrow. Can you text or call when you make it back to Philly?" He must be picturing that four-car pileup.

"Of course."

"Okay, great." He doesn't sound enthused.

After a few more words, we hang up. And I assess my level of consciousness. Steady hands. Clear vision. Full attention.

I'm finally awake.

By the time I climb the brick stairs of the townhouse, the promo has already aired. So I prepare myself for what I may find. The worst case scenario: Scott has seduced Rose somehow—his arm wrapped around her while she's in a vulnerable state.

My adrenaline is already spiked from the decongestant cocktail. Add in this unnatural fear—and my hand shakes before I turn the knob.

As soon as I open the door, my fear disintegrates into self-assurance. Scott and Rose aren't tangled on the couch together. She's not crying in his arms.

The living room is in an uproar. A chair is flipped over. Pillows have been thrown and scattered all along the hardwood. Rose has her heels in her hands, and she swats them at Scott like they're swords. But she's being restrained by both Daisy and Lily, who grip her waist, tugging her back.

I hate questioning my resolve to overcome bad odds, and I'm glad to have it back one hundred fucking percent.

I shut the door behind me, but no one hears my entrance. Lo is too busy spewing sharp insults that bleed my ears. Rose is violently cursing, layering on expletives like *cocksucker, son of a bitch, womanizer, dick, bastard, dipshit.* I hear *castrate* five or six times.

Scott has his hands defensively in the air, his back literally up against the wall furthest from the television. But he wears the biggest self-satisfied grin.

This is drama he created.

The cameras dance around the living room. Around Ryke, who clenches and unclenches his fist, one hand protectively on his brother's shoulder. Then around my girlfriend, who has completely lost her shit.

Everyone is screaming over each other.

I calmly walk straight ahead, towards the chaos. Rose slips out of her sisters' clutch, and she takes the opportunity to lunge at Scott, her heels barred. I slide into the space between them, and the sharp point of her heel digs into my chest.

My jaw muscles spasm, the only sign that it fucking hurt.

Her eyes widen in horror, and she drops her four-inch heels immediately, the shoes clattering to the floor. And then, just as quickly, her gaze becomes hot and ill-tempered. She points an accusatory finger at Scott. "He's a—"

"Douchebag? A pig? A fucktwat?"

She places her hands on her hips, fuming. I rub her arm, and she begins to calm. But hate is still present in her eyes.

My gaze flits between each of my friends. Their bodies begin to relax when I look at them individually, the tension in their muscles slowly loosening. Lo actually shuts his mouth, and Ryke unknowingly releases his fist.

People believe I have some sort of *magic* hold over others. That I can cause crowds to part without asking. All I have to do is stand at the edge of a mass and they'll slowly, effortlessly make a path for me. I can calm the most restless soul if I choose to, and it's not because I'm gifted with some inane supernatural ability.

My power is in my confidence.

It's that simple.

Their belief that it's something more—that it's something greater—is what makes the effect so strong. They need me to be their sturdy unbending fortress.

So here I am.

"Let me watch the commercial," I say. *And then we can decide whether Scott deserves a heel to the fucking face.*

I pick up Rose's shoes while Lily retrieves the remote. Rose reaches out for them, her nose scrunching at the hardwood that's most likely clean. But to Rose—it's not clean enough.

There's such malice in her features. I envision her impaling him in the eye. As much as I hate Scott—I don't want her to blind him. So I retract my arm, keeping the heels in a firm hand. "I changed my mind."

She gapes. "Give those back, Richard!" She doesn't want to walk barefoot around the townhouse. Fine. I lift her easily in my arms, cradling her body, and she inhales sharply. But instead of arguing with me, she holds on to my bicep. My eyes fall to her breasts, which rise with her heavy breath, and I internally smile.

I have the girl.

In my arms. Dizzy at my touch. I could have walked into something so much worse.

I carry her to the couch and set her down long-ways. She tucks her legs to the side, her dress rising to her thighs, despite her efforts to keep the hem to her knees. When I should be focused on the television, I ache to see *all* of her again. The curve of her waist, her erect pink nipples, her bare ass and her mouth wide and full of my cock.

She meets my gaze for a second, and we don't have to say a single word. She knows what's on my mind. She can see the longing in my eyes, even if everyone else can't. She glances at my belt, and my lips rise as I take a seat next to her.

I sit so close that I can practically hear her heart pounding out of her chest. I lean over to grab the remote from Lily, and as I do so, my mouth nears Rose's ear. And I whisper, "I'm going to tie you up again." I smile at Lily. "Thank you."

Her sister goes back to Lo, who's on a chair, and she lounges against his body.

Rose is stiff, but it's not out of fear. Her thighs press tightly together, and I rest my arm across her lap, my hand on the bareness of her leg. As I switch on the television, she scoots closer and leans her head on my shoulder, trying to relax, but I know she's imagining my belt, her wrists, our bed.

I want to make her so wet that she begs for me—that my name is the only one on her mind, the only thing she can possibly utter. I want to hear her scream in wild, crazed ecstasy. I want her to see how perfect we are for each other—mind, body, soul. No words this time. Just actions.

"You have to rewind," Rose tells me. She tries to reach out for the remote, but I pull it away from her grasp.

She glares. "Vous devez toujours avoir le control." *You always have to be in control.*

I try to contain a larger grin. "Vous aimez quand j'ai le control." *You love when I'm in control.*

Her lips tighten, but she watches me carefully the way I do her. "C'est encore à prouver." *That has yet to be proven.*

I rub the smoothness of her silky leg. "Ne t'inquites pas. Bientot ca sera un fait." *Don't worry. I'll make it a fact soon.*

"Hey," Ryke cuts in. "No fucking French."

"Yeah," Lo says, "Lily wants to hear you guys talk dirty in English." He adds a smile to his girlfriend.

She turns beet-red at his admission. "You weren't supposed to tell them that," she whispers, still loud enough for us to hear. But she doesn't seem to know that. "It was a secret."

"Aw, love, it was too good to keep." He kisses her on the lips, and he eyes the camera for a second while his hand slips up her muscle shirt, no bra underneath. Not that she's particularly top-heavy. Rose has the biggest breasts of her sisters and a fuller ass, wider hips. I could stare at her all day and have no problem getting hard.

I rewind to the beginning of the promo spot and press play. Everyone goes quiet as the commercial begins with all of us standing in front of a white backdrop. We shot the footage at a studio in Philly not long ago.

We were told to just act like ourselves while the cameras were rolling, and after thirty minutes of being ignored by makeup artists and gaffers, we all naturally fell into our roles. No acting required. It was real—even from me.

The commercial starts by panning down the row of seven, Scott on the end. The footage cuts to close-ups, starting from the furthest person on the right.

On screen, Daisy does a handstand, her white T-shirt falling down to reveal her bare stomach and green lacy bra. She sticks out her tongue with a playful smile. A caption appears right over her breasts.

Daredevil.

And then Ryke pushes her legs from behind, and she falls over with a laugh. On his chest, the caption scrolls the word: **Jackass.**

So they're labeling us.

The thought is silenced as the promo moves quickly. *Next in line are Lo and Lily. He has her tangled in his arms, and his mouth meshes against hers as they kiss hungrily, passionately, a desire so intense that it's almost hard to watch. It seems too intimate and too personal.*

At the same time, the words **Sex Addict** *and* **Alcoholic** *float across their bodies.*

And then here comes me, Rose and Scott. Rose looks mildly pissed off, her eyes ablaze—which is normal. But she's turned towards me, our bodies pulled together by something magnetically strong, and as I lean in to whisper in her ear, her face ignites.

I can't even remember what I said. I could have easily disagreed with one of her favorite feminists or I could have told her that her hair was pretty.

In the video, she shoves my arm. Twice. Waiting for me to get angry like her. Wanting to provoke me.

I just grin.

The word **Smartass** *quickly hits my body onscreen.*

On the couch, right here, I hold in a laugh that no one will appreciate. But I find this so fucking amusing. And what are they going to call Scott—a womanizer? No, that's far too kind. Maybe something like—Scumbag Motherfucking Producer (see also: Liar).

Beside her, in the commercial, Scott's eyes fall to her breasts.

I didn't notice that before, and any sort of amusement I felt suddenly flits away. How could I have missed that? I also didn't notice Rose . . .

She glances at Scott, ever so briefly. The attention is enough for him to tilt his head and sigh.

Please, this is a load of—

And then his caption appears. **Heartthrob.**

I choke on a laugh. That's five levels of ridiculous. So he's the white knight knocking on her tower. The hero. And I'm what the one who locked her there. It's wrong. But it's not necessarily backwards—I'm not the hero.

I'm the king to Rose's queen.

And then the camera begins to slowly zoom in on Rose while both Scott and I stare down at her, painting the love triangle he so desperately wanted.

Her caption pops up in big bold letters on her body.

Virgin.

I frown. Why would this upset her? Since we were fourteen, she's never been ashamed of being a virgin. She's never wanted other women to feel as though they *have* to lose it in their twenties—that holding on to your virginity post-college makes you unwanted. She's been proud of the fact that she's waited. Being ashamed of this now makes no sense to me. Unless she's more pissed by being labeled something at all.

That seems right.

The promo ends with the title logo for Princesses of Philly, *and below, a tagline scrolls:*

GET INSIDE THE CALLOWAY SISTERS THIS FEBRUARY.

It was short. Only thirty seconds. And it's enough to resurface hostile emotions. So I stand calmly before anyone starts screaming.

Lily shifts on Loren's lap and says, "I wasn't the only one who thought the tagline was dirty, right?"

She's completely serious. And it almost lightens the mood.

Lo nods to Rose. "Good thing you don't give two shits about being a twenty-three-year-old virgin."

"That's not the problem," she says. I know her well. She meets my gaze while I stand in front of the television that's mounted above the fireplace. "*He* stereotyped all of us with *one* word, as though we're caricatures." She's afraid of being made to look like a fool. But people have been stereotyping the Calloway girls on gossip blogs for months. This isn't any different.

"So?" I say to her.

Her mouth falls. She thought I'd be on her side. When she's wrong, I'm not afraid to disagree.

"People label you the moment they meet you," I tell her. "You're an ice-cold bitch. You're a man-hating prude, a rich stuck-up brat.

They only tell a fraction of the truth, and if you let them hurt you, you let them win."

Everyone settles down. No one wants to feed their stereotype either, and I think they're beginning to understand that if they throw tantrums, they're each going to look as two-dimensional as Scott wants them to be. They'd each fill the "rich-kid snobbery" part well. That image would hurt many of them.

Rose's lips tighten at the "man-hating" line. That one did sting her. I almost regret adding it in my explanation. "You're a conceited asshole," she tells me.

"You love me."

She shakes her head but her lips lift. "Stop."

"Stop what?"

"Being right." She groans and leans back against the couch in a huff. "I hate that we're all so worked up over it and you say a few words, and now everything makes sense again."

Lo rises with Lily in his arms. "He has a gift."

"Given by *me*," I say. I forget the cameras are even in the room until I hear the zoom of Savannah's Canon as she focuses on me while Brett's camera is on Scott. The blond-haired producer remains by the wall, glaring.

I came in and did exactly what he didn't want.

I calmed every single fucking person.

I flicked over his rook, his bishop, and protected my queen.

I mouth, *don't fuck with me.* These five people mean more to me than words can express. I've never once felt like I had a *real* family.

But with them—I know I do.

Seventeen

Rose Calloway

My parents have rented out the loft of a ritzy hotel in New York City, complete with thirty sprawling flat screens, hors d'oeuvres and two hundred of their closest friends. They call it a screening party for the first episode.

I call it a nightmare.

Let's be clear. This is a *reality* show. We're not going to look like proper, upstanding ladies of Philadelphia. I reiterated these sentiments to my mother and she waved me off. "I know what a reality show is, Rose," she said. "But this way, we'll be laughing with you and not at you."

I'm not sure that's much better.

4 months and 25 days until the wedding—Mom

I slip my phone into my clutch and snatch a champagne glass from the nearest server, who wears a signature-fitted Calloway Couture black pleated dress. Another reason why a hundred plus people are here to watch our antics: they have big checkbooks. Ones that may want to invest or buy some of the clothes that Lily, Daisy and I wear on the show.

I scroll through my phone, checking for the millionth time that the CC website is still online. God forbid it crashes during the show. That would be my luck.

The largest flat screen at the front of the room has a countdown before the show begins. Ten minutes. *Ten fucking minutes.*

Where the hell is Connor?

My nerves have spiked to new degrees, and I restrain myself from pulling out my phone and checking the website again.

I scan the crowd quickly, and I spot Loren and Lily standing off to the side, nearest a large potted plant. This is their first Calloway hosted event since Lily's sex addiction became public. Half the people in the room stare at them with curious, admonishing gazes. The other half gossip in whispers.

Lily and Loren look about as uncomfortable as they can be, shifting and avoiding eye contact. Lo has his arm around Lily's shoulder, touching her in comfort and rotating her body every time a camera edges too close.

There are twelve cameramen here. Just to ensure that every moment is captured for the show.

I'm about to walk over to Lily for moral support, but I barely take a step before Ryke approaches the couple. He hands Loren a can of Fizz Life and Lily his plate of Swedish meatballs. Whatever Ryke says, it has Lo smiling for the first time all night.

Two years ago, Lo and Lily would be standing miserable in a corner. Addicted and enabling. A few months ago, no one could persuade my sister to leave the house because of the gossip and ridicule.

Now they're here.

Smiling.

I'm usually not so sentimental. But watching my sister go from lying to broken to halfway-okay has moved me in immeasurable ways.

It's easier to be born strong than to find a strength that you never thought existed. For that, I believe she has more courage and prowess than I could ever possess.

My eyes linger on them before I start searching for Connor again. I find Daisy first, entertaining my mom with a few head nods. While Loren steals one of Lily's meatballs off her plate, Ryke watches Daisy from across the room, his smile fading and his features hardening in concern.

None of the guys like when we surround ourselves with our mother for long. I really don't want Daisy around her for more than an hour or two. Mom sucks our energy dry, but that's just her abrasive, all-consuming personality. Even if you never get used to it, you just have to deal.

When I finally spot Connor, all the built-up fuzzy, warm (generally foreign) feelings I had are replaced by annoyance.

I watch as my boyfriend greets a younger guy by hugging him and slapping him on the back in a typical bro-hug. It is *so* out of Connor Cobalt's nature—his true self that I know and love.

My heels clap loudly on the marble floor as I strut towards him. I tip the rest of my champagne in my mouth and set the empty glass on a tray before I land by his side.

"Richard," I say with heated eyes. I don't care if I look like a bitch. That's the point. I am who I am. Why can't he just let people see the real him? Who cares if people don't like him?

"There you are, babe," Connor says, hooking his arm around my waist. He nods to his friend. "Patrick, you know Rose, right?"

"We've never been formally introduced," Patrick says. He holds out his hand. "Patrick Nubell."

I don't shake it. "As in Nubell Cookies?" It makes sense. Connor doesn't schmooze anyone. He has to have a reason to give you his time. Money and prestige are two important factors. Nubell sits just below Kraft (Oreos) and Keebler on the marketplace. Though Nubell cookies are more natural and less appetizing.

Patrick laughs and drops his hand, realizing I'm not going to shake it. He doesn't seem affronted. Maybe he's heard of my reputation. In these social circles, I am frequently called an ice queen.

"Yeah, it's my great-great-grandfather's company," he explains. "You probably know how that is. People always asking you which flavor of Fizz you like the best. Well, I get *do you prefer nugget or cinnamon?*"

I stay quiet, which leaves Connor the opportunity to say, "Definitely, man." He nods like he is entranced with this nugget/cinnamon conversation.

Sure, I could probably relate to Patrick on some level, but now is not the time for bonding. I have—I check my watch—four minutes until the show airs. And I need a pep talk. Preferably from Connor Cobalt and not the twat he has impersonated.

"Could you give us a minute, Patrick?" I ask now.

"Yeah, of course." He leaves, probably searching for someone as young as him in the middle-aged crowd.

When I turn to Connor his eyes drop to mine. "That hurt me just as much as you," he says immediately. "Trust me, I had to use the word *killer* and *dude* in the same fucking sentence."

"You didn't *have* to do anything," I retort. "And *babe*, really?" I smack his arm. "And you gave him a bro-hug, Connor. Who are you?" I don't give him time to answer because I know it will be something profoundly aggravating. "And what were you doing with Nubell Cookies? Are you trying to partner with them? That sounds like a fantastic idea. Put magnets in the tins and make everyone sick."

I finish my rant and he full-on grins. But it's different this time.

He smiles at me like every word I said was special. Like they belonged to him and me.

"What?" I snap, but my voice softens when I see the look in his eye that says I mean everything to him.

He intertwines his fingers with mine and draws me to his chest. "Nothing, darling." His breath warms my ear as he leans down. "You look gorgeous in that dress. Is it yours?"

Is it yours? He's asking if I designed it. I nod.

He brushes my hair off my shoulder as I inhale strongly. His fingers run across the black fabric with studs on the collar, and he skims my neck with an even lighter touch.

"As gorgeous as it is," he says, "I'm going to love taking it off you tonight." He kisses my cheek, and I have to look around the room at all the faces to remember we're in public.

With hundreds of people.

My emotions have suddenly calmed, and as Connor squeezes my hand, I realize why.

Lo is right. He has a gift.

The countdown on the screen ticks down from ten.

Ten seconds.

That's all it takes to decide whether this show will fail.

Ten stupid seconds.

Thirty minutes in, and it's not looking so good.

Beside me at the screening party, Lily shields her eyes with her hand, peeking beneath as we watch the train wreck that is our lives. The six of us have congregated in solidarity by the fucking potted plant as the show continues playing. Scott chooses to stand beside my parents, whispering things to my mother, and she laughs with sincerity.

Connor's eyes flicker from the television screens to Scott and my parents every so often. I can tell he'd like to go interject and break up Scott's ploy to make nice with my mother and father, but he stays here. With me. And I appreciate that more than he knows.

We already watched the psychic disaster, and then I endured a five-minute clip where Daisy popped wheelies on her Ducati. She revved the bike too hard, and she slid off the back of the seat and ate it. Instead of crying, she picked up her motorcycle that rode off without her, and she tried again.

After watching that, our mother looked ready to storm over to us and scold her in front of everyone. The only thing that stopped her were the two hundred onlookers.

I finish my second glass of champagne and snatch another one before the server darts away. The interview segments are the most interesting part of *Princesses of Philly*. None of us have seen each other's tapes. Scott would stand behind Savannah's camera, conducting the interviews in our study, the walls lined with books. And he'd dictate questions to her to ask us—just so his voice wouldn't be recorded. God forbid anyone knows he's orchestrating the show.

"Lily and Lo f**k a lot," Ryke says, each f-bomb bleeped accordingly. He sits on a brown leather chair. "If we had to rank who's getting the most, it'd be my brother, his girlfriend, then maybe Connor Cobalt and his hand."

Beside me, Connor grins and sips his wine, finding Ryke's comment more amusing than I would.

Ryke's eyes float towards the door that opens.

Daisy peeks her head through, walking straight in. "I need you out front for a second," she says. "What was the last question? If it's important, I can come back later."

Ryke stands. "No it's fine."

I don't like where this is headed. Why would this be shown?

We hear Savannah's voice but can't see her. "He was ranking who has the most sex in the house. How would you rank everyone?" Savannah asks.

Daisy's face lights up with a smile.

"Don't answer her," Ryke says.

"Lily and Lo." Daisy ignores him with a playful grin. She bounces on her feet like she drank way too much caffeine. "They f**k a lot."

Ryke rolls his eyes.

By the potted plant, Daisy apologies to Lily, "I'm so sorry."

And then her eyes flicker between Ryke and Lo. "Please don't get upset." She directs that mainly to Lo.

Lo turns to his brother and just gives him a deep glare. "How many shades of inappropriate are we about to see?"

"Fifty," Ryke quips. His lips slowly rise and we all burst into laughter, despite the show still playing. People stare at us like they missed something on screen. They didn't. But finding the humor in our lives is much better than reliving the bad parts.

"And then who?" Savannah asks Daisy.

Ryke stares down at Daisy with a hard glare. "Don't answer her."

"You did."

"I didn't get that far."

Daisy grins like she's excited to be the first to divulge the information. She spins around and stares right at the viewers [the camera] and Ryke grabs her around the waist to stop her from speaking. But she says, "I'm totally getting more ass than Ryke Meadows."

She laughs as she squirms in his hold.

"She's not getting more ass than me," he says. He tries to pull her into his arms and turn her away from the camera. But she spins around quickly again and plants her hands on his chest.

"Oh yeah? I have a boyfriend. What do you have?"

*"A six-pack and big f**king c*ck."*

The crowd breaks into loud talk at that. Loren's eyes flash murderously at his brother. And Ryke just shakes his head at himself.

Connor can't stop laughing.

Daisy tries to wrestle with him again, and her shirt rises on her waist, revealing a purplish bruise on her hip. Ryke goes incredibly still, and Daisy stops moving as her face falls.

"It's nothing," she says quickly. "Come on, I need you out front."

We all turn on Daisy, who has taken a seat on the floor, texting in solitude. She's ignoring us on purpose. And I wonder . . .

When I gave Daisy pepper spray, it seemed like she was keeping a secret with Ryke. I completely forgot about that, and so I never badgered them for the information. I think I'm finally going to get some answers, and they're just going to be handed to me. No work involved. Look, the show has another perk. Who would have thought?

"Hey." Lo nudges Daisy's back with his foot. "What the fuck is going on?"

"It's taken care of," she says noncommittally, fixed to her phone.

Lo glances at Ryke. "Why didn't you say something?"

"Just fucking watch," Ryke says. "It doesn't matter now. They're airing it."

Connor sips his wine. "Clearly you hoped they wouldn't."

"A part of me did, actually. But I was protecting that one . . ." He leans behind his brother and points to Lily, who has her head on Lo's shoulder. "So give me a fucking break."

"What? Me?" Lily points to her chest sheepishly. "I'm okay." But her voice is small. She's had to see herself make out with Lo, and all of us had a three-minute heated debate whether this was considered soft-core porn—which she's not allowed to watch.

Then Daisy off-handedly admitted to being a porn-watcher— more to keep Lily from shrinking into herself in shame. And Lo made a face like someone stabbed ice picks in his ears.

I'm immediately brought back into the show after hearing one particular line from my sister:

"He threw something at me."

Ryke breathes heavily. "It looks like he f**king grabbed you."

She pauses. "Can you please come outside and I'll explain."

With locked shoulders, Ryke follows Daisy downstairs, into the living room and out the front door. When they reach the street, she leads him to her parked Ducati on the curb. The tail-lights and headlights are busted. And the handlebars are bent out of shape.

"*What the f**k? Mother ****ing, piece of sh*t **** **** ******* kidding me.*" He glares. "*Who f**king did this?*"

"*Some douchebag downtown. I came out of Lucky's, and he was smashing my bike with his boot. He told me, and I quote, 'Get out of here, you spoiled c*nt of Philly.'*"

Ryke cringes at the one swear word I've never heard him use. "*It wasn't your boyfriend?*"

"*No,*" she says. "*He wouldn't hurt me. I just . . . I was trying to get my bike back, and we had a bit of a confrontation, hence the bruise. It's nothing really. I was just glad the paparazzi didn't show up.*"

Lily gapes. "They're that angry at us for filming?" The fear blinks in her eyes. If Philly locals did this to Daisy—then what the hell are they going to do to my little sister whose sex addiction has been plastered on national news?

The heckling—it's not something I really thought about before.

"It wasn't that bad," Daisy tells both of us.

But Ryke's hardened jaw says differently. On screen and off.

Ryke inspects the damage on her bike, shaking his head more and more. "*We need to press charges.*"

"*I didn't get his name.*"

"*But you can describe him to the police.*"

She stays quiet.

"*He f**king assaulted you, Daisy. He's not getting away with this sh*t.*"

"*I don't want to cause more trouble, really. Let's just forget about it.*"

"*You want me to f**king forget about it?*" *His eyes fall to her waist where he saw the bruise. And then he stands and tries to pull her shirt up.*

Connor chokes on his wine. I rub his back with a mechanical hand. I really want to smack Ryke's head, but I'm restraining myself—something Ryke clearly cannot do.

"I gave you way too much credit," Connor tells him. "I thought you were smart enough not to do that on camera."

"On camera?" Lo interjects. "How about *not at all*."

Daisy waves her hand from the ground, still texting. "Right here, guys."

Ryke extends his arms. "What do you want from me? She just told me she got mauled by some fucking angry idiot on the street, and she wouldn't tell me how bad it was."

"For the record, it wasn't that bad."

"It was fucking bad." Ryke glares at her. "Your whole side was fucked up."

"What is *fucked up*?" I say in worry. "Do you need to go to the doctor, Daisy?"

"I already went," she says. "I'm fine. No internal bleeding—"

"I'm going to strangle you," I tell Ryke. I step towards him, and Connor clutches my arm, pulling me back to his chest. My sister was *that* hurt and no one thought to inform me?!

"Why are you fucking yelling at me?" Ryke shouts. "I'm not the one who tossed her to the ground."

"You should have told me!"

"Daisy didn't want you to know," Ryke retorts. "Is it that hard of a concept? You freak the fuck out, Rose. You're about to hyperventilate right now."

I'm not.

And then I realize that my chest rises and falls in a strange, uneven rhythm. Okay, maybe I'm not all there. But I hate that Daisy was hurt and I was purposefully left out of the secret. I should have remembered they were keeping something from me. I should have been by her side while she was at the doctor's. This is my fault. If we didn't have the reality show, she wouldn't have met such a hostile pedestrian *without* a bodyguard.

"Were you alone at the doctor's?" I ask Daisy.

"Ryke went with me."

At least she wasn't alone. But Lo glares at him, hardly thinking he's a good replacement. He's better than no one.

I glance back at the big screen. *Ryke and Daisy stop fighting each other. He holds her arms while she stares up into his brown eyes.*

"I'm fine," she says.

"The more you keep saying that, Calloway, the less I believe you. What'd he do, body slam a hundred-twenty-pound girl on the f**king ground?"

"No, we wrestled. In the mud. There were cheerleaders in attendance too."

"Shut the f**k up."

She grins. "It's funny."

"You being hurt is the least funny thing in the entire f**king world."

"And that's the biggest exaggeration I've heard all day."

They just stare at each other for three long seconds. Ryke tries to cut the tension by looking away first. He says, "I'll take your bike to the shop. You can ride mine if you need to go to a modeling gig."

People mutter again, and my mother's bony collar juts out as she inhales, her frame too skinny. With the scandal, she's eaten less and less. And it's not long before her hateful gaze finds her target, landing on Ryke. Direct hit.

"Momma Calloway is going to ream your ass," Lo tells him. He slaps his back and squeezes his shoulder hard. "Good luck, bro." He smiles.

"You're enjoying my distress way too fucking much."

"It keeps my life bright."

The commercial break airs, and I'm surprised my mother has the balls to stay here. She could cave in embarrassment at her daughters' impropriety and bluntness and their boyfriends' habit of telling it like it is. But she smiles and waves at her stereotypical WASP friends without carrying a morsel of shame. Either she's a terrific actress or she's grown to look past our unbecoming natures.

I'd love to think better of my mother, but people don't change that quickly, especially not stubborn middle-aged women who've been rooted in their beliefs for so long.

But maybe this reality show could help her forgive and accept rather than hate.

By the time the show starts again, my head spins with a decent buzz. I grab another glass of champagne, and Connor stands behind me, his hands on my waist. He gathers my hair onto one shoulder, and the cold nips my bare neck.

We're both suddenly distracted by the montage that plays—moments at the house when only Lily was home.

Lily squirms on the leather couch. She adjusts her feet underneath, her forehead wrinkled in distress. Her hand starts to descend towards her jeans. She retracts almost instantly, her cheeks heating. She looks around the room to see if anyone saw. And when her eyes hit the camera, looking directly at us, the viewers, she presses a pillow to her face in humiliation.

It doesn't end there. Her internet privileges have been restored only because she's taking online classes. And we've all trusted her to stay off dirty sites.

She lies on the couch, her laptop on her legs. She glances over her shoulder and then she immediately shuts her computer, fighting a dangerous compulsion. Her hand descends towards her jeans, but she stays above the fabric and touches the spot between her legs.

"How can they air this?" I ask angrily.

"The PTC will bitch tomorrow," Connor says calmly. "Just let it play out." The Parents Television Council—I'm sure they'll wave pitchforks at the network and producers, but it'll be all over entertainment news and blogs, just stoking the fire and causing more people to watch the footage.

Lily covers her eyes with her hands, and Lo has his lips to her ear, whispering to her rapidly while silent tears start to fall.

The clips keep coming in quick succession.

Lily rubs against a kitchen chair, unconsciously. When she catches herself, she reddens.

Lily rubs against the corner of the kitchen counter.

Lily's hand descends—three different times. But she always stops before she gets too far.

I don't get embarrassed about many things, but I sense the judgment, the weird stares pinning on Lily in the party room. I can practically feel my sister crumpling before I even look at her.

Lily turns into Lo's chest and she grabs at his black crewneck. She stuffs her head underneath, literally hiding inside his shirt while he's still wearing it. "I'm not coming out," she says. "Don't make me come out, Lo."

Loren touches her head. "Stay there as long as you want, love." When he looks up, he sends shriveling glares to anyone who so much as glances at him. His glares aren't necessarily like mine or like Ryke's. They're the kind that make you feel like he's about to go get a chainsaw and murder your whole fucking family. It's a sadistic, *I have nothing to lose* type of look that his father taught him well.

And it's enough to cause everyone to face the big screens again.

The footage has changed to a compilation of interviews with Daisy, Lily and me. I remember the questions being focused on sex. No surprise. Lily's addiction is what's drawing the viewers to *Princesses of Philly* in the first place.

Since we shot everything separately, they cut to each of our answers.

"Who's your celebrity crush?" Savannah asks.

Daisy smiles wide. "James Dean."

My eyes pierce the camera. "Audrey Hepburn."

Lily stares off in thought. "Uhhh . . ." She flushes. "Loren Hale."

Lo laughs and stares down at Lily, who's still hidden in his shirt. "Right answer, love."

She sniffs, and her arms wrap around his waist underneath his clothes.

"Have you read Fifty Shades of Grey?*"*

"Yep," Daisy says, "one handed." She wags her eyebrows deviously.

I say, "Any patriarchal c*cks*cker who makes a woman ashamed to read it should be slapped across the face with his—"

Lily blushes. "Uhhh . . ."

"Top or bottom?"

"My mother's going to kill me," Daisy says. "Both. Sorry, Mom!"

The people in the party room laugh, and my mother even cracks a smile. I think we all forget how young Daisy is because she looks older than Lily . . . and she's incredibly endearing.

But every time we cut to my answer, I look like a royal bitch compared to her, cursing the entire audience to hell.

"I'm a virgin," I say. "Why ask me that inane question?"

"Uhhh . . ." Lily's eyes widen.

"Back door or front door?"

"No c*cks have been near my a**h*le, sorry." Daisy shrugs after answering crudely.

Lo gives her a look. "You're spending too much time with my brother."

She just laughs.

I tilt my head to the side. "Really?"

"Uhhh . . ." Lily's eyes grow bigger with each question.

"What do you wear to bed?"

"*I sleep in the nude,*" *Daisy answers.*

"*A nightgown,*" *I retort, not elaborating whether it's silk or ankle-length cotton.*

"*Uhhh . . .*" *Lily turns her head to look at the door.* "*Lo!*"

"*Whips or handcuffs?*"

"*Oooh,*" *Daisy grins.* "*I like the idea of whips. But you know, me dodging the whips. Make it into a game.*" *She laughs.*

I swear the men in this room grunt in audible desire.

I must wear a look of pure disgust because Connor squeezes my hip and whispers, "We're not all pigs, Rose."

He's right. I know I shouldn't generalize the entire male species as vile, gross things that'll get off to my sixteen-year-old sister's image.

And just when I'm feeling apologetic, I spot a guy with a *clear* bulge in his suit pants. "What do you call that?" I whisper in detest.

"A boner."

I shake my head. "You're such a . . ." I trail off and then smile. "*Smartass.*"

He touches his chest mockingly. "Ça fait mal." *That hurts.*

"Je suis content." *I'm glad.*

His grin only grows. "They could have chosen anything else to label me, you know. 'Genius' would have been my number one pick."

"Pretentious," I argue.

"Or popular . . ."

"Conceited," I continue.

He flashes another smile. "Handsome."

My eyes flit from his white button-down that fits him perfectly to his deep blue eyes. "Maybe."

He takes a sip of his wine and waves me to keep going. "I have you *almost* giving me a compliment, why stop now?"

Our banter sets a fire underneath my heart. I could kiss him.

But I regretfully turn towards the big screen. I realize I missed my response to the *whips or handcuffs* question, which was evasive anyway. And Lily most likely gave her perfunctory *uhhhh*.

Now the guys are being asked a series of questions, cut together like our interviews.

Loren glares, waiting impatiently for Savannah to ask him something.

"Blondes or brunettes?"

Lo stares harshly. "Brunettes."

"I don't give a sh*t about hair color," Ryke says, his forearms on his thighs as he sits on the leather chair.

Connor is seated with his ankle on his knee, leaning back like a CEO of a multibillion-dollar company. He has his fingers to his jaw in mock contemplation. "What happened to redheads?"

Savannah clears her throat. She has red hair. "Or redheads."

"What about gray hair?" His eyes flicker up a little. He's staring at Scott, who stands off screen. "You're forgetting black hair too. And purple, blue, orange—"

Lo is back, glaring.

"Wow," Lo says, his hand on Lily's head, still concealed in his shirt. "They cut off your little rant, Connor. How'd that feel?"

"Chapped," Connor says easily.

"Come here, I'll rub your ass for you."

Connor smiles into his sip of wine. But it must be annoying that Scott has the power to shut him up with a simple edit. I can see his irritation in the tight muscles of his jaw.

"Who's the messiest?"

"Ryke."

"Me."

"Ryke."

"Have you ever been with a man before?"

Lo cocks his head to the side. And he flashes a bitter, dry smile, not giving anyone anything they want to hear.

"No," Ryke says.

Connor wears an unreadable expression. "*Many people want to be with me. I may give them all my attention, but I'll only be with a handful, and of those, I'll only really like a few.*"

"Who has the best legs?"

"Lily," Loren says. "*But she won't believe me if I say it.*"

Ryke rubs his lips in thought.

Loren glares at him like, *you better not have fucking said her name*—but I think we all hear *Daisy* in his head anyway.

"Rose," Ryke grimaces.

I laugh into my sip of champagne.

"Rose," Connor says. "*And then me, of course.*"

"Top or bottom?"

Lo glares. "Top."

Ryke shakes his head in annoyance. "I don't care."

"Top." Connor grins. "*Always.*"

"Do you think Daisy is as sexually active as Lily?"

Lo's eyes flash cold. He stands up. "*I'm done with this sh*t.*"

"What the f**k kind of question is that?" Ryke asks. He rises and chucks a pillow.

"No, she's not," Connor says definitively. He stands and buttons his suit jacket. "*That's enough for the day.*"

While we go to commercial break, Daisy picks herself off the ground, her cell phone in hand. She tries not to make eye contact with any of the guys. It's clear that the media is trying to determine whether or not my little sister will turn out like Lily.

And this fact only causes Lily to stay buried in Lo's shirt, not only doused with shame but now guilt.

My chest hurts for both my sisters, but there's nothing in my power that can reverse what's happened. Maybe my clothing line isn't worth *this* attention.

I scroll on my phone. My sales . . . they're up by ten percent so far. The little ads that cut to the commercials must be helping. They say, *Purchase the clothes worn by the Calloway sisters right now!* And they show the links to the CC website.

I wish my body didn't soar by the small success. A part of me wishes this reality show was a failure so I could easily choose my sisters' welfare over my dream. I should do it. Two years ago, I think I would have. But I wonder if Lily would ever forgive herself for driving my company to the ground. I think she needs to know that my company is okay too—that she didn't destroy everything with her addiction.

Daisy's phone slips between her fingers and clatters to the floor. She bends down to pick it up, forgetting that she's in a black backless dress I designed, short on her thighs. The dress immediately rides up, showing half her ass since she wears cutoff boy-short underwear.

My little sister has sufficiently mooned the crowd.

Ryke is the closest to Daisy. "Fuck," he curses, quickly standing behind her. He grabs the hem of her dress and tugs down.

The three guys look over their shoulders at the nearest camera.

"Did they see her . . . ?" Lo trails off, not able to talk about Daisy's ass without cringing.

"That one did." Connor motions to a photographer with horned-rimmed glasses, gesturing for him to come over to us. As the photographer nods and approaches, Connor pulls out his phone and makes a quick call.

Daisy struggles to pick up her cell.

"Daisy, grab the fucking thing," Ryke tells her, having to literally tug her dress down three more times as she moves.

She finally snatches the phone and spins towards him with a large smile. "Got it!"

Ryke stares at the hem of her dress, making sure it's not riding up. I should be the one doing it, but I'm slightly tipsy, and I fear moving the wrong direction in my four-inch heels. I already sway a little. If it wasn't for Connor's hand protectively on my waist, I would have stumbled by now.

"Are you checking out my ass?" Daisy asks with the raise of her eyebrows.

"Yeah, so did the rest of the fucking party."

"So what'd you think? On a scale of one to ten." She grins playfully.

"I'm not rating your ass."

"Will you ride it then?"

"Daisy," I interject. *Stop*, I mouth. She pushes Ryke too far, and he's not one to back down from these kinds of conversations.

Daisy's smile fades. "Sorry . . . I was just messing around." She flips her phone in her hand. "I'm going to go . . . mingle."

Now I feel bad.

"No," I tell her sharply. "You're staying."

"No, it's cool. I need to go talk to Mom anyway." She avoids Ryke, who stares down at her with a strong gaze—filled with this unadulterated concern. It's strange for such a hard-lined guy to have such potent empathy for others. But I've seen it come out on more than one occasion.

Connor speaks into the receiver of his phone. "Greg, you see this photographer nearing me?"

So he called my father.

Connor continues, "He has a picture of your daughter's ass. I'm going to take the camera if you don't send someone to do it."

I hear my father say, "Which daughter? And I have someone on the way. Thank you."

"Daisy."

My father lets out a large sigh. "That one's going to kill me."

Connor's lips slowly upturn, and his eyes glimmer with this unbridled longing. It's powerful but barely visible. Fleeting. Like an eclipse of the sun.

He truly wants children.

He wants the challenges that each one brings.

He smiles as though he can't wait for that day where he has to deal with the hard parental choices, the dilemmas, the chaotic situations he must calm.

He does want it all.

But I'm afraid I may not be able to give it to him.

Eighteen

Connor Cobalt

The screening party has been going relatively fine until I watch Samantha Calloway fawn over every bullshit line that comes out of Scott's mouth. He's complimented her brown hair three fucking times, and Rose's mother is close to melting at his feet. At least her father is on my side.

He texts me: I don't like him.—Greg

To the point, a heart with good intentions. No bullshitting around. That's Greg Calloway. His wife isn't as benevolent, intelligent or non-judgmental. She has a WASP elitist mentality that would make my mother internally roll her eyes.

It's mostly Rose's parents that have my stomach in knots. Because even though I've appeared only twice in the show, edited to look disinterested in my own girlfriend, it's their opinions that matter to me, not the public, not strangers—just people that I need to impress. Because one fucking day, I plan to marry that girl, and I want them to realize that I'm the best man for Rose. And that no one else can come even marginally close.

Rose's anxiety is sedated with five glasses of champagne, and she relaxes into my chest while I hold her around the waist. Since the aired footage has been mostly about the "love triangle" for the past fifteen minutes, Lily bottles her emotions and finally emerges from Lo's shirt, her cheeks tear-streaked and pink. I have a feeling

Lo will be carrying her out of the venue. Most likely in a front piggy-back.

We're nearing the last five minutes. I think they'll end with a Lo and Lily clip, but as soon as Scott Van Wright's face fills every big screen with the caption—**_Heartthrob. Rose's ex-boyfriend_**—I realize they're going to continue to capitalize on the love triangle.

So here we go, Scott. What do you have left for me?

"I think about her all the time," he says with an insincere, *wistful smile. "She's a firestorm that I won't ever smother. I'm the one who inflames her, who riles her to a new, confounding degree. She's my perfect match."*

My face falls. And I unwillingly let everyone see my shock. I can't hold it in this time.

Because those last lines are mine. I said them in an interview.

And he stole them from me.

"I hate him," Rose says under her breath, her eyes narrowed. She can't see my reaction since she stands in front of my body while I hold her from behind.

"What's wrong?" I ask.

"He plagiarized you."

I let out a breath. "Comment peux-tu le dire?" *How can you tell?*

"Who riles her to a new, confounding degree?" she repeats. "Only you would say that . . . and maybe me."

I kiss her cheek and wrap my arms tighter around her waist. She eases back into me. He can't come between us.

"I'm still in love with her," Scott says. *"And I can't help what I feel, but it's there. I love Rose the way she deserves to be loved. I just . . ."* He shakes his head like he's filled with worry. *"I just don't see Connor being the best thing for her. He's too self-absorbed to care for that girl the way I do. And I hope, over the course of living with her again, she'll realize that we're meant to be."*

"Murder is still illegal in Pennsylvania, right?" Rose asks.

"And the United States, and the world," I tell her.

"Dammit."

And then the screen fills with me.

Back in the study room where I sit on a desk chair:

"What do you think of Scott?" Savannah asks.

I stay complacent. "I find him comparable to a little teenager *jimmying the lock of my house." I stare right at Scott in the room, who's off screen, hovering over Savannah's shoulder as she films me. I add, "He's nothing more than a petty thief, trying to take what's mine. Is that honest enough for you?"*

"And what about Rose?"

"What about Rose?" This is where I said what Scott just did. I called her my perfect match, but it's edited out completely.

"Do you love her?" Savannah asks.

The abrupt cut makes me look more callous than I am. More inhuman and unfeeling than I ever want to be. *I stare off for a long time as I gauge my answer, picking my words carefully. To tell the truth. Or to lie.*

"Love is irrelative to some."

Most people let me stop there. They never make me elaborate. *But Savannah says, "And is it to you?"*

I have a couple fingers to my jaw, and I smile, something that looks empty and soulless on screen. "Yes," I say. "Love holds no meaning in my life."

The show fades to black with that last line. In the full-length interview, I added, "But Rose is at the epicenter of my world, whether I allow myself to love her or not."

It was all cut.

And as the large crowd claps and talks amongst themselves about the show, Lo and Ryke turn on me with dark scowls. Rose grabs another champagne glass off a tray and leans back into my chest, unaffected by my words like them.

"So was that the real Connor Cobalt?" Lo asks, his arm around Lily, who stares at me with the same furrowed brows. She glances at her sister with more concern. They're on Rose's side. As they should be.

"I spoke honestly," I say. "And that wasn't the first time I've done so."

"So you've never loved anyone?" Lo asks. "Not another girl-friend, not your mom, your dad or a friend?"

He wants to know if I think of him more than just a contact like Patrick Nubell. Am I using Loren Hale for his father's company, the multibillion-dollar baby product franchise? At first, yes. Now, no.

He's my *real* friend. Maybe my first one ever.

But have I loved him the way a friend loves another friend? I don't think I'm wired that way.

"No," I say. "I've never loved anyone, Lo. I'm sorry."

Rose points to Lo, her champagne glass pinched between her fingers. "Let it go, Loren. I have."

"Why," Lo asks, "because you're both cold androids?"

Rose shoots him a look that would be harsher if she didn't drink so much tonight. I need to get her to bed before she passes out. "It's just how he is. If you even understood half of Connor Cobalt's beliefs, your head would spin."

"Rose," I say, worried she's going to fracture my relationship with Loren. While he doesn't know me like she does, I've never lied to him. I just haven't shown him all of me. And that shouldn't be a bad thing. Some people are naturally private. I am.

She tries to defend me, stepping towards Lo and skillfully stay-ing upright. I hold her by the waist to steady her movements. "No, Connor has done nothing wrong."

"He doesn't *love* you," Lo sneers. "He's been with you for over a year, Rose."

"Lo," Lily warns.

"No," Lo says, "she needs to fucking hear this." He points accusingly at me. "What the hell kind of guy stays with a girl for that amount of time without anything in return? If he's doesn't love you, then he's just waiting to fuck you."

He pokes at the most vulnerable part of my relationship with Rose. "She doesn't need your protection," I say to Lo, trying to keep my voice even-tempered, but Rose wavers uneasily in my arms. "She knows who I am."

"So you're okay with that then?" Lo asks her. "He's going to fuck you, and then he's going to be out of here. Does that make you feel good, Rose? You've waited twenty-three goddamn years to lose it, and you're going to give it to a guy who can't even fucking admit that he loves you."

"I'm not going to admit something that I don't feel," I tell him. He opens his mouth, but I cut him off, "Would you like me to sit you down and fill your head with numbers and facts and relativities? You can't stomach what I have to say because you won't understand it, and I know that hurts you. But there's nothing I can do to change the way things are. I am a product of a mother as brick-walled as me, and trust me when I say that you won't ever see more than I give you. In order to be my friend, that has to be enough, Lo."

He lets this sink in and then he says, "And what about you, Rose, is that enough for you?"

Lily reaches out and touches her hand.

Rose nods stiffly, and she holds Lily's hand tighter. "I'm going to go to the bathroom. You guys can meet us at the car." Lily supports her sister with an arm around her waist as they head through the dispersing crowds.

I watch her, making sure she safely leaves, and then I glance back at Lo. The look he gives me—it asphyxiates me for more than a few seconds.

He stares at me like he yanked off my superhero cape and grounded me to the mortal world.

"I just want you to know," Lo says, "that I lost some respect for you tonight. And you're not going to get it back so fucking easily."

Ryke says nothing. He just wears a haunted, dark expression.

"Sure," I say. "I understand."

Lo rubs his lips; his jaw clenches, and he nods to Ryke. They head out to the car without me.

I stay still and try to gather my feelings that tangle in a muted mass.

What kind of person needs a therapist to tell them how they feel?

Am I not as smart as I believe or am I just human?

Nineteen

Rose Calloway

I can't come. I'm so, so, so sorry! Just make sure no lilies, okay? And remember that I like your taste better than mom's. THANK YOU!—Lily

I receive the text as soon as I arrive at the florist to pick out arrangements for the wedding.

4 months and 2 days—Mom

It's like the countdown to the Apocalypse.

I text my sister back, telling her it's fine. At least she didn't make up a stupid excuse this time. Her "stomachaches" for the past month have been more about her fear to come face to face with our judgmental mother.

Lily went from being ignored by our mom to being told to close her legs. To wear a lighter pink lip gloss (on the rare day she does wear makeup). To comb her hair so it doesn't look tangled in a post-sex haze.

She ridicules. And we both know it's not out of love, but her obligation to protect the reputation of the family.

I look around the flower shop quickly. Brett follows me today with his steadicam, nimbly keeping out of customers' way as he films me. I arrived twenty minutes early so I could pick out what I liked and so my mother would have a harder time bulldozing my opinion.

First, I choose pink and cream roses for the centerpieces. I wait impatiently while the florist demonstrates an arrangement. She has tinsel sticking out from flowers. "Simpler," I urge. "Just the flowers. We'll put them in one long row down the table. No separate vases, so it will look like one extended centerpiece." I look around and spot the table of white roses. "These for the bouquet. And we can wrap the stems in pearls." I'm not sure if Lily will approve, but at this point it's clear she doesn't care.

The only request for the past two months has been *no lilies*. Otherwise, I'm walking around blind.

While I wait for my mother, I click onto Twitter and type in #PoPhilly. A list of tweets pops up.

@RaderBull595: The Calloway girls are hot, but that tall one is such a bitch. I'd bang Lils though.

@TVDFan70008: Have you seen the way Lo looks at Lily? *swoon*

@thefieryheart: Brb building a shrine for Ryke and Daisy!

@RealityXbites4: I loooove this show!! #TeamScott

@SlightlySpoiled: Can't wait for Rose to dump Connor. Fry his dick! #please

Lovely.

The reviews for the show have been much better than any of us could ever expect. Even though we're labeled "foul mouthed, rich and conceited" most of the articles congratulate us for being real. For not trying to put on fake faces in front of the cameras. Daisy burps, Lily says sexual comments on accident and I threaten to castrate men. Some people like us for our flaws. Others still see us as caricatures. But I try not to let those comments bother me.

You can't please everyone.

@Fashion4Goddesses: Just received my Calloway Couture dress! Gorgeous!

My heart swells at that tweet. Soon after the first episode aired, my sales skyrocketed. And they have continued to grow exponentially with each new episode. Fizzle has even seen a spike in its stock. Hopefully the success will last.

The bells on the door clink together, and I quickly pocket my phone in my purse. My mother struts through like she suddenly bought the entire store. Her nose upturns at a vase of half-wilted daisies.

"You're early," I tell her. Ten minutes to be exact.

"So are you," she replies. "Where's your sister?"

"She's not coming." I don't use the stomachache excuse since I've overdone it already. Instead I try the truth. "She doesn't like how you talk to her."

"Lily has a voice of her own," my mother snaps. "If she doesn't like how I speak then she should tell me herself."

I don't say anything. I don't tell her that she's not the easiest woman to talk to, and it takes practice and skill—that even I come away feeling more neurotic and unspun.

"I already picked out the flowers," I tell her.

She doesn't seem surprised. "Then we have to choose between mine and yours because I already called in arrangements this morning." *Of course.* She walks haughtily to a cabinet where white and orange lilies are gathered together with teal ribbon.

"She specifically said *no* lilies," I say angrily. "I've already told you this ten million times." Not only that but *orange* and *teal.* Really? Maybe for Daisy but Lily is more . . . subdued.

My mother huffs and fingers the string of pearls on her neck. Her greatest tell. When she's particularly stressed or annoyed she touches them as though they're rosary beads, praying to the Holy Father for her argumentative daughter to be docile and content.

"What's wrong with lilies?" my mother asks. "Olivia Barnes's daughter had them at her wedding and they were just gorgeous."

"Her name is Lily," I say. "She doesn't find the pun as amusing as you do. And when she sees lilies everywhere, she'll be upset." Not to mention that we receive unsolicited bouquets of lilies along with fan mail almost every week. From men that fantasize about my sex-addicted sister. Those flowers are tainted in her mind.

"I already ordered them, so what do you want me to do?" she says. "I can't very well cancel, can I?"

"Yes, you can."

"I don't understand why you're so bent out of shape over the flowers."

I stand my ground. "I know Lily better than you," I remind her. "We're going to accommodate her one and only request."

My mother mumbles something that sounds like *but she's not even here to voice it herself.* Her eyes flit around the room before she huffs again. "What alternatives do you have in mind?"

I show her the white and pink roses I picked out.

She gives me a look. "Don't make this about you, Rose."

My lips press into a thin line and I'm sure my nose flares. "My name and the flower are not synonymous, Mother."

Poppy, my older sister, has never had trouble talking to her. Most of the time she just agrees willingly so that arguments don't begin. Same with Daisy.

I can't be agreeable with someone I know is wrong, regardless of her being my mother or not. I'm not sure when I had the courage to say no. But she still doesn't understand that my opinion isn't less because I'm her child. I'm twenty-three years old. She may see me as a little girl who stands behind her at dance recitals, who tugs on her arm for advice about other girls in school, but I'm an adult now.

I appreciate her advice, I do, but I also have the right to disagree with it. And yet, this direction only causes arguments and fights. Neither of us can win if we're in the same room.

My mother stares at the roses with narrowed eyes. I remember

Daisy's advice when I couldn't get my mother to stop arguing with me. *Tell her you love her*, she said. *That always works for me when I want something.*

I give it a shot. "I love you, Mother—"

"Oh, don't even start, Rose. I haven't heard you say that in five years."

I suppose she's right. Since I rarely show affection to my mother, it makes sense that Daisy's *I love you*s seem like blinding rainbows in comparison.

She spins on her heels and her eyes hit mine. They haven't softened. "You can cancel the order," she says. "But I'm not done discussing the flowers or the centerpieces. God knows we both can find something better than an ice swan."

I try to smile. "That sounds good."

"How is Daisy doing?" she asks.

"Good." I don't elaborate. She talks to Daisy enough. Whenever my sister is on the phone, it's usually with her. And I have no right to keep Daisy with me after the reality show wraps. There's nothing I can do but wait until Daisy's older—to see if she'd like to live with us and distance herself from our mother a little more. To finally breathe the way I know she wants to. It's going to be a long wait, but I'm willing to suffer through it.

"Good." She nods.

I pause for the rest of her question, but it never comes. "You're forgetting your other daughter."

"Lily is twenty-one," she refutes. "She's lying in the bed she made for herself."

I shouldn't have said anything.

"How can you plan her wedding if you're still bitter over the scandal?" I ask in detest.

"Because this wedding is the only thing that will return her reputation, and it'll wipe the stain she's set to the Calloway name. It's more important than my bitterness. It has to be perfect."

She looks me over, as if reminding me that the *perfect* element of the wedding is my job. "We need to schedule a venue by the weekend. I'll send you my top choices. Keep your phone on." She gives me a tight, rigid hug before leaving the store. And leaving me feeling more overwhelmed than before.

So much shit to do. Like planning a bachelorette party. I would have hired male strippers—but for a recovering sex addict, that's not the smartest theme. I think Lily and Lo want to have a joint bachelor and bachelorette party anyway.

As I head out the door and find my Escalade on the curb, my mind reverts back to everything that's been happening with Connor. His thumb. The shower. Love.

Loren may believe that Connor won't be there for me at the end of the line, but that night at the screening party made me realize how much I do trust him. How much I do know him. Lo was wrong on so many accounts, and that's only because Connor has let me see more than a couple sides of his life.

Whether Connor says it or not, he loves me enough to let me in more than halfway. And I know it's time for me to do the same on a different kind of level.

I pull out my phone and send a quick text to Connor.

Bring wine tonight.

Since Lo is sober, we try to keep alcohol out of sight, so I have a trunk in our bedroom that I'll store our stash in. I pause to think about my choice of alcohol. Wine? I'm probably going to need something stronger.

And tequila.

I take a breath and wait for the text.

Is there a reason we'll be drinking tonight?—Connor

Surprise, I reply back.

Can't wait 😊 —Connor

Twenty

Connor Cobalt

Frederick has spent the past ten minutes giving me the silent treatment. He sits behind his desk and pretends to be interested in *The New York Times* on his computer. He's pissed that I'm still taking Adderall. But I can't function without it.

I finish texting Rose and lean back in the leather chair. Frederick hasn't looked up yet.

"I'm not paying you to ignore me," I tell him.

His eyes remain on the computer screen. "You're right. You're paying for my counsel, which you are clearly not interested in." He starts typing on his keyboard, the pounding more aggravating than I'll let on. He has a squared jaw, tousled brown hair and broad shoulders—in his thirties, fairly good-looking, but he never married. His work is his wife.

I press my fingers to my lips in thought. "And you're not even the slightest bit interested in what Rose texted me?" I try.

His fingers falter as he types, but he regains fluidity. Frederick enjoys talking with me, whether he'll admit it to himself or not. I'm his most interesting patient.

"She asked me to bring home wine and tequila." I don't say anything else.

I watch the curiosity build in Frederick's eyes until he lets out a sigh and rolls his chair back, his body angled towards me.

"You're too easy," I tell him.

"So you've told me." He pauses. "How far have you been with her?"

I hesitate to reveal this, which surprises even me. I'm usually open about everything with Frederick, but being with Rose makes me want to keep every moment close to our chests, so no one can share what happens but us. It takes me about a minute to finally say, "She sucked my cock."

Frederick's brows rise in surprise. "You got her to blow you?"

"Rose had the choice." I don't want one of us to lose with sex. We both need to come out successful and fulfilled.

"How kinky?" Frederick asks.

I let out a mock sigh and stare at the ceiling. "We're not there yet." I tilt my head. "Give her time, Rick. She's a virgin."

"I'm surprised you're not pushing her harder. For years, you've talked about how you want to—"

"I'm going to push her as far as I think she can go without having her run out on me. She's packed a suitcase before, remember? She stayed in a hotel in the Hamptons for a week just to prove a point. And we weren't even living together then."

Frederick laughs. "I remember. You were both fighting about the Theory of Relativity."

"She loves to disagree with me." We argue a lot about theories because they're easily debatable, but we always, somehow, kiss in the end. When she finally returned to Princeton, I spent the day with her in bed, sucking on her neck, gently easing her to go further. She was too scared to do more. But I think, for once, she will now.

"When she went down on you, you didn't let her use her hands?" he suddenly asks.

"No." These questions are annoying me more than usual.

"Did she like it?"

"Immensely."

"You're very possessive of her," he states, taking out his notepad.

"How can you tell?"

"You sound irritated."

Wonderful.

"Did you go down on her afterwards?"

"No." I shift my jaw, trying to get my words to cooperate and not come out so damn coarse.

"Because you didn't have time?"

"No," I *almost* snap at him. I clear my throat as Frederick scribbles something down.

"Because she wouldn't let you."

I stay quiet since he phrased this one as a statement, not a question.

"She's frightened to let you touch her. The alcohol she wants you to buy will lessen her inhibitions and reservations. If she's afraid in the first place, maybe she's not submissive, Connor."

My eyes narrow, a territorial feeling boiling inside of me. "She responds the way a submissive would. She shudders in pleasure when I take full control. But she's still horrible at it; I'll admit that. I'm trying to get her to a place where she can accept what turns her on." I pause. "Outside the bedroom, you're right, though. She's not submissive. And she never will be."

"And you like that?" Frederick asks, his pen hovering over the notepad.

"Yes."

"Why does that appeal to you so much?"

"You know why."

"But I want you to hear yourself say it again."

I let out an exasperated sigh and clear my throat for the second time. "I enjoy being matched outside of the bedroom. It's a constant game that's fun to play. She keeps me on my toes." The words come out like I've rehearsed them, but it's only because I've said them so many times before. "But I love the part where I can give her everything she needs in sex, and I get the same in return. Through that bedroom door, I become in control again, and I can empower her. It's a dynamic that never gets tired or old."

I often thought about her when I was at Faust and Penn—remembering the conversations we had at academic bowls and conferences. I never believed she'd enjoy giving up control in bed. But the longer she shied from affection, recoiling from other men, I thought she was just scared. And how could a woman as powerful and unabashed as her be frightened of sex? And then it dawned on me. She didn't wish to rule a man in bed. *She* wanted to be ruled. But she didn't know how to ask without feeling weak. So she thought being alone, unfulfilled sexually was the better option. I'm here to tell her it should have never been a fucking solution in the first place.

Frederick nods.

"There's more." I need to be honest about what's going on recently. "She thinks once she gives herself to me, I'll leave—that our relationship is nothing more than a game because I won't allow myself to love anyone."

"And why don't you love her, Connor?" His chair creaks as he leans back, and a shadow of a smile plays at his lips.

He acts as though he understands what I can't, putting me at odds with myself. He's listened to my beliefs about love for years, but that doesn't stop him from routinely asking more.

"People relate love to insects fluttering inside their digestive system. I've never had that affliction."

He cracks a smile. "It's a metaphor."

"I know what a metaphor is, Rick."

"Then stop being a smartass and so will I."

I straighten in my chair, becoming more serious. "I've seen the kind of love that cripples. Take Loren Hale and Lily Calloway—when one is shot with an emotion, the other feels it. If you stripped one from the other, they'd be less than themselves. If that's love, I want no part of it." I want to be whole. I want to be the best possible version of myself without the chance of being wounded or broken.

"Can you empathize with Rose?" he asks me.

"Yes, but love is a weakness that I won't submit to."

"Sometimes you can't control everything, Connor," he tells me. "Even as intelligent as you are, there are things out of your grasp. Love, death—you can't predict either. They just happen."

"And you believe it's already happened?" I refuse this outcome. It's not computable.

"Why are you with her?"

"Attraction."

"And?"

"Affection."

"What else?"

"Amusement—these are just words, Frederick."

"Love is just a word."

"I can't love her," I tell him definitively as I stand and pocket my phone.

He stays seated, and yet I feel as though he has the advantage on me. He still sees what I can't. "And why is that?"

"Smart people do stupid things when they're in love. I've yet to do something inane."

Frederick grins. "Give it time."

I suppress the urge to roll my eyes. I wave him off and head to the door. "See you next week."

"I'm looking forward to it."

"Of course you are," I say back. "You get to hear about me spanking my girlfriend."

"Get out of my office, Connor." He returns to his papers, but his grin grows wider and wider until I leave.

I stop by the liquor store after my session with Frederick, and it's late when I arrive home. The lights are off in the living room, and I don't hear Lily's or Lo's climaxes through the walls.

When I reach the second level, I stop by my door, not about to knock. I haven't been that courteous since we moved in together. There are some barriers that I choose to destroy for her.

As soon as the door creaks open, I find Rose sitting on the bed, flipping through the latest issue of *Vogue*. Her eyes flit up to mine and she drops the magazine on her lap. "Did you bring it?"

I hold up the brown paper bag. "Wine and tequila as you requested, but I would advise only choosing one tonight. Unless you'd like to be ill."

"The wine is for you," she says curtly.

My eyebrows rise. So the tequila is for her. She's that nervous.

She pats the mattress. "Take a seat, Richard. You look like a scared little cat. Sadie would claw you for your cowardice."

"My cat loves me unconditionally," I reply. The bed rocks as I climb onto it, and I set the paper bag in between us. "And I'm fine, so you must be projecting your fear onto me." I smile, just so I can see that flicker of contempt in her eyes.

"I'm not scared." She straightens up and pulls her shoulders back. "I know exactly what we'll be doing tonight. I can't say the same for you."

"So what are we doing tonight, hun?" I ask. "Other than getting drunk."

She reaches into the paper bag and pulls out the bottle of Patron. I watch her unscrew the cap and start rubbing the lip with the hem of her black thigh-length nightgown. It's silk and looks like a slip underneath a dress.

I immediately imagine myself slowly lifting the thin fabric off her body, leaving her bare for my touch. I want her naked. Now.

Patience.

I place my hand on the smoothness of her leg, her skin nearly as silky as her nightgown and exceedingly warmer. The minute I pull her closer to me with that one hand, her chest rises. But she focuses on wiping the rim of her Patron.

Rose plans on drinking straight from the bottle. She's trying hard to progress our relationship, willing to forgo a glass. That's a big deal in Rose Calloway's world. Her effort hasn't gone unnoticed in my eyes.

When it's successfully clean for her lips, Rose takes a swig from the bottle. She nods to the bag. "Get your wine. And then we'll play the game."

"What game?"

"Truth or dare."

She says it with a straight face, almost challenging me to laugh. I keep my expression complacent, but I can't help what I say. "Shall we spend seven minutes in heaven too?"

She shoots me a heated look. "We're playing. Don't make me tie you up."

I laugh and rub my lips, unable to contain my amusement. "Darling, if anyone is going to be tied up," I say, my hand descending towards her ass, "c'est toi."

It's you.

Twenty-one

Rose Calloway

D on't be a pussy," I tell Connor. "If I can do it, you should be able to." Although with that confident declaration of *tying* me up—my brazen attitude feels more like a front than anything else.

"Name calling gets you nowhere in life," he refutes with ease. "And just so you know, I was only going to drink from a glass in case I spilled it on your comforter. But your loss."

He acts like he's going to tip the wine bottle *accidentally* onto my white-laced bedspread. My heart jumps into my throat, and fear bulges my eyes.

He grins and then puts the bottle to his lips, taking a large swig. The wine and tequila are strategic. I need more liquid courage than him, and I'd rather be buzzed. I've never seen Connor drunk, which means he could very well turn into an inebriated asshole. Someone I do not want to play truth or dare with. But it's a risk I'll take.

"Truth or dare?" I ask him after another sip of tequila. The liquor slides sharply down my throat, but I'm too nervous to care. Normal couples who share a bed would be fine playing truth or dare together. Another piece of evidence that I am not normal. *We* are not normal.

He doesn't blink. "Truth."

I don't want to ease in. "What's your favorite position?"

"I won't hurt you," he says, reading into my question. "I know you're nervous to have sex, but I promise I'll be . . ." He smiles at his own thought. ". . . no, that's not quite right."

"You were about to say *gentle,* weren't you?"

His lips rise further, validating my assumption.

The aftertaste of tequila sticks to my tongue, and my head dizzies at the idea of Connor being *anything* but gentle. I'm not the softest girl, so the image of being handled by a soft, careful boy makes me squirm.

"I promise I'll be me," he says, grinning into his next swig of wine.

"It's a good thing I like you then." My voice is still icy. The alcohol hasn't kicked in just yet.

"*Like* me? Qu'en est-il de l'amour?" *What happened to love?*

"You don't believe in love," I retort. "So you've lost the right for me to love you back." I nod assuredly at this new stance I'm taking. "But I still like you. Don't worry."

"I never worry," he says. "I do believe in love. When I was a child I thought it wasn't real, but I've come to see that it does exist for some people. Just not me."

Right. He can't love anyone. He's too analytical, I suppose. I've come to accept it, but there's a part of me that wants so badly to be his first love the way he's mine. His hand keeps descending, gripping my ass above my silk nightgown. I tip the bottle of Patron against my mouth, taking half a shot.

"You didn't answer my question," I say.

"What's my favorite position?"

"Yes."

"I have a lot of favorites."

"Choose one, Richard," I snap.

He smiles. "Missionary . . . with a few alterations."

"What alterations?"

His lips just curve higher, as if he's partaking in a personal inside joke. I kind of want to punch him for the smirk, but I also want Connor to kiss me roughly. It's an odd mixture that's pounding my head.

At least he doesn't want me to ride his dick like a sexy dominatrix. I don't think I could confidently pull that off. It's not something I've ever visualized either. Although when people meet me, I know it's their first assumption, their first wild picture. Of me in stilettos, a heel at a man's throat. All these years, I believed in the stereotype too. That to be a strong, confident woman outside the bedroom, I'd have to be as equally dominant inside. It's a reason why I rarely brought guys back to my apartment in college. Because I'd disappoint them. And I'd rather shove them out of my door and be called an ice-cold bitch than be laughed at for not making good on their fantasies.

We're all more than we appear to be.

"Truth or dare?" His question pops my thoughts.

"Truth."

"What's your strangest fantasy?"

"I change my mind. I choose dare," I say quickly.

He laughs. "Play by the rules, darling."

"Dare," I repeat, not backing down.

"Fine. I'll let you cheat this once."

Cheat. That is a *vile* word, but I stay my course.

"I dare you . . ." His eyes flit around the room before landing back on me. "To answer my question." He full-on grins.

"You're terrible," I deadpan.

"You love me. Even if you won't say it anymore."

"Maybe." *Ugh.* I stare at my traitorous bottle of Patron for loosening my lips and deteriorating my brain.

His hand dips further to my ass, and he pulls me so close that I realize I'm sitting on his lap, my legs sprawled to the side. He combs the hair off my neck and places a light kiss on my nape. He watches how my body shivers from the touch, warms from the alcohol and dizzies from his closeness.

"You wanted to play this game," he reminds me. "Somewhere in your heart, you wanted these things to be revealed."

I did. And that's why I had the alcohol. To build my courage. I take another small sip, my lips wet with the liquor. He rubs his thumb across them, slowly. As my breath hitches, he puts his thumb in his mouth, tasting the tequila.

"My strangest fantasy?" I repeat, studying him like he's the most interesting specimen in the universe. To me, he most definitely is. When the answer suddenly hits me, I pale. I'm not even close enough to being *that* drunk to tell him. But I can't lie. I hate cheaters so damn much. "Ask me something else."

"No," he says, not making this easy for me. He rests a hand on the back of my neck, so near now that his chest touches mine. He inhales strongly, my body closing in on him. The tension winds me in a taut strand, the place between my legs beginning to pulse for touch. He kisses right outside of my lips. "Answer me," he murmurs with a deep, husky voice.

"Define strange," I breathe.

He's abandoned his wine bottle somewhere. And I don't even care to search for it. "Not normal to society's traditional standards."

Yes, my fantasy is definitely abnormal. I've thought about it a few times before, and I have no idea why it aroused me. "I shouldn't be turned on by it."

"I'll be the judge of that." He brushes my hair out of my face again, his gaze steadily and slowly skimming every inch of me, heating me up more than the alcohol now.

"I think my fantasy is weird, even for your standards."

He stops stroking me and his eyebrow arches, pure curiosity pouring through his gaze. "Now you have to tell me."

"I picture you." My vocal cords freeze.

"Good. Keep going."

I smack his arm.

"I picture you as well," he says. "I have since I was seventeen."

"Really?"

"It wasn't fair to the other people I was with, but you've been the most fascinating person to me. And no one could really compare in my mind."

I rephrase his words and hear *I love you*. Even if *he* won't ever say them. This proclamation inflates my courage. And I sit up a little straighter on his lap. I lick my lips and continue, "I picture you and me."

"We're getting somewhere close, I suspect."

I glare. "We can move on if you don't want to hear it."

"Rose," he says affectionately, "I would sit here for eighty more years and listen to you talk. I love the sound of your voice and every meaning behind your words."

"So you love my voice but you don't love me?"

He grips my butt hard, and a gasp catches in my throat. "Maybe *you* should be labeled smartass after we fuck."

I actually laugh.

He smiles with me. "Tell me," he whispers, his lips tickling my ear. "N'ai pas peur." *Don't be afraid.*

I swallow. "I may not like it, even though I've imagined it."

He groans, half in frustration, the other half in arousal. He breathes more heavily than before. "You're killing me."

He hardens beneath me. I really, really love that power. "Maybe I should draw out the suspense then and *never* tell you."

"*No.*" He cups my face in a strong hand. "If you could live inside my mind right now, you'd realize how crazy you're making me."

"I want to be in your mind," I say honestly, the alcohol doing its trick as I run my hands across his chest, popping the buttons of his white shirt.

"You're almost all the way there."

That does it. I take a deep breath and I tell him. "I'm always sleeping when it happens." I don't break his gaze. I stay strong. I can tell him my fantasy. I can do this without balking like a coward. "And I wake up to you inside of me . . . thrusting . . ." I trail off as I try to read his expression that stays blank.

I can't tell whether he thinks I'm weird or not.

His hand rises from my neck to the back of my head, and he kisses my unmoving, frightened lips before he whispers, "I've done much stranger things, Rose." I hear the smile in his words, and I immediately relax. "Your turn," he says. And just like that, he brushes it off so I don't keep fretting.

It felt good to share that, to be more open sexually. I think I could do this more often with him. It's not so hard. "Truth or dare?" I ask, my knuckles whitening as I grip the bottle of my Patron, pent up the longer he touches me.

"Truth."

"What rouses you more, my body or my brain?"

His eyes drift to the tops of my breasts while one hand slides up my nightgown, settling on my bottom above my panties. "Both, equally."

If I wasn't so intoxicated by his presence and the liquor, I would make him give me a definitive answer, but I let it slide.

"Truth or dare?" he asks.

The last truth was difficult, and I know he won't make it any easier. So I say, "Dare."

He exhales deeply, so very aroused. Places in my body are clenching that have never clenched before. "I dare you," he says, "to let me take off your nightgown."

Before I even nod, his hands slip all the way beneath the silk, and he slowly lifts the fabric over my head, my breasts visible for his intense, heady gaze. My nipples already stand at attention.

I love the way he's staring at me. It makes me feel more than just beautiful. I feel like I'm his. Like no one else could possibly compare to me. He doesn't even have to say the words. I see it in his eyes. I can practically read it in his mind.

I sit on his lap, only in black panties, while he's fully clothed. I want to strip him, but when I try to take off his unbuttoned shirt, he grips my wrists hard in disapproval. Right, we're still playing the game. "Truth or dare?" I ask him.

"Truth."

My eyes narrow. "You were supposed to pick dare." I'd love to see his cock again, but it stays hidden in his pants. Just staring at the large bulge makes me wet.

"But I didn't."

"Fine. If you could cut off any part of my body and store it in a jar, what would it be?"

"Your eyes." He doesn't miss a beat.

I glare.

"And they'd look at me just like that." His fingers glide across my hip, but he stays away from my breasts on purpose. I've never wanted him to press against me so badly. "Truth or dare?"

"Dare." *I'll do anything.*

"Let me play with you for . . ." He checks his charcoal Rolex. ". . . ten minutes." It's as ambiguous as he wants it to be. And before I can ask or accept (which I would have), he has me pinned flat on my back.

His lips touch mine in a big inhale, causing my body to buck up and meet his.

And then his hand descends towards my belly, his mouth trailing my jaw to my breasts. He sucks my nipple and bites the bud, the pressure grasping my throat.

I want more force on my neck, but I can't speak to ask for it.

I'm lost in these feelings.

He sits up for a second, on his knees. And then he splits my legs open. In one swift motion, he slides me forcibly towards him, my heat digging into the hardness beneath his slacks.

Holy shit . . .

I don't want to shut my eyes, but my lids flutter with each rupturing nerve. His hand disappears beneath my panties, and he slips two large fingers inside of me, pulsing them with mastered speed.

"You're incredibly wet, darling," he says with a heavy breath. "You've been a bad girl, not giving your body what it craves." He lifts me a little higher and rocks against me while he's fully clothed. The force feels so damn good. He slaps the side of my thigh.

Fuck me.

My limbs are tight in his clutch, and it's everything I can do not to scream. All the noises just lock tight in my chest. I think I've spent so much time holding in sounds when I touch myself that it's hard to let go.

"Let me hear you."

He rocks harder. I wish his pants were off. I wish I could see his ass that tightens as he pounds into me, in sync with his fingers.

He slaps me again, more towards my ass this time. I let out a wrangled cry that even surprises me.

"You liked that," he says.

"God . . . yes . . ."

"God's not in this bedroom, Rose."

My arm covers my eyes. I barely hear his words. "Fuck . . ." My lips part in a silent scream. I clench my comforter, and a wetness seeps beneath my ass. I look up and see the tequila spilt all over the bed.

And I don't even care.

"Connor," I breathe. ". . . Connor . . . harder."

I see his lips lift before my lids close again. And he obliges by quickening the movement of his fingers and slamming into me. Then his hand finds the length of my neck. I open my eyes as he wraps his fingers around my throat and squeezes so tight.

I can't breathe.

All the blood rushes to my head. He chokes me, not hard enough to hurt me, but enough to be lightheaded. This is what I wanted only minutes earlier. The fact that he understood this without me asking—it drives me to a new point, a new climax that I have never, ever experienced before.

I come in a turbulent, blissful wave. I can feel myself contract around his fingers as he keeps them inside of me. A thin layer of sweat coats my body, and when he pulls out his fingers, he grips my chin, forcing me to look at him.

He makes me watch as he puts his fingers in his mouth, licking off the wetness from between my legs. The image kick-starts my sluggish breathing into a rapid-fire pattern.

When he takes his hand out, he says, "Just as I thought."

"What?"

"I love the taste of you." He leans over me and slips those same two fingers into my mouth. He licked most of me clean, and I taste mostly him—his mouthwash and minty breath. I suspect he knew I'd taste more of him than myself.

He checks his watch. "Three more minutes." His lips skim my neck and he whispers, "What I could do to you in that time . . ."

And just as he slips his tongue into my mouth, a huge crash bangs against the wall. I jump in fright, accidentally biting him. *Shit.*

Connor places a hand on my collar, keeping my back to the mattress while he sits up. "I'm fine," he assures me.

But I taste the bitter iron of blood. And I know it's his. Before I can inspect his tongue, something else slams behind us again.

I flinch, but I glance back at him. "Let me see your tongue."

"No." In a single word he reminds me that I can't push him around. "And my tongue is fine. You barely sliced it."

Good.

The next crash in the wall comes with muffled yelling.

Connor stands from the bed, no longer hard. As he changes pants and underwear quickly, I realize he came too. I hadn't even noticed. I was too enamored with my own climax.

"It's probably just Lily and Loren screwing," I tell him.

His eyes narrow at me. "I must have fingered the brains out of you."

I frown.

"That's Daisy's room."

I bolt upright and spring off the bed, grabbing a black silk robe. I slip it on and knot the tie at my waist. Another bang hits the wall hard. My heart leaps to my throat.

"You should stay here," he tells me, zipping his black slacks.

I glare.

"It was worth a try." He places a hand on the small of my back. "After you."

The moment I reach the doorframe with Connor, we find Scott standing here, watching the scene with crossed arms. Not doing a damn thing to stop whatever's happening.

And then I look, and my jaw hits the floor.

A glass lamp is shattered on the ground, a bookshelf toppled over, any fragile knickknacks destroyed on the hardwood.

Ryke wrestles a medium-built guy in the center of the room. I discern his age quickly. Forties. Red hair that sticks up from being pummeled. His lip is busted, and he manages to put up a good fight against Ryke, who's shirtless in a pair of track pants. The man shoves Ryke back and flings two punches, one connecting with Ryke's jaw.

"Get the fuck off me!" the guy yells.

And then Ryke socks him right in the gut. The man crumples forward, coughing.

Daisy is in the corner, smashing something on the ground, hidden behind her bed. I give Scott a long agonizing glare for being a horrible human being and just standing here. And I go to my sister's aid while Connor tries to separate the guys.

"You motherfucking pervert," Ryke sneers, grabbing him around the throat. He's about to slam his head into the ground, but Connor grips Ryke's wrist hard and throws him off.

All I can think is that Ryke found Daisy's boyfriend. Who's a gross older man. That's my first assumption.

"Don't wake up Lily and Lo," Connor says in a hushed voice. "Calm down."

Ryke's features are so dark. He's almost hard to look at.

And then the man tries to escape, about to sprint out the door, but Connor snatches him by the shirt and drags him in front of his body. The man struggles in Connor's forceful grip.

Right when I reach Daisy, I realize what she's smashing.

A camera.

Now on her knees, she slams the device repeatedly on the ground, little plastic pieces flying in every direction. She screams furiously each time the mangled lens meets the floor.

"Daisy," I whisper, but I grab her arms before she hurts herself with the sharp debris.

She drops the remains of the broken camera and slowly sits, shivering in my arms. It wasn't her boyfriend in her room, I realize now. It had to have been the paparazzi—what looks to be a stupid one, a loser who obviously has no concept of the law. I glance over my shoulder at Connor and Ryke.

Connor has his phone pressed to his ear while he grips the man's shirt. Every time he struggles, Connor throttles him with one hand. Composed, tall and strong. He speaks quietly to someone on the other line.

I make out Connor's words, "We need to keep this out of the tabloids . . . Lily and Lo don't need to know. They feel guilty enough for the media attention . . ."

"What happened?" I ask Ryke, who nears the bed. Scott continues to just stand by the fucking door, watching. It's not as though this is being filmed. We're in a *bedroom*, which means there aren't cameras here.

"Daisy called me on her cell," he says.

She stares at the ground, her face as pale as a sheet.

I shake her arms, not very maternal or soft, and she almost blows over with my force. "Daisy? Talk to me."

"He barged in my room," she says under her breath.

I collect her waist-length hair out of her face, trying not to freak out. "And?" I say, clenching my teeth. *If he put a finger on her . . .*

Her gorgeous face contorts in a series of violent emotions. ". . . he started taking pictures of me . . . I didn't know what to do, so I called Ryke . . ." She shakes her head and tears splash onto the floorboards. ". . . I'm so tired . . ." I hold her to my chest while she begins to cry.

I look up at Ryke, and he stares at her with that same look I saw during the screening party. Concern. Dark empathy.

"Shh," I whisper to her, combing my fingers through her hair. I rest my chin on her head and keep her close.

". . . I'm so tired," she says again, her voice trembling. When our mother's not preoccupied with Lily's wedding, she pulls Daisy in five different directions. She makes sure she's booked for photo shoots, and for the past three weeks, Daisy has been working tirelessly. If she's not at school, then our mom carts her to New York to visit her new modeling agency. I've hardly seen her at all this month.

I even had to convince our mother to let me throw Daisy a birthday party. She would've had to cancel one of her shoots so she could celebrate. It took four screaming matches over the phone before I won out. But that was just one free day I gained for her.

"What's going on at school, Dais?" Ryke asks.

I glance over my shoulder to make sure Lily and Lo aren't here. At least they're still sleeping.

Daisy chokes on a sporadic breath. "I . . . I'm fine . . . really."

I exchange a worried look with Ryke.

He mouths, *It's not fucking good.*

I know, I mouth back.

But what can we do? She has to finish prep school, and I can only guess the kind of ridicule kids are casting on her. She's famous now. Her sister is a sex addict, and she's been painted as a sex-addict-to-be. Her photographs are everywhere—sometimes deliberately from modeling, other times not consented from paparazzi. It's an abrupt change from her old life, and none of us can relate to her current situation. We're all in our twenties, out of prep school by now. We don't have to worry about bullying like that.

"We're going to take care of this," I tell her. I'm going to surround the fucking townhouse with security. We had iron fences and a guarded gate at our home in Princeton. We should have had better things in place here. "How'd he break through the front door?" I ask Ryke.

He glares. "I didn't have time to fucking ask."

My lips tighten. "Did he touch her?"

Ryke stares back down at Daisy. "Did he fucking touch you, Daisy?"

She shakes her head repeatedly. "No . . . I'm sorry . . ." She wipes her eyes quickly and tries to bottle her emotions.

"Don't you ever fucking apologize for another guy's offense," he growls. He layers on a few more curse words as he glares at the ceiling.

Wow. Ryke jumped up twenty points in my book. Not for the swearing, to be clear. "When did you become such a feminist?" I ask him.

"Since I learned my alcoholic father cheated on my mother. Then he fucking left her so he could raise his bastard son." The bitterness and resentment pours from his harsh words.

"I shouldn't have asked." *His family tree is fucked up.* I smooth Daisy's hair.

Connor pads over to us, pocketing his phone. He no longer has the guy by the shirt. In fact, the man is gone. "Your father's security came and took him," he tells me. "He broke through the front door with a bump key."

"We need—"

"Your father already hired extra security to stand outside. He's taking care of the incident quietly. No one will know about this unless Scott decides to air it. He has footage of the man coming up the stairs and through the hallway."

I look for Scott, but he's gone too.

"Lily and Lo . . ." Daisy murmurs, rubbing her eyes.

"They won't ever find out," Ryke says. "This stays between the four of us."

And Scott. But no one adds him or my father's name to the mix.

And we don't ask why Lily and Lo can't know. It's what Connor had told my father on the phone. The guilt would hurt them so much. The crazed media was spawned from Lily's addiction being publicized. But I bear some of the guilt myself—for putting my sisters through a reality show with awful security, for ditching their bodyguards. But I can withstand that guilt and come out strong.

Lily and Lo can't. They're addicts. This is naturally going to tear them apart, and they could turn to their vices to numb the feelings. And none of us want that. We'll be the walls that shield these terrible events from them. We can endure the pain for however long they need to heal.

It's what the four of us agreed to the moment Lily was afraid to step out of the house and meet the world. The moment Lo looked sick each time he tried to convince her to go outside and face the coldhearted media.

There was a very dark point where we all believed they'd die together. Where they'd call it quits. There were moments where I wondered how any girl could endure what she was going through. And I think the only reason they both didn't leave the world was because they refused to leave it together.

Leaving separately—causing the other to suffer that horrific loss—I doubt that was even an option in their minds.

Twenty-two

Connor Cobalt

What is it?" I ask Rose while I pay for the check at the crowded restaurant. The seven of us—Scott included, who feels more and more like a tagalong as Rose and I grow closer—ate out at Valentino's for dinner.

The more popular *Princesses of Philly* becomes, the more the press has latched on to us. Besides the droves of photographers outside, families in booths snap pictures of us with their phones as we sit at a long table.

But that's not why Rose's brows have pinched together. She cups her cell on her lap and concentrates on the blue-lit screen.

I hook my ankle to her chair and drag her closer to me.

"She's relentless," Rose says stiffly.

I read the text.

3 months and 24 days—Mom

"Should I even ask about wedding dress shopping?" Last time I questioned about the cake, Rose almost went manic, spouting off things that her mother told her in a discordant mess. I couldn't understand anything she was saying, not even as she spoke in French. She kept pacing in our bedroom and breathing abnormally. It took me an entire hour to calm her down.

"Lily said she didn't want to go," she says. "I can get Daisy and Poppy to be fitted for bridesmaids' dresses without Lily there, but

I can't just go pick out a wedding gown for her." She stays relatively at ease, so she must have thought of a solution.

"And?"

"I'm going to sew her one," she tells me. "I've been designing it for the past week. I think I can finish it in the amount of time I have left."

I don't want to reiterate what Frederick has been telling me, even though I know it's true. She's taken on too much. She's not only planning Lily's wedding and her bachelorette party, but she's been working tirelessly on reviving Calloway Couture. She refuses to hire employees until her profit margin increases, so she's tasked with all of the social media and inventory, not to mention calls from hopeful investors and department stores.

It's a lot for one person to handle. I can't see how designing a wedding dress will alleviate any of her anxiety, but I'd rather not be a hypocrite in this situation. My body is being fueled by Adderall. It's not the noble solution, and I wouldn't want Rose to take it.

"I'm sure you'll find time," I say, trying to believe the words so they don't feel like such a lie.

"So do you really have a boyfriend or are you just fucking with us?" Ryke asks Daisy as he tosses his napkin on the table, servers clearing away the last of our dirty plates.

"Yeah, how come he's never been in an episode?" Lo asks.

Daisy leans back on two legs of her chair and shrugs. "I don't know. Ask Scott."

"Let's not talk about production," Scott says casually. Maybe he has trouble not being a complete and utter dipshit because his eyes do a number on Daisy—staring at her makeup-less face, her natural beauty enough for him to stare longer and harder. His eyes even fall to her breasts, the sides exposed in a Calloway Couture gold sparkling top, the neckline plunged.

"Eyes up here," Ryke forces, waving his knife towards his own face in a threatening gesture.

Scott doesn't peel his gaze from Daisy, which is starting to aggravate the fuck out of me. The public has been clear that they're overwhelmingly Team Scott in this fake love triangle. I think the last blog comment I read said something like: Connor is getting on my mf-ing nerves!! What the hell does Rose see in HIM?! Scott loves her soooooo much.—LadyBug345

I've also learned that many people want to fight me. I get "I want to punch Connor Cobalt!" all the time. I almost choked on my coffee this morning, laughing hard as I went through comments. Behave, Connor. If you were my son, I'd wash your mouth out with soap.—DeeDeeJohnes

DeeDee, I admire your fervor, even if you're not on my side. That's what I feel with each disdainful remark. At least these people care about something so deeply that they're willing to shout about it online.

An impassioned spirit truly paints the gray world with color.

What the public hasn't realized is that Scott has been shying away from Rose more and more. He's refocused his attention. Two days ago, he showed Lily a photoshopped picture of her head cut and pasted on a humping bunny. Some guy made it online, and it spread through Tumblr. Even *Celebrity Crush* reposted the image on their website.

And Lily has been purposefully avoiding any criticism about her or the show. Scott took it upon himself to change that.

Lo almost went postal when he came home to find Lily bawling in Rose's arms. Literally, I had to cover my hand over his mouth so he'd stopped threatening to cut Scott into tiny indistinguishable pieces.

There was one benefit from this. Our mutual hate for Scott has trumped any sort of disagreement we've had since the screening party. I've seen only a small change in my relationship with Lo.

When we joke around, his features sometimes sharpen more quickly, as though remembering that I don't love him the way he probably believed I did. That I don't even love Rose. He questions what's real and what's fake between us now.

I wish he wouldn't, but I can't change what's happened. I just have to move on.

"Do you like dares, Daisy?" Scott asks, his eyes flitting from her breasts to her face.

"Sure," she says.

Daisy is considered a weak link in our group. But Lily is definitely the most fragile. Scott is redirecting his attention on them. Rose and I worry about how far he's going to go to break her sisters and fracture our group of six.

"I dare you," Scott says with a creeping smile, "to go flash the paparazzi when we leave."

Ryke tosses his knife onto the table nearest Scott. It clatters in his lap. "I dare you to go fuck yourself," he sneers.

Scott just tauntingly keeps his gaze on Rose's little sister.

Daisy stands up and everyone goes rigid. "I dare all of you to chill out. My top is staying on, thank you very much."

I wrap my arm around Rose's waist as we all rise to leave. Savannah, Brett and Ben are already on their feet, filming us.

But Rose points a finger at Scott. "You're disgusting."

"She had strippers at her seventeenth birthday party. Taking off her top for a few cameras is nothing in comparison."

"They were dancers, and they stayed fully clothed," Rose retorts with a deadly glare.

"Let's go," Lily says in a soft voice. "Please, everyone . . ."

People in the restaurant are beginning to stare. Lo rubs her shoulders.

I toss Ryke the car keys to Rose's Escalade since I've been drinking and she had a glass of wine with me. He catches them easily and heads out first with Daisy. When Scott tries to stand by her side, Ryke literally puts a hand on his chest and forces him back.

"No," he says. "You're not allowed to fucking talk to her for the rest of the show."

Ahead of them, Daisy glances over her shoulder, and her lips lift in appreciation. Scott must be annoying her as much as he is the rest of us.

"I can do what I want," Scott says, lowering his voice so others can't hear. "I own you and her. And these three behind me. Don't ever forget that."

I don't restrain Ryke. Neither does Lo. But surprisingly, he restrains himself, pocketing his fists in his jeans. He passes Scott, shoving him hard, shoulder to shoulder, before reaching Daisy's side and leading her out.

Scott stumbles back, but I'm more concentrated on what happens as soon as the tinted restaurant doors open. The blinding flashes of cameras are as bad as a flickering black light in a club. And the shouts of the paparazzi, screaming questions for us to answer, blare into Valentino's candlelit, serene atmosphere.

Lily shrinks into Lo's chest. "I wish my invisibility superpower would kick in," she mutters to him.

"Don't ever wish that," he says and kisses her cheek. "Then I wouldn't be able to see you."

"Teleportation then."

"Yeah, I'm still fucking praying for that one." He squeezes her shoulder.

Rose and I watch them closely, waiting for them to safely exit the restaurant and grow the strength to move forward. Scott has already followed Ryke and Daisy outside.

I study Rose for a second. Her neck is rigid, her shoulders locked back, and she looks ready to enter a fiery ring of hell. But she's not breathing.

"Tout va bien se passer," I whisper. *Everything will be fine.*

"Comment sais-tu?" *How do you know?*

"Because I'm here," I say with all of my confidence, willing it in my voice, my posture, my *being*.

Her lips rise, but she doesn't mention how arrogant I am today. Her hand drops to mine, and she holds it tightly. And we watch as Lo finally encourages Lily to take her first steps outside.

Twenty-three

Connor Cobalt

One hour. That's how long I slept. My mother called me in to *file* paperwork at midnight. It wasn't a job a CEO would ever have to do, but she likes to test my tenacity—how badly I want the position.

Well, I want it badly enough that I need a second prescription of Adderall. How's that?

I took a nap on the couch, but I had to get up to finish a research project, so here I am. Sipping my sixth cup of coffee and submitting a paper via email. My phone buzzes on the kitchen counter as I refill the coffee pot for Rose.

I glance at the screen and read the caller's name: **FREDERICK.** I collect the phone, making my way onto the back patio before I answer it. "I'm heading to your office in fifteen minutes," I tell him, resting an elbow on the edge of the large hot tub. My breath smokes the chilly air.

I hear the *click click* of a camera, and I spot paparazzi on the street, their arms and lenses sticking out of car windows. I don't spin around, not caring whether they have a photo of me or not.

"That's why I'm calling," Frederick says. "You're not seeing me anymore."

I know this is about the Adderall. I texted him last night to sign off on a refill of my prescription. He never replied back.

I take a long sip of my coffee, ignoring his comment and the firmness in his voice.

"Did you hear me?"

"I heard you try to predict the future. You failed by the way."

"That prescription was supposed to last you six months, Connor. You weren't supposed to take those pills every day. And I don't want you coming to sessions anymore, not when you can use that time to sleep."

"I sleep just fine."

"Then you'll be *fine* if I don't sign off on your refill." He's not bluffing, and my silence prods him to continue. "Get some sleep. I don't want to talk or see you until you're in a healthy routine."

"You would desert your patient just like that?" I say calmly. I have to sit down on the steps of the hot tub, the rejection like a slap to the face, even if I don't show it in my voice, even if Frederick's actions come from a place of sympathy. It hurts that he'd be so quick to dismiss me when he's been my counsel for twelve years.

"If I believe it's in your best interest, yes, I would."

"What's in my best interest," I say, "is to talk to my therapist, not to sleep my day away."

"We can talk in three weeks when you're back on your feet."

"I'm always on my feet." I glance at my position right now. I am literally and figuratively sitting down. Wonderful.

"Connor," he says, drawing out my name so I listen closely, "you're not inhuman. You don't need me to remind you of what you're feeling. It's there inside your head."

I rub my dry, scratchy eyes as I process his words. After a couple seconds, I say, "You're not expendable to me, Frederick. You're necessary to my life."

"I know. This is only temporary."

"Okay." I give in. I lose this fight. Only with Frederick do I concede so easily. I trust his advice more than I do my own at times. That's the highest praise you can get from me, by the way. "I'll sleep and see you in three weeks." No more Adderall. I already know that Wharton is going to be the first to suffer from this choice. And yet, I don't care as much as I would have months ago. My priorities keep shifting. "I have a lot to talk about," I add.

"Category?"

"Rose. Sex." I only say this as bait. I have no real desire to share the details of my sex life with anyone but Rose, but maybe it'll entice him to change his mind about today.

"Have you—"

"Not yet. But she's comfortable enough to do it. We just haven't found the time." I can almost feel Frederick smiling over the phone. My sex life is the most intriguing topic we discuss, especially since my beliefs would be considered sideways from society's norms.

For me sexuality is about attraction.

Whether it's men, women—it doesn't really matter. The human race is filled with passion and lust. And to coin terms like heterosexuality, homosexuality or even bisexuality makes no sense to me. You are human. You love who you love. You fuck who you fuck. That should be enough—no labels. No stigmas. Nothing. Just be to be. But life isn't that kind. People will always find things to hate.

"I look forward to it," Frederick says, "in *three* weeks."

"Right." We both say our goodbyes before we hang up. I return to the house and place my empty coffee cup in the dishwasher, trying not to feel weird by Frederick's dismissal. I'm going to take his advice and sleep. But I don't want to wake Rose by crawling into bed, so I head downstairs to sleep on the lower level—the room that Daisy used to share with a few rats. It's clean now, but we've been using it for storage.

As I climb down the stairs and walk along the short, narrow hallway, something bangs against the wall. I face the door and listen closely before I enter, focusing on the sounds. Maybe . . . groaning and grunting.

The noises grow louder, and I distinguish an unfamiliar male voice from the heavy panting.

"Ahhh . . . yeah . . . baby, right there. Good girl."

I feel justified in opening the door because whoever's having sex shouldn't be having sex down here. So I turn the knob, but it clicks. Locked.

I hear some muffled cursing from the guy. "Someone's trying to come in," he says.

I don't want to jump to irrational conclusions. Like it's Rose on the other side. There's no reason it would be her. Logic says it's not. But I begin to stupidly imagine Rose on her knees with some other fucking guy.

I pound my fist against the wood. "Open up." A lump lodges in my throat at this unnatural, senseless fear. *She's not in there, Connor.*

The door swings open within seconds of my request, and I stare down at Daisy. I try to shelve whatever sudden concern I have and look at the situation a little more analytically.

She just barely cracks the door, and she blocks the inside of the room with her body, consequently hiding her boyfriend (I hope) from view.

I study her form. She's fully dressed in sweat pants and a tank top. Not flushed. Not sweaty. Not glowing or happy. But she doesn't look pissed either. Just disappointed. Unsatisfied. And maybe even a little glad that I interrupted.

"What do you need?" She gives me a congenial smile, and it's rather convincing. If I wasn't so brilliant at reading people, I'd think she was having the best day of her life.

"Who's your friend?" I ask, choosing to be direct.

"Oh . . . you heard him . . ." She taps her fingers against the doorframe and cranes her head over her shoulder. "I told you, you were being loud."

"That happens when a girl gives good—"

"Breakfast," Daisy says, her smile brightening. "I think I should make breakfast for everyone."

"Do that," I tell her, "and I'll talk to your friend while you cook."

She waves me off casually. "There's no need for that. You'll see him in the Alps." She clears her throat. "Production is making him go on the trip." She rocks on her heels nervously, her only give-away right now.

So this *is* her new boyfriend. "And you don't want him to come?"

She shrugs. "I'm happy that we're going to get away from the paparazzi for a week, but I'm not too excited at the idea of Lo and Ryke giving him the third degree."

"He should start with me then, ease him in," I say, manipulating her a little. But it's for a good cause. "I just want to have a civil conversation."

"Sure. That sounds good." But I see the worry behind the façade she's created. Daisy has a talent at hiding her true feelings, something I'm an expert in.

Before she leaves, she turns around in the hall and talks while she walks backwards. "Could you . . . maybe do me a solid and not mention to Rose that Julian was making those noises?"

That's strange.

Rose knows Daisy is sexually active. She's also a proponent for women exploring their sexuality, even if she's been too timid to explore her own. Based on the lack of sweat and flush, I assume Daisy wasn't having sex.

"Rose won't care," I end up saying. But Daisy knows this, so what's the real problem?

Daisy clasps her hands together. "Right. Good." She jabs her thumb towards the stairs. "Breakfast then." She disappears, leaving a sinking feeling in my stomach.

Something's not right about Julian.

I push open the bedroom door to find a tanned guy with tousled brown hair and an unshaven face. Most likely Italian.

My first reaction: he's definitely a model. I can tell by his striking features alone, and I'm sure he's someone she met at work. And then the minute he stands in front of the mirror and combs his fingers through his hair to style it, I see the real problem.

This guy isn't a teenager. Not even close.

"Hey, man." He nods at me. "You wouldn't be her brother, would you?" He grimaces, already expecting harsh words. He doesn't even know that she only has sisters.

"So you're Daisy's new boyfriend?" I ask, intentionally not answering his previous question.

He shifts uncomfortably on his heels. "Kiiind of . . ."

"Well the term 'boyfriend' doesn't have more than one implication." I lean my shoulder against the doorframe. "You're either dating or you aren't."

He narrows his eyes like he's confused.

"Well, we're not fucking at all. She's underage." He grabs his coat off the chair. "What do you call that?"

A lie.

"You can still be convicted of sodomy for a blow job," I refute. "So I call it fucking."

His face goes pale. "Look, I'm a model. I've known Daisy for almost a year. We're just good friends."

"You're about . . . twenty-two?" I ask.

"Twenty-three."

Fuck. Ryke is twenty-three. He's going to kill him.

I shake my head.

Daisy is confused. I read it across her face almost every time I see her. She has a career and has been treated like an adult from the fashion industry, from agents, photographers and models like Julian, since she was fourteen. But there are people, like Lo and

Lily, who see her as a little sister. Who treat her like she's sixteen going on seventeen and not her maturity level.

Age is a number that doesn't reflect circumstance, environment or psychology. Age matters very little to me when some thirty-year-olds act like children and some teenagers take on the responsibility of households.

I don't judge people based on two numbers. I judge them from the inside out.

I've contemplated talking to Daisy about her situation. Letting her know that as confusing as it seems, it's merely the construct of society that's causing her to feel lost. That, no matter how many boxes people try to put you in, as long as you know yourself, you'll be fine in the end.

And you may have to play by their rules, put up with their labels and use their terms—I've done so all my life—but it's what *you* believe that matters most.

But I'll never have this conversation with her. Frederick often reminds me that I am not the world's psychiatrist. I can see through people, but I have to choose who and what I want to fix. Daisy is smart enough to get there on her own. She just needs some time.

Forbidding her friendships and relationships won't solve her problems. It will just be another confusing reminder that two numbers matter more than her level of maturity. So I have to suffer being pleasant to her boyfriend.

"Word of advice," I say casually. "If you're going to have sleepovers in this house with your *good* friend, keep your orgasms to a minimum. I may not be the one to catch you next time, and it sounds like you enjoy your balls."

"So . . . who exactly should I avoid?" He laughs.

"Everyone but me," I tell him.

He laughs again as if this is a joke. I don't break my even gaze and his smile falters. "Oh . . ." he mumbles. "Shit, that bad, huh?"

"Yeah, man, that bad." I inwardly cringe at my vocabulary, but he seems to respond better to it. His shoulders have slackened and he puts on an easy smile again. It's almost like we're friends.

Another one to add to my collection.

How fucking sick is that? *Frederick*—oh wait, I can't call him. The annoyance builds and builds. I just need a fucking nap apparently.

"Julian, you think I could get your number? You're coming to the Alps with us, right?"

"Yeah." He recites his number for me and I categorize it in my phone. I have no intention of ever calling him, but if something happens to Daisy and she's with him—it would be important information to have. "You think you can call Daisy back down here when you go upstairs? We were kind of in the middle of something, you know." He gives me one of those looks that would accompany an elbow nudge to the hip.

He really is an idiot. "No," I say flatly. "You can use your hand to finish up. She needs to make breakfast." *And something tells me she doesn't want to touch you.* I can't look at him without wanting to slam his face in the crease of the door.

So I leave after I secure his number. I'll just go upstairs and try not to wake Rose as I crawl into bed.

Thanks to Frederick, I can now sleep this day away.

Twenty-four

Rose Calloway

D id you see what happened at the airport?" Lily asks me with a big, silly grin. "Not one person even blinked in my direction. And all I had to do was wear sunglasses." She lets out an appreciative sigh before collapsing on the bed. "I think I love France."

I can't help but smile. Seeing my sister happy is a special event.

Our trip to the Alps has been scheduled for a while since production wanted to film in a vacation setting. But it couldn't have arrived at a better time. We all needed a break from the rabid paparazzi. The cabin has been rented out and stocked with wood, the climate still biting and snowy at the end of March.

3 months—Mom

Three months and Lily will be married. Three months and I need to finish sewing the gown. After five sketches, I think I've designed the perfect one, and I brought some fabrics here to start. Connor says I should just hand it over to a seamstress, but I want it to be perfect. If this is the only thing I get right for Lily—then the whole wedding is a success in my eyes. Maybe not for my mother, but for me—definitely.

Everyone unloads groceries while Lily and I scope out the beds to assign rooms. I hate to ruin her suddenly cheerful mood with wedding talk, but she's created the perfect opportunity.

"So since you like France, you won't mind that your wedding is in Paris."

Lily lifts her body up on her elbows. "Does that mean that the reporters won't film it?" The wedding is supposed to be national news, broadcasted on multiple cable networks sponsored by Global Broadcasting Association, as if Lily and Loren are royalty. GBA bought the rights to film us, against other big names like ABC, NBC and CBS.

"I think they'll fly out for it."

"Oh . . ."

The silence stretches longer than it should, the tension heightening. "I can change it if you'd like. You just haven't given me any ideas or hints as to what you want."

"I want to still be engaged in three months."

"Lily—"

She holds up her hands. "I know," she exclaims with a sigh. "That's not a choice." She thinks for a second. "I guess Paris will be fun." She grins. "Can we have crepes at the wedding?"

"Already ordered."

She jumps off the bed and throws her thin arms around my waist. "Thank you, Rose . . ." She pauses. "I'm sorry I'm making this hard for you to plan."

"It's okay. I like the challenge," I lie. That's Connor's thing. Challenges. Games. I'd prefer my path to be an easy one.

Ryke lets out an exhausted huff as he barges through the front door, supporting my fifty-pound suitcase in his arms. "What the fuck did you bring, Rose?"

"Sweaters and jackets take up more room than bathing suits," I defend from the kitchen. Lily, Daisy and I start stocking the wooden cupboards, and we make soup for dinner. Ben, Brett and

Savannah are still here, but they're silently buzzing around, trying to unload their camera equipment as quickly as possible.

Savannah is the fastest, and I refrain from cheering her on, but she deserves the praise. Those steadicam contraptions are heavy. She's already on her feet, heading to us.

Loren traipses in behind Ryke with Lily's duffel slung over his shoulder, trekking in snow. He watches his brother struggle to keep my suitcase in his arms. Loren looks unsurprised by my over-packing, considering he's attended *many* family trips with us.

"It has wheels, you know," Loren tells him like he's a moron.

"It's fucking snowing," Ryke growls.

Loren turns to me. "Don't you already own a slav—I mean a boyfriend." He flashes a sardonic grin.

In perfect timing, Connor walks through the doorway easily carrying my other two duffel bags without an issue. Yes, I have a problem over-packing. I need choices, and I would have gladly brought my own luggage inside but we divided up duties.

"We were just talking about you," Loren tells Connor.

"I heard," he says. "In terms of ownership, we're both on equal footing . . . unless you're talking about in bed."

"I can see how she'd be bossy."

Connor grins and slides past Loren and Ryke to drop off my bags. Loren's brows bunch together in confusion while my neck heats.

Lily tugs my arms. "You've done things, haven't you?" she asks in a whisper-hiss. "And you haven't told me?"

Savannah edges close with her camera, her red braids against a black chunky sweater with mini pink skulls. Her goth look is actually quite cute, and she's more apt to crack a smile than porky Brett, who only looks happy when he catches Lily doing something sexual.

He's *still* my least favorite of the three-person crew.

"Maybe," I answer Lily evasively.

At the stove, Daisy stirs the soup with a large ladle, smiling brightly until she looks up and her eyes lock on someone.

I follow her gaze and find her "boyfriend" strolling into the cabin as he texts on his phone. Tall, dark-haired, Italian, a quarter Spanish. I had a five-minute conversation with him on the plane, and it was clear Daisy didn't hide Julian from us because he's dumb.

He's six years older than her.

To say that most of us were displeased would be an understatement. None of us have done the yelling bit yet. Mostly because the cameras have been heavily up in our faces during the trip, waiting for us to explode on Julian.

That's why Scott withheld airing footage with him. They wanted *that* moment. And so far, no one has given it to him. Which put Scott in quite the pissy fucking mood. I am abnormally chipper because of it. I could twirl around in a dress and hold out my hand, waiting for a bird to come land on my finger. Imagine the Wicked Witch doing that dance number, and that's pretty much me right now.

I turn to Lily. "Apparently we all keep secrets."

"Hey," Daisy says, knowing I was referring to her. She waves her hand at me. "I knew you'd disapprove. If production hadn't forced me to bring him along, he'd be back in Philly."

"I *only* disapprove because it's illegal if you two hook up," I remind her. "One year. That's all you have to wait."

"Back to the point," Lily insists. "Connor said *unless you're talking about in bed*. That implies you did things."

Months ago, Lily would have crawled underneath a table to avoid discussing sex. Now she prods for details. It's enough to break my silence. "We did some things," I tell her in a whisper. But I know Savannah catches every word.

"Things? What things?" She grins from ear to ear, excited *for* me. I wonder if she remembers her first time, or if it was something hazy like her other sexual experiences.

"Wait, I want to hear," Daisy tells us. She steps away from the stove and closes our little circle.

"We haven't had sex yet, so don't get too excited."

"*Things* can be better than sex sometimes," Lily says, poking my arm with her bony finger.

Daisy stays quiet, her gaze drifting.

"Daisy disagrees with you, Lily," I say.

"What? No I . . . okay, I kind of do." She grimaces a little as she recalls a few memories, waving her hands theatrically with each word. "They're pretty much equal for me. Fingering, oral, sex—it all sits somewhere in the *meh* territory. I think I'm just not programmed to like sex. I'm like the anti–sex goddess. The opposite of Lily, you know?"

Lily turns bright red. "Ugh . . ." She places her hands to her hot face. "My body betrays me all the freakin' time! I don't know why those words embarrass me."

"Because you're a sex addict," I remind her. "Stupid people make you feel like you're a whore if you say them." And then I turn on Daisy. "And that's ridiculous."

Daisy is all smiles but I see her fear—that she really isn't ever going to have a proper fucking orgasm.

"You can orgasm," I tell her. "You just have to find the right person." I thought she had reached that peak with a guy before, but she explained to Lily and me what happened, and it did not sound like an orgasm. It sounded more like she settled with what was given, which was nothing much at all.

"And what if there is no right person for me?" she asks seriously. And then she plays it cool, shrugging. "I mean, I have no problem being a casual dater, a single lady for life. You were going to do that before you met Connor, weren't you?"

"Yes, but I never had a problem pleasing myself."

Daisy has said on numerous occasions that she can't orgasm from masturbation, no matter how hard she tries. The only thing

I can think of is that she's doing it wrong. I even found a book that literally shows her how to touch herself—and she still said nothing happened.

Lily's eyes widen at me like *you're making her feel bad.*

Oops. Tact. I lose it sometimes. "You'll find someone," I tell her, squeezing her shoulder encouragingly. But I think I squeeze a little too hard because she winces. I let go. ". . . Just keep dating. And when you find a loser, ditch him quickly. Please."

Daisy nods. "So how far did you go with Connor?"

"I thought you were going to forget about asking."

"No way," Daisy and Lily say in unison.

"We did things . . ." I remember him choking me for the first time as I hit an excruciatingly blissful peak, and then the many times after where he made me come with his fingers. Almost every night we play around, but we haven't had sex yet. And we haven't done anything kinkier than tying my wrists to the bedposts.

"We want details," Lily says with wide eyes. "Like . . . what things?"

I feel the hot gaze of the camera. I want to keep *some* things private from them and *many* things private from the nation. "Good things," I say evasively. I gesture my head a little at the camera, and they both catch on, starting to drop the conversation. I end it with, "He's better than anything I imagined." *Suck on that, Scott.*

Daisy beams, a longing in her eyes for something similar to what Lily and I have. I truly hope she finds love someday and way more than *meh* sex.

Her gaze drifts. "Look who showed up."

Scott stands in the doorway, typing on his phone. He stopped in Los Angeles for a production meeting with GBA before he flew to France. He tucks his cell in his pocket, and his eyes find mine. The smarmy smile only heats my chest. He's no longer as pissy as he was at the airport. I seriously consider pouring the vat of bubbling hot soup over his head.

But I don't.

Because then I'd go to jail for assaulting him. And I'd probably be called a man-hater more than I already am, which is a title I don't think I warrant. And if I do . . . I need to work on that.

Jail and my pride are really the only two things stopping me. I can handle him going after me, but when he picks on my sisters with mean and offensive comments, like he's been doing this past month, *murder* sounds so worthwhile.

This week is supposed to be a break from the chaos, but I have a feeling it's all just beginning.

Twenty-five

Connor Cobalt

So you guys are like nasty rich," Julian says, gripping the stem of a beer bottle. Lo, Ryke and I have pulled Julian outside after dinner. Since Daisy doesn't have a brother, the three of us are in charge of questioning her new boyfriend.

I'm really just here to make sure Ryke doesn't hit him and Lo doesn't make him cry. Ben lost a game of rock-paper-scissors with Brett and Savannah, so he withstands the cold to film us.

"Our *parents* are nasty rich," Loren tells Julian. "We live off their generous donations."

"Trust funds," Ryke amends.

"I make my own money," I interject and take a sip of my wine. Lo and Ryke both have Fizz cans in their hands, not drinking alcohol per usual.

Loren gives me a look. "Yeah, from your mom's company."

I shake my head. "She gave me five thousand dollars for my twelfth birthday. I invested it and made good money. I don't have a trust fund." I refused the one she offered me.

"We should play a drinking game," Lo says. "Every time Connor Cobalt makes me feel stupid we take a shot."

"You're fifteen months sober," Ryke reminds him.

"Always gotta put a black cloud on everything, *bro*," Lo refutes, though there's more humor in his voice than hostility.

"What do you think?" Ryke asks Julian.

Julian shrugs, hardly affected by Ryke's hard-core glare. "What do I think about what?"

No one elaborates because there's nothing to elaborate on.

"You're not sleeping in her room," Lo warns.

Julian swishes his beer in a brief moment of contemplation (not long enough apparently) because he stupidly says, "I've already slept in the same bed as her before. I don't see the big deal."

Lo lets out a short laugh like *is this guy for real?* "You don't see the big deal?" He steps forward. "Let me spell it out for you, Julius—"

"Julian—" he barely has time to correct him.

"You're twenty-fucking-three," Lo says, not missing a beat. "How old are you, Connor?"

"Twenty-four."

Lo turns to Ryke and mockingly tilts his head. "What about you, Ryke?"

"Twenty-three," Ryke says.

Lo touches his chest. "I'm twenty-two myself."

"That's great," Julian says, a little dumbfounded as to what's going on. *Just wait, Julian. He's getting there.*

"I consider myself fairly smart," Lo says, "but you must be a real fucking idiot if you think we'd be okay with someone our age sleeping with our girlfriends' seventeen-year-old *little* sister."

Julian's not even intelligent enough to catch the obvious flaw in Lo's statement—that Ryke doesn't even have a girlfriend in this scenario.

He shrugs, still not seeing the issue. "She's a model, man. We've spent nights at our friends' flats in New York City together. She's snorted coke before. I think she's past the overprotective-brother routine. Maybe you haven't noticed, she's pretty mature."

Lo grits his teeth and turns his head to me. "Can you believe this guy?"

I can believe he's a moron, yes. But his argument is valid. It doesn't mean I think he should be spending the night in Daisy's bed. I'm not even sure she wants that. "You're sleeping on the couch," I tell him calmly.

He just shakes his head with a pouty lip, not even considering it. "No, I'm not."

"I'm seriously going to kick his fucking ass," Ryke says to us.

"I'm standing right here, man," Julian retorts. "What's your deal?"

"You're twenty-three," Ryke snaps, "and you're fucking a girl who's seventeen."

"We're not fucking. And aren't you the one on *Princesses of Philly* who's *always* around Daisy?" His eyebrows rise in accusation. "Maybe you're the one fucking her. Or maybe you're just jealous. Yeah, that's probably it."

Before Ryke has the chance to lunge, Lo steps in front of his body, blocking him from Daisy's boyfriend.

"Julius," Lo says, purposefully using his name wrong now that he knows it irritates him, "maybe you're feeling a little goddamn disgusting being with a seventeen-year-old. Keep your shitty feelings to yourself. Don't project them onto my brother."

"I'm not projecting anything. Have you see the way he looks at her? He wishes he was me right now."

Lo would normally have a snide retort ready, but he's busy restraining Ryke, who tries to charge forward, probably to sock Julian in the face. Lo rests his arm against his brother's chest, forcing him back.

Ryke stares disgustedly at Daisy's boyfriend, and the guy just leisurely sips his beer. But I sense an antagonizing quality in Julian's fixed stance, in the way he watches Ryke with a hawkeyed gaze. He's the type of guy who'd love to fight him—just to prove he's the bigger fucking man. Ryke, on the other hand, just wants to protect that girl inside. It's an interesting dynamic. One that I'd almost love to witness, but stirring that shit just gives Scott what he wants. And I'd rather smash in his face than help grow his in-gratiating smile.

"We all win some," Julian says to Ryke, "and we all lose some. You'll find another girl who's a better fit for you. Though she won't be as hot as Daisy, and there's no way she'll lick cock as well either."

Lo's jaw unhinges.

Ryke almost loses it. He shouts a string of curses at the top of his lungs. I catch *motherfucker*, *cocksucker*, and a new one—*dickfucker*. I would laugh, but I want to throw Julian off the porch just as badly—I just don't express myself with such vehement ag-gression.

Veins pop in Ryke's neck, his face reddening as he shouts and points at Julian, who starts to scream back.

"You don't know shit about that girl!" Ryke yells.

"And you do, right?!"

"Fuck you!" is Ryke's only response.

This has turned into a moron battle. Fists would be more ap-propriate right now. But the only thing keeping Ryke from laying into Julian is Loren, who stands between them, a human barrier.

I don't even try to calm him down. A deep part of me just wants Ryke to hit him.

"Sorry, man," Julian taunts as their voices lower. "You should have started dating her a year ago when she was single. You can have her when I'm done."

A foul taste rises in my mouth.

Lo glares at Julian like the world shifted without his consent. "What the fuck did you just say?"

Ryke wears pure darkness in his eyes, nothing else. His muscles flex the longer he has to withstand this guy.

"He can have her when I'm done," Julian repeats. "I can give you the exact date. I'll need about three hours on February twen-tieth of next year. Then you can have her. Mark your calendar."

February 20. Her eighteenth birthday.

And right as Lo is about to move out of the way and unleash his pissed-off brother, the back door opens. Lily steps outside, wearing Rose's black fur coat, which swallows her skinny frame. Everyone stays tense, but no one makes a move to hit Julian in front of her.

"Hey, guys." She shuffles to our group as we go silent. She notices the strain between the guys, and she quickly slides in the middle of Lo and Julian to try to diminish the prospect of a fight.

The girls are clever.

"Rose and Daisy want to play a game." She tucks her hair behind her ear. "A drinking game though."

Ryke peels his gaze off Julian and stares down at her. "The three of us don't fucking drink, so how does that work?" He gestures to Lily and Lo.

Lily shrugs. "I think we should participate somehow. It'll be fun."

I chime in, "You three can play the strip version."

Lo lets out a short laugh. "Always trying to get me naked."

My lips rise.

"Oh, and Rose wants to talk to you." Lily nods to Julian.

"Great," Julian says with added sarcasm. He even rolls his eyes, probably wishing he'd stayed home. He leaves our group and Ryke loses his chance to lay a fist into him.

Lo watches Julian disappear inside. "That was the first time I didn't warn a guy to protect his balls before talking to Rose."

"That's because we all hope she crushes them," Ryke says roughly.

I remember how delicately she held my cock for the first time, and I try my best to hide my smile into my next sip of wine.

I know her better than anyone.

Twenty-six

Rose Calloway

We've switched games three times to help Lily, but she's still losing. Luckily before we started she layered on clothes in her bedroom, waddling out like a little snowman. She even stuck my bobby pins in her hair and has been throwing them off as a "clothing" item.

She's down to a sweater and pajama pants without any accessory to fling off, and Scott refuses to switch to another game this time.

I'm a little tipsy, but nothing like Daisy, who stumbles around the kitchen trying to find a bag of marshmallows for the fireplace.

"She's going to hurt herself," I say, but when I stand to help, everything spins. Okay, I've definitely *surpassed* tipsy. I plop right back down on the couch and try to recover. Maybe no one noticed.

"You okay, Rose?" Loren asks with a knowing look.

Connor combs his fingers through my hair, which feels so damn good that I forget to snap back at Lily's boyfriend.

"Hey, stay away from the fucking knives!" Ryke yells angrily as Daisy clatters around. He's about to shoot up from the couch opposite of us, but Julian, her real boyfriend, beats him to it, sauntering into the kitchen.

After I lectured Julian about statutory rape and sodomy, he's been pretty much exactly the same: dismissive and lackadaisical. It's really fucking annoying. I tried to capitalize on cutting off his balls during our talk, and he just *shrugged* at me. I swear he was seconds from patting my head like I was a little girl.

Connor saved him from the wrath of my purse. I could have hit him over the head with it. But Connor drew me away and distracted me with a promise of something new tonight in bed. Although he never specified what *new* entailed. So I'm left to guess.

Connor's hand falls to my neck, and he rubs the bareness of my skin with his finger and thumb. I lean into him, snubbing the couch cushion, which was warm from my back. But he feels much better, my buzz tingling my body.

Scott refills everyone's empty shots, which line a log coffee table. A bear-fur rug covers the hardwood, and flannel blankets drape over the chilly brown leather furniture. Ryke keeps stoking the fire so no one grows cold. It's nice. All of us here. Even Savannah and Ben have relaxed in the kitchen with drinks while Brett singlehandedly films our game.

I hiccup and touch my lips. I think the last game we played was designed to get us wasted. Only problem is that Daisy and I weigh less than the guys playing. Ergo, we are getting fucked up faster. The game we've chosen now, Never Have I Ever, targets the most experienced person in the room, which means Lily is at a serious disadvantage. I should be winning, but Lily and Loren use phrases like, *never have I ever made an A on a math test.*

I turn to my less-than-tipsy boyfriend. Despite how much wine he consumes, he never gets drunk. "How many shots have you taken?"

"Less than you." Translation: *He's winning.*

"Who's next?" Scott asks. He's been the game pusher all night. I think he has his eyes set on Lily, trying to get her naked or nearly naked in front of everyone. She sits on Loren's lap, looking petrified to continue a game without another bobby pin to remove.

"I'm next," Ryke says, watching with a hard gaze as Julian guides Daisy into the living room.

Julian has his hands on her hips, whispering in her ear and forcing her back towards his chest. Even drunk, she looks mildly uncomfortable to be in his arms while in our presence. And it shows as she squirms out of his hold. She smiles at him and places a chaste kiss on his cheek to make up for it.

He doesn't let her off the hook. He literally grabs her face in two hands and plunges his tongue in her mouth.

"Hey, Julius, sit the fuck down," Loren snaps. *Thank you, Loren.*

I don't ask why Loren just mispronounced Julian's name. Everyone knows Lo's favorite comic book character is Julian Keller from *X-Men*, and Lo has declared (to the entire townhouse) that Daisy's boyfriend doesn't deserve to share the same name as him.

Daisy puts her hands on Julian's chest and breaks apart from him. Then she settles in her seat beside Ryke, Julian slouching on the other side of her. She sits up on the edge of the cushion so he can't wrap his arm around her shoulder.

Connor's lips brush my ear. "She's okay. Lo and Ryke have an eye on him."

I nod, realizing that I can't fixate on my little sister all night, even though I see how much she just wants to push Julian into the snow and leave him there. But she's not rude enough to do that.

I most definitely would.

"Ryke," Scott urges. "Go."

Ryke scratches his jaw. "Never have I ever . . . faked an orgasm."

"That's just mean," Daisy says, reaching for a full shot.

"Maybe you shouldn't have done it then," he retorts.

"And hurt the guy's feelings?"

Scott motions from the shots to me and I shake my head. I've had no reason to fake an orgasm with Connor. And he's the only guy I've ever been with.

Connor holds me closer, and he leans forward and grabs the

shot. I glare at him as he brings it to his lips. "Not with you," he tells me. I'm not even sure how a guy can fake an orgasm, but he's creative enough that I wouldn't doubt him doing it for personal gain.

"That's what they all say," Scott adds like a five-year-old.

Ugh. His interjection immediately makes me side with Connor, believing my boyfriend more.

"I hate this game," Lily complains, the only other person who lost this round. She looks down at her available clothes to remove.

"Really?" Ryke says. "You're a sex addict. I honestly didn't think you'd need to fake an orgasm." He must have been trying to help her out.

"Not all guys are created like Loren Hale."

"Jealous," Daisy says.

Julian's lips part in disbelief as he watches her.

"What, I never faked with you," she lies easily and pecks him lightly on the cheek. She whispers something in his ear that relaxes his shoulders. She's good at pleasing "people," so I'm not surprised that skill has translated over to pleasing "boyfriends."

"Here," Loren says, grabbing a plaid flannel blanket off the large recliner he shares with Lily. He wraps it around her shoulders and cloaks her body from view. "Take off your sweater."

"That's breaking the rules," Scott informs him from a rocking chair nearest the coffee table.

Loren glares. "Yeah, and maybe I'd abide by them if there wasn't a goddamn camera in our faces." He doesn't want the world to see Lily in her underwear. None of us really do. There's already enough sick fan mail sent to the house. It's easy to assume what men would do to a near-naked image of her.

Lily skillfully pulls the sweater off from underneath the blanket and tosses it to the floor. She looks more at ease.

"Rose, it's your turn," Scott says.

"Never have I ever . . . peed in a sink." Easy.

All the guys take a shot, except Ryke and Lo, who strip. Ryke removes his shirt, and Lo pulls off an arrowhead necklace.

And then Daisy reaches for another shot.

Both Ryke and Julian freeze and stare at her with raised brows while Connor and Lo try to contain their laughter. The booze is making my lips upturn more often than usual too.

"What?" She shrugs and throws the shot back, coughing a little as she sets the glass on the table.

"Explain," Ryke says, handing her a shot of orange juice to chase the alcohol with.

She mouths, *Thank you*, before drinking that too. "I was at a party in New York," she says, setting the glass down, "and I had to go badly but my friend was using the toilet. So I used the sink." She touches her chest and hiccups. "I'm not weird." She hiccups again. "You all did it."

"We have dicks," Ryke says bluntly.

"True." She smiles.

I rest my head on Connor's shoulder, the alcohol loosening my inhibitions that stay locked tight in front of others. He smells so good—his expensive cologne like citrus. "I love fruit," I whisper to him. I imagine myself placing a kiss on his neck, but moving to do so sounds like so much work.

He stares at me with a growing smile. "I'll keep that in mind, darling."

"Never have I ever . . . been engaged," Julian says, a cheap shot at Lily and Loren.

Lo glares at him while he pulls off his black long-sleeve shirt, and Lily wiggles off her pajama pants underneath the blanket.

Connor says, "Never have I ever . . . been cheated on."

No one moves. And Scott blinks at Connor like he's the devil incarnate, drama-blocking him.

My boyfriend just smiles. "Perfect."

Scott prods Ben to say one from the kitchen. With a mouthful of chips, he says, "Never have I ever snorted coke."

Lily sighs. "I hate this game." Before she goes for her panties, she touches her hair and smiles, revealing a hidden bobby pin.

Lo strips down to his boxer briefs, and Lily's eyes gleam in excitement at seeing him *almost* naked. He shakes his head at her, but he can't stop smiling.

In a wave, everyone takes shots. Scott, then Julian, then Daisy. And Ryke unclips his watch. Both Connor and I stay seated. I'm not surprised that almost everyone has experimented with drugs, but I've never had the urge to try out cocaine. And if someone peer pressured me, I'd say *no, no. No.* I really have no problem looking like the stuck-up prude in the room who refuses to blow a line with her friends. Hate me all you want. I'm not the one running around naked with dilated pupils.

Loren frowns at Connor. "You really haven't snorted coke? Not even once?"

"I have a rule about drugs."

"And what's that?"

"Don't do them." He grins. "My body is a temple."

"One that only Rose can enter," Loren banters.

"I'll let you in sometime, darling. Don't worry."

Loren laughs.

I roll my eyes, but I'm actually smiling at their "bromance," which has been heavily praised on blogs. People *only* like Connor when he's with Loren. It's weird. And I really don't need another reason to be annoyed by Loren Hale, so I've let it go. Brushed it off the shoulder. Like dust.

Okay, I think I'm getting drunk.

Lo's laugh fades quickly, and he stares off in thought. Since the screening party, he does this often. Just ending their quips with a silent, faraway gaze. As though remembering he's supposed to be in a fight with Connor.

Ten minutes later, I have gained a *serious* buzz and we've reached Scott one last time. I verge on my limit, so I'm hoping he's choosing a girl-friendly response. "Never have I ever . . ." His gaze pings from each of my sisters to me. ". . . swallowed a guy's cum."

"Fuck you," Lo says, defending the three of us, who Scott has been singling out the whole game.

Daisy's eyelids droop a little as she reaches for her shot. She knocks over two more.

Ryke leans forward and cleans her mess. "You can skip this one, Dais."

"She can handle it," Julian says, grabbing a shot for her. "Here you go, baby." He passes the glass to her. She downs it (messily) before Ryke can steal it from her hand.

Lily is now naked underneath the blanket, so the game is over.

And I quickly do a shot, the liquor sliding down my throat easily since I'm feeling good. But not *bad* yet. Anymore and it'd be a different story.

But Daisy has most definitely exceeded her limit. She's gone, but as Connor and I watch her, she does something really interesting.

Right as Julian nears her a little, Daisy stands, teetering, and she sits on the other side of Ryke, away from her "boyfriend." She whispers something to him that sounds like a slurred mess. But he nods like he understands.

And I realize, in this moment, how much she trusts Ryke to protect her—even from her own boyfriend.

Julian reddens in aggravation. But I have no verbal hostility in my throat to chastise him. Alcohol has softened me into a gooey state. I like it once in a while.

We try to ignore Julian's silent rage, and a few minutes later, we're on our electronic tablets, scrolling through gossip blogs for *Princesses of Philly* and trying to find the funniest comments.

Lily squirms on Loren's lap, having trouble controlling her

urges while she's naked underneath the flannel. Loren tightens his arms around her waist and she stops moving.

Connor's hand descends down my thigh of my long black cotton dress. The fabric is thin, and I can feel his fingers near a spot that truly begs for him. My lips touch his shoulder, and my eyes flit up to meet his, full of intense desire.

His expression matches mine, and I feel the wetness soak my panties.

He says under his breath, "I'm going to fuck you hard, Rose." He strokes my head and leans me to his chest. "So hard that you're not going to be able to walk in the morning." Why does that sound so good?

I touch his microphone battery pack for a second, realizing that the cameras caught that. But they probably won't air it anyway. It's too dirty for network television.

I glance back to the group and notice that Daisy has passed out, her head resting on Ryke's lap. Julian watches her, but he makes no move to grab her from Ryke yet. I want her to stay with Lo's brother. I trust Daisy's judgment, even drunk, and she just chose him.

Connor flips open his tablet, and he scrolls through long lists. I read from his screen as he holds it up to us. The words keep blurring together the longer the alcohol sets in.

"Here's one," Loren says. "*Ryke Meadows is the biggest jackass.*"

"How is that funny?" Ryke asks with narrowed eyes.

"Oh, I thought we were just reading comments." Loren grins while Ryke rolls his eyes.

"I've got one!" Lily clasps her hands together. "*Connor is a prick, but I'd bone him.*" Lily's eyes widen at the camera. "Just so we're clear, I was reading a comment!"

Connor smiles beside me. Whoever that girl is, she can't have him. He's all mine. Or maybe I'm his.

We own each other, I think.

I look down at Connor's screen, and the words don't make sense to me. That never happens. "What does this mean?" I ask Connor, almost rolling my eyes when I utter the phrase. I can already feel his ego inflate. "*Lo and Lily are so my OTP forever.*"

Lily lets out a delighted squeal, her hands shooting to her mouth. She bounces giddily on Loren's lap, and he holds the blanket around her body to keep her covered. "Are you serious?" she asks excitedly. "They called us OTP? Lo, did you hear that?"

"I heard, love," he says with a smile. "But I didn't need anyone to say it for me to believe it."

Her entire face glows at his words.

I'm still stuck on OTP. I turn to Connor and he shakes his head like *don't look at me for this.*

"What does OTP stand for?" I ask my sister.

"One True Pairing. Like couples that fans think are meant for each other," Lily says quickly. "It's used for fandoms. I guess, since we're on a reality show, now we qualify." Weird. But she would know that information, seeing as how they're both into comic books and general pop culture things.

"Neither of you knew that?" Loren asks with a grin.

"It's slang," Connor says like that explains it all. It doesn't matter. The fact that my sister and her boyfriend stumped us, the smartest people in the room, literally makes them beam in pure glee.

"Okay, what about this: *I ship Ryke and Daisy so hard it hurts.* What the hell does that mean?" I end up slurring the end of the sentence. *Oh my God. Get your shit together, Rose. He's going to fuck you so hard. He can't fuck you if you're passed out!* I swallow, but my throat feels like cotton and clouds . . . which is one of the stupidest thoughts I've ever produced. I really am drunk. Dear God.

Connor runs his fingers across my arm, so light that I shiver. He tucks me closer to him. *Please don't pass out, Rose.*

Lo groans as Connor rereads what I said aloud, only more coherent than me.

"What?" Ryke frowns.

Lily is all too excited to explain. "Ship is like *relationship.* When you ship someone you want them to hook up. Like I ship Magneto and Mystique in *X-Men: First Class.*"

"But they're not canon yet," Lo interjects, adding another term that makes little sense to me.

Lily clarifies, "They're not really together. We just want them to be, but once it happens, they're canon. I'm still holding out hope."

Connor looks between Lo and Lily. "So let me get this straight. People are rooting for Ryke and Daisy to be together, but they're not canon because it's never happened."

Lily claps and smiles brightly. "I'm a great tutor."

Connor laughs.

"And it will *never* happen," Lo adds, nodding to his brother to make sure he understands. I think Lo just fears abandonment again. That if Ryke dates Daisy in the faraway future, he'll lose his brother and that sense of family. It's not true, but you know, people believe what's in their heart. You can't change that so easily.

Julian stays quiet, digesting all of this information even though we're talking like he's no longer her boyfriend or even in the room. As far as I'm concerned, she just broke up with him tonight. I'm beginning to think Daisy stays with these losers because she doesn't have the heart to reject them.

"Hey," Ryke says, purposefully locking eyes with Julian. "I have fucking fans." He raises his glass of water, and it's hard to overlook my sister's head in his lap.

Julian stands and nears him. "I'm going to take her to bed."

I open my mouth to refute, my eyes narrowing, despite the booze softening me. But Ryke (sober) is way faster.

"She's *not* fucking sleeping with you. Sorry, *man*."

"Okay, just hand her over, dude. This shit is getting old."

"Is it not processing in your fucking head?" Ryke asks with one of the worst glares I've seen him use. "You're not fucking taking her. You're not sleeping with her. She's staying here."

"With you, right? That's not happening. I don't fucking trust *you* with *her*."

Lily perks up on Lo's lap. "She can sleep in my bed, and Lo can go in Ryke's room. Right, Lo?" she asks.

He nods. "Yeah, sure." But he looks worried about leaving *Lily* alone. Not only for her own safety against Scott, but she'll also be tasked to protect Daisy from her boyfriend. What if Julian crawls into their bed? We don't know him that well.

"I'll sleep with them too," I announce, knowing that I drank too much to do anything with Connor anyway. But I do regret the words, even as I say them.

If Connor's disappointed, he masks it perfectly, his face entirely unreadable.

"Great," Julian says, "I'll go put Daisy in her sister's bed."

Ryke stands with Daisy cradled in his arms, her legs dangling lifelessly. He readjusts her so she's turned towards his chest, looking more passed out and less dead.

Julian waits for Ryke to hand her to him.

"Over my dead fucking body," Ryke growls.

Before they have a tug-of-war with my sister, Loren steps in and pries Daisy from Ryke. "*I'm* taking her to bed."

Lily wraps the blanket tight around her naked frame and follows Loren out of the living room.

Julian puffs his chest out like he could push Ryke and pummel him. But Ryke pretty much has a look like, *I'm going to rip your head off and chuck it in the snow.* I'd say Ryke would win based on expressions. That is, if I had to bet on this stupid fight at all.

I really just want to be alone with Connor, even if I already committed to sleeping with my sisters. I can creep in their room later, right? Drunk me says *hell yes.* Sober Rose would say, *where did your loyalty go, bitch?*

Drunk Rose is so powerful right now.

Connor stands, my armrest gone. I almost fall into the cushion, but I catch myself with an unsteady hand.

"We should all go to bed. It's late," he says. He turns to me and easily grabs my hand, lifting me to my feet and supporting me with an arm to the waist.

Scott speaks to Brett, words that I can't catch, and then they head over to Savannah and Ben in the kitchen to review old footage.

"Yeah, whatever," Julian says. He shoots Ryke one last threatening look before backing up and climbing the stairs to the loft bedrooms.

When we hear the door close, Ryke's shoulders slacken. He shakes his head repeatedly and runs his hand through his hair.

"What'd Daisy say to you?" Connor asks. I didn't realize this was an important piece of information. Okay, I am *not* drinking anymore for the rest of the trip.

Ryke stares at the ground, his features darkening. "She said, *don't let him touch me.*"

My face clouds with worry. She really thought he could have taken advantage of her while she was passed out? "I don't like him," I say with the shake of my head.

"Join the fucking club."

Connor sets a hand on the small of my back. "Let's just be civil with him for the rest of the trip. Daisy has to work with Julian, so obviously she's treading some muddy waters here."

"I don't see anything fucking muddy about it," Ryke retorts. "She doesn't like him. So she needs to dump him."

"Not everything is black and white, Ryke," Connor says. "You should understand that, considering your situation with Daisy."

Ryke scowls. "There's no situation."

Connor tilts his head. "Act stupid in front of your brother, but that tactic won't ever work with me."

"You like her," I add, saying each word slowly so I don't slur them together. "It's okay to like her." Hell, I like any guy that makes my sister happy and treats her well. Julian does neither.

Ryke glares at both of us. "It's *not fucking* okay. I'm not into her like that. I *can't* be. She's seventeen."

"What about when she's eighteen?" Connor asks with an arched brow.

Ryke shakes his head adamantly. "You think I'm going to sacrifice my relationship with my brother for a *girl*? Then you don't fucking know me, Cobalt."

"Lo will get over it."

"Yeah, I don't see that happening. And maybe you're fucking right—all of this shit is confusing." His nose flares as he breathes out. "I'll try not to hit her boyfriend, okay? Only because they work together." Ryke doesn't give us the chance to respond. He disappears upstairs, shutting the door to his room.

I spin back to Connor and place my hands on his hard chest. "Maybe . . ." I say, trailing off. "I can go sneak into Lily's room later?"

His eyes roam my body, and he brushes my hair off my shoulder. Instead of answering, he leaves my side and walks confidently to the refrigerator.

At the kitchen table, Scott looks up from the camera equipment and stares between us. But I'm so entranced with Connor, the way he commands the room at six-foot-four, his self-assuredness so unquantifiable and so, so attractive.

I unconsciously sway, waiting for him to return to me in the living room. He procures a carton of strawberries and kicks the refrigerator closed on his way back. He bites into the fruit, staining his lips red for a single second before he licks off the strawberry juice.

As he nears me, he twirls my body towards our bedroom on the main level. And then he presses his chest to my back, guiding me with a firm hand to my hip. Wild thoughts jumble in my head, spinning madly with the help of the vodka shots. What is he going to do to me?

Once in our room, decorated with bear cabin décor, he closes the door behind him and sets me on the edge of the bed, a red and brown quilt underneath me.

"Are we going to have sex?" I ask him, my neck straightening in alarm as I process those words. *Am I about to lose my virginity?*

"No, Rose. You're drunk," he reminds me. "You're going to remember our first time together for the rest of your life. And alcohol isn't going to take that away from you or me."

I glare, my shoulders curving backwards in defense. "So you're just going to put me to bed then?" I'm clearly horny.

He pops open the carton again and eats another strawberry, not saying anything one way or the other. His domineering posture causes me to slowly sink back, my elbows propping my body on the mattress. His penetrative gaze rakes me from head to toe, traveling across all the places that crave his powerful touch.

Images of him on me, *in* me, breeze through my brain in a wonderful, toxic mess. And I swallow hard as I realize what I want. "Can you be rough with me?" Without the alcohol, I'm not sure I would have had the balls to ask, despite gaining more courage in bed these past couple of months.

He places the strawberries on the mattress, moving casually, easily, contentedly. The uncertainness of what he's going to do quickens my heart, and then his eyes meet mine, his one forceful look saying everything: *I'm going to give you that and more.*

He lifts me and throws me further onto the bed, the air rushing out of my lungs. He climbs on before I can orient myself, and he spins me so my stomach is flat against the mattress. "We're going to play a game . . ." He digs his pelvis into my ass before he strips me crudely with two hands, tossing my dress aside. The cold nips my bare skin, and he snaps my bra off but leaves my blue cotton panties on.

"What game?" I ask breathlessly.

I turn my head a little and watch him unbutton his shirt and shrug off the fabric. He unbuckles his belt, and the spot between my legs aches for him. I stifle a moan and try to sit, but he puts a hand on my back, forcing my breasts to the quilt.

The only way I can watch him is by pressing my cheek to the mattress. He allows me this at least. He takes off his slacks, only in his navy boxer briefs. He's incredibly hard, and as he lowers his underwear, his cock springs out, ready to enter me.

But he's already made it clear that's not what he plans to do tonight.

I can't stop staring at the size of him. "I know you're going to be able to fit," I say. "I'm not an idiot, but when you do, I think it's going to hurt . . . a lot."

"Most likely," he tells me, not denying it. He kneels on the bed and leans me on my side, my bottom facing him. He gathers my wrists and ties them behind my back with his belt.

My lips part as soon as the leather digs into my skin, the buckle cold against my wrist. I close my eyes as the sensations ripple through my middle and settle in tortured places.

His lips find my ear. "Are you scared of being sore?"

I shake my head once. I could beg for that force right now, but the words are lost inside my tangled mind.

He yanks my panties up, hard, the fabric digging into my heat.

"Connor," I gasp, my arms tugging against his belt restraint.

He groans, and lets out a deep, husky breath. "I can't wait to fit inside of you." He kisses the small of my back and exposes my ass without taking off my panties, his lips sucking on my tender cheek. "Hard. *Rough.* Wet, volatile sex, with no letting up."

"Who will concede first, you or me?" I ask him.

He bites my ass, and I press my forehead to the mattress. *Ahh.* A sharp breath catches, and I let out a high-pitched cry.

"We'll come together," he tells me. "Always." Then he opens the fruit carton. With my cheek back on the quilt and in his mercy, he has control of what I see. All of a sudden, the flesh of a strawberry is against my lips.

"Open wide. Don't eat it. Treat the fruit like my cock," he says. "You bite down too hard, and you're going to be spanked *hard*. Understand?"

"I'm not an idiot," I remind him.

"You're drunk, darling. I'm just making sure you're coherent. Otherwise, this ends."

"No, I'm here," I say forcefully. "You're not leaving me."

He leans forward and kisses me roughly, hungrily on the lips, his tongue nearly choking me with the pressure. I clench my legs as I throb for more of this and him. He peels away abruptly and says, "I give the fucking orders." And then he spanks me.

Hard.

I grit my teeth, my face heated, but the spot between my legs reacts much differently. I ache for him to slap me there. *God yes.* My insecurities about him leaving, not loving me completely, become shelved in the back of my head. And I concentrate only on how this feels. I leave my mind behind, something that I can only do when I am riding a boozy wave.

He slides the strawberry in my mouth, the green end sticking from my lips, and I rest the fruit on my tongue, careful to not dig my teeth into it.

Connor massages my ass with his large hand. I hear his heavy breaths behind me as he strokes his cock at the same time. I'd like to watch, but I have no say in that. So I'm left to imagine what he looks like as his cock swells, as his lips part in heady pleasure and his head tilts back. I've seen that adrenaline-fueled *I am close to passing out* look before. I've seen his muscular ass tighten as he jerks forward. And there's nothing more I want to see than all of that while he's so deep inside of me.

His fingers dip into the wet, dying spot, nudging my panties to the side.

And I spasm at the sudden touch. I taste the sweet strawberry before I realize I've bitten it clean in half. I chew and swallow. Maybe he won't notice. *Yeah fucking right, Rose. His IQ is higher than yours by one percent.*

His hand whips my ass, and I gasp, then wince, and glare. "That fucking . . . hurt," I retort slowly. But as soon as I say it, his fingers return to the needy spot, and he rubs my clit. Ohhh . . . I melt instantly, and I think I whimper into the mattress. I don't know what else to call that foreign sound.

"You're too drunk to have my cock in your mouth," he says.

I scoff at that declaration, but the aftertaste of sweet strawberry says he's right and I'm very much wrong. But even drunk, I can't surrender so easily. "I am not."

He suddenly sits me up by pulling at my tied wrists, but my spine still faces him. I feel him shift on his knees, the bed rocking with his weight, and his hard cock poking at my back. "Connor," I moan, close to begging.

"How do you feel?" he asks. "Besides dizzy from the alcohol." He clenches a chunk of my hair and pulls so my chin juts upward and I can see his eyes as he stares down.

"I feel . . ." I blink a couple times as I try to form the words. I lick my lips and say, "Like I want you to do anything to me." Just uttering the words shallows my breath.

He stares at me with a hard, possessive gaze, and his arm extends over my shoulder, and his fingers fit back inside me again. But he doesn't move.

"Elaborate."

"I . . . need you . . . to move."

He takes out his hand quickly, and he forces me on my knees. The blood rushes to my head, and he spanks me again, the sting more numbed by the booze than before. He must notice because I don't whimper or moan or flinch forward.

He sighs in frustration and starts untying my wrists.

"Wait, no," I say. "Stop."

"Just months ago, you were telling me to stop from touching you. Now you want me to keep on doing so, and I'm still not going to comply with your order, Rose." He tosses the belt aside and turns me onto my back, my head relaxing into a pillow. "You know why?" he asks, his hands on either side of my shoulders as he hovers over me.

"Because you're an asshole," I snap.

He pinches my cheeks with one hand. "Because you're wrong. I won't fuck your mouth, your pussy or your ass when you're drunk. I'll fuck you when you're sober." He kisses me roughly on the lips before saying once more, "Elaborate."

On what I feel.

I stare into his deep blue eyes. Lost in the power inside them. And I take his hand for a second, and I fit it between my legs, his gaze never breaking from mine. "This is yours," I tell him. "That's what I feel."

I've never wanted a man to toss me around how they want, how they like, using me to their desires so much before. And in this moment, I realize it doesn't matter what I believe outside the bedroom. In life I can be powerful, but here, I can trust him to fill me with his power, his strength. That has to be okay. Because beyond all thoughts, all logic, it's what makes me feel so fucking good.

His lips rise. "Ca vous a pris pas mal de temps." *It took you long enough.*

"How long do we have left?" I ask him softly, his body beginning to blur.

He strokes my hair. "Pour toujours." *Forever.*

I smile as everything fades to black.

Twenty-seven

Connor Cobalt

I dry my wet hair with a towel and button my pants, watching Rose sleep peacefully, tucked in a red and brown quilt. Before I put a shirt on, she stirs with a low groan and squints in the darkness. The only light comes from a sliver in the bear-printed curtains.

"Good morning, darling." I sit on the edge of the bed and grab the water off the nightstand. "Comment te sens-tu?" *How do you feel?*

She slowly rises against the headboard, a hand to her temple. Her hair sticks up in five different places. I try hard to conceal my smile, but seeing Rose this disheveled happens—almost never. And I adore this side of her just as much as any other.

"I have no idea what you just said," she yawns with a hand to her mouth. "My hangover has destroyed your French."

"Impossible," I tell her. "Your hangover can't defeat me."

She's too tired and hungover to banter. She just yawns again. "Really . . . what did you say?"

I pass her the water and she takes a small sip.

"How do you feel?" I repeat.

"Like I spent five weeks prepping for the Academic Bowl Championships."

"So not that bad then?" I smile.

Her eyes narrow. "Not all of us were able to study for two hours and retain every single piece of information."

"I studied more than two hours for the collegiate championships." I reach over and grab the Advil on the nightstand and pop the cap. "You just weren't at Penn to see me, which was a shame. We could have studied together." I pause before I add, "I'm an excellent tutor. Just ask your sister."

She rolls her eyes but there's a smile behind them. Because if I didn't tutor Lily in economics, she believes we wouldn't be here today. But I make my own fate. We came together because we both wanted to be here more than anywhere else. We both had choices, and we both said yes to this, to us.

That's not fate.

It's just desire.

And determination. Ambition. Resolve.

We have it all.

"How much do you remember from last night?" I ask, expecting the answer to be something I hate. I'm almost certain everything with the strawberries and beyond has been swept from her mind by vodka. I've already come to terms with it, but before I drifted off to sleep, all I wanted was for those moments to be recorded and ingrained for life. What if they never happen again?

It's the *what if* that clenches my heart in five different ways.

"How much can *you* remember?" she shoots back, drinking more water. I almost have her hostile nature back completely.

"All of it."

"And how is that possible? You drank more than me."

"You remember that?" I frown.

"Yes, Richard."

After a long pause, I say, "I have a high tolerance." It's not entirely true. I've been on Adderall for a while now. Ever since I returned to Frederick's office, I went on a one-week silent streak until he prescribed me Adderall again. He caved on the seventh day, wanting to discuss my life so he could analyze all the details.

Mixing Adderall and alcohol is not a good or smart combination. The pills diluted the effects of the alcohol, so I was coherent for longer.

She stares off for a second. "I also remember . . ." She blushes. "No wonder my ass hurts."

My chest swells. "What?"

"You spanked me." She slaps my arm. ". . . and I liked it." She adds, "I'll be sober next time. I promise."

I break into a smile that turns into a laugh. She remembers. I exhale deeply, my world brightening. I can't contain the joy that fills me. I kiss her cheek, her lips. *She remembers.* The words lift me to a new plane of existence. I feel higher now than I did swallowing Adderall.

"What happened after you said *forever?*" she asks as I kiss her nose.

"You passed out," I say, "and I tucked you in this bed and made sure you didn't vomit on yourself."

She glares. "How romantic."

"How *real*," I retort. "Just remember our romance isn't the fake kind."

"Unless you're watching *Princesses of Philly,*" she notes with the raise of her chin. Before I can reply back, her eyes slowly widen.

"What is it?" I ask.

"Wait . . ." She grabs my wrist and her mouth falls as she recalls something.

"Rose?" My heart lurches. She shoots to her feet, and I follow suit, grabbing her waist.

"My sisters," she says. "I promised to sleep in their room. But I'm here. I woke up *here*. Which means . . ." She bolts out the door, wearing the same black cotton dress from last night.

I walk after her with ten times less alarm. As soon as we pass the kitchen to go upstairs, Ben hurriedly stands from the breakfast table, deserting his cereal. He grabs his camera and rushes after us. Of the cast, we must be the first ones awake.

Scrawny Ben fumbles with his Canon, and he tries to bypass me on the staircase and film Rose, but I keep an arm out so he has to stay behind. I'm going to be the closest to her in this situation. He can take a back seat.

She swings open the door to Lily's room, stampeding inside. I lean on the doorframe, and Ben stays in the hallway, his camera pointed at me since he can't film inside the room. He's nice enough to keep his distance.

Rose comes screeching to a halt at the sight of her sisters. Daisy is sprawled on the bed, the comforters kicked all around her. Lily is on the other side, lost within a mound of blankets. Untouched. Unharmed.

Two guys sleep on the floor.

Ryke wakes at Rose's thunderous entrance. He lifts his head off the pillow and kicks off a quilt. Lo holds his knees and rubs his eyes, trying to get oriented to the light from the hallway.

"What the fuck?" Ryke whispers, trying not to wake the girls. He glares at me. "Why didn't you tell her?"

I give him a look. "And she would have believed me?" Even if I said, *Lo and Ryke decided to camp out in Lily's room to keep your sisters safe*, there's a hundred percent chance she would have barged in here regardless. Plus, I was reveling in the fact that she remembered last night's events.

Ryke glances over his shoulder, checking on his brother, who watches Lily yawn and stretch her arms. When Ryke stands and heads over to the door, Lily slides out of bed, wrapped in a blanket.

She finds Lo on the floor and beams at his appearance. She bites her lip and then impulsively straddles Lo, his back leaned against the wall. She kisses his cheek and they talk softly, but she digs into him as she leans forward. I'm not even sure she realizes she's doing it, but Lo's neck tenses as he holds in a groan.

And Rose—she's watching them with pursed lips.

She's going to cock-block him for about ten minutes. It's one of her favorite hobbies. I'd stop her, but her cold, bitchy attitude amuses me far more than people ever understand.

I nod to Ryke. "I'm surprised you slept on the floor. You're usually a walking billboard for REI. No hammock in your suitcase?"

I smile and wait for the perfunctory *fuck you*. But it doesn't come. He catches me off guard by stopping in the doorway, his face shadowed with worry and anger. I see it in the hard cut of his jaw.

"I need to talk to you," he says under his breath. Daisy shifts on the bed, waking with all the chatter. He quickly hands me his phone, a text conversation popped on the screen.

I scroll through it.

I'm going to come inside of her wet pussy before I hand her off to you. I may even get a few friends to join.—212-555-9877

I try not to jump to conclusions, but my heart begins to speed, the Adderall not helping slow it down.

Who the fuck is this?—Ryke

Julian—212-555-9877

The conversation ends there. My eyes flicker up to him. "Did you punch him last night?" I whisper so only he can hear.

"No."

"I can't imagine you reading this . . ." I check the timestamp. ". . . at four in the morning and doing *nothing*." I picture Ryke slamming doors, darting to Julian's bedroom and beating the shit out of him. But I forget that Ryke isn't a testosterone-fueled idiot. He's intelligent in ways that most aren't.

"I'm hoping it's not his number. I was waiting to see if you had Julian's so we could match them."

I grab my phone from my pocket and scroll through my contacts quickly. Ryke looks over his shoulder and meets Daisy's gaze while I search.

"Don't look at her," I advise. "She's going to know something's wrong."

"She won't," he says, stuffing his hands in his pockets.

"You're wearing your emotions."

Ryke tries to blanket his face with contentedness.

I stare at him with raised brows. "Now you look constipated."

"Fuck you." There it is. I smile while he goes back to his brooding self, not masking his concern.

When I read both numbers side by side, the bottom of my stomach falls.

"Now who's wearing their emotions?" Ryke retorts. "It's the same fucking number." He shakes his head. "I should have beat the fuck out of him last night."

"Lower your voice," I whisper. "Ben is right here."

Ryke glances out of the doorframe and spots Ben hanging in the hallway. He eases back inside and says, "What are we going to fucking do?"

"What's wrong?" Daisy slides between us. She's about to go into the hall, but both Ryke and I stick out our arms to stop her here.

Rose, Lily and Lo bicker behind us, deeper inside the room. I ignore their voices as best I can. But I hear Lo say, "Go vomit in your Gucci handbag, you'll feel better. And maybe you'll expel some of that *bitch* inside of you."

"Says the guy who's more sloth than human. Go hug a tree and eat an ant."

I tune out the rest. Ryke and I exchange a look before staring back down at Daisy.

She rubs her temple, her long hair tangled at her waist. "I feel really short when you guys do that whole *towering over* me thing." She swallows. "I think I need some water." She tries to leave again, but we block her. "Okay, really, what's going on?"

I hand Ryke's phone to Daisy. We both know that she can handle this information. Lo and Lily don't need to hear it, which is why Ryke has kept this to himself.

"Wait . . ." Daisy frowns, her brows scrunching. ". . . this has to be a wrong number."

"It's not," I say. "We just checked."

She shakes her head. "He wouldn't say this to me. He's not that crude."

"He didn't say it to you," Ryke tells her. "He sent the text to *me*. He's a fucking guy, Dais—he's going to be cruder to me, not his girlfriend."

She stares at the ground in thought. "What . . . what happened last night? Did I do something . . . ?"

"*Fuck*," Ryke curses and he glares at me. "She can't remember anything."

Well, if it had to be either Rose or Daisy, I'm selfishly glad it was this one who blacked out. "It's fine. You didn't do anything out of your nature, Daisy."

Her worry doesn't dissipate with that fact, which is why I said it. I want her to break up with Julian. We all do. And somewhere in her head, she does too. She's just too frightened to do so.

"Okay . . ." She hands me Ryke's phone. And she tries to run her fingers through her hair, but it catches on a giant knot. She clears her throat. "Okay, I'm going to think about this—"

"What is there to fucking think about?" Ryke growls.

She stares up at him, and her eyes expand a little more than usual. She's scared. "I have a shoot with him soon, a jeans campaign. I can't . . . I can't afford for there to be weird tension between us. He may . . ." She shakes her head. ". . . he might complain to the designer about me. And I'll be the one sacked. They really like him, and Mom will be . . ." She struggles to breathe fully.

And then across the hall, the door to Julian's room slowly opens.

Daisy's eyes widen, and she mutters, "I have to . . . run." And she dashes out of the doorway and down the flight of stairs.

"Fuck," Ryke curses before sprinting after her.

As soon as they're gone, I shut the door behind me, concealing Rose, Lily and Lo inside so they don't see what's about to happen.

Julian comes out, nodding to me with tired eyes. "Is there any hot water left?"

"Yeah," I say. "Hey, man." I put a hand on his shoulder to stop him. "I have to ask you something." He thinks we're cool. It makes getting the truth that much easier from him, but my muscles constrict the longer I have to withstand Julian. I see the text and the threat of gangbanging Rose's little sister in my brain—like a warning of who he really is.

He groans. "If this is about your friend Ryke, you can save it. I've had to deal with a lot of bullshit being with Daisy, but that was ridiculous. She's *my* girlfriend, and I had to put up with him grabbing at her."

I can't defend Ryke right now even though I want so much to do so. He grabbed Daisy *once* to keep her safe from him, at *her* wish.

I blink. "I thought she wasn't your girlfriend."

He runs a hand through his messy hair. "Friends with benefits, whatever. We're dating."

"Exclusively?"

He glares. "Yeah, that's what I said." *No it's not, you asshat.*

I hold up my hands. "I'm just trying to get things straight here."

"Well get this straight," he says. "Your friend isn't going to be with her. He needs to go find another girl and stop staring at mine."

"Okay," I say. "Did you text him last night though? He said you did . . ."

Julian frowns. "What are you talking about?"

"At four this morning—"

"I was asleep."

I hand him Ryke's phone so he can verify.

"What the hell is this?" He shakes his head and pushes the phone into my chest. "I didn't send this."

I want to believe him because he appears confused. But if all models are like Daisy, then they're really good actors.

"Right," I say, pocketing Ryke's phone. "I'll let him know. It must have been a prank."

Julian just shakes his head again. "Everyone here is fucking crazy." He nudges my arm. "At least we're the two normal ones."

"Yeah, man." I nod with a smile and he heads to the shower without another word. I rub my jaw that hurts after concealing a scowl. I don't know who to believe, but I think we all want Daisy far away from Julian until her photo shoot—when she can actually break up with him without fearing being fired and subsequently her mother's disappointment.

I head downstairs to make breakfast. Ben follows me. Before I go to the kitchen, I peek out the living room window.

Daisy runs through the snow. Barefoot. Without a jacket.

Ryke catches up to her easily, and he wraps his large coat around her body. He picks her up before she can protest, holding her beneath her legs and her back. Her feet are reddened and frostbitten, and she buries her head into Ryke's bare chest while he talks to her to calm her down.

I back away.

For as much as I give Ryke a hard time, I can't imagine another person with a kinder soul.

Twenty-eight

Connor Cobalt

Rose and I spend three days teaching Loren and Lily how to ski. They admitted to never learning during family trips. They'd ditch lessons to goof around, and when they reached a certain age, they replaced normal adolescent behavior with more dangerous activities. Lo would stay at a bar all day, drinking until he passed out, while Lily would sleep with anyone willing.

Daisy opted to snowboard, and even when she chose the black diamond slopes, both Ryke and Julian went with her. Savannah was the only one skilled enough to film them. I can only imagine Ryke and Julian at each other's throats. That episode is going to draw millions of viewers.

Scott's the only one who stayed back at the cabin. A rarity. He usually loves tagging along, which means his tactics are changing. I don't know what he plans to do yet, but I'm constantly on guard.

Everyone changes out of their wet and puffy clothes by the front door. I make it into the living room first to start a fire. Lily is by my side next. I glance back and notice Rose removing her third sweater and brushing her hair off her reddened cheeks. Lo bickers by her side as he stumbles to take off his boots.

Lily clears her throat.

Obviously she wants to talk. "Yes?" I ask.

She raises her hands to the stone fireplace to warm them.

"You really don't love her?" Lily blurts out.

I let out a breath. This is why I don't tell anyone my beliefs. I have to explain myself for weeks and months just to be understood.

"It's complicated, Lily," I try.

She opens her mouth to refute, but her phone jingles in her pocket. I squat and turn over a log in the flames with an iron poker.

She answers her phone after checking the caller ID. "This is Lily." She frowns and then taps my shoulder quickly. "Can you talk to my lawyer?"

I stand, and she hands me the phone, a more distressed look coating her face.

Brett's boots thud against the floor, now changed out of his winter gear to film us from the corner.

I press Lily's phone to my ear. "Hello?"

"Hi, this is Mark Cole from Red Hot Films. We want to make Lily Calloway an offer to star in one of our productions."

Porn.

This isn't the first time she's been offered a role, but it's the first time someone has called her personal phone. Usually they go through her father's lawyers and managers.

"How did you get this number, Mark?"

"We had a contact," he says, "we're prepared to offer two million if she stars. One million if she directs, and that would be behind the scenes business. She doesn't even have to appear on screen." But her name would.

"She's not interested," I say calmly.

Lily gives me a thumbs-up and an encouraging smile.

"She's the daughter of a multibillion-dollar mogul. No amount of money or exposure will sway her. Stop calling." I hang up at that.

"Thanks," she says as I hand her the phone. "Whenever I try to say *no* people usually cut me off."

"They shouldn't be calling you anyway."

She nods like she knows this too. "I think my number was leaked. I might get a new one and give it to only . . ." She counts in her head. "Six people."

"Lo, your sisters and your parents?" I ask.

She shakes her head "Not my parents. You and Ryke. If that's okay. I just don't really trust my parents to keep the number to themselves."

It's strange to be included in someone's close personal contacts. I'm used to being on the outskirts of a network, a connection that people use if they really need one. To be so closely tied to Lily and the Calloways makes me truly realize what I've gained by being with Rose.

I have a family. A *real* family. It's not something you can win. I didn't manipulate a soul to get here. I have it because they like me for me.

Each day, I'm more thankful for them. And I'm more aware of how much I can lose.

"Perfect," I tell her, "so I can call and remind you to study for your tests."

Her eyes grow big. "When is my next test?" Studying and school (even online school) seem to be last on Lily Calloway's priority list, whereas academics have always ranked high on mine.

"Two weeks," I say, having memorized her schedule when she showed it to me. I admit, it's not completely selfless, even though I do care about Lily. I know the way to Rose's heart is through her sisters.

Her shoulders slacken, probably glad it's not in a couple of days.

"Lily!" Scott calls as he enters the living room. "I have something for you."

Brett rotates the camera to catch Scott on film.

He holds a manila envelope in his hands, large enough to contain a paperback book.

Lily frowns, as confused as me.

"I wanted to get you a little thank-you gift," Scott explains. "The ratings for the show these past months have been off the charts, and we all know the success is from you."

After he hands her the package, she unwraps it quickly to find a DVD of *Magic Mike*. Unfiltered anger surges through me. Loren has expressed *multiple* times on camera that he doesn't want Lily watching the movie, afraid it may trigger her cravings for porn, which is a major compulsion of hers.

The fact that Scott went behind his wishes is low.

By the front door, Rose and Loren continue to argue, slowly peeling off their wet outdoor clothes, not noticing what Scott has just given Lily.

To make matters even worse, Scott leans into Lily's ear, his hand on her arm as he whispers to her. She turns bright red, obviously uncomfortable by his closeness and maybe even his words.

I step in. "Scott, leave her alone." I add, "And take your inappropriate gift with you." My insides twist in unmanageable knots. All I can think about is Lo. He's right there, by the doorway, a couch and a chair apart from us. And I know how much this is going to hurt him.

Our friendship means something to me, despite what he said at the screening party. And I have to stick up for him and for Lily.

Scott pulls back from her ear, but Lily remains flushed and motionless. A statue solidified in the middle of the fucking room. He turns to me. "It's the perfect gift for her, actually. She's been saying how much she wants to watch the movie."

Lily stares at the movie, tight in her grip. And after a long moment of contemplation, she pops it open and inspects the disc inside.

Scott has crossed a line. Maybe he sees this as a drama-inducing ploy, but this is beyond that. It's beyond just giving Lily a movie. He might as well be passing a drug addict a joint. I've seen the amount of porn she's had to trash. I've seen her cry at the foot of her bed until Rose consoled her. There were three months when Lo was in rehab, when she was struggling to recover from her addiction, and she had no one but me and her sister. And we were trying the best we could to get her to stay sane, to get better.

And shit like this—it's how something bad starts. One *small* moment can change everything.

"We need to talk," I say to Scott. "Alone."

He obligingly follows me to his bedroom on the main floor, Brett close behind, but as soon as Scott slips inside, I shut the door. The wood almost hits the camera. I lock it, and I ignore Brett's disgruntled look.

Two computers are sprawled on his bed. I scan everything quickly. The papers that splay on his pillow, a camera opened and on pause. I can barely make out the image on the tiny screen, but it looks like footage from the drinking game.

"What is it?" he snaps. "I don't have all day." He glowers like I fucked with his show.

He fucked with my friends.

But we're not even. I'll never be even with him.

"Say whatever you want," I refute, my complacency slowly and painfully leaving me. "Call me a prick, call Rose a man-hating prude. Call Lily a slut and Loren a bastard. But don't fuck with their addictions."

"I gave her a movie, Connor," he says like I'm being ridiculous. If Rose was here, she'd spit in his face. "Not a dildo."

"You don't understand sex addiction. And that's fine. Not everyone does. But you know *exactly* what you're doing. I'm asking you nicely to stop. The next time, I won't be as kind."

Scott laughs a bitter, dry laugh that spikes my irritation. "It's funny," he says, "this is the first time you've been in my face in a while, and it's not even for Rose . . ." He eyes me up and down. "Does she know you're attracted to her sister?"

I near him, gritting my teeth. "You are *grasping* for drama. Literally pulling at anything ridiculous you can latch on to. Shall I educate you then?" He opens his mouth but I don't give him the chance to refute. "I'm secure enough in *my* relationship with Rose that I don't bite off the cocks of men who wrong her or call her a bitch. She's more than capable of biting them off herself. I'm here, now, in your face because that girl in the living room has no teeth."

Brett knocks on the door, and I hear a muffled angry yell against the wood.

I don't take my eyes off Scott. "They're addicts, Scott. You kick Rose and me down, we're going to feel like shit but we'll get back up. You kick Loren and Lily, and they may not. This isn't drama for television. It's real and painful, and if you put them in those places, you don't need to be scared of anyone but me. I will kill you myself."

And I mean it.

Not because Lily is Rose's sister. Not because Loren is my friend.

But because there are some things in this world that are just wrong.

Scott nods. Whether it's sincere or not, I don't know. "I'll take that into consideration." *Not.*

I can't stay here. I might punch him. And hitting people is something I consider stupid. It solves nothing.

I turn around and leave, passing an infuriated, pudgy cameraman as I do so.

In the living room, Lily is talking to Lo. "Please. Just once. It's not porn, Lo. We can even fast-forward all the dancing. I just want to watch a movie like a normal person again."

"We can watch movies," Lo retorts. "Just not ones that might trigger your compul—"

"*Might!* Keyword. And I won't! I promise!"

His face twists in pain. Lo has told me how much he hates

saying no to her, but it's tough love he's slowly sunk into. "Lil, if I asked you for beer, what would you do?"

"It isn't the same thing!"

"It is!" he yells back. "And the fact that you don't get that worries me."

Silence lingers between them for a long moment before she says, "Okay . . ." She hands over the DVD. "Lo . . . I just want to be normal."

He pulls her into his chest and kisses the top of her head. "I know, love."

I step farther into the living room until Lo sees me. His eyes meet mine. "Where is he?" he growls, referring to Scott. He detaches from Lily and charges forward. I put a hand on his chest.

"I talked to him."

Lo's eyes redden with hate and hurt. He knows what Scott's attempting. "He can't fucking do this, Connor."

"I know."

Lo searches my face for what . . . maybe strength, comfort, reassurance. I try to give it as best I can.

"I won't let anything happen, I promise. He won't screw with your relationship or your addictions." It's a big promise. I usually only give out ones I'm one-hundred-percent confident I can keep. This one is a toss-up really.

"Thank you," Lo says, his amber eyes full of gratitude. I see something else in them. Apologies. For doubting our friendship after the screening party. For doubting me.

It feels nice to be back in Loren Hale's good graces. I think that's the thing about friends who aren't quick to let others in.

When they do give you their friendship, it means something more.

Twenty-nine

Connor Cobalt

We reach a frozen lake on our run, which turned into more of a walk with the heavy snow. Ben, who's proven to be clumsy, has tripped over his gangly legs three times, even stumbling over a root buried beneath thick white powder. Ryke helped him up after the second and third fall to make sure he didn't sprain an ankle. Ben was assigned to follow Lo, Ryke and me only because Brett can't run, and Rose has latched on to Savannah, picking a favorite. I'm not surprised it was the girl.

It's hard to ignore the guy holding the camera, especially one that has face-planted twice. But we've all somehow adapted these past few months.

Lo turns to Ryke and me with a focused look. "So I have some big news."

"Please tell me Lily isn't fucking pregnant." Ryke immediately jumps to conclusions.

Lo sends him a patented Hale glare. "It's about the wedding, you asshole."

"You didn't give me any fucking hints. Don't be pissy."

"Not that I don't enjoy these brotherly spats, but it's cold. Can we get to the point?" I ask.

"My bachelor party is coming up," Lo explains. "And I have to pick my best man . . ." He looks between us. "So you can see I'm at a dilemma."

"How?" Ryke asks, his brows bunched in confusion. "I'm your fucking brother."

"Yeah, but I've known Connor longer."

"By what? A couple months." He points accusingly at me. "He doesn't even fucking *love* you." Ryke's voice carries, disturbing the birds as they fly from their tree branches.

"It's nothing personal," I defend, my voice easier and calmer than Ryke's. "I don't love anyone."

"There you go," Loren says, like I make complete sense. I must have really been forgiven yesterday. "It's a tough choice. My best guy friend . . ." He motions to me, adding the obligatory *guy* since his best friend happens to be Lily. ". . . and my half brother. One of you will be royally pissed at me if I make the decision."

"Connor doesn't get pissed," Ryke says.

"I do," I reply. "I just don't let you see my anger."

Ryke gives me an annoyed look. "You don't even want to be his best man."

"That's not true. I'd love the position." I wait for my choice of words to crawl under his skin.

"You don't love anything," Ryke groans in distress.

"Hey!" Lo cuts in and physically pushes Ryke back as he steps closer to my body. But I'm not afraid of getting punched. "To make it fair, you two can flip for it."

"No," I say quickly. "I'm not leaving this up to chance."

Lo shrugs. "Then you'll both just have to share it." He puts a hand on each of our shoulders, standing between us. "Co–best man," he says to Ryke and then looks to me. "Co–best man."

Ryke glares at me.

And I say easily, "I'm toasting first at the wedding, just so you know. I'm afraid you'll scare the children."

"Fuck you."

"My point exactly."

He restrains himself from flipping me off. "I'm standing closest to Lo when Lily walks down the aisle."

I don't like losing this part. "You can stand behind me," I tell him.

Ryke glares harder.

"Or beside me. On the right side."

"Fuck off."

"We can always tie you to the arch." I'd actually really enjoy that. "I'll set out a bowl of water so you don't get thirsty."

Lo laughs while Ryke just shakes his head.

"There isn't going to be an arch at his wedding," Ryke reminds me. "It's indoors in a fucking church."

Right. I forgot. Formal. Traditional. Lily and Lo seem more likely to be married in the middle of a comic book convention—or something else far from the norm. When Rose proposed an outdoor wedding to her mother, she quickly rejected it. Three times. Through text, phone and email. That was not a good day for anyone.

"I'll tie you to a pew then."

Ryke takes another step forward, and Loren puts his hand on his chest.

"You should be honored," I tell him. "I only tie up the people I really like."

Ryke rolls his eyes dramatically and shakes his head. "I'm not backing down from this."

He's his brother. He should be his best man. The loss is going to sting, but I can manage. Just as I go to relinquish the title, I notice the questioning in Lo's eyes, the narrowed gaze, wondering how much I'm going to fight for this. If I care at all. He's naturally insecure about friendships since he's had very few.

So I look back to Ryke and say, "Let's just flip for it."

"Really?"

"Yeah. Why not?" *Because my odds are now fifty-fifty.*

Lo brings a quarter out of his pocket. "Who wants to call it?"

Ryke nods to me. "Go ahead, princess."

"Stop, you're making me blush," I say flatly.

He actually laughs, and both Lo and I share a smile. His brother hasn't relaxed this whole trip, not with Julian here and Scott threatening to unhinge his brother's life.

Hearing that sound from him lifts the whole mood of our run. "Heads," I tell Lo.

He tosses the coin in the air, and it comes down into his palm. He cups his hand over the quarter, and I hear the mechanical groan of Ben's camera as he zooms in over my shoulder.

Lo uncovers the coin.

Tails.

This is why I hate gambling.

I usually lose.

Thirty

Rose Calloway

This week went by so fast," I say, watching the snow fall outside, the dark sky illuminated by the ski resort's bright lights in the distance.

We fly back home soon. Back to rabid paparazzi. American television. And my mother. Even though Ben, Brett and Savannah have followed us around, it's been nice to have a house that isn't rigged twenty-four-seven with cameras.

Connor sidles up behind me, and his hands slip around my waist. I sink back into his chest, the action so much more natural now. It's hard to believe that months ago I was scared of this intimacy. Now all I think about are ways to be closer.

He pulls my hair off my shoulder and kisses the sensitive skin of my neck, marking a line up to my ear. My nerves prick with each feather-light touch. "This week may have gone by fast, but tonight will feel so . . ." His warm breath tickles me. ". . . unbearably . . ." He brushes the straps of my nightgown, and they fall off my shoulders. ". . . slow."

The air nips my skin, and he runs a hand from my thigh along the curve of my hip and settles his palm on my breast. He tugs the silky fabric to expose them. A breath hitches in the back of my throat as he kneads my breast with one hand, standing behind me while I stare at the snowfall. His muscular body overtakes my frame, no space between us, and I eagerly wait for his skin to meet mine, for his shirt to be gone, his pants to disappear. *Please, yes* . . .

He massages my breast with force and want, rippling a new feeling through my core. I ache for him. All of him. His thumb flicks my hardened nipple back and forth, shivers cascading down my spine.

And then he spins me around, his eyes grazing my breasts and the way the nightgown bunches at my waist. "Step out of it," he tells me.

I wiggle the nightgown to my ankles, my head starting to re-adjust, to make sense of what's going to happen. "Are we . . ." I trail off, lost to the way his eyes bore into each crevice and curve of my body as I stand bare, only in a pair of black cotton panties.

When he finally meets my gaze, he says, "I'm going to fuck you."

Not *we're going to make love*. Not *we're having sex*. Just, *I'm going to fuck you.*

A demand that drops my mouth and soaks my panties. Right there. That's it. I'm done for. He can take me any way he wants.

I cast out any nerves that try to attack me because I'm still a virgin. Despite being with him for over a year and gaining confidence, this is still new. I imagine most girls are anxious their first time.

Connor grabs me around the waist before I descend further into my head. He hoists me over his shoulder, and I let out a gasp. He pats my ass while my head dangles upside down, all the blood rushing to my brain.

"Stop thinking," he orders, throwing my body onto the soft mattress. My breath and thoughts leave me at once.

Holy . . . I watch him slowly unloop the leather belt from his pants. My heart races as he leans over and takes my wrist in his hand, wrapping the leather around it and a rung in the wooden headboard. When he secures the buckle, he bends to his suitcase and finds another belt.

For my other wrist.

"My first time is going to be tied up?" I ask, fear suddenly bursting in my belly. *So much for not thinking.*

"Yes," he says after he has my left wrist tethered to another rung much farther apart. He strokes my hair, and our eyes lock. "I'm going to take you deep . . ." His eyes fall to my lips, and my chest collapses. ". . . hard . . ." *Oh, fuck* . . . The spot between my legs clenches, beginning to pulse for something large, something powerful. ". . . rough . . ." He bites my lip, and I moan.

Just come inside me already.

He smiles with my bottom lip caught between his teeth. He lets go and says, "Patience."

He has plenty more than I do.

My whole body flushes in hot, agonizing *want*.

He straddles my waist and meticulously rolls my panties down my hip bones, past my curved bottom, down my thighs and slender legs, right off my feet. I am completely naked now. His to play with. His to take care of and consume.

But then he crawls off the bed.

"What are you doing?" I ask.

"No more questions, Rose."

I glower. "I'm about to lose my virginity. I can ask whatever the hell I want."

He steps closer, his shirt unbuttoned, and he covers my mouth with his large hand. He bends down so his lips skim my cheek, his breath warming my skin. "You may compliment my cock, you may beg and you may politely ask for more. I don't want to hear anything else, and if I do, I'll stuff your mouth with your panties so you can't speak." His fingers dig a little deeper in my cheeks. "But believe me, I don't want that. I want to hear all your noises. I want to hear you come."

Translation: *shut the fuck up.* And holy hell it turns me on. My body is like a taut rubber band ready to be snapped.

Before he removes his palm, he reminds me why I don't need to ask questions. "Vous êtes en sécurité avec moi." *You're safe with me.*

He kisses my forehead and draws back, retreating to the closet and leaving me naked and tied to the bed. I have to trust that he locked the door—that no one will dash into the bedroom while we have sex. Wouldn't that just be my luck?

When he returns, he carries a towel, and I stay quiet even though my stomach overturns with anticipation and nerves. He approaches me again and lifts my waist, spreading the towel underneath my bottom. And then he sheds his shirt off his shoulders, revealing defined, rigid muscles across his abs.

He turns his back to me before I can stare too long, and he disappears below the bedframe, rummaging in his suitcase again. I only have a view of his wavy brown hair.

"I have something for you," he tells me, standing with a slender black box. I've seen enough jewelry boxes to know it's a necklace.

Hopefully diamonds.

They're my favorite.

My eyes sparkle and my anxiety dissipates as he climbs onto the mattress, sitting near my waist. I jerk my wrist, wanting to not only touch the box but his body, from his shoulders to his waist to the hem of his pants. The restraints fix me to this one spot, but I cross my ankles, waiting for him.

He lingers, his palm rubbing the soft black velvety box, teasing me. How much I'd give for that hand to be caressing *me.*

"Is this where I'm supposed to beg?" I ask, not able to soften my eyes that narrow in a glare.

His lips lift, and his eyes flood with arousal. "That's a wonderful idea," he says. "Beg for this box."

I glare harder. "I was joking."

"I'm not."

Like hell. I'm not about to beg for a *box.* I stare harder at the case and imagine the jewelry. It's taunting me. I bet the necklace is gorgeous, something I would love. My resolve begins to weaken. It's not like I'm pleading for his cock . . . although, I think . . . I think I'm almost there too. The object of my desire is jewelry . . . diamonds. I would beg for diamonds.

But begging sounds weak. *Internally*, I can plead for his cock. Outwardly, how the fuck am I going to grovel?

"Please, can I have that box?" I ask, softening my usual coarse words. I didn't do so awful, right?

He doesn't move. "Didn't you say something about graduating with honors?" he asks in amusement. Yes, I often remind him of this fact in arguments. It's not really a winning point considering he graduated with the same accolades.

"Highest honors," I refute anyway, my eyes swimming with challenge. I like arguing with him far too much. I have a feeling it's going to get me into trouble tonight.

"*Highest* honors." His lips twitch. "Well then, if you're so smart you should know how to beg properly."

"I said please."

"Say it like you mean it." He sets the black box on my bare chest, the velvet smooth on my skin. With my hands tied to the headboard, there's no way to open it myself.

"Do you want me to call you *sir*, is that it?" I have no idea how far we're taking this.

His eyes darken. "I have my own way of doing things, my own rules." He skims my leg with his fingers, which tightens the aching, pissed-off spot that dearly, dearly wants him. "*Sir* is impersonal. You can call me Connor, or if you're really good, I'll even let you call me Richard."

His words relax my shoulders. My eyes drift back to the box on my breasts, and impatience strikes me cold. "Just open it, *Connor*," I say angrily.

He squeezes my kneecap in a firm clutch, and that hand descends to the top of my thigh, his fingers gripping my flesh. "*No.*"

How can one word carry so much force? I clamp my thighs tighter, my bony ankles hurting as they dig into each other. I am so naked. So aroused. And I have to beg to get what I want. I can feel how wet I'm becoming, and he raises his eyebrows knowingly.

The spot between my legs clenches.

Jesus Christ.

The longer the anticipation, the more torture. So I suck up my pride and take a deep breath.

"Please, please, *please* open the box," I plead in a whispered tone. "I want it badly."

To my surprise, he snaps the velvet case, flipping the lid. My heart careens as I absorb all the diamonds, strung together in long rows. The entire necklace is made of them. It shines and glitters in the dimmed light, the jewelry turning me on almost as much as his words.

And then I finally see past the linked gemstones to realize what type of necklace this is. Not just a choker. No. These diamonds are embedded into a leather band with a silver buckle at the back.

It's a collar.

Anger boils in me like nothing before. "I'm not your pet."

"You are my pet." He climbs further onto the bed. "You're also my girl. My lover. As I am your man. The only difference . . ." He pauses, drawing out the tension between us. "I'll always be on top." With both of his hands, he has hold of my legs and in one motion, he spreads them apart. I try to writhe against him and return my thighs to the "locked-you-can't-have-me" position, but he glares. And a Connor Cobalt glare is very, *very* hard to come by. His new dark expression causes my body to go utterly still.

And then the corners of his lips curve upward. Like a fucking prick.

"Gloat all you want. I'm not wearing it," I snap.

His smile spreads from his mouth to his eyes. "Stop me then," he challenges. But he has pinned me down with his body. His pelvis in line with mine, his erection hard against a spot that hates and loves him.

I can't stop Connor.

Even if I truly wanted to.

I'm barely breathing as he delicately wraps the leather choker around my neck. His fingers graze my skin as he buckles it in the back.

My anger is replaced by this feral need for him. My entire body screams for his touch, to know what he would feel like within me. And for the first time, I'm about to find out.

He leans back to soak in my body, my position and readiness. I watch his eyes flit from my new diamond collar to my breasts, reddened from his hands, to my naked flesh that cries for him. *Just come inside me already.*

He rests a hand on the mattress beside my head, and he kisses my temple, his lips sucking a line down the nape of my neck, grazing over the fullness of my breasts, tantalizingly slow.

"Connor," I moan, needing him to hurry.

"No talking," he says huskily, his lips closing over my nipple with a strong suction. The force bucks up my hips for more contact with him. He digs his hardness down into me, stifling my movements and stirring my desire.

"Con—"

His hand flies to my lips, muffling my voice. He resumes his exploration of my body with his tongue. I am at the mercy of his mouth, descending at a sluggish, tormenting pace.

All forms of intelligence have deserted me. My thoughts have resorted to a stupid, ridiculous chant. *Lower, lower, LOWER!*

"Lotherrr!" I mumble against his hand.

Connor bites down on the soft flesh of my hip—*hard*. The pain shoots up and ignites something new inside of me. Something stronger and headier. Spanking—I like. Choking—I like. So I shouldn't be surprised that biting my hip flushes my cheeks and neck. But it does.

I like to be bitten.

Like a goddamn vampire.

Dear God.

"Shh," Connor whispers with a forceful tone. He kisses the reddened mark on my hip and continues his descent. His lips finally graze my clit, flicking against the sensitive bud, and my entire body responds by jumping, my heart taking the biggest leap. A high-pitched noise catches in my throat, and I whimper.

His lips part at my sound, his breath deepening. He removes his hand from my mouth and lifts his head from between my legs. My eyes immediately fall to his pants, where his erection tries, pathetically, to remain hidden.

He's big, even beneath the fabric.

Any words that I anticipated saying have been lost to rawer senses. Like the way he sheds his pants slowly, without ever peeling his eyes from mine. Desire, passion, lust, they all spin inside me like a whirlpool with no bottom, no end, no resolution to these feelings.

He slips off his navy boxer briefs, his cock in full view and closer than ever before. Connor nudges my legs open with his knees, locking them to a position for his use. He grabs my ass, squeezing and lifting me into his hands, stretching my arms, which stay fastened to the headboard.

I'm horny and so confused.

Because he never slows, never hesitates. Not to put on a condom. The nerves that I kicked aside abruptly crash into me like a hundred-foot wave.

Connor freezes, going still, concern shadowing his powerful gaze.

I must wear confusion on my face, a rarity for me.

"Speak," he orders.

My throat has gone dry. I'm doing this all wrong again, I think. He continues to hold my bottom in his hands, my legs wrapped around his waist, but he sets me on the bed, no longer prepared to enter me.

Fuck.

"Dammit, Rose." Connor glares. "Just tell me what's wrong."

"You're going to wear a condom, right?" I phrase it like a question, which makes me cringe. Normally I'd just command him to wrap his dick.

Connor's shoulders slacken, and he lets out a breath of relief. I realize I scared him, an emotion *he* rarely feels. I suppose we're bringing out new sentiments in each other.

I tap his thigh with my ankle. "I have one in my bag."

A smile slowly overtakes his face. "Do you? Were you expecting to get laid on this trip?"

"I'm always prepared," I remind him, trying to hide my own smile.

He picks up my foot and places a light kiss on the bottom of my heel. "No condoms," he suddenly says.

"What?" I snap.

"I don't want anything between us," he tells me. He scoots forward, his hardness so very near, and his hands slide from my knees to my thighs. "I want to fill you, Rose, even after I pull out and hold you in my arms." *He wants to come inside you, Rose.* I could stare at the ceiling and say, *Thank you, Lord,* but Connor would be so pissed. The thought almost urges me to do it, but the sensible part of me returns.

Because if he doesn't use a condom that means . . . "We can't . . ." I shake my head. "We can't be hypocrites. Loren and Lil—"

"Are irresponsible," Connor finishes for me. "Lily forgets to bathe and eat, and we both know she regularly forgets to take birth control, which is why we remind Loren to use condoms. And you, Rose, are the most responsible woman I know."

His words have a way of placating worries, even mine.

I nod. This is it.

I can't help but stare at his blue eyes that swim with a familiar ambition and passion. *This is Connor*, I remind myself. For ten years, I've known him. And not very many people ever truly do.

He's roped to my gaze, inhaling a deep breath. He brushes a piece of damp, sweaty hair from my cheek. "I've wanted so many things in life," he says softly, "but you're the one that has meant the most to me."

Translation: *I love you.*

His thumb skims my bottom lip. Oh, that thumb . . .

And then he plunges in, so hard and fast that I cry out. The pain comes all at once, but it's slowly usurped by more pleasant sensations. He thrusts, pulsing each one in deep succession, the rhythm blinding my vision. I tilt my head back, my eyelids fluttering, trying to stay sane. The fullness drives me to a new place, but it's the way his hips pound into me, his force as I stay bound to the headboard, that truly sends me over.

He grips my thighs for support as he pushes deeper. He lifts one of my legs higher to fit more of him inside me. I gasp and struggle against the belt restraints. *Connor* . . .

My whole world spins.

I'm drenched in sweat while a hot layer gathers across his skin. I'm also soaked between my legs, and if I concentrate on just how deep he stays, just how far he goes, how it seems like his cock rides into my belly, my back begins to arch. My rotating world lights on fire.

He groans as he hooks my leg underneath his arm, holding it up, rampaging my body like it belongs to him for this purpose.

God yes . . .

Why the hell did I wait so long?

The headboard *rap rap rap*s against the wall, and Connor breathes in low ragged breaths through his nose, the determination in his eyes fucking me just as much as his cock. I want him to choke me. To steal my oxygen for a second.

And just like that, he grabs my leather collar while thrusting, not missing a beat. And he uses the collar to lift my neck up to his face, our lips meeting. He kisses me hungrily, passionately, *eagerly*—and he chokes me of air this way, my lips swelling underneath his, numb to the pressure, his minty taste swirling in my mouth with his tongue.

As he thrusts again, he hits a spot that breaks my lips from his and mangles my voice. It was a noise from a place five thousand feet high, in a cloud.

He watches my excitement, and his arousal continues to grow, his muscles tightening, never letting up. He increases his speed. *Faster.*

Holy . . .

No breaks. Not even as more sweat beads our skin. We create heat like we're gods.

I don't know how he deepens his movement, but he does. My noises escalate until I can't contain anything anymore. And he pulls at the collar again, kissing my parted lips once and twice before setting my head back on the pillow. Then he reaches up to my hand on a rung of the headboard. He interlaces his fingers with mine, holding me as he drives me to my climax.

My sex clenches around him, three or four times, my entire body writhing. My toes curling, my moans morphing into deep breaths of dizzy pleasure.

"Let it out," he whispers in my ear as he continues his mind-numbing pace.

Tears prick my eyes as I fall down from the high, but he's not done. I realize he hasn't come yet. He continues to rock against me, building me back up.

I never want this feeling to leave.

As if he senses this, he makes the moment, somehow, pass like an eternity.

And then we both reach the peak in unison. When he comes, he thrusts forward, hard, and then he rocks his hips against me, milking his climax until we're both light-headed and breathing heavy.

As everything slows, I become acutely aware of my surroundings and thoughts again. Of what happened. I was the virgin in this scenario. He's done this before, and I want to know if I was awful. Or if he's had someone better. I'm competitive by nature. In bed—I want to be the best he's ever had. It might be too much to ask.

His chest rises and falls as he tries to catch his breath. He hovers above me as if preparing to do it all over again.

I kind of hope so.

And then he begins to laugh, his smile enveloping his face—not in humor but in happiness.

"What?" I ask softly.

He stares at me like I'm the only one he wants here. Underneath him. "You and me," he says and licks his lips. "We fuck like winners."

I grin. He didn't say *I* fuck like a winner. It was *we*. Us. Together.

"You have ten seconds," he tells me, "before I take you again. You ready?"

Oh yeah. I'm ready.

Thirty-one

Connor Cobalt

We didn't do it once. Or twice. Or even three times. After I exhausted her mind and body, I finally begin to untie her from the bed.

Her eyes flutter wearily, but she fights to stay awake, a quality I admire.

"What, no more?" she asks softly, humor to her voice.

"It's time to sleep." I toss my belt on the floor and kiss her reddened wrist. Faint bruises and marks blemish her naked body, and I can't wait to see what she thinks of them in the morning.

I place her hands gently by her side, and I carefully wipe the spot between her legs with the towel. Rose cringes just slightly. She was tighter than I expected, but she was also incredibly wet. Still, I didn't want to take her slowly. She'll be sore in the morning. I grin as I imagine how every time she aches and moves she'll remember me inside of her.

Quickly, I throw the towel in the hamper and clean myself off. I find another pair of boxer briefs from my suitcase and pull them on before I head back to bed.

Rose's eyes have closed, but they open a fraction when I slip underneath the covers next to her. She scoots closer, a gesture unlike the guarded girl I know. I take advantage and grab her around the waist, tucking her in my arms.

She rests her head on my chest and her lips softly kiss the bare skin. She doesn't say anything, and my hand falls to her round bottom. I could get used to this vulnerable side of her.

"I think I understand how someone could get addicted to sex," she says softly.

"Yes, well, your sister doesn't have sex like that." I stroke her damp hair, and my comment stirs her almost fully awake.

"And how would you know?" she combats, as if presuming I slept with Lily. *And there goes that vulnerable side.*

I smile. "Maybe we should take it slower next time," I say. "It seems all these endorphins and hormones have made you a little—"

Her eyes burst into flames. "If you say stupid—"

I kiss her lips, cutting her off. She settles down, probably more out of exhaustion than true surrender. She is an awful submissive. But that's what I adore about her. She's a challenge. *My* challenge.

I glance down at Rose and her eyes are barely open now. "I'm glad I have you," she tells me before her lids sink closed, and she drifts asleep in my arms. But I'm the one who should be glad.

I had no one before Rose. No true friends. No family, not really.

Now I have her. I have people I care about it. People that I want to protect.

Now I have everything.

The only thing about having everything is that you can lose it all.

Thirty-two

Rose Calloway

I can't walk. Literally. I am so fucking sore that the short trek to the bathroom had me moaning in pain, but when I think back to last night, I feel like a little school girl who can't restrain a blinding, giddy smile. I used to glare at those girls, the ones who drooled over boys. But I understand now. Some things just make you overwhelmingly happy. Having sex definitely did it for me.

The aches are worth these unrestrained feelings. Plus, there's nothing in the world like being pampered by Connor Cobalt.

He brought me breakfast in bed and alternated between kissing and biting my neck, a sensation that I have begun to love too much. I plan to spend most of the day on the couch or tucked in bed, but I had to go to the bathroom to at least do my hair, wash my face— half of my normal morning routine.

My robe hangs on my arms as I brush my teeth, careful to distance the sleeves from the running faucet. After I rinse, I wipe my lips on a cloth, and my eyes lock on the diamond collar. It's gorgeous, even if it makes me look like his pet. I zip up my toiletry kit, and my robe falls off my shoulder. I go to lift it up, but I notice the outline of a bruise on my arm.

I inspect the rest of my body, some faint and some prominent marks all across my breasts, arms, legs, wrists, more reddened than anything. I drop my robe completely and spot the bite mark on my hip, Connor's teeth imprinted. My fingers graze the tender area, and I smile.

I like these bruises.

They're like my war wounds.

I survived wild sex.

I *still* can't stop smiling, even as I grab my panties and step into them, my limbs protesting at the movement. Okay, now my smile has vanished. I grimace as the fabric sits against a sensitive place that wishes to be free of touch.

I stare angrily at the bra on the counter. My nipples hurt. The left one is red and raw, having gone through hell at the mercy of Connor Cobalt's mouth. That bra might as well be iron spikes, and I haven't even put it on yet.

Before I make this crucial decision, the bathroom door opens, and my arm flies to my breasts. *Not Scott. Please not Scott.*

I exhale as soon as Connor shuts the door behind him.

I drop my arm, and he peruses my body quickly. I focus on the bottle of lotion he carries. "Where did you get that?" It looks expensive and feminine.

"I bought it in New York before we left," he says, almost in disinterest. "How do you feel?"

I draw my shoulders back in confidence and mask the pain from my face. "Fantastic," I say, combing my fingers through my hair. "Ready for round . . ." How many times did we actually do it last night? I'm so aggravated that I lost count. I don't lose count of anything.

Shit. My thoughts are even pretentious.

Connor must be rubbing off on me. Or maybe I've always been this way.

"I'll be the judge of when you're ready," he says, leaning an arm on the sink as he watches me.

I give him a look. "I think I know my body better than you."

He raises his brows in challenge. "That's debatable, and secondly, you're stubborn and competitive. Two qualities that make you a terrible judge." He uncaps the lotion and squeezes it into his palm.

"I can do it myself," I say, regretting the words immediately. I'd much rather be indulged by him.

"But the wonderful thing about making these bruises is that I get to tend to them." He (thankfully) ignores my statement and rubs the lotion onto one of the faint bruises on my shoulder, careful and tender, the exact opposite of his demeanor in bed.

A girl could get used to this.

He massages the bite mark, and only once does the pain intensify. I try to hold back my grimace, but I must be unsuccessful because he kisses the spot. Then he talks to me in French about everyday things. Calloway Couture. Cobalt Inc. What we'll do when we return to Philly tomorrow.

Being taken care of has never felt so good.

When he finishes checking my bruises, he focuses on the spot between my legs. He cups my sex, and I clench my teeth, refusing to show how much it aches—and not in the *please fuck me* kind of way.

"These need to go." He slowly removes my panties, sliding them down my legs. I hold on to his shoulders as I step out of them. He helps me slip my arms back through my robe, and he ties it at my waist. The silk gently caresses my skin, unlike the cotton of my underwear.

Connor looks at my diamond collar and reaches for the buckle.

I take a step back, possessively touching the leather at my throat.

His entire face lights up, and he holds in a laugh, rubbing his lips to stifle the sound. "So now you like it?"

"They're diamonds," I say like he's insane. "And it was a gift. You can't take it back."

"I'm not going to return it," he assures me. "I'll keep it safe." He approaches, and I don't withdraw this time. He unfastens the buckle, my neck bare without the warm leather.

"Why can't I keep it on?" I ask softly, eyeing his lips. I watch the way they move when he speaks.

"Because you'll wear it when I play with you," he says. "And today, I'm taking care of you." He gathers my hair in his hand and rubs lotion where the buckle dug into my skin. His fingers dance so skillfully along the tender areas. I muster all of my willpower to stop from moaning and submitting like a drooling puppy.

He caps the lotion, pockets the collar and leaves the bathroom without another word. I frown, confused at first. But then he returns with another black case, the same size as last night's. Another necklace?

My eyes widen in excitement.

He doesn't make me beg this time. He merely opens the box. "This one is for days like today."

He untangles it from the box, and then he steps behind me, swooping it around my neck and fastening it in place. He's given me jewelry before: a teardrop necklace when we first started dating. But this means more to me. Not just because a *diamond* pendant rests against my chest, but because it's simple and refined, on a feather-light chain that I could wear with almost every outfit. He thought about that, I can tell.

I think I might cry. And I never cry.

I suppose it's okay to shed tears over jewelry. That doesn't make me more of an ice queen or a materialistic snob, right? Oh, who the fuck cares?

My tears are apparent.

"Thank you," I say.

He kisses my lips and slides his arms over my shoulders. "Always."

Connor and I spend all morning switching between the Discovery and History channels, trying to avoid the reality shows in favor of the educational segments. (Yes, I realize this is a little hypocritical, but just because I'm on a reality show doesn't mean I like to watch them.) We've secluded ourselves to the bedroom, and when my sisters asked about me, he told them I wasn't feeling well. They bought it enough to leave us alone.

His phone rings just as a piece on the Black Death begins to play. "You can't leave now," I tell him. "You're going to miss all the pictures of pestilence and gangrene."

He looks up from his cell. "Tempting." He smiles to let me know he means it.

I think back to literature involving the bubonic plague, unearthing the knowledge I've stored from college, quiz bowls and my own leisurely studies. "Even with the utterly lost, to whom life and death are equally jests, there are matters of which no jest can be made." I quote *Masque of the Red Death*, quizzing him and distracting him in one sentence.

His eyes gleam in challenge, and his hand drops, ignoring the buzz from his phone. "Edgar Allen Poe," he answers with ease, and devours my bait in one swoop.

Connor slides beside me on the bed, his legs nestled against mine. He fingers my diamond necklace, smoothing the thin chain and inadvertently tickling the hollow of my collar. I clasp his hand before the sensation makes me squirm.

He stares at me deeply, whispering, "Love all, trust a few, do wrong to none."

One of my favorite quotes. I turn a fraction, just enough so that our lips don't suddenly collide. "Shakespeare," I breathe.

"Very good."

My thoughts migrate to my heart. A kiss is at a breath's distance, and despite my sore body, I want a repeat of last night.

Love all. Love. I've accepted Connor for who he is, even his anti-love beliefs. But why the hell did he have to choose that quote?

"You can't seduce me with Shakespeare." I command my thoughts to return to my brain. *Come back, Non-Gooey Rose.* I put a considerable amount of distance between our lips, scooting to the right. "Especially with a quote about love."

"Darling, I don't need to seduce you," he says. "I already have you."

His face blankets with lust as I narrow my glare. The more I glower, the more I arouse him. I've learned that fact over the years, and yet, I still can't seem to bottle my irritation to win a round.

He licks his lips and delivers another quote. Only he recites the lines with heavy, bated breath. Almost like he's making love to the words. "We know what we are, but not what we may be."

Why is that so sexy? And why does intelligence turn me on more than muscles and taut abs?

"*Hamlet*," I reply. I sit up straighter, leaning against the headboard, and I try to hide the fact that the spot between my legs thrums with newly lit passion.

"We are such stuff as dreams are made on, and our little life is rounded with a sleep."

I internally grin from ear to ear. Our very first date, we saw this play together. "Easy. *The Tempest.*"

"All right, Miss Highest Honors . . ." He sets a knee on either side of my waist, not straddling my lap. He stays above me like this, towering as he presses a hand to the headboard and stares down at me. He has sufficiently confined me in his muscular, tall cage. *I can't believe he's my boyfriend.* That's literally all I can think right now.

"Love is merely a madness."

It takes me a moment to process his words. *"As You Like It."*

He lowers his head. He's going to touch his lips to mine, but he tricks me, his mouth diverting to my ear. "Though she be but little, she is fierce." He says each word with such conviction that my heart backflips.

Oh God.

Think. Think. I have to win. *"A Midsummer Night's Dream."*

With one hand still on the headboard, he uses the other to caress my right breast, one that is vastly less sore. "What's past is prologue."

"The Tempest again."

He tilts my chin up and brings his lips down upon mine, his tongue parting them and stealing my breath at once. My nipples pucker, and he retracts as he recites, "What's done cannot be undone."

I watch his hand fall to my neck, rubbing my tender skin. Then to my breast. To my arm. I can hardly concentrate on his words. I'm lost, and my arousal has built all over again. "I . . ." Shit. ". . . repeat it."

"What's done cannot be undone."

Think, Rose.

He gives me a new quote from the same play. "Life is a tale told by an idiot, full of sound and fury, signifying nothing."

I squint as I faintly recall this one. "Did you abbreviate?" He hates abbreviating, and he must have done it to stump me.

"Maybe."

I am about to call him a cheater, but he covers my mouth with his hand and says, "I didn't have to give you a second quote to help you, Rose."

True.

He kisses my forehead and then says, "Life's but a walking shadow, a poor player that struts and frets this hour upon the stage, and then is heard no more. It is a tale told by an idiot, full of sound and fury, signifying nothing."

"*Macbeth*." I straighten in pride, and he actually shares it. Instead of sulking in the loss, he grins at my win.

But then he adds, "Time is but a fool as we are to the mercy of its hands."

I frown. I don't know this one at all. I glare, not taking this loss as well as he did.

"A Connor Cobalt original," he tells me.

I throw a pillow up at his face, and he catches it before uncaging me from this spot. I'd be more than okay imprisoned on this mattress all day long by him, and only him.

But he climbs off the bed, his feet setting on the hardwood with his phone in hand. "I'm going to call Frederick back and then we can watch a city die together." He jabs his thumb towards the television, where the Black Death has begun to ravage Europe.

"Are you going to talk about me?" I wonder.

"Yes," he says. "I'm going to gloat, so I think maybe I should go outside." He motions to the patio.

"Tell him I said hi," I say with a tight smile. I've met Frederick once, and he was pleasant but short, probably worried he might let something slip. He knows more about me than he lets on, that's for sure.

Connor disappears out the sliding glass doors, and I find my own phone on the nightstand. I'm about to dial Poppy's number when I remember it's six in the morning in Philly. I invited her to the Alps, but she said she'd rather stay home with her daughter. Poppy is only four years older than me, but I feel like we've already grown decades apart.

She has her own family and has begun to distance herself from Lily, Daisy and me in favor of Sam and Maria. Is that what happens when you have children? You gain new family members but have to sacrifice the connection of others?

It scares me. The fact that the relationships I have with my sisters now could dissolve when we all get married and start "new" lives. Will this be the closest we ever are?

I hope not.

A fist raps against my door before it opens a crack. "Shhh," Lily hisses. "She could be sleeping."

I fold my hands on my lap and cross my ankles like a lady, waiting for them to enter, my smile peeking through. If we part ways in a few years, I might as well enjoy this now.

"No . . . I see her. She's awake," Daisy says, craning her neck above Lily's to look into my room.

Lily opens the door wider, and Daisy slips in front, holding two mugs with marshmallows floating on top.

Lily cups her own red mug in her hands. "We made you hot chocolate."

"We thought it might help your migraine," Daisy adds.

She hands me a dark blue mug while they plop on the mattress by my legs.

A migraine? That was Connor's lie? He could have done better, but I suppose he didn't want to worry anyone with a fib.

Lily nods to the television, where dead bodies are being thrown into big ditches. She looks mildly horrified. "What are you watching?"

I smile into my cup. "The Black Death." I take a long sip and then feel Daisy's hand drift to my neck, examining the diamond pendant.

"Is this new?"

I nod. "A gift from Connor."

"Pretty," she says with sincerity, delicately placing it back against my chest, but I see a lingering sadness behind her eyes. She tries to conceal anything out of the ordinary by twisting her hair into a giant knot with one hand.

"What'd I miss?" I ask Daisy.

"Besides Scott being a douchenozzle, nothing," she says easily. My eyes narrow. "What'd he do?"

"He's not the douchenozzle," Lily says, giving Daisy a strange reprimanding look that she rarely produces.

My mouth falls. "Are you defending Scott, Lily?" Did Connor fuck me to another dimension?

She reddens. "No," she says quickly. "I mean, Scott is still an asshole. He keeps whispering *slut* when he passes me in the hallway. But . . ." She shrugs. ". . . I'm learning to ignore him like everyone else." She sets her sisterly glare back on Daisy.

I stiffen. "What is it then?" I connect the dots faster than Daisy forms words. "It's Julian, isn't it?"

Daisy shakes her head, but Lily nods and points a finger at her. "He put his hand down your pants, in front of *Ryke*. That's not nothing!"

"And I took his hand *out* of my pants," Daisy says in a hushed whisper. "No harm done."

Lily clues me in on the rest. "Ryke almost punched him."

"I bet," I say before sipping my hot chocolate.

Lily's eyes form tiny slits as she scrutinizes me. "You're calm about this."

"Julian has been marking his territory since we arrived in the Alps. I'm not surprised he chose to do it by grabbing her ass."

"*Underneath* her jeans," Lily clarifies.

"I'm right here." Daisy waves her hand.

"You are," I say. "Where's the pepper spray I bought you? If you don't scald his eyes, I'd be happy to do it."

"He's my boyfriend. I don't want to hurt him."

"Is he really your boyfriend, Daisy?" I ask, a little too icily. But I can't help that.

"Yes."

"Then describe what it's like to kiss him."

She cringes.

Lily points another finger at her. "Aha! You don't like him."

Daisy's shoulders fall. "I'm working on it."

"Promise me you won't *always* be working on it," I say. "He's older, and he shouldn't be trapping you in a relationship."

"He's not. I promise. I can get out at any time. I'm just waiting for the right moment to strike." She pats my leg, dodging quickly. "So how are you feeling, anyway?"

I'll take her distraction this time, only because that conversation was going nowhere, not until she can reject Julian. And if she can't, I have absolutely no problem stepping in and burying his face in the fucking snow.

I clear my throat and straighten my neck. "So . . . I have news . . ." A few months ago, I made a promise to Lily that I'd tell her when I lost my virginity, only if she agreed not to make it a big deal in return. I try not to smile as I say it. "I had sex."

"*Ahhhhhhhh!*" Lily's excited squeal sounds more like a frightened scream.

The bedroom door flies open in response, unsurprisingly. Both Loren and Ryke rush in while the patio door slides for Connor's quick entrance, his phone still in his hand.

"What the fuck happened?" Ryke asks first, looking between the three of us girls, who have gone utterly quiet. Daisy acts like she's enthralled with a marshmallow in her hot chocolate.

Lo's cheekbones sharpen the longer he stares at Lily in concern, trying to figure out what's going on like his brother.

The silence must eat at Lily because she grabs the throw blanket, pulls it over head, and hides.

I'm about to explain, but Brett tries to maneuver his camera through the doorframe to capture a view of the bedroom—an area off-limits from filming. His intrusion annoys Ryke enough to slam the door *on* his face.

I hear the *oomph!* and the cameraman stumble in the hallway. I'd be more upset if it was Savannah or Ben. Otherwise, I don't care so much about Ryke's bout of aggression.

When I look at Connor, he raises his brows, and a smile plays at his lips. He knows I told my sisters.

Loren sidles to the bed and prods Lily's blanket-covered body. Even shrouded, I can tell she looks ready to melt into my mattress.

"What's going on, Lil?" Lo asks. He rubs her back.

She shakes her head and then shifts her body so she faces me. I think. Her nose sort of sticks out. I'm not sure how that helps since I can't see her beneath the plaid flannel.

"I'm sorry, Rose," she says. "I was just happy for you." It's like some blanket monster apologizing to me.

"It's fine, Lily," I tell her. "I don't really care." They were bound to find out one way or another. I'm sure Connor would have told them eventually. This current situation may be a little odd, but welcome to my life.

"You girls need to work on your fucking happy noises," Ryke says angrily. "They shouldn't sound like someone is being assaulted."

Loren pulls off Lily's blanket, and her hair sticks up from the static. "What are you happy about?"

She goes silent and a little pale. *For Christ's sake.*

"I had sex," I blurt out for the second time.

All eyes immediately fixate on Connor, who has been very quiet. His phone is gone and his hands are in his pockets. "Yes, it was with me," he answers the nonexistent question. But it relieves some of the awkward tension in the room.

"Really?" I feign confusion. "You were there?"

"Je te rappellerai plus tard." *I'll remind you later.* Words sound so much sexier in French.

"And that's my cue to fucking leave." Ryke disappears through the door, careful not to let any cameras in.

"Congrats, sis," Daisy says with a huge smile. She gives me a hug and follows Ryke's footsteps.

That leaves Connor and me with Lily and Loren.

I wait for Loren to hit me with some insult. He'll probably talk about "becoming a woman" now as if having sex makes me older and wiser. It doesn't. It just makes me a little more experienced. So what?

He rubs the back of his neck before he says, "I'm happy for you two."

I wear my shock, and Lo rolls his eyes. "What? I can't be nice for once?"

"It's weird," I admit.

He nods to Connor. "You sticking around then?" He still thinks Connor might ditch me now that he's had sex with me?

"Yeah, Lo," Connor says, his eyes tightening with a flicker of hurt. I'm surprised he allows Lo to see it. "I'm sticking around."

Lo nods again as he tries to absorb this as truth. "Congrats, man, for a second I was worried Scott was going to beat you to it." He flashes a dry smile.

"The only thing he's beaten me at so far is—"

"Rose," Scott says, slipping into the room with his cell phone in hand. He holds the device out to me, but I don't make a motion to crawl from my ladylike spot on this bed.

I have just announced my deflowering, and of course he'd find this as an appropriate time to interrupt. He clearly wants to cut Connor down from his highest achievement, and mine too.

But then he says, "Your mom is on the phone. She wants to talk about the seating arrangements for the wedding."

Connor steps between the bed and Scott before the producer reaches me. My boyfriend's eyes heat with malice that I haven't seen before. He snatches the phone out of Scott's hand.

Before he presses the receiver to his ear, Scott adds, "Be sure to tell Samantha thanks for the hour-long chat. I loved hearing about her day. It was . . . informative."

He's fucking with him.

My mother is pliable, easily manipulated by sweet-talking men with money. Hell, she likes *Loren Hale*, who is only nice when he wants to be. I didn't think any parent would shove him on their daughter, but she's been praying for a marriage between Lily and Lo even before they were together.

I am starting to wonder how much the reality show has warped her mind. If the rest of the public hates Connor with me—which they do since he's been snippy on screen and edited as a pretentious ass—then her friends won't support my relationship. They'll vote for Scott, and my mother usually goes with the majority.

Just lovely.

"Samantha . . ." Connor says as he puts the phone to his ear, eyes never leaving Scott as he does so. "She's unavailable . . . yes . . . of course . . ." He drops his gaze and glances at Loren, silently asking him to stay in my room. He nods, and then Connor seeks privacy on the patio again to talk with my mother. The sliding door shuts, and I consider moving my pained muscles to join him.

"Get out," Loren immediately says to Scott.

The producer raises his hands in defense, but his smarmy gaze zones in on me, descending to my breasts, the tops visible in my low-cut nightgown. "You've definitely left the nunnery, Rose Calloway." He lets out an amused laugh. "I'll see you all later." He pauses in thought. "And you know, you and your sisters should all put on that . . . gold top that Daisy wore at Valentino's. Great ratings with that episode." He whistles. "You should see how many people reblogged that picture. Side-boob sells."

I am going to kill him. I picture myself crawling on all fours towards his body and springing like a lioness, a wild cat, something feral that will claw the eyeballs right out of his sockets. But then I imagine him smirking at the perfect view of my cleavage during the assault. So I regretfully stay seated. Like a lady.

"Get. Out. You *shitty* fuck," Loren says slowly like Scott's a moron.

Scott raises his hands in defense, but he still acts like he holds all the cards. Maybe he does. He owns us and the townhouse we live in. And he has footage to tamper with. We're just marionettes in his play.

The door shuts. But the tension never leaves. I don't think it ever will.

Not until the cameras finally stop rolling.

Thirty-three

Connor Cobalt

S he's twenty-three, in a yearlong relationship—"
"Over a year."
"*Over* a year, and she's *never* had sex. Something is wrong with that girl."

I watch *TMZ* from my office desk at Cobalt Inc. before I call it a night and head home. The hallways are desolate, only a janitor left, vacuuming the gray carpet in the break room.

"She definitely has herpes," a reporter from one of the cubicles says. And the newsroom breaks into laughter. "What else explains it?"

The Alps trip aired last night on GBA. No mention of Rose losing her virginity. But if she saw *TMZ* slandering her right now, she'd be pissed. They're shaming every girl her age who wishes to wait.

Rose had no problem with production keeping her virginity a secret. But on the plane ride home, just to test Scott—to see what he would do—she stared right into one of the cameras and professed that she had sex with me. It let Lily, who had been so unnaturally quiet in fear of spilling the secret to the whole world, off the hook.

He never showed the footage, probably to keep her "virgin" label on the show intact. And because I'm everyone's least favorite choice to be with Rose. Her mother so much as said so on the phone. That was one of the hardest conversations I've had. I wanted to tell her off, but I bit my tongue and stomached her chiding about not being more caring towards my girlfriend, her daughter.

I mentioned bad editing *once* and she scoffed and told me to stop using excuses. So I just said, "*I'm sorry, Samantha. I'll be better about it.*" And she threatened, "*You better. Or I'll convince Rose to give Scott another chance, which he deserves.*"

She truly believes that they dated before. It's . . . a new level of insanity for me.

I hate Scott.

But at least he never ruined some of the best sex I've ever had. I just want to go home and fuck Rose, forget about all this bullshit and do something that makes both of us feel good. But time isn't on our side. I fight for more constantly. Wharton is killing me. Cobalt Inc. is manageable. But I'm lucky to make it home by 2 a.m. each night before she falls asleep.

I stand and gather any papers, stuffing them into a briefcase. Before I leave, I flip through the channels one last time and land on a rerun of *Princesses of Philly*. I caught a portion of it before, but not this part—where Lo pins Lily on the couch at the cabin. Where he passionately kisses her lips, bringing her into his arms each time he draws her up with a strong inhale.

But his eyes lock on the camera as he does it. As though he's literally *fucking* the viewers with his mouth. I rub my lips and try not to laugh. Rose would be infuriated, but Lo has done this so often. I've seen a few bumper stickers around Philly that say *Fuck me, Loren Hale*. Especially after Lily's latest interview aired. She went into a lengthy explanation about how Loren is the only man able to satisfy all of her sexual needs.

Celebrity Crush even wrote an article, trying to determine the size of his dick. It was horrible journalism, but it's articles like those that really put into perspective how popular the reality show has become.

And how famous we all suddenly are.

Lily can't even watch herself make out with Lo during these segments. He covers her eyes. It's that arousing for her.

I shut off the television, flick off my lights and swallow a couple Adderall. I have a half-completed Wharton project for a management class left to finish. I want to say *hell with it* and have rough sex with my girlfriend instead.

Tying her up and watching her come beats every other task on my to-do list. My body heats just remembering her face the first time I filled her with my cock. Her mouth fell open, and she choked on some of the most gorgeous sounds.

I've never felt like she belonged to me more than in that moment. She let me do whatever I wanted to her body, all trust, no barriers or restrictions. I took her as hard as I knew she could withstand, her tightness gripping my cock in a vise that I don't ever want to forget.

Which is why I plan to go home and do it again.

The elevator is in sight, and I'm already picturing what position I'll put her in. Face down on the mattress. Hands tied behind her back.

I think I'll spank her.

"Connor!"

I stop dead in the hallway. There's only one person who could ruin these beautiful thoughts. Only one other person who'd be working while the janitor finishes his routine. I turn around to confront my mother, who quickly approaches me with determined steps.

"I just put my proposal on your desk," I tell her. *Let me go*, I silently plead.

"I got it," she says breezily. "I scheduled a reservation at L'Bleu on Saturday. Seven o'clock. Bring Rose." She spins and disappears down the hall, leaving no chance for an excuse.

Something foreign presses against my chest. I think it might be anxiety. I open my phone to call Frederick, but I see a missed text instead.

Come home now, please. We have a Lily and Loren problem.—Rose

Shit.

I don't let my imagination try to predict what kind of problem that could be. I just make a quick exit to the elevator and brace myself for what's to come.

As soon as I walk through the door, I spot Lily and Lo curled up on the couch, reading a comic silently together. "Problems" with those two usually involve screaming, maybe even crying. It's odd. But I try not to pass judgment until I know the facts.

Before I can even begin to question them, Rose marches down the stairs and grabs my wrist with a lot of force, fire blazing in her eyes. I should be more concerned about the shit storm she's going to unleash, but my cock has its own agenda, painfully begging for her to redirect that pressure. She tries to lead me to the second level, but I pry her fingers off my wrist.

"I think I know where the bedroom is," I say.

Her lips tighten in a line, and she blushes. "We're not having sex right now."

I tilt my head, my brows pinching. "All I meant was that I can lead myself upstairs. I said nothing about sex." I pass her on the stairs and walk in front of her.

She huffs. "We don't have time to accommodate your ego." She's pissed that I took precious time away from the dire situation.

She tries to pass me on the stairs, and I hold out my arm and give her a look.

"Move faster!" she commands.

"Is the townhouse on fire? Did someone steal your shoe collection?" I ask with a growing smile.

Her neck is so stiff. She barely even inhales. "I'm going to slap you."

I actually think she may.

I'm too curious about the Lily and Lo drama to start that fight, but it's really tempting. I can already see her hand scorching my cheek. And then I'd shove her against the wall, bite her lip and fuck the anger out of her, replacing it with content, vulnerable submission.

She finally exhales as she watches me, so deep that I know she must see the longing in my eyes. But we can't have sex in the hallway. It's rigged with cameras.

I break her gaze and go to the bedroom without another word. She shuts the door behind us, and I notice Ryke already here, pacing in front of the bed with clenched fists. I recognize Savannah's Canon Rebel on the mattress. Before I can ask what the camera is doing here, Rose explains.

"The tequila and wine are gone," she tells me, her hands planted firmly on her hips. She says she searched the house, and then Ryke found the bottles in Lo's closet—empty and hidden beneath a pile of dirty clothes.

I blink a few times, trying to ignore emotions that want to pummel me backwards. I'm not used to feeling so much from something that has no direct effect on me, no cost that'll weigh down my benefit.

"There wasn't much in the tequila bottle. We spilled most of it on our bed," I remind Rose with an even voice, but a lump scratches my throat. I have to cough into my fist to clear it.

"It doesn't matter." She points a finger at the door. "He's been sober for *sixteen months*."

"I know." Breaking his sobriety—it's a big deal.

I turn on Ryke, who fumes, trekking forwards and backwards with hostility.

"And you haven't stormed downstairs to confront your brother?" I ask in disbelief.

He stops in the middle of the room and points at the door just like my girlfriend did. "I'm so fucking *close*," he growls. "But that's exactly what those dickfuckers want."

I cringe. "Can you not use that curse word? It's ridiculous."

Both of them glare at me.

"I'll take cocksucker for one hundred," I banter, hoping to ease Ryke's flexed muscles and Rose's hot-tempered eyes. But I realize it's more for me. I'm dodging. I never dodge. I just don't want it to be true. I don't want Lo to drink again and go down that dark path. I can't save that kid from his demons, and watching him drown is not a show I want a front row seat to.

Ryke chooses to ignore me, finishing his rant, "They want me to scream at Lo, and then the whole world will think he's relapsing like an irresponsible rich prick. And maybe he is . . ." Ryke rests his hands on his head, breathing heavily.

"You don't believe that," I say.

His features break, and his eyes glass as he shakes his head. "Every day I think, *that could be me*. I spent twenty-two fucking years with my head up my ass," he says. "I didn't give a shit about my fucking half brother who I *knew* was living with our father— *our* father . . ." He can't say the rest out loud.

Rose stares at Ryke with the most empathy I've seen her convey, her face pained like his. My stomach is in knots, and I don't know how to untighten it.

Production never airs these intimate, painful details—the parts that shape us into the people we are. I think we all hide them too often. Sometimes from each other.

Lo has been verbally abused by their father all his life, and Ryke escaped it.

That's the truth.

It's what we all know.

If production truly wanted to show *all* of Ryke Meadows, they'd tell the viewers that he spent his last year in college helping his half brother get sober. That he stopped hanging out with college buddies, going to parties for athletes, just to make sure that Loren didn't turn out like their alcoholic father, to guide him towards a better road.

I admire Ryke for many reasons. But I think this is the greatest one: Loren Hale is the bastard child that destroyed Ryke's family. Their father got another woman pregnant, conceiving Lo. And Ryke subsequently lived with his single mother after the divorce. Yet, Ryke stands here today, wanting only to protect a guy who was the catalyst for his broken life.

But Ryke doesn't even understand the impact he's had on Lo's life. He really can't see all the good he's done. Because he's not finished blaming himself for being so selfish those first twenty-two years, for ignoring Lo because he was attached to their father by blood and proximity.

He needs to forgive himself. I'm not sure how long that'll take, if it will ever come to pass. We just have to wait and see.

Ryke rubs his reddened eyes. He looks like he needs to scream. Or maybe kick something. "I don't know what to fucking do."

"Ryke," I say calmly, filling my voice with the most reassurance it can handle. "If he's relapsing, you're not alone in this. We're going to help you take care of him."

Ryke nods to himself, trying to believe this.

I want to add, *You didn't fail your brother.* But it sounds trite and cliché. But it's also true.

"That's not all," Rose says, her voice slightly shaking.

Fuck.

She heads over to the mattress and picks up Savannah's camera. It's Lily.

Whatever's on there—it has to do with her sister.

We lock eyes for a second before she adjusts the screen, the volume and the playback. Sometimes I feel as though Lily and Lo are the heart of us all. When they go down, a force inside of us slowly decides to break. It's a painful reminder that we're all human; we all have foibles and no matter how hard we think we're keeping ourselves together—it's other people that can hurt us the most.

Love is an asshole. Or a bitch. I wonder how long we've been fighting each other.

I watch the screen as Rose hits the "play" button.

Lily and Lo are at a bookstore—a rarity for them. Usually they're holed up in their rooms or they hide out at Loren's office, where he's trying to build a publishing company for comic books and graphic novels.

I watch as Lily pulls Lo into the *public* bathroom.

Shit.

They have rules based on Lily's recovery plan. No public sex is one of the big ones. Savannah films from outside the door, but the audio picks up their voices from the microphones they wear underneath their clothes.

"Everyone is staring," Lily whispers.

"You're a sex addict and I'm an alcoholic," he reminds her, *"and the whole world fucking knows it. We have to get used to people staring, love."*

There's a long moment of silence before Lily asks, "Can I give you a blow job?"

I glance up at Rose, who still holds the camera. Her yellow-green eyes pierce me with an internal rage. I wrap an arm around her shoulder, so rigid she might as well be a marble statue.

Lo doesn't exactly answer Lily. But noises emanate from the bathroom. Sucking. Slurping. Groaning comes soon after.

Rose turns off the camera. "That lasts for thirty minutes," she says coldly. "*Thirty minutes*, Richard. He knows better."

"And your sister is innocent in all of this, of course," Ryke snaps. "She shouldn't have asked him to have sex in the first place!"

Rose squares off with him like they've been tapped in to battle for their respective siblings. "Lily has been doing really well—"

Ryke lets out a dry laugh. "That's doing well?" He points to the camera. "She might as well have jumped on his—"

"She's dealing with a lot of anxiety," Rose cuts him off. "Her entire sex life and addiction has been put up for public mocking. Let's see how you handle thousands of people calling your dick a disease-infested wasteland."

"She's clean," Ryke refutes. "She knows it. *We* all know it." He motions around the room. "What other people say shouldn't fucking matter."

"She's trying to be stronger!" Rose screams at him, her nose flaring. I walk forward and touch her waist to calm her, but she only moves out of my hands. "Your brother, however—"

I cover her mouth with my palm. She grips my wrist to try to pry it off, but my force keeps her head in my possession. She's not going anywhere or saying anything that will turn this situation from bad to unmanageably shitty.

"Enough," I say calmly. Both of them fall into silence. Well, Rose is being forced into it, but her shoulders thankfully begin to relax, less on the defensive. "When you two compete over who has the better sibling, we accomplish nothing. They're both fucked up. Leave it at that."

"They shouldn't be together," Ryke declares. It's a statement he throws out almost every time the three of us have these little talks about Lily and Lo.

Rose politely slaps my arm this time instead of just tearing at it. So I release her.

"You break them up and see what happens," Rose threatens, peeling a piece of hair off her lips. We could do it. We're the oldest of our so-called group, and it wouldn't be hard to force Lily and Lo to separate for a couple years. I think we all consider it for about five minutes before we realize what that means.

They love one another deeply. And the only reason they're still trying to be healthy is for each other. Take that support away and they might as well be slaves to their addictions again.

Instead we sit for hours discussing alternative plans. Like taking both of them to a comic book convention. We did that months ago, trying to get them out of the house and out of their heads. Little things matter.

They have no clue we talk about them in detail. They'd probably feel guilty that we all care enough to obsess over their welfare.

"We don't even know if he drank the alcohol," I tell them. "It could have been Lily or . . ." I shake my head at the thought. "Production."

"They wouldn't," Ryke says, his eyes dark. "If they fuck with their addictions, I'm done. I'm fucking off this show and they can fucking kiss my ass."

I swear I become stupider when I hear curse words strung together.

"The only way we'll know is if we ask Lily and Loren," I tell him.

"They'll lie. You think they want the three of us shoving our disapproval and disappointment down their throats?"

"So let's not even ask," I say with a casual shrug. "Let's just act like they're two dishonest, despicable addicts who don't deserve to explain their side of the story."

Ryke narrows his eyes at me. "You know what, I'm fucking glad that production has been editing you into a giant fucking prick. Because this . . ." He waves his hand. Ryke becomes *overly* animated with his body gesticulations whenever he's angry. A huge part of me wants to tie him up just so he stops. ". . . is the most annoying shit I have to deal with in my fucking day."

I have so many rebuttals to that, but provoking Ryke takes time. Which I don't have right now.

"So we agree to talk to Lily and Lo?"

Ryke glowers.

"I'll get them," Rose cuts in and slides between us to leave out the door.

Thirty-four

Rose Calloway

ily and Loren take a seat on my bed, and Lily keeps shaking her head the longer Connor and I explain the situation. She finally cracks when Connor mentions the empty tequila bottle. "He would have thrown up if he drank! He's on Antabuse."

The drug is for recovering alcoholics, causing them to be ill if they ingest liquor. It doesn't curb your cravings; it's merely an incentive not to drink.

Loren stares at the ground, his eyebrows bunched in confusion.

"Are you still taking it?" Ryke asks roughly.

Lo glares. "Shouldn't you know that? You count my pills." He's acting abnormally sketchy, deflecting instead of outright answering his brother. I almost charge forward on the offensive, but Connor holds me by the waist, two firm hands on my hips.

Ryke rubs the back of his neck. "I stopped because I was trying to trust you."

"I don't know why you even ask me," Lo says angrily. "You already think I drank."

"Honestly, I don't know what to fucking think."

Connor speaks before Lo can blow up. "We can squash this really easily. We haven't seen you sick these past couple weeks. All you have to do is show us your pills so we know that you're taking them."

"It's not your fucking body, Connor," Loren sneers. "This

doesn't affect *anyone* in the room but me and maybe Lil. I don't have to tell you shit." He stands like he's ready to leave, and Lily's face falls in confusion.

I am boiling. I am on fire. I want to punch him for being so clueless! I tear through Connor's hold on me, and I sidestep to block Loren's body from the door, outstretching my hands to either frame. "Your addiction affects *everyone* in this room. If you can't see that—"

"I see just fine," he interrupts, his voice carrying an edge that sharpens with each word. His cheekbones are so severe, his features beautiful and terrifying all at once.

"Don't be an idiot."

Lo lets out a short, bitter laugh. "That's so fucking easy for you, isn't it?" he says with malice. "Being *smart*. Miss Perfect. What do you have to worry about? Does my hair look good today? Do my shoes match my dress?"

"Lo," Connor warns.

But this doesn't stop him.

Loren watches my breathing deepen in pure rage. All I see is my sister. He said he was going to protect her, and he's enabling her again. Why the fuck would he do that? Why is the most significant person in her life her savior and her demon?

I want to hurt him so badly. He makes it way too easy to do so. That's the problem.

Lo saunters over to my neatly arranged bookshelf. "Let's see, Rose . . ." He grabs a hardback and carelessly flips through it before shaking the book by the spine. My chest caves. "How does this feel?"

Horrible.

And then he opens my manila design folders and rattles them until all the papers flutter to the floor. "Stop it!" I shout, trying to collect them, every misplaced item like a knife in my side. My anxiety pitches.

"This doesn't bother you, right?" he says. "Nothing's fucking wrong with Rose Calloway? *I'm* the idiot. I'm the fucking moron in your world who's so stupid and selfish that he would *drink* again and again."

"No . . ." I say, but my head spins so much as I rearrange the papers. My hands tremble as I reach for my sketches in charcoal, some in color.

More than a couple I drew when I was only a teenager.

He spilled part of my childhood on the floor and scrambled the years.

Thirty-five

Connor Cobalt

Rose is close to manic.

Her eyes dance wildly over the papers in distress. The last time I saw her like this, she was pacing her room, crying, shouting things that made no goddamn sense. It was after her best friend betrayed her—helping Lily cheat in Princeton behind her back and blaming it on me.

But this is so fucking different.

Because it's Loren Hale. No matter if he curses us both to hell, I can practically taste his pain that throttles his body. He says cruel things in hopes that we'll say them back and hit him.

It's that simple.

And neither Ryke nor Rose has to consult with me to learn this. We all understand him by now.

So no matter how much I want to throw Lo against the fucking wall for putting Rose in a state of distress, I can't *touch him*. I can't curse him to hell. I can't punch him in the fucking face. It's like abusing a kid that's been shit on his whole life. I'm not going to add to those bruises.

I just need to concentrate on my girlfriend, who breathes sporadically, tiny sharp gasps leaving her lips. I bend down behind her and whisper a line of French in her ear to gauge her response. She hardly pays attention, shuffling hurriedly through papers, accidentally smudging the charcoal on one. And her blackened finger-prints stain another.

She pauses in a horrific daze, and for a split second, my whole world tilts.

I make an impulse decision. I grab her around the waist from behind and lift her from the papers, most fluttering from her hands.

"No!" she screams, kicking out to try to reach them.

"Stop," I force in her ear.

She screams again, a high-pitched wail that rips out my heart.

I only want to calm her. I grip her wrists in front of her body, about to whisper to her again, but Lo interjects.

"It took you twenty-three goddamn years to finally lose your virginity." He pulls at another loose thread, this time, hitting me full force. "And you lost it to a guy that's just fucking you for your last name."

"LOREN!" I shout. My face pumps with an unbridled, irri-tated, hell-bent rage. I don't think Lo has ever seen me this upset. I want to kick him as badly as he wants to be kicked. I would *never* go after Lily the way he's going after Rose. She may be strong, but she has her moments of fucking fragility. And he's purposefully breaking her.

His face immediately falls, blanketing with an intense guilt. His mouth opens, and I worry that an apology won't be on the other end. I can't have him tearing at my girlfriend anymore today. She can't handle it.

I cut in, "*Don't.*" The word is controlled and powerful enough to quiet the room. "Give me a minute." I pick up Rose around the waist while she breathes heavily, no longer fighting me.

I glance back at Lo. He stares at the ceiling, his legs a little loose like they're going to give out on him. Ryke tries to talk to his brother, but Lo just shakes his head and stares out the window. I look for Lily, but she stays seated on the edge of the bed, rooted there with a faraway gaze.

I set Rose by a vanity in our room, placing her on the bench.

"Darling," I say, wiping her hot, stray tears. I hold her face between my hands while I bend in front of her, eye level.

She raises a shaking hand to my face, as though to say, *give* me *a minute.*

I take her hand and tenderly kiss each one of her fingers. Her eyes finally focus on me, and they soften considerably before she grips the sleeve of my shirt. I slide on the bench next to her, and she tries to hide behind my body so no one sees her splotchy face.

"It's already past," I tell her in a breathless whisper, my thumb skimming the black mascara beneath her eyes.

She once told me that as a child, she would lock herself in her closet after she fought with her mother. The arguments revolved around many things. Like her schedule for the day, being forced on a date with a boy she found repulsive, being made into a person she didn't want to be.

She'd grab an old fur coat and scream, muffling the noises in the clothes. She made sure to have her mental breakdowns in private. Even in her madness, there's still a level of control.

She takes a deep, trained breath, blowing out of her lips like she's meditating. And then she grazes my features and says, "Thank you."

My heart beats rapidly and I fight the urge to pull her away from everyone, this situation and the worries. To lock ourselves alone and find solace in silence. She frightened me tonight. I realize how easily this could have escalated. How it could have gone another way. What if it had? What if she writhed in my arms until her screams punctured the sky? What if I lost her to emotions so deep they'd swallow her whole?

I want to protect her. From everything, even herself.

Her breathing steadies, and I place a hand on her cheek and my lips linger on hers. She responds by shifting her body towards me, and my tongue encourages her lips to part. I grip the back of her head, pulling her closer.

We kiss desperately, and I draw her so near that she sits halfway on my lap.

She breaks away abruptly, her breath heavy, but at least she's breathing this time. "I'm sorry." She apologizes for making a scene, for being a handful, for having a moment of pure panic. "I'm—"

"Human," I finish for her. I tuck her hair behind her ear. "You're human, Rose. We all are."

I glance at the rest of the room. At Ryke, Lo and Lily, who waver in uncomfortable silence. We have things we need to get to, but I'm not moving until she's ready.

She holds my arm in a half-tight, half-frightened grip and nods to me.

"Let's finish this then," I say, rising with her, right by my side. Where I always want her to be.

Thirty-six

Rose Calloway

I may be calmer after Connor's short talk and reassuring presence, but no one else looks as mild-mannered. Ryke has his arms crossed over his chest, staring between Lily and Loren, who uncharacteristically start fighting.

She asked him if he drank booze. And the one question pummeled him backwards. Her words, her feelings towards him, mean more than whatever Ryke, Connor and I can say or do.

"I just . . . I don't understand why you wouldn't get your pills to prove it," she says in a small voice.

"So you're going to take their side over mine?" he chokes.

"I'm not taking sides." Her face contorts as she thinks about everything. "I just want the truth, Lo."

"I didn't drink." He shakes his head repeatedly, but his eyes redden the longer he does so, telling us a different story. "But I can't prove it. I stopped taking Antabuse months ago."

"You did what?!" Ryke shouts.

Lo touches his chest in defense. "They were driving me nuts! I'm paranoid about everything I eat—if it's accidentally cooked in alcohol. I picture myself puking from a shitty fucking meal. I can't do that for the rest of my goddamn life!"

Before his brother can respond, Lo turns his attention back to Lily. "You have to believe me," he says, desperation lacing his voice.

"I do," she says, no hesitation.

Relief floods his face. He walks to the bed and reaches for a hug.

But then something strange happens. Lily pushes Loren in the chest and then she points her finger at him. "But it's not okay. It's not." Her chin quivers and she tries to gather this shadowy strength that likes to flit away from her. "You can't stop taking them just because it drives you nuts. And it's not okay that you kept this from me . . . from *us* . . ."

They're both crying now, and it feels intrusive watching them fight like this.

"My chest is on fire," I tell Connor. I really want to leave. But we still have to talk to Lily about the videotape.

He rubs my back and kisses my temple.

It feels good. To have him. In these moments, I can't imagine reverting back to being alone. I would feel outnumbered and unspun.

Loren holds my sister in his arms. Or maybe she's holding him. It's hard to tell.

"We're in a fight, just so you know," she whispers. "I'll sleep in Daisy's bedroom."

His face twists in hurt now. "You haven't had sex in three days. I was going to . . ." He drifts off as Lily shakes her head.

"I don't care about sex. I care about you being healthy and not drinking."

I'm grinning. I can't stop it. It's fucking happening. My chest lifts. Doused with water. Those words *I don't care about sex* have never left that girl's mouth.

Loren looks just as surprised, just as in awe as I do.

"We have another issue," Ryke interjects.

I glare hatefully. "We don't have to bring that up now," I say. My sister just denounced sex, the compulsive, harmful kind. We should throw her a party, not question her about the alleged bathroom blow job.

Ryke looks at me like I lost brain cells and then grabs the camera. "Watch this," he tells Lily and Loren.

They stand behind the camera as the footage replays, and Lily's cheeks redden the further along. When we all hear her say, "Can I give you a blow job?" her eyes bug, and her hand shoots to the air like she's ready to answer a question in class.

"I was having a bad day," she defends.

"Shhh," Loren hisses, his eyes narrowed at the camera. The moaning and groaning begin and Lily suddenly shares his confusion. "What is this?" Lo asks. "Is this some kind of fucked-up joke?"

"You tell us," Ryke refutes. "You're fucking in a public bathroom in the middle of the afternoon."

"*Nooo*," Loren says the word slowly. "We didn't fuck in the bathroom. We don't fuck anywhere but our bedroom. Someone must have tampered with the video."

"So you didn't ask to give Loren a blow job?" I question my sister.

Her rash-like flush spreads to her neck and arms. "I did do that . . ." she mutters.

"And then I told her no," Loren adds. I don't know what to believe. I want to put faith in them, but the evidence is convincing. How does a person even edit a video on the actual camera? It's not as if we're watching the footage from a computer.

"What were you actually doing for thirty minutes in the bathroom?" Connor asks casually. His questions always seem less like an interrogation and more like a conversation.

Ryke and I fail on that front.

"I was giving Lily a pep talk," Lo explains.

"I needed one," she agrees. Her eyes flicker to his in gratitude, but then she must remember her earlier declaration because she takes a step to the side to put distance between them. "We're still in a fight."

Loren's throat bobs at her words. "I'm going to start taking Antabuse again, Lil," he whispers.

"Good," she says with a nod. Then she looks to Ryke. "Fast-forward to the end. When we come out of the bathroom, I know I'll look disappointed."

Ryke presses a button and the footage speeds up, when he hits play, we all wait in anticipation, as if this is the only piece of evidence we have left.

On screen, Lily and Lo exit the bathroom, and before anyone says a thing, Lily goes, "Ah-ha!" She points to the footage. "I look *so* upset."

I frown and bend closer to the screen. She needs her eyesight checked. I put my hands on my hips as I lean further. Really, what is she looking at? All I see is Lily's flushed face and her hand in Lo's. Their demeanor is natural, almost content.

"That's you disappointed?" Ryke says in disbelief. "You're sweating and your face is red."

"It was hot in the bathroom," Lily defends.

"It was," Loren agrees, but his voice has changed. Where Lily is frantic, Lo looks resolute, as if he's accepted the fact that this looks bad for them.

"Are they going to air this?" Lily wonders.

"Probably," Connor says, "but it helps promote your wedding. The bad edit would be you slipping into the bathroom with another guy."

"We're just concerned about your health," I say.

"I didn't have sex, Rose," Lily tells me with pleading eyes. "I'm doing better. I mean, I shouldn't have asked Lo that . . . that question. But besides that, I'm doing better."

I have to trust her. I know this.

But if Lily didn't blow her boyfriend in a public restroom and if Loren didn't drink, then there's only one other guilty party.

Production.

Scott Van Wright.

I'm going to kill him.

Thirty-seven

Connor Cobalt

I convinced everyone to keep their production-tampering suspicions to themselves. If we give production a reaction, they win. They all agreed after a few hours, but Rose, Ryke and Loren have short fuses. It's only a matter of time until one of them detonates.

Five days later and I have other obligations to attend to. Like an apocalyptic dinner with my mother and my girlfriend.

I wait for Rose in my limo, which hugs the curb. The townhouse is lit by bulbs in the dining room, flickering through the windows. Our home is also guarded by her father's hired security. I'm about to call her to see what's taking so long. I doubt she'd want to be late the first time meeting my mother. If I could, I'd drive this limo past the restaurant and into a hotel or Rose's office. Anywhere to avoid the chaos of the night.

Rose has expressed about twelve times in the past three hours that she wants to impress my mother. The confession nearly had me laughing. Rose Calloway wants to *impress* someone, a feat she has never been a hundred percent successful in. But for some reason, I feel like if she fails this time, I'm partially to blame. Katarina is *my* mother after all.

My phone pings before I call her.

Daisy, Lily, me—Rose

My eyes narrow at the list. We started playing *Fuck, Marry,*

Kill again on the plane. And when I gave her three inanimate objects, she almost whipped out her pepper spray and used the whole canister on me.

She's been simmering. Waiting for a chance to get me back.

She definitely has.

I cringe as I try to find a suitable answer without offending anyone.

And then I press send.

Thirty-eight

Rose Calloway

I'd fuck, marry and kill you.—Connor

Oh. He is not getting out of this one that easily. He made me admit to fucking a tree, killing an orange and marrying a book. He is not cheating. *I* didn't.

With the phone in one hand, I struggle to text him back and snap my high heels at my ankles. My old silver peep-toes betrayed me today. The heel broke when I walked down the stairs, so I've had to hurry for an alternative, which happen to be black heels with too many buckles.

"LILY!" I shout.

After a long pause, she says, "I'M NOT COMING OUT!"

I purse my lips. I forgot. Loren and Lily have been isolating themselves in their room for three days and counting. They're waiting for Scott to apologize for the *Magic Mike* ploy and generally every vile comment he's made to Lily. I think what finally tipped the boat was when he told her to *go suck a cock* with Lo right there. Just to start a fight.

Instead of attacking Scott, they're both hoarded in their rooms, outsmarting him. He's not getting *any* footage with the couple unless they have to sneak to the bathroom. I don't know how they're eating because neither I nor Ryke will feed into this crazy plot.

Being isolated from us is a way to fester their addictions. I don't like it, but I can't coax them out without letting Scott win.

I *do* have a suspicion that both Daisy and Connor have been supplying them with breakfast essentials and microwaved meals. I caught Daisy with three empty bowls of cereal in her hands. And since her photo shoot for Marco Jeans is quickly approaching, I highly doubt she's eating that much.

And I can't call Daisy down here either. She's not at the townhouse. I've seen her for maybe three hours total in the past two weeks. That's how busy she's been with school and modeling. I asked the guards when she got in last night and they said 3 a.m.—riding home from New York. The perks of being wealthy: we have a family driver that each of us can use if we want, so no one has to worry about her sleeping or drinking at the wheel. But it hardly helps diminish the other concerns I have for my little sister.

Savannah points her camera at me, and she gives me a look like she wishes she could help me with my heels. I asked all of the cameramen to kindly stay behind while Connor and I go see his mother, who does not want to be filmed. They've all graciously accepted, and Connor had a guard sweep the limo to make sure there weren't any hidden cameras.

Besides Savannah, the only one in the living room is Ryke. He drinks a bottle of water, his hands chalky from climbing some mountain.

I'm not joking.

He does it for fun. No ropes. No harness. He's as crazy as my little sister.

"Ryke," I say with the fakest girly voice I can muster. "Can you please come help me?" I feel like I just choked on a steak bone.

He nods, and I forget that he's not his brother. He's not going to put up a fight with me. Thank God. I don't have time for that. He kneels at my feet, and before he touches my heels, I flinch back.

"What?" he asks roughly.

"Your hands, they're dirty." I crinkle my nose.

He glares as he wipes the chalk residue on the burgundy rug.

I cringe even more. My poor rug. But if I had to choose between my rug and my heels, I'm going to choose the heels every damn time.

He raises his hands to show that they're *slightly* clean. Fine. It'll have to do. I stick out my feet again, and he buckles them at the ankles while I text Connor.

I don't fuck cheaters. Send.

That should get him to speak.

My phone buzzes, but the new text isn't from him.

2 months and 13 days—Mom

"Who died?" Ryke asks.

I stare down at him with furrowed brows.

"You look upset," he clarifies, fumbling with the last buckle.

"Worry about my heels," I snap.

He shakes his head and lets out a short, irritated laugh before standing. "Finished, your highness."

I smooth my dress as I head to the door. "Thank you." See, I do have manners. "Try not to dirty the couch while I'm gone." Translation: *go take a shower.*

"Love you too, Rose," he says with a tight smile.

My lips rise as I walk outside, down the brick stairs. The limo sits on the street, and I have to pass a couple guards to get there. He better text me before then.

Like he's read my mind, he's finally made a real decision.

Fuck. Kill. Marry.—Connor

He'd fuck Daisy.

Kill Lily.

Marry me.

He barely gives me any time to think this over before he texts again. Lo, me, Ryke—Connor

Now I have to level the playing field.

And it's pretty easy to do so.

Kill. Marry. Fuck.

I send nearly the same answer as him. Now I think I'm ready to meet his mother. I take a deep breath. It can't be as hard as having to admit to fucking Ryke Meadows or hearing that your boyfriend wants to kill your closest sister.

This will be easy in comparison.

Right?

Thirty-nine

Rose Calloway

can't believe I did that," I say with wide, petrified eyes, my chest rising and falling so heavily that it feels like I'm one small step from hyperventilation. We climb back into Connor's limo after a dinner that literally lasted *ten* minutes. We didn't even order food yet. "I stooped to the level of a child."

Connor smiles, the first real smile all night. He grabs a bottle of champagne out of the ice bucket as the limo bumps along the road.

"There is nothing to celebrate!" I shout and slap his arm as he leans back next to me.

"I'm celebrating the fact that the dinner is over seventy minutes earlier than I expected." His grin overtakes his whole face.

I gape. "Your girlfriend just threw wine on your mother's *silk* blouse!"

He tries to hold in a laugh. He's unsuccessful.

"It's not funny," I deadpan. "It probably cost a fortune. Can you tell her I'll have it dry cleaned or replaced, whatever she wants?"

I haven't been this embarrassed since the sixth grade at the Smithsonian science museum. I had started my period, and to make the event even more memorable, a stupid boy pointed and told me that my Uranus was bleeding.

This might be worse though. *I* was the immature one in this scenario.

"I'll talk to her," he says calmly. I expel a breath of relief. "I'll let her know that I fully supported your decision to act like a child, and if you didn't do it, I would have."

I attack his bicep with my purse, whipping the black sequined clutch at him. "You're not helping, Richard!"

He grabs my purse and tosses it aside before I have anything to say about it. And then he passes me the uncorked bottle of champagne. "Drink," he orders.

I gladly take a swig, trying to sweep away the humiliating memories that I've created. The first two minutes had been cordial enough. She asked about Calloway Couture, and I told her that a couple department stores were interested in stocking my clothes. And then she brusquely swerved the conversation to my relationship with Connor.

She said, "While I admire your ambition, it's going to ruin my son."

"Excuse me?" I retorted, my spine arched and prepared for attack.

"He needs someone better than you by his side," she elaborated. Her dyed red hair suddenly looked animatedly devilish. I understood that she was trying to protect her son, and she happened to be a very blunt woman.

Well, so was I.

I said, "And what makes you the best judge of your son? He spent his childhood in boarding school."

"And you'd be a better judge? You're just a silly little girl," she retorted, cupping her white wine.

That line did it.

The *silly* part—saying I'm stupid. And the *little* girl. I've been called so much worse, but by her, it was like a punch-gut blow.

And I blew back. I stood up on impulse and splashed my red wine all over her cream blouse.

Her eyes went big like saucers as she sprung from her chair in alarm.

I froze.

Connor set a comforting hand on my shoulder, silently telling me it was okay.

And Katarina pursed her lips, but she didn't curse me to hell or make a bigger scene. After collecting herself, she calmly set down a napkin and pushed in her chair.

She neared us on her way out, stopping for the last word. "You think you have time for each other now, but when you both get older, you'll see." She looked me up and down. "You two continue this path, and you'll realize that something has to give. And your ambitions will always trump each other. And you, Rose, will be the one sending off your little son to boarding school. Years will pass like minutes, and it will be too late before you realize you've missed *everything*."

With this, she passed me and Connor to reach the door.

That woman was so full of regrets, and her words suddenly seemed less like insults and more like warnings. My cheeks burned. They still do. I feel so *stupid*. Like the little girl that she called me.

"She hates me," I say, pinching the bridge of my nose after I chug the champagne.

He steals the bottle from my hands. "She hates herself more," he replies. "She's been really nostalgic lately. You just caught her at a bad time."

"If I gave up my profession for you, would she like me more?" I ask him.

"Yes," he says. "But I would like you less. You can't please both me and my mother. You can only make one of us happy."

I narrow my eyes. I don't like this fact. I want to squash it immediately.

But he leans close, his hand beside my thigh on the leather seat, and I smell the sweet champagne on his breath. His sultry gaze rakes my body. "Don't *ever* quit Calloway Couture for me. Your drive turns me on." He kisses me roughly, his lips hard against mine. His hand rises up the length of my bare leg, slipping beneath the hem of my black dress and plummeting between my thighs.

I let out a gasp. *We're in his limo*, I remind myself.

And then his other hand falls to my neck, unfastening the thin chain.

I clutch the diamond pendant protectively. "What are you doing?"

"I'm going to play with you." He meets my eyes, and his lips curve in that arrogant smile. Instead of wanting to slap *him* for it, I only want Connor to take control of me.

He pockets my necklace and reveals another familiar piece of jewelry.

"You had the collar in your pocket the whole time?" I ask.

"Yes." He reaches around my neck and snaps it on carefully, making sure not to pinch my skin.

"Even during dinner?" I say, aghast. His mother was there! . . . briefly.

He squeezes my chin between his fingers. "It's a necklace, not a vibrator."

"It's a *collar*, Richard," I rebut.

"And it looks beautiful on you."

I go quiet more at the way he's staring at me than his words. His deep blue eyes consume my features like he wants to fuck all of them. An ache fills me, and as it builds, he places a strong hand on my back and forces my stomach to the leather seat.

I sit up on my forearms and my knees. His movements are so fast and domineering. In a matter of seconds, he hikes up my dress, rips off my panties and kneels behind me, his pants at his thighs, his boxer briefs down. His cock hard and exposed.

Fuck . . . me.

Before he pushes in, he rubs my ass and dips his fingers towards the spot between my legs. "What do you say?" Connor asks.

I smile into the leather. "Please, sir?" I nearly laugh at the words.

He smacks my ass so hard that tears crease the corners of my eyes.

"Don't call me sir, *smartass*," he reminds me sternly, no humor to his voice. I turn to see his face, to check if his eyes say the same. But he grabs me by the collar and forces my face straight.

Fine.

Be that way, *Richard*.

"What do you say?" he asks again, more huskily this time. He lets out a low groan as he edges closer to me. And he drops his hold on the collar so he can massage my breast, lowering my dress so I'm free for his touch.

When he pinches my nipple, I gasp again.

"*Rose . . .*"

I swallow. "Please . . . fuck me," I beg. I check to see if the privacy screen is still up in the limo. Yes. Thank God. Gilligan, his driver, has no view of this. But I wonder if he can hear my voice pitch high while my mouth opens in a giant O.

Connor is doing a number on my breast with one hand while his fingers rub my clit with the other. And then his fingers dive into me, filling me so much, and the short plunges try to catapult me into the door.

He scoots me back so I stay a safe distance away from it. And he grips one of my shoulders to fix me to this place.

His motions are decisive, hard and unrelenting.

"Connor!" I cry. He fucks me with his hand so fast that it's not long before my eyes flutter, and I feel myself clench around him. The high is there—in sight. At the top of the hill. Just a few more—

He stops.

Pulls his brilliant fingers out. Every part of me, mind and body, pleads and aches for him.

I think I hate him now.

"I know you're glaring and I can't even see your eyes," Connor tells me. "Would you call that intuition or magic?"

Well, Connor doesn't believe in magic. If Hogwarts actually existed I'm sure they'd send an owl to shit on his head.

"I'm sorry," I say rather than answering the question. I try to relax my face.

And then his long, hard cock barrels into me. *Holy* . . .

My arms weaken beneath me and I moan into the seat, biting the leather at one point. *Fuck* . . . *fuck* . . .

My thoughts have been fucked into submission—only curse words pass through.

Fuck . . . *me* . . .

He holds on to the crease of my hips and ass as he slams into me from behind. Thank God, not *in* the ass. I am nowhere near ready for that.

His breathing is more controlled than my ragged gasps. But he lets out deep, satisfied groans that vibrate my core. Each thrust against my body jellifies my limbs until I am being supported only by his hold around my waist.

Fuck . . . *ahh* . . . *fuck, fuck, fuck* . . . "Connor!"

And then the driver turns sharply, and my whole body jerks forward with the car, my head slamming into the door handle. Hard. My vision darkens to black for a split second before dots flicker in my eyes.

"Dammit," I barely hear Connor curse.

I'm disoriented from the climax and the cranial impact.

I gather my senses when I'm in his arms, on his lap, his boxer briefs and pants back up on his waist.

"Rose, Rose." He snaps in my eyes. "Look at me. Rose!" His

head spins to the privacy screen. "Gilligan, we're going to the hospital!"

What?

"No," I say softly, finding his gaze and trying to meet it clearly. I blink a few times. "I'm . . . okay. Just let me . . ." I touch my head, a knot swelling. I wince. Lovely.

Connor inspects the spot with concern tightening his eyes. "I'm sorry," he immediately apologizes. He rubs my arm and holds me tenderly, like he's trying to mend his favorite toy that he dropped on the ground. The possession feels good. Because it means he's not going to leave anytime soon, and that he won't ever hurt me. On purpose, that is.

"It's not your fault. It was an accident."

He grimaces at that word. "I'm not a child who wet the bed. This is serious."

"Adults have accidents."

"You were unconscious for a few seconds, Rose." He carefully slips my dress back over my shoulders, covering my breasts. The tender affection is a side of him that I dearly love. "I should have held you tighter." He lets the pain pass through his features. Maybe he doesn't care if I see his emotions anymore. "Gilligan," he calls again. "The hospital."

The driver's voice sounds through the limo's speakers. "Already on the way, Mr. Cobalt."

"I'm okay," I say again, "just dizzy."

"I still want to get you looked at." He places two fingers on my neck, checking my pulse. He studies my features with a focused gaze.

"What are you doing, Richard?" I ask softly. I blink a couple more times to keep his face in my line of vision.

"Making sure you're fine."

"You're my doctor now?" I ask. "How inappropriate. You're sleeping with your patient."

He smiles only when he's satisfied by the tempo of my breathing and all the other parts of me that he was examining.

I know what's in his heart.

And if he didn't love me, he wouldn't care so deeply. I just wait (rather impatiently) for the day when he can admit it to himself. If it never comes, then at least I'm smarter than him, able to see something he's blind to. I'll take that win if it's all he'll give me.

I rest my head on his chest while the limo speeds down the road. Connor strokes my hair, keeping a trained eye on any bad signs in my movements.

"I feel safe with you," I tell him, "even if you let me bowl into four car doors."

"There won't be a second, third or fourth," he whispers, his lips beside my ear. His hot breath tickles my skin. "It won't happen again, I promise."

Promises from Connor Cobalt are like oaths spilled in blood.

Translation: *I will die for you.*

I smile widely.

I will die for you.

That will never get old.

Forty

Connor Cobalt

1 month and 20 days—Mom

I read the text on Rose's phone after it buzzes on the desk. She's downstairs cleaning the kitchen with Daisy. It was taco night, which meant the entire place exploded in cheese and chips, only adding to Rose's neurotic hysteria.

I'd be helping if it wasn't for this damn term paper. I can almost see the finish line for the first semester, but papers and finals stand in my way. I doubled my Adderall dosage last week just to concentrate.

The door swings open, and I swivel my chair to watch Rose walk into the bedroom. She glares at Brett, who stands in the hallway. "I'm in the no-film zone. Run along, now." She waves him off and then shuts the door. She'd never be as rude to Ben or Savannah, but Brett and Rose get along about as well as her and Lo.

When she turns to face me, I notice a . . . bulge where her breasts are. No wonder Brett followed her up here.

Curiosity compels me to my feet, and I cross the room to Rose. "Something's a little off about you," I say, and my eyes drift up to her hair as if I'm focusing on her nonexistent bangs.

I reach towards her breasts, and she slaps my hand away.

"I'm a lady," she chides. "I don't let boys touch me there."

Fuck. My cock stirs at her words. I grab her waist and pull her body against mine in one swift motion. She sucks in a sharp breath when her hips knock into me. She's still in her five-inch-fucking-heels. Almost the same height as me, a few inches off.

"What about men? Do you let them touch you?" I ask, holding her tight.

"Definitely not." Her eyes drift to my mouth.

I lick my bottom lip, moving my tongue slowly, as I watch her chest inflate with the motion. I slide my hand up her leg, her thigh, between them—her lace fabric already wet to my touch.

"And here?" I ask.

"Never," she says in a whisper.

When she's sufficiently distracted with my hand, I take the opportunity and reach down the top of her dress, grabbing whatever's hidden in her bra.

"Hey!"

I already have the baggy in my possession, and I hold it above her head.

She doesn't make a pass to retrieve it, just pushes me in the chest for tricking her. I'm too fixated on her contraband to respond.

"Why do you have a bag of marijuana?" And *where* did she get it? Four messily rolled joints fill the plastic. The papers don't have neat creases, which means that Rose didn't roll them. It takes her two hours just to meticulously fold her panties and place them in her drawer.

My eyes fall to her with interest.

She stays quiet, twisting her diamond necklace in her fingers.

"Care to explain?"

"I thought we could do something different tonight . . ." she says. "I usually don't try new things, and with you . . ." She trails off, lost for words. This must annoy her, because she rolls her eyes.

"I accept," I say instantly.

Her eyes brighten in surprise. "Really?"

I nod, willing to try anything with her. I want her to experience as many firsts with me as she possibly can. I've smoked only once—my first and only foray into illegal drugs. It was strategic. Boarding school. Trying to gain a connection I needed for Student Council.

"On one condition," I reply. "You tell me who gave these to you."

"Daisy." She doesn't even hesitate. "If I have the drugs, then she doesn't have them. They're much safer in my position." She grins.

Devious and intelligent. I like this side of her.

My face suddenly falls as I remember something important.

I'm on Adderall.

And I'm not a hundred percent positive it's safe to smoke pot on the stimulant. The small percentage of doubt is not something I'm willing to live with. I'll never forgive myself for impairing my brain or my body over something so stupid.

"What's wrong?" She touches my arm in concern.

The one question makes me frown even deeper. I'm getting worse at hiding my emotions from her. Or maybe . . . maybe I just don't care if she's sees this part of me anymore.

For the first time, I really want to be honest with her.

Not just my half-assed attempt at honesty. I want her to know me as well as I know myself. So I prepare to admit the one thing that could cause her to storm out, pack her bags, sleep in Daisy's room and maybe even sling my clothes out the window.

"I'm on Adderall." I let it go. One sentence. One breath.

She drops her hand from my arm, and her *I'm-going-to-rip-your-dick-off* glare heats her eyes. "Bullshit," she says. "You would *never* take Adderall."

"I wouldn't," I agree. "But I was losing sleep, and I wasn't putting a hundred percent into Wharton or Cobalt Inc., so I decided to start taking it."

"For how long?" Her collarbones sharpen as she holds in a breath. I remember what Frederick once told me when I was only eighteen and I thought I was finished discovering who I was and what I wanted to be. He said, *Lies tear at relationships until they're nothing but unwound threads.*

I hate that my own has begun to unravel.

I hate that, in this moment, I am ordinary.

"The end of January."

"Almost four months," she says, dumbfounded. But she doesn't attack me, doesn't throw up her hands and call it quits. Her eyes are on the ground as she thinks it over.

"You would've given up something if you didn't, right?" she asks, her eyes flitting to mine, so many questions swimming in them.

"Not you," I tell her. "I would have never given up you."

"Wharton?"

I nod, and she shakes her head in dismay. "I don't want you to choose me over your dream," she says. "But I can't stand here and be okay with you choosing me over your health."

It's not fair for me to put her in a position, to trap her into giving me an ultimatum. I know what I have to do. Even if the semester is almost over, I still have a year and a half left. I'm not even close to graduating and earning this final degree.

I notice the space between us. Five feet away. Five feet too many. I imagine that space so much further if I make the wrong decision right now.

Frederick is right.

My mother is right.

I can't have everything. So I'm going to have to fucking choose.

"I'm withdrawing from Wharton." I deliver the lines with finality. It hardly topples me backwards. It doesn't even make me sway. In fact, a weight rises off my shoulders—a heaviness that I didn't even know was there before. Dragging me down.

It's not as earth-shattering as I once believed it would be. Sometimes the dreams you construct for yourself at ten, twelve years old aren't the same ones you thought they would be at twenty-four. And it just takes a while to finally make peace with that.

I think I just have.

"Connor—"

"I'm going to quit taking Adderall." I step towards her and place my hands on her shoulders.

"Your MBA—"

"I don't need it."

"You never needed it," she reminds me. "That's not why you were trying to get one." I see the guilt in her eyes. I've chosen her over my dream, and I told her never to do that for me.

I cup her face with my hand, skimming her bottom lip with my thumb, her lipstick a dark red that makes her look as fierce as she is. I want to be with her every day of my life. I want to be here, not in class. And I have the means to do so.

"My dreams have changed," I say. The future I once imagined is gone. Where I proudly accept my diploma, where I prove to myself that I'm the best because I can be. The longer I've been with this girl, the faster it's flitted away.

I kiss her deeply, and she reciprocates in reply, silently telling me that she's accepting my decision.

"That was easy," I say as we part, holding her around the waist while I stare down at her smooth skin, her cheeks reddened with blush and heat from the kiss. "I thought you would fight me harder."

She shakes her head. "You should see the look in your eyes."

I frown.

And she smiles. "You're wearing your emotions, Richard." She runs her hands over my chest, smoothing down my navy-blue shirt. "I can tell you don't care about Wharton as much as you used to, and I want you, my sisters, their boyfriends and Lo's brother to do whatever makes them happy. Isn't that the goal?"

It is for me now, but I'm not so sure it's always been that way. "Your sisters' *boyfriends*?"

Rose's nose scrunches in disgust. "Daisy is still with Julian."

"And I'm *not* happy about that," I tell her. "What were we saying about happiness?" I feign forgetfulness. "We . . . do what makes us happy." I keep her in my arms, one hand lowering to her ass, glad that five feet no longer separates us. "I'd *happily* like to remove him from your sister's life." I see the gangbanging text he sent Ryke, which worries me the most. I don't want him with her for longer than he has to be.

Rose says, "I'd happily cut off his dick and toss it into a tank of flesh-eating piranhas." She flashes a cold smile that would shrivel his balls too.

"Creative." I grin.

Rose saw the text like the entire nation did. On television. Production aired my conversation with Julian in the hallway. I thought people disliked me, but I learned it's more of a love-hate after the intense backlash Julian has received.

No one has started an online petition to have me thrown in jail.

He definitely beat me on that account.

Julian should be fired from the Marco Jeans campaign that he booked with Daisy. But the designer won't let him go. He likes the media attention, even if it's negative. So Daisy has to work with him.

I try to not think about Rose's little sister, whose life is more complicated than any seventeen-year-old's should be. And I glance down at the joints in the plastic baggy, still in my hand. I step back from Rose and pull my phone out of my pocket.

"Who are you calling?" she asks curiously.

"Frederick. I need to know if I can mix Adderall and marijuana." I put the phone to my ear.

Her face fills with surprise. "You still want to do that?"

"Yes, darling." I rub her bottom lip and kiss her once more, right before the line clicks.

Forty-one

Rose Calloway

Connor won't feel the mental sluggishness of pot, but he'll still feel the body high. At least those were Frederick's words. He wasn't pleased about the drug-mixing, but Connor put me on speaker phone, and I softened Frederick's worries, explaining how Connor just threw away his Adderall. I didn't mention dropping out of Wharton, or the fact that he took a giant immeasurable leap for me.

I'm sure they'll discuss that on Monday.

I cough into my third drag since I never learned how to smoke properly. I was too focused on my company, grades and extracurricular activities (which did not include pot) to dive into any sort of illegal paraphernalia. But I'm twenty-three. It's not too late to experiment and try new things. If I told my seventeen-year-old self that I'd be choked and spanked by my number one academia rival (and I would like it) and I'd pass a joint with him six years later—I would have *never* believed *me*.

But I think my seventeen-year-old self would be so damn tempted towards that image. I think she would want it to be true.

I watch Connor blow a line of gray smoke from his lips, not hacking up a lung like me.

I attempt to glower at him, but it loses its potency when I'm choking on air.

"Here . . ." Connor tosses a throw blanket over our heads, caging us in a man-made tent. He pinches the joint between his fingers, places it between his lips, and sucks deeply. His eyes stay on mine, and I wonder if he wants me to study him, so I can do it right next time. But he would have uttered a smartass remark about "tutoring" me.

Even so, I scrutinize the way he inhales deeply, the smoke sucking down his throat. I've never found smoking sexy—not until now, when my overly intelligent, cocky boyfriend exhales like a champion, a god, some immortal being with a grin that could light the world and create an eighth great wonder.

And I would *NEVER* say this to him. Just so we have this clear. I narrow my eyes so he can't read the high praises and exaggerations on my face. But he's near laughter, so I must be doing something wrong then. I reach for the joint, and he shakes his head. He takes another long drag, but this time, he keeps his mouth closed, holding in the smoke.

Then he grabs the back of my head with one authoritative hand. Before I blink, my lips touch his and part on command. Smoke rushes into my mouth and tickles the back of my throat. An incoming cough threatens to ruin my high once more. But Connor stifles it with a kiss, his tongue slipping into my mouth, easing the sensations. I breathe in his intoxicated air, and he takes on mine, the most intimate kissing experience I've ever been swept into. Breath for breath. Inhale, exhale.

His fingers run through my soft hair, and with his other hand, he urges me onto his lap. I straddle his waist, and yet, it feels like he's more in control of the moment than me.

It spikes my pulse with pleasure, and I swoop my arms around his neck. When our lips finally break apart, we both blow a small puff of smoke up in the air. Our grins are unmistakable.

"Let's do it again," I say, excited to finally inhale without my throat burning in refute. I sincerely thought my body wouldn't allow poison to flow through it. *Good job, body.*

"Every junkie's favorite words," he says with a playful smile.

"Weed isn't that bad," I rebut.

He takes a small hit and then blows the smoke away from my face. Our tent has filled with the thick smoke and pungent smell, hotboxing our little area. We're going to reek.

"You're right," Connor says dryly and appraises the joint. "It doesn't fry brain cells. Only kills ambition. How can that be worse?"

Anything that makes a person into a lesser version of themselves is malevolent. At least in Connor Cobalt's mind.

I'm not going to ruin this by arguing with him. "I do have one problem with it," I admit.

He raises his brows in curiosity.

"The smell," I say. "It's disgusting. Worse than cigarettes. I'm going to have to bathe in bleach."

He smiles and kisses me deeply. I love that. Drawing a man in with my opinions and words. It feels headier than enticing him with my body—though I enjoy that too.

When we part, I say, "Someone would make a lot of money if they invented odorless weed. Oh! Or perfumed marijuana!" I giggle. *Giggle.* That high-frequency girly noise is so unfamiliar. This hotbox is definitely working.

He kisses me again, silencing my laughter and filling my lungs with smoke and delight.

We stay under the blanket for a while. When I try touching my face, my hands move in slow motion, and my leg seems to take forever to shift, too sluggish to really go anywhere. So I stay positioned on Connor's lap. But when I turn my head, it speeds faster than the rest of me, like it's not attached to my body. It's a weird combination that has me in a fit for two minutes. Was it two minutes?

Connor watches me, drinking water, and when he tries to pass the bottle in my direction, I reach out and hit his elbow. I laugh again.

"Here," he says. He puts the rim to my lips and tilts the bottle up, helping me drink. The water feels good against my sandpapered throat. After wiping my lips, I become suddenly entranced by the buttons on his shirt. My fingers play with them. Wow. The buttons fit perfectly into that little hole. Such simple mathematics, and yet someone, somewhere discovered it first.

Connor says very little. I like the silence. It makes all the feelings stronger. Like how he brushes his fingers through my hair. Each part of me becomes more sensitive than the next.

"I'm hungry," I suddenly say.

"I know the solution." He scoops me up quickly, tossing the blanket aside. My heart races faster than before. He nuzzles his nose into my neck. "Time to feed you."

I laugh, his skin tickling mine as we exit the room. I don't care that we're venturing into the camera-filled house. It's not like we're smoking on camera. No one has proof of anything.

And plus, it's past Savannah, Brett and Ben's hours. They're probably fast asleep in their own homes, leaving the cameras on the walls and in the rafters to film us.

Connor descends the stairs with me in his arms. Once we reach the main level, he sets my feet on the ground. The living room is *right there*. But Lily and Lo have their backs to us on the couch, staring at the television above the fireplace mantel. They stayed barricaded in their room for a full week before Scott apologized. Which Lo said was *half-assed and insincere*, but it was enough for them to *finally* venture downstairs.

I open my mouth to speak.

"Shh," Connor whispers softly, pressing his fingers to my lips. We both smile. Why is that so funny?

We stay hidden by . . . nothing really. They can see us in the open space if they just turn around, but they're both absorbed by the movie.

"Why are we watching this?" Loren asks.

"Because you need to know why I think you're Peter Pan incarnate," Lily replies.

I'm about to laugh again. I really don't know why, but Connor covers my mouth with his hand to suppress my noises. How is he keeping me standing with just one arm?

He's strong, Rose, don't be stupid. Oh my God. Does weed make you stupid?

"And if I'm Peter Pan, who would you be? Wendy?"

"No," Lily says. "Wendy chooses mortality over the boy she loves. I would be . . ." There's a long pause, and I run my tongue against Connor's palm.

He presses his lips together, trying so hard not to laugh.

"Tinkerbell," Lily concludes. "She never leaves Pan. She loves him more than anything."

"So you're like my little fairy?" Lo asks, but I sense the adoration behind his words.

And yet, as cute as it is, Connor and I can't keep our laughter in. It bursts forth and crushes our secrecy.

Their heads spin over their shoulders, catching us beside the staircase with crinkled brows.

"What the hell are you two doing?" Lo asks with the tilt of his head, scrutinizing our positions and faces and—what else is there to look at?

"My feet," I say.

Connor has to bury his mouth into my neck to smother his next bout of laughter. Mine comes out full-force, no stopping that.

"What?" Lily squints at us in confusion.

Connor hunches over to rest his chin on my shoulder before he says, "We're eating."

Lily gasps. "Are you stoned?" She's up off the couch before I can throw out an excuse. She's not even ten feet near us and she stumbles back and pinches her nose. "*Ugh.*" She gags. "I hate that smell."

Loren wears a supreme grin. "You two . . ." He shakes his head as he sidles next to his girlfriend. "Who would have thought the most responsible people in this house are the ones who get baked? Congratulations, you officially fit in our group."

"Our friendship circle," Connor clarifies.

I erupt into another fit of laughter. Connor picks me up in his arms again, carrying me towards the kitchen and setting me right on the counter.

"Can we stay and watch?" Lily asks excitedly.

"We'll be seeing this on the next episode," Loren reminds her.

"I want the unedited version though."

Connor touches my leg. "You okay?" he asks, concerned even when he's stoned.

"I'm not paranoid. Maybe it's good weed." But as long as I have Connor, I know I could ride out a bad trip.

What a weird version of love.

And it's all mine.

Forty-two

Connor Cobalt

The living room has been cleared out. Soft padded mats line the floor. Daisy is already jumping up and down, preparing for the self-defense lessons that Ryke, Loren and I have promised the girls. I offered to hire a real instructor, but Ryke told me he was practically licensed.

I reminded him that being able to beat someone up doesn't make him a good teacher. And then he said, "Stop fucking annoying me and go light a joint."

I've been insulted far better.

Scott Van Wright aired the small segment of Rose and I giggling stupidly and devouring the leftover tacos. Since there wasn't actual footage of us smoking, the backlash from the episode was minimal. There've been too many reality stars lying in their own vomit to be shocked by two young adults in unintelligible fits of laughter.

The only downside, I looked stupid for the first time in my life.

And I don't care. It took twenty-four years to obtain this type of apathy. In college, if someone saw me as less than smart, at the bottom of the class, it felt life-ending. If they thought I was a prick, fine. If they thought I was a social climber, fine. Weird, whatever.

"Stupid" was the word that sliced me cold. Failure was the act that would leave me dead.

In one day, I had failed Wharton. Failed my "supposed" dream.

And then I did something that made me into a stupider version of myself.

And today, I can say, *I don't care*, and mean it.

I'm twenty-four years old. I always thought I was done growing up. But being with Rose has made me grow into the version of myself that I love the most.

My fears are no longer so selfish and so pretentiously vain.

Rose tells me, "If I'm being attacked, I'm taking out my pepper spray and Taser. I won't use my fists first. That's a last resort."

"What if you don't have time for all of that?" I ask her. I can't help but smile every time I eye her clothes. No tennis shoes. No yoga pants or T-shirt. She chose wedges, leather shorts and a white cotton top, tucked in like she's about to attend a lunch meeting. Loren told her to go change, and she looked like she wanted to rip off his face.

I know better.

"Not all paparazzi are despicable," she says. "I'm sure someone would have a moral bone and help me against angry hecklers."

"What if the paparazzi aren't around?"

She holds up her finger. "One time," she tells me. "Only one time in the past four months have I been *alone* in public. And that was when Lily drove down five wrong streets in a row."

"Hey!" Lily speaks up. She's on the ground in proper workout clothes like Daisy. Only she wears her furry white cap that's more suited for the snow than warm, mid-May weather. It has tusks and apparently it's something called a Wampa from *Star Wars*. The only reason I can see her wearing it is Loren. Every time he glances her way, his breathing deepens and his amber eyes glaze in desire, looking ready to mount her.

Lily stands to her feet, abandoning whatever move Loren was trying to show her. "I only drove down the wrong streets because the GPS was in French."

Rose gives her a look. "You were the one who put it in French."

"Only because I'm trying to learn the language," Lily explains, "so that I can know what the hell you two talk about behind our backs."

Last episode was the first time they aired us speaking French to each other. Production included subtitles.

Our conversation revolved around Lily and went something like this on TV.

ROSE: She's losing weight. I can see her ribs.
ME: That's a shadow.
ROSE: It's not a shadow. It's her skeleton.
ME: I have a physics book upstairs. I'm sure it talks about light and shadows. Do you want it?
ROSE: Why would you have a physics book? You're a business student.
ME: For moments like these.

It was one of our more calm exchanges in French, but Lily wasn't amused by the fact that we were discussing her weight—right in front of her.

Apparently they all thought that we just argue about "smart people" things (Lily's words) and that we have a rule to not talk about them in French.

I do have a rule.

If you want to understand me, learn my language.

Ryke and Daisy don't seem to care that we could have talked about them, but Lily and Loren are aggravated.

"And just so you know," Lily says, "I can say five whole words in French already. So at this rate, I will be fluent in no time."

Daisy walks over after jumping up and down. "Didn't you fail Spanish and Latin in prep school?" she asks with a smile.

"That's a mute point," Lily defends. "Those aren't even the same languages."

Rose gives me *another* look, but I can't stop myself. "Moot point," I correct her.

Lily stares at me, dumbfounded. "What?" Loren wraps his arms around her waist as she explains, "It's mute. Like it doesn't make a sound, so it doesn't matter."

"It's moot," I repeat. "I assure you."

Rose elbows me, and Lily's eyebrows bunch in even more confusion.

"No one likes the fucking grammar police," Ryke tells me.

"That's scary coming from a guy who used to write for the city's newspaper in college," I say. "Did your editor hate you?"

He flips me off.

"Wait." Lily holds up her hands. "What's a *moot* then? That's not a word."

"It doesn't matter," Rose says quickly and waves me off.

"It does," I refute. "I want to educate your sister."

Rose punches me in the arm and then points. "That's for your indirect insult. She's not stupid." I open my mouth to speak and she punches my arm again. "And apparently you need self-defense lessons. You don't seem to be doing a lot of defending."

She goes to punch me again and I grab her fist in my hand.

Her lips purse. "Fine."

I just notice Ben, Brett and Savannah circling us when they start to flock Ryke. I look around for Scott, but I realize he must be locked in his room. Working. He's shifted his tactics once again. No longer annoying the Calloway girls as much as he used to. He's been almost absent for the past two weeks. I don't know if this house is making me more paranoid, but I keep thinking he's up to something. I just haven't determined what he could possibly do to me without physically taking Rose. He's already failed at that. So what's left in his arsenal?

Rose and I look over as Ryke tosses his shirt to his side. He has better lean and defined muscles than both Lo and me. We'll both admit that because we're not the ones ascending mountains with our bare hands every other day.

"I didn't know this was naked self-defense class," I quip.

Lo laughs. "Damn, you beat me to that one."

Ryke glares. "No one fucking hit my right shoulder. It's off-limits." That's all he says in reply. But we know what he's talking about. He's spent over a month getting an intricate tattoo. One of the most popular episodes was when Daisy went with him for company. It was one of her few free days, and Rose and I both noticed she chose to spend it with Ryke of all people.

Princesses of Philly aired about fifteen minutes of "did Daisy get a tattoo with Ryke or didn't she?" until they revealed the answer at the end.

She's tattoo-free.

Her mother would have killed her if she marked her body, which is pivotal in furthering her modeling career. And Samantha would have also found a way to destroy Ryke, probably by throwing him in jail for some ridiculous charge. I have no doubt about this, which is why I've been cautioning Ryke to stay away from Daisy until she's older.

But he's a masochist; I swear he does things he knows will hurt him in the end.

We all stare at his finished tattoo. A phoenix with wings in shades of red, orange and yellow engulfs his right shoulder and chest, the feet near his abs. A gray and black chain is wrapped around the ankles of the bird, and it descends down his side, an anchor inked at his hip.

Lo shakes his head. "At least you didn't get a tribal tattoo."

"Fuck off," Ryke says. He stretches an arm behind his head and ignores our stares and the three cameras.

I tilt my head. "You did make sure the needle was wrapped and sterile?"

"I'm not a fucking idiot."

"Well, when you say it like that, I believe you more," I deadpan.

"I think it's hot," Daisy chimes in. She grins impishly while everyone (except me) groans. "What?" she laughs.

"That's my brother, and you're like my little sister," Lo says with a disgusted look. "Just, *no*."

Ryke's jaw hardens, not saying a word. He just grabs his shirt off the floor and puts it back on.

"Thanks for that strip tease, *bro*," Lo says.

Ryke shoots him the middle finger.

But I watch his eyes meet Daisy. Her bright grin has already completely vanished. I didn't catch the moment when the humor left her, but maybe Lo's comment did the trick.

Ryke and Daisy stare at each other for a long moment that's filled with words I can't hear and things I can't read. I almost look away, irritated by this lack of knowledge.

Then Daisy mouths *sorry* to Ryke.

"Just don't hit my arm, okay?" he tells her. "It still fucking hurts."

Her lips slowly rise.

"I know how to defend myself." Lily suddenly makes a giant proclamation. She's been in Lo's arms, but she steps out and raises her hand at him, giving him the Vulcan salute from *Star Trek*. When we went to a comic book convention, Rose didn't know what it was named, and Lo chastised her when she called it the "Spock thing."

While Lily continues to part her fingers in a V shape, Lo looks at Lily like he wants to kiss her and block the rest of us out.

No one says a thing, and we have our brows raised, standing still like *what the hell?*

"See," Lily says. "Everyone's too confused to attack."

And then Lo playfully grabs her wrist. He leans down and

sticks his tongue through the gap between her fingers, making a crude gesture. With her hand and his mouth.

The cameras veer off Ryke and pin on Lily and Lo.

Lily gasps and punches him in the shoulder. "You just desecrated the Vulcan salute!"

He wraps his arms around her hips with a grin. "Yeah? Who does the Vulcan salute while wearing a *Star Wars* hat? You ruined it first." He rubs her head with the furry white cap. And then she stands on the tips of her toes and kisses him. He grins as he kisses her back.

"Shall we get started?" I ask. Daisy just came home thirty minutes ago, and it's already one in the morning. And she arrived *earlier* than usual.

"Shhh!" Rose yells, extending her arm over my chest hysterically, her eyes ablaze as she whips her head from side to side.

Everyone frowns and goes quiet for a second.

What is she . . .

And then I hear a jiggling sound, like bells clinking together on her collar. Sadie emerges from the bottom-level stairs, not hesitating to enter the main floor like she owns this part of the house too.

Rose reaches for her pepper spray on the ground, her eyes narrowed at Sadie like she only has bad intentions.

But the worst reaction comes from Lily, who apparently was "haunted" by Sadie last week in her bedroom. She said she'd wake up and Sadie would just be sitting there, watching her sleep. It was so ridiculous that I started crying in laughter when she told me.

"Ohmygodohmygod," Lily says. I think I heard her say *demon* once or twice, but she slurs her words together in a frantic state. She starts running in circles around the living room, looking for a place to hide, but we pushed all the couches and chairs against the wall. The space is open for Sadie to find her.

And my cat lets out a low hiss the longer Lily makes jarring, spastic movements.

Daisy tries to reach out and collect Sadie in her arms, but Ryke pulls her away instantly, drawing Daisy to his chest. The last time she attempted to grab my cat, Sadie raked her leg, three long claw marks bled, and her mother had a fit, shouting at me for at least an hour at a Sunday luncheon. I actually sold Sadie after that, but I came home the next day and found that Rose and Daisy went out of their way to buy her back.

For as much as I like my cat, I care about these women more.

Lily sprints around until she finds a solution. She climbs on Lo like a monkey, crawling up his back while he struggles to contain his laughter and keep her from falling. With her furry hat and bugged eyes, she truly looks like some kind of gangly animal.

"I'll take her downstairs," I tell everyone.

"If we can't protect ourselves from a cat, then what hope is there left for us?" Daisy says dramatically, a bright, playful smile spreading back across her face.

"I can defend myself," Rose refutes, shaking her pepper spray canister.

"Darling," I warn her, "we really don't need a call from PETA in the morning."

"Fuck PETA."

Shit. "Rose." I shake my head at her. This is where we're different. She can't hold her tongue when it matters.

"Someone's going to throw a bucket of red paint on you after this episode," Lo tells her. He has Lily on his shoulders, where she seems content, her legs dangling on his chest. She eyes Sadie, who saunters around the room with too much pride.

Rose looks *slightly* regretful, and I leave her side to usher Sadie downstairs. "I love animals," she says mechanically to make up for it. She smiles icily at the camera, and then adds, "And if anyone ruins one of my fur coats, I'm going to bill you and then rip out your goddamn eyeballs. Because you don't deserve to look at beautiful clothes, *ever* again."

I watch Sadie slink down the stairs while everyone laughs. I smile as I glance over my shoulder, at these people, at my friends.

I wouldn't want to miss this for Wharton.

I wouldn't want to miss this for anything.

Right here is where I'm happiest.

Forty-three

Rose Calloway

I stir to a body rocking against me, my eyes fluttering open in a half sleep.

I squint at the fuzzy morning light, and my mind starts to collect my position and what's happening: the fullness between my thighs, the hands on either side of my shoulders, the body that hovers above me with determined thrusts.

I'm still naked from last night's rough sex, and the collar is firmly snapped around my neck.

My heart quickens as I meet Connor's eyes. He watches me wake completely, making good on my *strange* fantasy that I once spilled. I always imagined I'd be aroused right off the bat, but it takes a little while to lead me there.

Connor facilitates my needs, rocking slowly to build up these electric sensations. I grip his biceps, which flex with each push inside of me. It's one of the few times I've had use of my hands during sex. When I glance down and watch the way he disappears between my legs, I feel myself start to clench around him.

He bends his head low and kisses me deeply.

I like this.

I can't believe I like this. But more than that, I can't believe he was willing to make it happen. I love him for it.

A layer of sweat glistens on our bodies the longer he thrusts.

His mouth opens as I squeeze my legs around his waist, tightening the way he fits inside of me.

"Rose . . ." he groans, his face marbleized in pleasure.

And then he pumps hard, and I turn my head into my pillow and moan, my toes curling. He slowly pulls out while we both catch our breaths. He rolls over and lies beside me, our chests rising and falling together, in unison.

Waking up to a cock thrusting into me—it's a turn-on that I can now fully admit to.

I summon my strength to meet his powerful blue gaze again. He grins, knowing exactly how much I desired this.

"Morning . . . darling," he says with his last heavy breath. He leans over and kisses me once more.

Right as he parts from me, I'm about to tell him how much I loved it, but loud *thumping* splinters my thoughts. The sounds come from the wall near our dresser, not behind us.

The *thunk, thunk, thunk* continues, and then there's the added moans and groans. I frown. "Didn't they have sex last night?" We have thin walls, and I try to ignore them as best I can.

But there is a perk to having an adjacent room to Lily and Loren. I know how much sex they're having, which means I know when Lily is regressing in her recovery.

Connor swings his legs off the bed. Completely naked, he walks over to the wall and slams his hand against it. "Hey!" he yells, but even his screams seem calm and assured. "You two, cool it!"

The humping suddenly ends, only to be replaced by a worse sound to my ears—Loren Hale's voice. (Though it's muffled from the wall.)

"We're not doing anything!"

"You had sex last night," Connor says loudly. "Only one time within a twenty-four-hour period. Remember that?"

Lo and Lily usually only wait twelve hours between fucking,

but they're trying a new rule and asked us to help enforce it if they get weak.

"Then keep *your* noises down!" Loren yells back. "My girlfriend is a sex addict. She can't be hearing you two going at it."

"I promise to be quiet," Connor says. He turns back to me, and we lock eyes. "Next time, you'll be gagged."

I narrow my gaze, but my lower body responds much differently.

Connor just smiles as he disappears into the closet to change. I don't move off the bed. I grab my binder from the nightstand and start working on my daily to-do list. I have to pick out the music for the wedding today.

1 month—Mom

One month.

It's almost here. I need a little more time, but we can't push back the date without the media howling with suspicion.

I asked Lily to help last week and she nearly burst into tears. It's too close for her.

And the televised event doesn't help. She confessed she's had nightmares about tripping down the aisle and the clip being auto-tuned and made into a viral video for YouTube.

It's hard to appease those worries.

Because I can see it happening.

Besides the wedding, I'm swamped with Calloway Couture inventory. The show has sky-rocketed my line, but this isn't the first time I've seen a spike in sales. I used to be booked for campaigns, even Fashion Week at the height of my career. My triumphs have been so up and down. Every time my line goes in a store, it gets pulled right out. I can't enjoy this sudden success, not when I know how fleeting it may be.

There is no happiness in ambition.

Only fear of losing it all or belief that it's never enough.

I wish I could settle for something less. Connor seems content without his MBA, but I don't expect the same outcome if I compromise my dreams.

And I don't know how to change what I feel.

"You okay?"

I look up from my binder and see him towering close to me. He sits down on the edge of the bed and tilts the binder in his direction to read my to-do list.

"I'm just stressed," I confess. "Too many things to do, not enough hours in the day." I wave my hand like I'm brushing off the worries. "You know how it is."

"I can help." He taps the second chore I've written down. *Reorder the ugly centerpieces that Mother picked out.* "This looks like something I'll ace."

I give him a look. "You quit Wharton," I remind him, "not to help me plan a wedding. You have a job. Go to work." I push him off our bed.

His feet hit the floor and then he snatches the binder from my lap. I give him a hard stare and he returns it. "Just so we're on the same page—I quit Wharton to be with you," he rephrases. "Not for Cobalt Inc."

I tighten my robe around my waist and stand, ignoring his admission. I motion for my binder, which might as well be my sanity at this point. "Hand it over."

He flips open the binder and scans the list once more. "I think . . ." he muses. "I'll take all the wedding responsibilities, and you can have your Calloway Couture tasks." He looks up. "Sound fair?"

"No, Richard. It sounds like you're bailing me out of my problems."

I reach for the binder and he holds it up over his head. "We're a couple. I want to bail you out of as many problems as I can. And I'm not asking for you to accept my help, Rose. You'll have it whether you agree to it or not."

I cross my arms over my chest. "What if I don't like your

taste?" I argue. "You could choose even uglier centerpieces than my mother."

He raises his eyebrows like I said something truly stupid. I let out a huff and drop my arms. Fine. He has good taste. His shampoo costs more than mine for Christ's sake.

"Consult Lily before you make the final decisions, even if she doesn't really give you a straight answer," I say. He grins, totally reveling in the win.

When his eyes fall back to the binder, his smile disappears. "Why do you have Scott's name on here?"

I don't even have to refresh my memory to know about number twenty-seven on the list. "It was a reminder," I tell him. "I wanted to ask you if Scott seemed different this past month."

"How so?" he asks. But I think Connor has his own theories; he just wants to hear mine first.

"At the beginning of the show he was a misogynistic pig, making disgusting comments and always in my face. But ever since the Alps, or maybe a few weeks after that, he's backed off. I thought maybe it was because you and I had sex. Somewhere, deep down, Scott has a sense of respect."

Connor's already shaking his head.

"Yeah, I know," I say. "It doesn't add up."

"Timing is everything," Connor tells me. "I think he's just waiting."

"For what?"

"I don't know yet."

Shivers run up my arms.

One month left.

I wonder if Scott has been waiting for the wedding. Or if he's planning on fucking something up sooner.

For the first time, I'm as nervous as I was when we first started the show.

I didn't think that was possible.

Forty-four

Connor Cobalt

"Don't do this," Daisy pleads. "I beg of you." She cups her hands together in a praying fashion as her head whips from Rose to me. She sits on the edge of her paisley green bedspread while we stand in her room, the door shut so no leering cameras can peek inside.

"We gave you three whole days to break up with him," Rose reminds her little sister. "If it hasn't happened already, it won't be happening in the near future."

The Marco Jeans campaign ended almost a week ago, which means Daisy can break up with Julian without fearing "bad" chemistry at the shoot. But Daisy has a weakness for hurting people's feelings.

I'm supposed to escort Julian out of the townhouse when we deliver the news. And I am *greatly* looking forward to it. I no longer have to be nice and put on a façade that hurts my fucking jaw. He's of no use to me anymore.

Daisy groans into her hands. "I don't want my older sister and her boyfriend breaking up with *my* boyfriend for me."

"Fine. Will you break up with him?" Rose raises her eyebrows.

"Ye—"

"Right now?"

Daisy's face drops.

"So let's lay out the facts," I interject. "Everyone in this house dislikes Julian. *You* dislike Julian. And I don't like to generalize, but I'd say a very large portion of America *hates* Julian. But you're still dating him because . . ."

"I don't like breaking up with people," she admits. "It's awkward and horrible. In all my past flings, I would just stop talking to the guy and he'd kind of go away. Julian's not like that."

Rose snaps, "If you can't break up with someone, you shouldn't be dating them."

"Okay, but still . . . I say we reconvene this powwow in a month or two. Like, chill on it until Julian gets tired and moves on."

Rose looks to me and her lips lift. "I think this might be on my bucket list. You and me, crushing the heart of my sister's disgusting boyfriend."

"Was this boyfriend on your list named Loren Hale?" I ask with a smile.

"Maybe. But we can always have an addendum."

Daisy lets out another long groan.

"If it's so embarrassing, next time don't date someone you can't break up with," Rose refutes.

"She's watching this, right?" I ask my girlfriend.

"What?" Daisy gawks, her eyes widening. "No*ooo* . . ." She draws out the word like she's coming to terms with what's about to happen.

"You'll watch," Rose says with a nod.

"And take notes," I add.

Rose turns to me, her face lighting up. "Look at us. We're already pretty good at this."

I slide my hand into hers, joining in her excitement, maybe even more than her. I see us ten years from now. The same incredible team. Only with little versions of us running around. But her fear of motherhood is another battle for another day.

"After you," I tell Daisy, gesturing towards the door.

"He's here? Right now?" She blinks in a daze.

"Yes," Rose snaps, "so reconfigure your sense of direction and make your way downstairs. Chop chop." She snaps at her sister until Daisy springs to her feet.

"Okay, I can do this . . ." Daisy says, brushing her hair off her shoulders. "I've swam with sharks before. What's so bad about listening to my sister tear the soul out of a guy?" She cringes and gives Rose a pleading look. "Go easy on him. He's already half ape, Connor said so."

I laugh when Rose glares at me. "What?" I say. "I watched him open a can of soup in the Alps by smacking it against the counter. There are tools that humans invented for such complicated tasks."

Rose shakes her head repeatedly and then she marches towards the door. "If no one is going to move their ass, then you all can follow mine."

"Fine with me, darling." But I wait for Daisy to walk ahead of me. She's the type of girl who would jump out of a three-story window for the hell of it. And we've just given her a reason to do so.

Daisy sighs and heads downstairs with Rose. In the living room, Julian waits for me to show up, thinking I've invited him over for beer—like we're friends. He sits on the couch and flips through *Rock and Ice*, a mountaineering magazine that Ryke reads.

Daisy lingers by the staircase, unable to approach the couch any further. She looks like she's about to flush a pet fish down the toilet. Ben is already sitting in one of the chairs, his camera positioned at us.

"Hey, man," Julian says with a nod, standing up. He tosses the magazine on the table.

I don't say a thing. I just head over to the couch. "You can take a seat."

He frowns, but he sits on command. Rose and I choose the loveseat across from him. She crosses her ankles and rests her hands on her knees.

"Julian," Rose says flatly. "It comes with my utmost pleasure to inform you that Daisy will no longer be seeing you, ever again."

"What?" Julian scratches his cheek, more unshaven than I last remember.

"She's breaking up with you," I clarify. "Don't call. Don't text. Don't show up on the doorstep expecting a quickie of any kind. You're done."

Julian rotates, looking over his shoulder at Daisy by the staircase. "What the fuck? Are you dumping me?"

"Hey." Rose snaps her fingers at him, and the noise draws him back towards us. "She didn't want to hurt your ugly little feelings."

Julian immediately rises. "This is bullshit." He stares at Rose's sister. "Did they put you up to this, baby?"

She's about to answer, but the front door suddenly swings open, banging against the wall. Rose and I stand up at the same time. Wild, angry voices pierce the room.

"I'm not being overdramatic!" Lily yells . . . dramatically. She carries a towering stack of magazines in her arms. Loren and Ryke push forward, past Brett and Savannah, who try to squeeze through the doorway before them.

Lily rushes into the kitchen.

This doesn't look good.

I make my way to the kitchen to deploy whatever airbags they all need to survive this crash.

Lily throws the magazines into the sink and then opens a cupboard. She pulls out a bottle of lighter fluid for the grill outside.

"Whoa!" Ryke and Lo yell in unison. They dart for her body as she squirts the liquid all over the magazines. I pry the plastic squirt bottle out of her grip, and Rose starts cleaning. She trashes all the magazines in a garbage bag before Lily has a chance to light them on fire.

Lo has Lily around the waist, and I stare at her eyes, filled with hatred and hysteria. "What's going on?" I ask her, trying to be calm so everyone else feels reassured enough to relax.

But my tactics aren't helping Lily right now. "People suck!" she screams, half crying on her words.

That explains nothing. I reach for one of the magazines in Rose's hand before she tosses it. The paper is wet, and pages stick together. I don't need to flip it open to understand the root of her anger.

The headline reads: **LILY CALLOWAY, NYMPHOMANIAC AND REPORTEDLY SLEEPING WITH BROTHERS.**

The photograph shows her walking down a street in Philly with Loren and Ryke on either side of her, which isn't uncommon, especially when everyone is concerned about the girls' safety without bodyguards.

"I don't fucking care about the rumors." Ryke extends his arms. "How many times do I have to say that?"

"I'm not a cheater! I don't even like being an alleged cheater," Lily says angrily. She points a threatening finger at the magazines. "And I hate being called a nympho!"

Nymphomania encompasses all hypersexuality, not just sex addiction. For someone like Lily, who identifies with being an addict, being labeled a nymphomaniac strengthens the debate that sex addiction is a myth.

"What do you want to do about it, Lil?" Loren asks. "Throw a tantrum in front of the cameras. Done. They've got your reaction on film."

She settles down, and her face contorts in hurt. Before Lo can share in it, I speak up. "Or you could light this on fire." I throw the magazine into Rose's trash bag. "It might be cathartic."

Lily's eyes brighten at my permission.

Rose shoots me a disapproving glare. "Don't encourage her." She lets go of the bag and holds out her hands far away from her clothes. I can smell the lighter fluid on her from here. I'm about to help her clean up, but a loud voice overtakes all of ours.

"Are you fucking serious?!" Julian yells, his nose inches from Daisy's. His hands rest beside her head on the wall, her back pinned against it.

She turns her face and winces, shutting her eyes tightly.

"Do you know the *hell* that I went through for you?!"

"HEY!" Ryke shouts, immediately sprinting over to Julian, his features darkening in a split second. Brett races beside him, whipping his camera towards an impending fight.

Rose curses and tries to turn off the faucet with her wrist, her hands dripping with water. Lo has Lily, calming her down. And as much as I want to stay and help Rose, she gives me a look that says, GO.

Crisis management #2.

The fact that we started this issue makes me want to resolve it even more. And I don't begin running until Julian slams his fist into the wall beside Daisy's head, screaming so loudly that veins protrude from his neck.

She flinches, and Ryke grabs Julian by the shoulder and slugs him in the jaw with a hard right hook. Julian stumbles back a couple steps before barreling into Ryke, trying to force him to the floor. But I grab Ryke and keep him upright from behind.

Ryke shakes Julian off him, and then hits him again in the face.

Julian curses and staggers back—further this time. He stops, breathing heavily as he touches his reddened eye.

He deserved a lot more than a fucking shiner for screaming in a girl's face. I was kind of hoping Ryke would break an arm or a leg. I'm sure Rose wanted a detached penis, but we're going to have to settle for this.

Julian looks up, his nose flaring as he glares at Daisy again. "You're just going to fucking stand there?"

"What do you want from me?" Daisy asks.

"For you to give me back *months* of my life that I wasted with you, you stupid cunt."

Instinctively, I grab Ryke by the shoulders as he tries to lunge for Julian. I hear Lo start cursing from the kitchen, about to storm over here, but Lily has climbed on his back to stop him. Rose's heels clap towards us.

"Go fuck someone who actually likes you, Julius!" Loren yells from the kitchen. "Oh *wait*, that leaves *no one* on this planet. Better go find someone who can take you to Mars, you motherfucker!"

Ryke struggles in my grip, and he turns on me for a second. "I swear to whatever fucking weird god you believe in, Connor, if you don't let me beat the shit out of him, I'm going to fucking punch you in the face."

But Rose is faster than him. She has a can of pepper spray directed at Julian as a warning, and she pushes his arm. "Get out," she says. "Or I will burn more than just your eyes."

Julian raises his hands, the skin above his cheekbone beginning to swell. He shoots all of us one last glare as Rose opens the door and forces his body onto the brick stoop.

"Connor," she says in a stiff voice. "I need you to lead Julian out and to tell the guards to put him on a blacklist, please."

"Of course." I look at Ryke. "If I release you, do *not* run after him."

His muscles stay flexed. "Sure."

He's not convincing at all.

But then Daisy says, "Sorry, guys." Her voice cracks. We all look at her, even Rose in the doorway. Daisy clears her throat. "I should have broken up with him myself, to avoid this." She nods and stares at the ground, her blonde hair shrouding her face.

"No," Rose says, "I'm glad we did it—or at least *tried* to do it." Rose's cheeks redden with guilt. "It's our fault for not finishing what we started."

Ryke adds, "I can't even fucking imagine you breaking up with him alone. He would have probably . . ." He cringes and shakes his head, pissed all over again. I picture the same thing. Julian saying,

Baby, come on, don't be like that. Don't listen to your friends. We're so good for each other. And if she refuted, he'd probably pin her against a wall and scream all the same.

At least we were here to lead him outside.

As I pass Rose in the doorway, my chest brushes her body, and I meet her hot gaze, which warms me in a single instant. I'd very much like to be in control right now and have her look at me *just* like that.

My eyes flit over the length of her in a Calloway Couture black dress, short on the thighs, higher at the collar. And I whisper in her ear, "I know how I'm going to take you tonight, darling." I skim my hand over her hip before I drop it to her ass, squeezing.

Her breath shallows, and then I walk down the stairs towards the half ape who kicks over our trash can.

I can practically feel Rose smiling behind me.

Forty-five

Connor Cobalt

I steady her in my arms, maintaining my intense rhythm. Rose sits on my lap, her legs wrapped around my waist while I lean against the headboard of the bed. Even with her on top, I guide her. I make the decisions and route the path. My hands grip on to the flesh of her hips, and I buck up into her with rough exhilaration.

She moans. I think I hear my name from her muffled voice. She can't speak, even if she wants to. I've shoved her panties in her mouth. And her hands have been tied behind her back with my leather belt.

I stop moving, and her head lolls like she's been riding a roller-coaster for the past twenty minutes. And maybe she fucking has. I've been alternating between taking her by the waist and maneuvering her own body up and down on my cock, and then keeping her still as I thrust my own body up. My chest rises and falls, and I try desperately to ignore the throbbing sensation in my groin. But I want to play with her, not just fuck her into submission.

"Pop quiz," I say in a ragged breath. "One word to describe what you're feeling. Only one." I remove her lace panties from her mouth, and her breathing deepens as if trying to catch the air she didn't have.

"Don't be so dramatic," I tell her. "You have a nose to breathe through. Or have I fucked your anatomy knowledge right out of you?"

Instead of glaring, her lips lift and her eyes lighten. I press my fingers underneath her chin and lift her gaze. "You like that," I say, not asking. "You like me fucking you so hard that your brain empties of all those traversing thoughts."

She sways on my lap like she might fall backwards. I hold her tighter, one hand on her back to keep her upright while I slip my fingers into her collar, gripping it forcefully to support her head.

"One word," I remind her. "Even if it's as ineloquent as the word *cock*. Right now."

She licks her bottom lip and my eyes train to it. *Don't move, Connor.* But it's a struggle. Everything she does makes me want to take her hard and fast. And then she gives me her answer in a single, soft breath.

"Concupiscent."

My eyebrows rise. "That's a big word."

She gleams with pride. *Oh no, Rose. That was not a compliment.* I pull her collar and she leans forward on my command. My lips brush her ear. "You're still thinking properly," I tell her. "Apparently I haven't fucked you hard enough."

I feel her sex tighten around my erection in quick, short pulsing motions. Her mouth needs to catch up with her body. It has no trouble begging for me.

I don't move yet. I let her soak and squirm while I wait, trying my best to harness my own aching needs. "One word," I say again. My fingers dig into the soft skin on her hip and then I slide my fingers, edging up the length of her thigh.

"Lascivious." Her pronunciation slurs on the end and her head falls back, her eyelids fluttering as I begin to thrust again.

I stop after two short pumps. "One word." I yank the collar and her eyes shoot open.

"Passion." *Better.*

I let go of the collar and place both hands on her hips, and then I lift her off my shaft. I watch the way her body responds in distress. Not liking that I'm taking her away from me. When I bring her back down, filling her up, I do it hard. Our bodies make noises together. Flesh on flesh. Groans against moans. Ragged breathing that fills the silent air. I do it three more times, basically bench pressing her on my dick.

It might be my second favorite position. Right behind having her spread apart, tied up, gagged and left soaked and waiting on the bed.

On her third or fourth sharp gasp, I pause again, keeping her motionless with me deep inside. "One word."

She doesn't hesitate. "Fuck." *There we go.*

I take her in my arms again and make sure it's the last word she remembers.

We talk for a while, Rose on her stomach, the comforter at her waist while I have an elbow propped on my pillow. I run my hand over her lower and upper back, massaging any tense muscles and engraining the velvet of her skin in my mind.

I adore these moments after sex, almost as much as the actual act. Her stress has been reduced to a minimum. Even when she talks about her to-do list—her worries and fears—it's with an easy breath, not a strained one.

"I don't think I'm going to be able to keep Daisy with us after the show ends," Rose says softly. "I talked with my mother, and she won't let her leave." She has her cheek on her pillow, turned to me. "Maybe if there's a season two, she'd be able to live with us."

A season two? Another six months dealing with Scott, with invasive cameras following our every move? "You'd want that?" I ask.

"No," she says frankly. "I already have what I wanted out of the show. Fizzle stocks are high. A couple retailers are looking to store my pieces. People sympathize more with Lily than they ever have." This last fact has her smiling. "That's the best part," she admits.

It's hard to deny Lily's love for Loren or his love for her when they're always together on the show. "They're easy to root for," I say, kissing her shoulder. "You just have to understand them first." That's the hard part. Being willing to look past their addictions and see a person.

She shuts her heavy eyes for a second, but I don't want her to sleep just yet. I have to ask something important while she's in a complacent mood.

"About the wedding," I start. And before I can finish, she interjects, her eyes shooting open.

"Oh, I've been meaning to tell you, I showed Lily her wedding gown the other day, and she was *happy*, Connor." Rose smiles like it's a fantasy. My stomach twists in knots. She supports her body on her forearms to look at me better. "She squealed and bounced like she was excited. I think she's finally ready to get married."

"That's great," I say, not able to control my stilted voice. "I'm happy for her."

She frowns, and then she hits my arm. "You don't sound happy."

My hand stops on her lower back. "I'm with a girl who refused to take part in childhood games of marriage, and now you're fawning over someone else's wedding." She's told me before that when Lily and Lo pretended to get married as little kids, she destroyed all of the flowers by ripping them off the stems, and then she called everyone "stupid" and stormed away.

"If you're worried whether I'll mutilate the flowers at their wedding, don't be. I picked them out. They're having orchids."

"I changed them."

Her eyes jolt further open, and she sits all the way up, holding the sheet to her chest. She points at me. "If my mother swayed you to orange lilies and teal ribbon—"

I cover her mouth. "I didn't consult your mother on any of the final arrangements, I promise."

"Then what's this about?" she asks. "You look like you failed a math test."

I edge close to her and kiss her temple. "I was just thinking about us."

She freezes. "And it upset you?"

I've always been the most confident, the most prepared, but never the most forthcoming. And all of these are being overturned. How can you be confident when someone else holds your fate? I can't make my own if she's won't deal me some cards.

"I'm all in," I tell her. "I want the kids. I want the wedding ring on your finger. I want all of it with *you*, Rose. Where's your head at?" We haven't talked about this in months. The last time we did, she denounced my vain concept of children, but after dealing with Daisy, Lily—she has to see that we'd be good together, beyond academic rivals, beyond great sex. We're compatible in *life*. And that's what matters most.

She shakes her head as she stares off in thought.

My chest constricts, and I try to make this easier for her. "Imagine yourself in two years. What do you see?"

After a long silence, she says, "I see you working for Cobalt Inc. beside your mother, and I see us taking vacations together with my sisters and their boyfriends or husbands, whatever they've done in two years." She rolls her eyes but smiles at that future.

I wait for her to finish, but that's it. "What about Calloway Couture?"

"I don't know. I'd probably have more employees to help me. I wouldn't be so focused on it, or at least, I don't want to be."

I frown, not expecting this answer at all. "But you love fashion."

"You loved Wharton."

I shake my head at her. It's not the same. And I'll show her why.

"Can you really quit your business, Rose? Would that make you happy?"

She lets out a deep breath like she's combatted with this all before. "No. I would be miserable without Calloway Couture, but I'm miserable trying to keep it running. I have no control in what happens to the line once it goes in the store. It could be pulled in a year, less than that. And then I have to work hard all over again. For what?"

"So that women may wear your clothes, darling."

"It's foolish."

"It's not even *close* to that, Rose," I tell her with narrowed eyes. "You give women clothes that they can feel confident in. You empower them in a way you know how, and *that* will never be foolish. That's beautiful and brilliant and something you can't forget."

And then she kisses me. Her hand clenching my hair as her lips press against mine. I smile and urge her lips open for a second, our tongues meeting in an embrace that clutches my mind and refuses to let go.

But she breaks first, holding my cheek in a delicate hand. "Thank you," she says. "You're right—" She puts her fingers to my lips. "Don't you dare gloat."

I try not to grin too much.

Her lips rise. "I'm going to try to find a way to be happy with what I have. I don't want to keep thinking it's never enough. And I'm not ready to give it all up either."

I grab her hand, dropping it from my mouth. "That's a smart decision." I brush the bottom of her reddened lip. "And in ten years, when your sisters and their husbands have children and families of their own, what do you picture for yourself?"

"I can't look that far," she refutes.

"Lies," I scoff with the click of my tongue. "You've mapped out your life already."

"How do you know?"

"Because that's what you and I do. We envision our futures and we make it happen."

She squeezes my knee. "Now you make us seem utterly shallow and vain."

"We are," I say. "But in the best way." I grin and wait for her to tell me. I want to hear it.

"I see you and me together, and we're eating Thanksgiving at our house. Loren and Lily come over. They don't have kids, but they're happy with that. And Daisy will arrive on her motorcycle with some drifter boyfriend we all hate. Ryke won't be there. He'll be . . . climbing some mountain in another country, backpacking or something insane. And you and I will be drinking wine by the fire after everyone goes to bed."

No children.

Anywhere. Not even for her sisters.

That's how scared she is. "What frightens you about having kids?" I ask her, skimming her palm with my fingers, tracing the lines while she comes to an answer.

She goes rigid, and I sit all the way up and rub her legs that peek beneath the sheet. "Failure," she says with a tight voice. "What if they hate me? What if I don't show them the love they deserve? What if I turn out like my mother and suffocate each one?" She pauses. "I don't want to ruin a human being, Richard."

I stroke her hair, pinning a strand behind her ear. "You won't, Rose. I'll be here to help you, and I have no doubt that you'll love each of our children as much as the next one."

I wait for her to refute. To shoot me a dark glare and snap about me not knowing anything about kids since I have none. But I know her, and I know she'd be a great mother if she allowed herself the chance to be one. And to believe this—all anyone needs is a glimpse into how she treats her sisters. With compassion, dedication and soul-bearing love. She gives all of herself to the people she cares for.

"In our *late* thirties, if we're ready, if you *help* me, I can imagine a little girl or two . . ." She trails off as she stares at my face. "What?"

My mouth has fallen, and then my surprise transforms into the purest fucking joy. I smile so bright; I can't do anything but kiss her on the cheek, on the lips. I tackle her on the bed and pin her to the mattress.

"Richard," she says with a smile. "Stop for a second."

I grin. "You want children?" She said yes.

"When I'm *thirty-five* or older," she retorts.

She wants children.

I kiss her deeply.

"You have to *help* me," she says between kisses.

Help. She's asking for help. A girl who struggled to take my college blazer to hide a stain is willingly opening her arms to me—to us. "All I've ever wanted to do was be on your team, Rose." I laugh as I remember. "You, Miss Highest Honors, were the one who chose to be my rival by attending Princeton."

She tilts her head. "I like competing against you." She sits up on her elbows, her lips so close to mine as she says, "But I like being your teammate more."

"Me too, darling."

Me too.

Forty-six

Rose Calloway

7 days—Mom

I try not to let the countdown alter my mood anymore. I'm more upset that Poppy, my oldest sister, decided not to come to Lily's bachelorette party. Since we're spending the weekend in Vegas with the cameras—and *Scott*, tall, villainous Scott—she chose to stay back in Philly. At least she wants to be a part of the wedding.

Lily dances beside me, wearing a pink sparkly *Bachelorette* sash and tiara. Her happiness makes Scott's looming presence worth it. We're in a huge club with multicolored strobe lights and half-naked girls gyrating in cages.

I grab Lily's hands, all of us a little buzzed. Usually Lily doesn't drink, but when I ordered shots with Daisy, she said she wanted to be a part of it.

"You're getting married!" I shout over the music, swinging her hands.

She beams from ear to ear. "I'm getting married!"

I don't really understand her sudden change of heart. But why question it? I'll just ruin *this*, and I'd rather enjoy tonight and the next seven days.

Daisy twists her sweaty hair into a bun on top of her head. Savannah and Brett try to film us without being shoved by other dancers.

"Hey, look who it is!" I hear a guy shout.

Great.

"Go back to Philly, sluts!" The guys don't near us, but the longer they yell, the more likely they will find the courage (or stupidity) to do so.

"Get out of Vegas!"

"Should we take a bar break?" Daisy asks. "Beer time?"

Lily tries to ignore the heckling too. She nods quickly. "Beer time."

"You girls want beer?" I say. We have the option of fruity cocktails, dirty martinis, tequila shots, and they're going to choose *beer*. Really?

"You've *never* had beer before," Lily refutes. "This is the day for us to try new things together. Come on."

She tugs my hand.

"But you don't even like beer," I retort. Beer is not my alcohol of choice. Although, I've never tasted it. It kind of looks like piss in a glass, which makes complete sense why frat guys love it so much.

"I do like it," Lily tells me. "I just don't drink it often."

"I love beer," Daisy says with a nod.

"You love everything," Lily and I say in unison.

She smiles and shrugs. And she would probably try to eat everything if she didn't have to worry about her weight.

"Go back to—"

"We heard you!" I shout at the air, not sure where the voice is coming from. It must be close considering I hear him over the music.

We reach the long black granite bar with blue lights underneath, and we pick three stools beside each other. Lily is seated between us, and a guy with a scruffy jaw and tattoos sits on my left. From here, we can see our guys over in the VIP roped area, a balcony above us. They sit on leather couches and talk.

Scott doesn't join them. He leans his forearms on the balcony railing, his eyes pinned to me. *The whole time.*

It's aggravating, but I feel worse for Loren, who has to put up with Scott during his bachelor party. And I *rarely* pity Loren in settings like this.

I glance at Lily, who pockets her phone as soon as my eyes hit her.

"What are you doing?" I ask.

"Texting Lo. Let's order."

If this bartender would respond to my waving hand, that task would be much easier. But she's having a nice time flirting with the male customers who'll tip her more. I *would have* tipped her well. Now I'm reconsidering. I snap my fingers.

Lily grabs my hands, flushing in embarrassment. "She's not a dog."

Well she's not a good bartender either. But I tone it down because Lily looks as red as the bartender's formfitting dress.

I guess we'll have to wait.

Patience—it's something I don't have.

Forty-seven

Connor Cobalt

Scott keeps looking at Rose. It's creepy. Can you do something?—Lily

I pocket my phone. I've tried to stand up and distract Scott from Rose, but every time I do, Lo pulls me back down and Ryke tells me not to give him the time of "fucking" day. But it's about Rose, and I don't want her to be uncomfortable because of him.

"Go back to Philly, assholes!" someone screams from one leather couch over.

"I'm getting the sense we're not wanted here," Lo says dryly. He tries not to provoke the hecklers, but I can see the irritation growing as he flashes a bitter smile.

I glance from the text to Scott. "Give me a minute," I tell the guys. "I need to talk to him. Seriously." I have to see what he's plotting.

"No, we thought you were *joking* the last four times," Lo says.

But I stand up from the leather couch anyway, expecting Lo to tug me back, but he just nods to me and says, "Tell him I hate him."

"Any other messages?" I look at Ryke.

"Tell him to fuck himself."

I nod. "Didn't expect anything eloquent."

He flips me off, and I leave both of them to go to Scott. I rest my arm on the railing like him, not saying a word as I stand by his side. I just watch what he does.

Rose.

She argues with the a brunette bartender in a red dress, and even from afar, I notice the way she cranes forward with heat in her eyes, obviously on the offensive about something.

"So here you are," I say, feeling the gleam of Ben's camera lens behind me. "I have the girl, and you're left with what?" I finally turn to look at him.

"I never wanted the girl," he says.

I try not to seem shocked. I thought this was a pissing contest from the start. "You wanted fame," I state, throwing it out there for him to catch.

"No." He stands straighter. As do I. And we face each other. "If I wanted fame, do you really think I'd be the producer of a reality show? You think someone's going to award me a fucking Emmy for filming six rich college students?"

I don't make a point to announce that I already graduated college. He knows this. "So you just want money from the show," I say. "*Princesses of Philly* is a hit. You have your payoff. There's no reason to keep looking at Rose. The charade is *over*, Scott. You're not her ex. You've never been." But I stop myself. The more I say these things, the more his lips curve in a smug grin. I inhale in detest, rubbing my mouth as a bad taste rises.

"There's no season two, is there?" he asks.

"No."

"I figured as much when she signed the contract. I thought there's no way she'd want to do this for longer than six months." He shakes his head at me. "It's not over, Connor."

He wants more money.

What the fuck is he going to do?

Before I have a chance to continue, my phone repeatedly buzzes in my pocket. I answer it, not checking the caller.

"You have to get down here, right *now*!" Lily yells so I can hear over the loud music.

"What's going on?" I ask while I look for them at the bar. Rose is no longer arguing with the bartender. The thirty-something guy next to her is *in* her fucking face. And she's in his as they scream.

I can hear her voice in the background of Lily's receiver.

"Just order the fucking beer!" he yells. "Who cares what size it is?!"

"For you to understand me, you'd have to open your tiny, infantile brain," she sneers, "and try to step onto my plane of existence!"

"Girl size or guy size, it's not that fucking hard of a concept! Small or large!"

"FUCK YOU!" she shouts, not even that drunk.

I race down the balcony stairs at that last curse word. And I feel Ryke and Loren behind me; the distress must be clear in my muscles that constrict from my neck to arms.

When I reach the first floor, still on the phone with Lily, I sprint ahead, the crowds parting as soon as they see me. The bar is in sight. Maybe fifty feet away.

And then he punches her.

In the face.

Everything moves quickly.

The momentum knocks Rose off the bar stool. Lily crouches down to help her, and Daisy shoves the guy, screaming and trying to hit him back.

My heart is in my throat. The sensible, reasonable part of me that I have *always* listened to says to go to Rose, to make sure she's okay. But the livid, boiling side that Rose is familiar with has a mind of its own. I'm already making my way to him, my hand clenched around my phone, my knuckles white with hatred. Who the *fuck* punches a woman? I've met some assholes—some really fucked-up people who would sell their child if it meant living an A-class lifestyle. But this shit is something new and foreign and disgusting.

I almost reach the guy.

But as soon as he says, "Oh, you're that prick on the show. Come to restrain your fucking crazy girlfriend? She needs her mouth taped shut—"

I lay one fist into his stomach before the bouncers separate us. My grip was strong enough to break the screen on my phone. These stupid, raging emotions collect as I realize Rose is still hurt. On the ground.

I find her within a second. Lily has her arms above Rose so no one enters her space. And Lo is right beside Rose's head, holding a napkin filled with ice that he must have grabbed from the bar to her cheek.

"Tell me you hit him," Lo says the moment he sees me.

I nod once.

"Thank God."

"Thank *me*," I say, dropping to my knees while Lo just laughs. It's easy to joke right now. This is the hard part. "Rose?" I inspect her cheek that swells. Not a shiner, but she'll have a bruise on the bone. I can barely breathe without seeing a fist in her face. Her body falling off the stool. The motion is repeated over and over again. I want to fucking puke.

"He *hit* me!" she growls, her eyes flickering hot. She tries to sit up to go attack him, but Lo keeps his hand on her shoulder, forcing her down.

"I have her," I tell Lo, and I swiftly cradle her in my arms. She holds on to my bicep, not trying to go after the guy. Lo passes her the ice and she keeps it to her cheek, silent again.

"How bad is it?" she asks. "Oh my God, the wedding pictures." She grimaces. "What an asshole!" She growls again.

"There's such thing as Photoshop," I tell her with an even-tempered voice. I hate that she's hurt, and another guy was the cause. From the sound of it, he wasn't even a heckler.

"LET ME AT HIM!" Daisy screams.

We all turn our heads. Ryke has Daisy thrown over his shoulder, beelining towards the exit. I follow with Rose in my arms, Lily and Lo behind me somewhere.

Daisy tries to climb down Ryke's back to go attack the tattooed guy who's seated at the bar again. Her head is near his ass until he pulls her back up on his shoulder.

"HE HIT MY SISTER!!!"

"Say it a little louder, Dais!" Ryke shouts at her. "The world can't fucking hear you!"

She screams incoherently and then yells, "If someone hit Lo, you'd kill *them*!"

"Someone did hit Lo, and I didn't do a fucking thing," Ryke retorts, "so calm the fuck down!"

I remember that night. It was when they met each other. He didn't really know Lo then. I try to concentrate on Rose, who looks murderous at any person who passes, as though every dancer in the club wronged her.

"You're okay," I tell her.

"I should have punched him back."

"You were on the ground."

She huffs. "How do I look?" she asks, her eyes softening as she stares up at me. Her cheek continues to swell.

"Beautiful," I say, and I kiss her forehead before she can refute.

"At least he didn't break my nose," Rose says, pinching the bridge with two delicate fingers in gratitude.

If he broke her nose—I think my mind would have truly ejected at the sight of her blood.

Just as Ryke disappears through the door to go outside, I glance over my shoulder to make certain that Lily and Loren are following. But I notice Scott close by, speaking to Brett, both of them laughing and smiling together.

I have a horrible feeling.

Forty-eight

Rose Calloway

've willfully handed over my pleasure and the wedding to-do list to Connor Cobalt. I've either gone mad or he's put a spell on me. I smile at the thought. He doesn't like when I accuse him of witchcraft.

My phone buzzes as I finish clipping the buckle to my heel in my bedroom, back in Philly.

4 days and I bought new makeup for you—Mom

I head to the vanity just to check my face once more. It can't be that bad . . . Well, it's not *good*. A purplish bruise puckers on my cheekbone. It could have been worse. My eye could have swelled shut and oozed puss—that's what Connor told me to lessen my misery. It worked. Now I'm just happy I don't have a puss-filled eye to deal with.

And I can also say I've been punched. The bachelorette party hasn't aired yet, but if anyone thinks it's my fault, I don't really care.

Connor walks into the bedroom, shirtless and in a pair of black slacks. His muscles ripple across his abdomen, dipping down towards a place that I saw early this morning. He's sexier than he realizes—no, *no*, he definitely knows how hot he is.

He holds up two button-downs by the hanger. "White or blue today?"

"Did you just come out here to show off your body?"

His eyes gleam with mischief, telling me that's *exactly* what he did. "I need your impeccable fashion advice, darling. White or blue?"

But I like this more than he knows. It feels comfortable and normal. Sharing space. Sharing each other. I want to wake up and be the woman who chooses what color he wears for the day, and I want him to be the man who chooses what position we'll take at night.

"White," I say easily. "I like you in white."

"Blue it is," he replies casually.

I glare and his eyes rake my body, taunting me even more. He loves to make me mad. He rests the blue shirt on the desk and takes the white one off the hanger.

"What are you working on today?" I ask as I head towards the door, my purse hung on my forearm.

"My proposal for Cobalt Inc.," he replies. "The board members approved it this morning. It will go into effect within the next few months."

He still hasn't revealed what he's doing to the company.

I think he just wants to surprise me.

I slip into the hallway, wearing a dark purple peplum dress. Before I can go downstairs, Scott ascends them. His ugly gray eyes latch on to mine. Really, whatever part of him was decently *cute* or *hot* has suddenly become putrid, like a rotten sulfuric swamp.

"Rose, how are you?" he asks cordially.

"Brilliant," I say. "As always." *What? I never claimed to be humble.*

"Of course. You're a member of Mensa, you graduated in the top one percent of your class, and you know random facts that no one cares about."

Prick.

He flashes an oily smile.

And there goes my future children. Sorry, Connor. My ovaries just withered and died.

Before I can combat with something much nastier, he says, "Where's your necklace?"

I frown and my heart jumps in fear. Did I lose it? I quickly touch my chest, and I relax once my fingers find the smooth diamond pendant. I even glance down to double check. The thin chain is still clipped.

Now he's just trying to pointlessly irritate me. "Go annoy someone else," I snap, "preferably someone from a different universe. Maybe you'll reunite with your ancestors."

I try to shove past him, but he sidesteps and blocks me. "I was talking about your *other* necklace. The one with more than one diamond."

"I have many diamond necklaces, Scott," I retort, not realizing how bitchy and snobbish I sound until it's too late.

"Not this many diamonds," he says, taking a step closer to me. "The inside is leather." And then he drifts to the left, stuffing his hands into his pockets and sauntering away.

I stay frozen, too stunned to force my heel down the stairs.

He was talking about my collar. *My* diamond collar.

The one I only wear during sex.

And I've *never* had sex outside of the bedroom or anywhere the cameras can film.

Something is wrong.

I sense it deep in my gut.

Dread mixed with paranoia, a nauseous combination, carries my feet downward. I'm on autopilot, trying to shake Scott's words and continue my daily routine.

Breakfast. A vanilla yogurt with strawberries and granola and then I'm off to New York to introduce myself to the new Calloway Couture staff.

My heels clink against the hardwood in determined steps. Two stairs down and I stop, worried thoughts creeping back, despite my urgency to brush them away.

What the fuck are you doing, Rose? If Scott knows something, I need to confront him. Or talk to Connor. I almost turn around, but I hear the television from the living room below. Two more stairs down, and the voice becomes distinguishable.

". . . a top story. Another Calloway girl in a scandal," the news anchor says. "*This* time there's legitimate proof."

Daisy.

Something happened to Daisy.

I walk hurriedly, reaching the bottom of the staircase in no time. Loren, Ryke, Lily and Daisy sit on the couch together, their backs facing me. They watch the television above the fireplace, and I march further into the room to have a better look at what's on screen.

"Oh shit," Ryke says, seeing me first.

Loren quickly snatches the remote, and the television flickers to black.

I set my hands crossly on my hips and direct my hostility towards my sister's boyfriend. "I'm not five years old, Loren," I snap. "You can turn on the news." *Especially* if it's about Daisy.

"No," Lo says, flipping the remote in his hands nervously. "I'd rather not."

Ryke runs his fingers through his brown hair—a clear sign that he's anxious too.

Lily and Daisy huddle together on the couch, cupping their hands by their mouths as they whisper. I frown and scan the area for Ben, Savannah or Brett, but the camera crew is nowhere to be seen.

That's . . . strange.

And why are my sisters acting like gossipmongers in front of me?

Unless . . .

I refuse to believe what's right in my face. I don't want to accept it yet.

I stomp over to Loren on the couch, my five-inch heels never letting me down. They keep my body sturdily upright, confident and fucking poised. I try to snatch the remote from his hand, but he holds on to the other end tightly—as if we're about to have a tug-of-war.

I glower. "Let go, Loren, unless you'd like me to dislocate your arm."

He narrows his eyes. "Aren't you tired of making all these empty threats?"

I twist his arm, just like Connor taught me in the self-defense "class," and Lo winces. His grip loosens on the remote, and I take it quickly from his hand.

As he massages his shoulder, he says, "Bitch."

"Yes, but I'm a bitch with *real* threats." I power on the television. When the news pops up, I freeze. Again.

Fixed to the floor. Too cold to move.

"Bet you feel like a bigger bitch right now," Loren comments.

"Shut up, Lo," Lily calls out. "Rose . . ."

I wave her off and turn up the volume. But the headline on the bottom of the screen is vitally clear. Yet, I still have to reread it five times just for the letters to sink in.

SEX TAPE OF ROSE CALLOWAY AND CONNOR COBALT
SOLD TO PORN SITE FOR $25 MILLION

Porn site.

Sex tape.

I didn't sell *shit*. That little scumbag forged our signatures to a porn distributor? The only satisfaction right now is picturing Scott's head behind bars because if I imagine the other *thing*—everyone watching Connor fuck me—a tingling sensation crawls up my arms like thousands of centipedes.

The news doesn't even bother to explain who we are. Through

the reality show and blogs, we're already famous. Now, I suppose, we're *infamous*.

My head buzzes with all the noise from the television, from my friends and sisters. "The producer is none other than Scott Van Wright, Rose's ex-boyfriend." I barely catch that line. He's still my ex-boyfriend? I concentrate on that stupid lie that's still being aired. When the real shit hits the fan—Scott still manages to keep half his mask on. I hate him.

I have to be stuck in some fucked-up nightmare.

Loren tries to grab the remote out of my hand, and I jerk back and turn the volume up. "I'm watching this," I snap. And there I am.

They play a clip from the sex tape. I'm lying on my bed in this house, naked. Black bars censor the tape for network television, my breasts and vagina sufficiently covered now.

But somewhere online the unedited version is being circulated. And how can I stop it? Lawyers. Lots of them. But I can't even bring myself to call my father or to dial the family's attorney. I am hypnotized by me. On screen. With Connor.

My arms are tied to the bedpost with Connor's belt, and the expensive diamond collar glints in the dim candlelight. I remember that night. It was right after the Alps. My second foray into sex and it's public for everyone to see.

I turn the volume higher, my finger stuck on the button as it blares.

"Rose," Loren complains, his hands on his ears.

"Rose." Lily stands and tries to touch my arm, but I jerk away again.

"Don't touch me." *I need to see this.* No one tells me to turn it down, probably afraid I will kill them for it. I feel murderous. I feel like I could go kill a coalition of baby cheetahs and not bat an eye.

The news anchor's voice escalates to an intolerable level. But I don't lower the television. Not yet. "Scott Van Wright has sold the sex tape to Hot Fire Productions for a multimillion-dollar deal. There's been no comment yet from either Connor Cobalt or Rose Calloway, but it appears to be a legal transaction between all four parties."

My mouth drops. *That fucking liar.* There is *no way* in hell this is legal.

"The summary of the film says the hour-long session is rough and for mature audiences only." *Clearly.*

I turn the volume to the highest level.

"What the fuck are you doing?" Ryke asks, putting a hand to his ear to block the noise. Lily is the only one standing up by my side. Her face twists in pain, and I remember she's been in this position. Sort of. She's never had her sex life distributed. No one has *seen* it online.

She was just called a sex addict, and everyone took it as truth. Which it was. But this is clear, physical proof that I've had sex. I'm no longer a virgin.

"Maybe she's like . . . having a mental break . . ." Daisy says.

I spin on my heels, taking the remote hostage with me. I carry myself with some morsel of dignity. In the kitchen, I rummage in a cupboard that squirmy Brett loves to hide his booze under. Since we have a "no alcohol in sight" policy in the townhouse, most everything is kept out of reach. I land on my knees and dig around the dishwasher soaps for the bottle of Jack.

"Seriously though, Rose!" Lily says loudly, trying to talk over the blaring TV. "Are you okay?"

I rise to my feet, snagging a wine glass from another cupboard before I return to the living room. Everyone watches as I pour whiskey to the rim, practically overflowing the glass.

"Rose, not to lecture you at this really sensitive time in your life," Loren says, "but that's not how you drink whiskey. And as an expert in liquor, it offends me."

I give him a sharp glare. "You're not an expert in liquor. You're an alcoholic." I set the bottle of Jack on the coffee table and take a large swig. It burns the back of my throat, but I hardly even cringe. The sting is numbed by my anger.

"Which makes me an expert," Loren argues.

I wave him off. My go-to move at this point. *Wave it off.* If only I could magically wave away that sex tape.

I take three more gulps from my wine glass. I am so pissed. My body *throttles* with rage. I am *shaking* I am so fucking livid. Yes, it's embarrassing that the world has seen my breasts and vagina, two parts of me that I was unwilling to show Connor for an entire year.

Yes, I'm slightly nervous the world will view me as a doormat now that they see me gooey and submissive in bed.

No, I will *not* cry.

I won't shed a tear for Scott Van Wright. He deserves only my nasty, vile words. Not emotions that I reserve for people I love.

"What's going on?" Connor asks, his voice coming from the stairs. *Perfect.* He's heard my call. The loud, obnoxious television. And his gaze traverses to the TV.

"Look, honey," I say, "we have a sex tape together."

Everyone silences, probably wondering if the unflappable Connor Cobalt will suddenly lose his shit. It takes him less than ten seconds to unglue his feet from the floor—beating me by a whole minute. I expect him to take out his phone. To do the responsible thing and start dialing attorneys and crisis management centers.

Instead, he stops right in front of me. His eyes swim in mine, as if searching for my mental state. *I'm fucking fine*, I want to scream back. But I choose to take another large swig of the biting whiskey.

Raw concern encases his features. I want to explain how angry and *not* sad I am, but the words don't form. And then he glances at my wine glass. He better not take this away from me like I'm a child. If he pours my drink down the sink—

And then he snatches the wine glass right out of my hand.

Before I have time to complain, he puts the rim to his lips. And I go quiet, watching him take a huge, brazen swig—washing away his own fury with the alcohol. I smile. Because we cope in the same way. Not usually with drinking, but with pulling our shoulders back and taking it like a fucking champ.

He hands the wine glass back to me and says, "Ce n'est pas la fin." *This isn't the end.*

I nod in agreement. He steals the remote from me and softens everyone's ears by lowering the volume.

My phone buzzes in my pocket. I don't even check to see who it is. I just sit on the armrest of the couch and watch the television.

". . . *Princesses of Philly* has promoted Rose as a virgin. Many people are speaking out about the validity of the show . . ."

Connor changes the channel to cable.

". . . either she lied or she lost her virginity during the time of the show. Go to our website for a poll—" He flips to another station.

I yell spitefully at the flat screen, "The world doesn't have ANYTHING better to do than talk about my virginity?!" I motion to the TV with my drink.

"Or lack thereof," Loren adds.

I ignore that comment and turn to Connor. "My vagina has trumped national news." I let out a manic laugh. "What do you think our friends from Model UN would say about *that*?"

Connor's eyes rake me like he's diagnosing my hysteria.

I ignore *that* too.

After a quick moment, he sidles behind me and wraps his arms around my waist. He presses his lips to my shoulder. I lean back against his chest. It feels familiar and warm, safe even, knowing that I have someone here—on my team.

Daisy clicks away on her laptop. "It looks like most people are voting in favor of you in polls. They say that you can't be a liar or a hypocrite. Not when you've stated in the show that you would—and I quote—'jam my five-inch heel in the eye or asshole of liars and cheaters.'"

That was a little dramatic, even for me. But the interviews riled me to a new degree, and I spouted every threat I could think of. Like roasting Scott's penis by flinging it at the sun. I would *love* to execute that one if humanly possible.

Tink, tink, tink. Little bells clank together as Sadie pads over to our group. She looks as feral as I feel. And a wicked, crazy impulse drives through me. I disentangle from Connor's safe embrace.

"Rose," Connor says, half with worry and half with warning.

I don't listen. Still holding my wine glass, I squat down in front of the tabby cat. She's a hostile bitch (like me). She has scratched my arms. Hissed at me. And I swear she pissed on my Jimmy Choos, although I can't confirm that.

But in this moment, I feel invincible from all offenses. The media. Scott. And this fucking cat. I reach out to her.

"Don't do it!" Lily yells at me from beside the couch. "You're going to lose an eye."

Ignoring my sister, I slip my palm underneath Sadie's furry belly and pick her right up with one hand, my other still clutching onto the stem of the wine glass. I stand and stare straight into her eyes, which almost match the color of mine. I am channeling my hatred into one supreme death glare.

Sadie moves and Lily lets out an audible gasp.

But the cat doesn't claw me. No.

She *licks* me. Her scratchy little tongue brushes against my chin like a puppy and not a feline.

"What the fuck?" Ryke says in shock.

I hold her close to my body and she purrs against my chest. "We're friends now." I state the obvious and take another sip from my wine glass.

"Or she thinks you've grown balls," Loren refutes.

"I've always had them," I say, offended. I turn to see Connor, who stares with concern and a little bit of fear. The bottom of my stomach drops in effect. He can see right through the barriers I build to protect myself.

I'm okay. I try to convey the words through my eyes. But I'm not so sure I succeed.

Lily's phone rings loudly on her lap. "Shit, it's Dad." She looks between Connor and me. "What do you want me to do?"

I don't say anything. I just kiss Sadie's head as she continues to nuzzle into my ribs. Her change of demeanor calms me and gives me a little more strength.

Connor mutes the television and takes the phone from Lily, putting it on speaker. "Greg, this is Connor." His voice is relaxed, even if his tense posture and hard eyes don't agree.

"Good, I've been trying to call you and Rose. I assume you've seen the news," he says quickly, his anger underneath his urgency. "I'm on the phone with my attorneys and Cobalt's. We're looking through the contracts all of you signed. Until we can come to a clear picture of what's going on, I need you to get my daughters out of that townhouse. No more cameras."

Translation: Princesses of Philly *is canceled.*

Hooray. I can hardly celebrate *no more Scott* when the result comes at the expense of my name and image. And then it hits me like a freight train—Calloway Couture. *Everything* I've worked for can go to hell all over again. This sex tape could ruin my fashion career.

And I care. *A lot.*

My stomach roils like I need to puke. I think I may vomit. I hold my belly, and Connor puts a firm hand on my shoulder, squeezing tightly to reassure me that he's here, that everything is going to work itself out.

I try to believe it.

"We'll pack today and leave," Connor says to my father.

"Let me know when you make it safely back to Princeton. If there's too much press around the house, you should all stay at our place in Villanova."

"Sure," Connor says. "Do you know where Scott is?"

"No idea, but Loren's father is about to rip him a new asshole. To be honest, I'd love to see it happen." My dad can be as soft as a flower petal whereas Jonathan Hale is the thorn. "Is Rose around?"

"She's on speaker."

"Rose," my father says, his voice turning gentle. "Honey, how many lawyers looked over the contract before you signed it?"

Everyone stares at me, waiting for the answer. I already sense their judgment. I stroke Sadie, who purrs again. She's my only ally. "Just me," I say.

"What . . . the fuck?" Ryke says, his mouth falling.

Loren groans, leaning back into the couch like a wave crashed into him. "Why did we trust you?"

Connor rubs his eyes and shakes his head.

Lily looks petrified.

Daisy's face is frozen solid.

"I've taken multiple law classes at *Princeton*," I refute. "I understood every line of that contract." I've always shared Achilles' fatal flaw. Hubris. Excessive pride. I couldn't look weak in front of Scott, so I decided to do everything myself. I needed no one's help.

And if I misread any line in that contract, it's going to cost me. And Connor.

My dad lets out a disgruntled sound. "It'll . . . be complicated from here on out, Rose. I'll talk to you when the lawyers have read through the contracts in detail."

"Wait," I say. "How's Mother handling this?"

"Terrific, actually. She's been slinging Scott's name in the mud all around the house. She said she'd call and apologize to you later today, Connor." I can hear my father smile by the end of that statement. Connor shares it. Her precious Scott showed his true self today. I'm glad that my mother is back on my boyfriend's team.

"Stay safe. All of you," my father says.

With this, he hangs up. No mention of the actual sex tape, no chiding. He only seemed disappointed by my refusal to grab a lawyer.

Connor gives me a reprimanding look as he hands the phone back to Lily. "I thought you took my lawyer to the meeting, and I thought he read the contracts."

"I thought I told you I left him behind."

Connor shakes his head. "You must have mentioned that to someone else, darling." He takes my wine glass again and finishes it off with one long gulp.

"What the hell was that?" Loren asks Connor. "Greg gives me a two-hour speech about sobriety after our scandal, and he doesn't even acknowledge yours."

"To be fair," Connor says, "you lied to Greg and Samantha about being addicts. That news is a bit more jarring than a sex tape . . ." His voice drifts off on the last words.

We all turn to see what stole his attention.

There he is.

Standing by the staircase like nothing's wrong.

Scott Van fucking Wright.

The room silences in an uncomfortable wave. My body is vibrating in rage, and I realize I'm squeezing Sadie too tight when she lets out a small, dissatisfactory hiss.

Scott looks between all of us, and then his lips lift into that shit-eating grin. "Did I miss something?"

Before I can respond, Connor walks *casually* towards Scott, my boyfriend's face utterly blank and unreadable. I can't predict anything, and that unknown has all of us on edge, no one but him making a sound or a move. I just hear Connor's expensive shoes tap the hardwood until he stops right in front of Scott.

And then Connor holds out his hand, like he wants to shake the producer's. "Congratulations," Connor says. "You outsmarted me. Not many people ever do. And I admit . . . I never saw this coming."

His wooden voice frightens me.

Scott stares at his hand and then back at his face. He shrugs like *what the hell?* and then he clasps Connor's palm.

What is this? A truce—

And then Connor decks Scott in the jaw with his free fist. Scott slams into the wall forcefully. "That's from me," Connor says, anger lacing his voice.

Scott gathers himself quickly and swings back.

Connor dodges the attack and then kicks Scott, *hard*, in the penis. Scott groans in horrific pain. *Fuck yes!* I am cheering on the inside. There are cannons shooting out confetti in my brain. Halle-fucking-lujah.

"That's from Rose."

Scott is in a crouched position on the ground, his eyes watering. He grimaces and slowly stands, clutching on to the wall for support.

Connor doesn't back away, not even a little scared of being hit back.

Scott chokes on a cough, looking like he doesn't want even the slightest *chance* of that happening again. ". . . I'd love to see your face when you realize what you've signed."

"You're seeing it now," Connor tells him calmly, not giving Scott any more satisfaction. I love him for that. "I'm positive you have full rights to anything we ever film, which gave you permission to sell the sex tape to a porn site without our signed consent. I don't have the contract in front of me, but I'm sure there's something misleading about the part where you weren't allowed to film us in the bedrooms."

"I *read* that line correctly. I know it," I say. There was a stipulation about the bedrooms . . . wasn't there?

Scott hunches a little, still recovering from the blow to the balls. "It said that we couldn't *air* anything from the bedrooms on *television*. We never did. The contract said nothing about filming. And any of the footage from the bedrooms and the bathroom can be used for movies and web content. Just not network TV."

OhmyGod. I blew Connor in the bathroom.

Scott laughs devilishly as he watches my face fill in horror. He has . . . so much footage of us. I recollect every time we had sex. He has it all. Hours of us, fucking.

Lily and Loren . . .

Scott must read my stricken gaze, which travels to my little sister. "Lily was almost always in her room," Scott says, "so we weren't able to install any cameras to catch anything." Right. They had to reinstall cameras because I made Connor and Loren sweep the bathroom and the bedrooms when we first moved in.

I glance at Ryke.

"I didn't fuck in the house," he says.

I turn to Daisy. Her face pales.

Connor eases her worries. "It's illegal to film minors in pornographic situations." He glares at Scott.

We've caught him.

He's going to jail.

"We didn't," Scott says. "All that footage was destroyed."

Fuck you! I unleash Sadie, about to ram my heel up Scott's ass. But Ryke stands behind me and holds me back, two hands on my shoulders. It takes me a moment to realize that Connor is staring at Ryke, giving him a command through his eyes to restrain me.

"You're disgusting!" I shout at Scott with an extra-high-pitched scream.

Scott stays calm. I am the only one freaking out. How is that possible? He dropped a grenade on *my* life. I want everyone to be as fucking *pissed* as me.

But I realize that when I'm angry, there's almost no room for anyone else to be the same. I am a hurricane. A typhoon, and I will *destroy* everyone in my wake.

Yes, dramatic.

But that's just how I fucking feel.

Get out of my way. Or I'll drown you.

"The text message from Julian?" Connor asks Scott.

"Planted. Brett took Julian's phone in the middle of the night and texted it to Ryke." *That pudgy asshole. I knew he wasn't on our side.*

"Lily and Lo in the bathroom with the slurping audio?"

"Edited. We did it in advance and uploaded it on the camera for you to find." *That motherfucker . . .*

"The alcohol in Lo's closet?"

"Planted. Savannah and Ben put it there when Lily was taking a nap. They were supposed to install a camera too, but they ran out of time."

. . . Savannah and Ben. I hate them all. *Where's the loyalty?*

Ryke takes his hands off me and starts to near Scott.

Loren doesn't do a thing. He's just whispering in Lily's ear and she nods back.

"You're going to fucking hell for this!" Ryke says with darkness swirling in his brown eyes.

Connor shoves him back the moment he's close. And then Connor turns to Scott. "I'm going to let Ryke go if you don't get out of this house. And his fists are going to hurt a hell of a lot more than mine. So take what's on your back and *leave.*"

Scott straightens up, not exactly exiting with his dignity. But he has millions of dollars in his pockets from *multiple* sex tapes. He can sell them for much more than the first one.

He's set for life.

He won.

We lost. How did we lose?

Oh yes, *hubris*.

I am a Greek tragedy. Or a Shakespearian comedy—it's going to end with a wedding after all.

When the door closes behind him, the room blankets in tension, only disrupted by Sadie's collar, which jingles as she rubs her body against Connor's calves.

"So . . ." Loren looks from Connor to me and back. ". . . is there going to be a boxed set of you two for sale?"

"Most likely," Connor says. And every dime will go to Scott and the porn site. Fuck my life.

He comes to my side and kisses my temple. There's nothing we can do. We just have to deal. With Connor here, I think I can.

I clap my hands together to alleviate the leftover strain in the room. "Everyone, go pack. We're leaving, you heard Dad."

I picture my gated house with the black shutters, large kitchen and most importantly—private bathrooms. *Dear God*, I'm already salivating over a nice hot shower alone with *no* threat of cameras.

I glance at Connor, who collects my hair off my neck. Maybe he can join me too.

Daisy shifts on her feet. "I guess I'm going back to Mom's."

My stomach falls again. She's seventeen. There's nothing I can do about that, as much as I want to. And then my eyes drift to Ryke, the other one who will be left in Philly. It's weird. We've been together in the same house for so long that breaking our routine feels odd. Like a puzzle piece out of place.

We've become something of a family.

A dysfunctional, fucked-up family. It's hard to let that go.

But things are changing again. The reality show helped Calloway Couture, and in one moment, this sex tape could topple all I've sacrificed.

I'll have to confront the public at some point, and it'll have to be more than just waving a glass of whiskey at the television.

I could be hated and condemned like my sister.

I hear the criticism already. And I don't wilt by it. I'm just angry.

So bring it on, motherfuckers. Try to hurt me. Because I won't let you.

You've won the right to see my body, but you're not taking my pride.

It's too excessive to destroy anyway.

Forty-nine

Rose Calloway

The townhouse is empty except for my heavy cedar table in the living room. I set my small duffel bag on the kitchen counter as Connor descends the stairs.

"All the rooms are checked," he tells me. "Nothing's left behind."

"Except my dignity."

His eyes deepen in concern, the same look he's given me the entire time we've been packing. I've shut down any conversation revolving around Scott and the sex tape. But now I'm no longer fueled by my liquid courage, and I've had two hours to shake off the shock and process what's happened.

"I'm sorry," I immediately say. He comes over and touches my cheek. But I take a step back, and his hand falls.

"Rose—"

"Just let me get this out." I take a deep breath. "It's my fault that we have a sex tape . . . soon to be sex *tapes*." I grimace, but I don't back down from his gaze. I don't cower. "It was my fault. *Mine*. And I'm so, so sorry. Your penis is now all over the internet, and that's on me."

He smiles at the last line. I narrow my eyes as he nears me again and cups my cheeks. "Rose, you don't have to apologize to me," he says sincerely. "It was a mistake."

I cringe again.

"I know," he says. "You and me, we don't have many of those." Connor combs my hair away from my eyes. "But they happen."

I exhale and nod. I've been holding so much in—looking more like a wooden board, like someone shoved a broom up my ass, on red alert, waiting for the next attack. I'm trying to let this go, but it's a little difficult. My naked body is all over the internet, and my world has changed in one millisecond and moment of time.

What's done cannot be undone.

"Can I try something?" he asks me.

I frown deeply, not understanding. Not until he clasps my wrist and pulls me into his arms. And then he places his large hand on the back of my head, guiding me to his chest so that my forehead nestles safely in the crook of his shoulder.

Darkness is here.

The kind I don't like to meet.

Emotions so cavernous stir within me, and a powerful surge bubbles them to the surface, a force I can't stop. The layers I wear to muffle the pain start to peel off quickly. The tears come first. Silent. And then the sobbing. Louder. The type that shakes my whole body. I have fucked up so badly, and it's not just me that's paying the price. I *hate* that I dragged someone else down from my mistake.

Connor may lose his job over this. Cobalt Inc. may not take kindly that their future CEO is a porn star. The loss of Calloway Couture will hurt me, but knowing that I ruined someone else's dream—that's unforgivable.

I can't stop crying. I hate tears. I hate what they mean, but in the confines of Connor's body it feels safe to show this part of myself.

He holds me tighter, and I clutch on to the fabric of his shirt.

"Let it out," Connor coos as he strokes the back of my head.

My privacy has been stripped, and I'll *never* get it back. I feel so incredibly violated, but Connor has somehow muted this pain that tries to pummel me. The way he holds me, with reassurance, with commitment and confidence, makes me believe that I can overcome anything. I think all my life he's helped me find power inside of myself so that I may barrel forward and never look back.

I don't know how long he holds me while I cry, but when I feel drained, when the tears have ended and I master the strength to lock away the guilt, I withdraw from his warm chest.

Connor rubs the wet streaks from my face.

"Can you fix my mascara?" I ask in a whisper.

"Look up," he tells me. I stare at the ceiling while his thumb removes the black smudges I've caused. When he finishes, he places his hands on both of my cheeks again. "Rose," he breathes. "I'd rather you cry in my arms for ten minutes than pace manically for two hours. I'm always here when you need me."

"Literally a shoulder to cry on," I say with a small smile.

"Literally, yes." He shares it.

He kisses my lips chastely before he says, "We're going to get through this. There's no challenge we can't defeat together."

He's right. My chest lifts with a newfound strength, just in time for the front door to swing open. We both look over, Loren and Ryke walking in.

"So the movers just left," Loren tells us. "They said that they couldn't fit your cedar table in the truck, so we have to carry it to your Escalade." They stop by my coffee table like they're going to lift it, but then they just wait there for a second, staring *knowingly* at me. This is a level of weird that I'm not used to.

They've seen me have sex.

They've most likely seen me naked or partially naked.

I have no idea if they watched the unedited tape on accident, on purpose, or not at all, but the option is there. Instead of being plagued by embarrassment, which threatens to creep up, I set my hands on my hips and say, "What are you waiting for? Take the table to the car." I *almost* snap my fingers at them. But I withhold that impulse.

Loren cocks his head, and his mouth curves in a wicked grin. "So you like to be tied up?"

My nose flares. Embarrassment sufficiently gone. Anger intact. I am about to lunge (with poise and class) and swing my purse at him, but Connor wraps his arms around my waist.

"What?" Lo says mockingly. "I'm just stating the truth."

Ryke gives his brother a look. "Stop making her ashamed."

Lo touches his chest innocently. "I just find it funny that a girl who invents new ways to mutilate dicks every single day likes to be fucked hard by one."

Connor speaks before I have the chance. "She likes what she likes. Let's leave it at that, Lo." He says it casually, but we all sense the warning behind his words.

"Okay," he says, but he's having trouble holding back a smirk and a laugh. Ryke shakes his head at him, but he's about to laugh too.

"I hate both of you," I tell them.

Ryke looks a little apologetic. "We're not laughing at you. Honestly, it's just . . ." His eyes flicker between me and Connor. He smiles again. "You go through life, seeing people one way. And in one fucking moment, what you thought was commonplace becomes something else, something . . . different." He shrugs. "That's all. I see you guys a little differently. Not bad, not good. Just fucking different."

It takes me a moment to digest that. I can be okay with different. Connor is trying to stifle an even larger grin. I can practically hear his thoughts: *Ordinary is boring, darling.* He *loves* every word that just came out of Ryke's mouth. And that rarely happens.

Loren nods to Connor. "You going to help us lift this?"

Connor's eyebrow arches. "Is it really that heavy?"

"It's *solid* wood," Loren says, about to kick the table to demonstrate.

I glower and hold a finger to him. "Don't *scuff* my table."

His foot freezes mid-kick. He sets it back on the ground while Connor goes to the middle, each brother on either side.

Before they pick it up, Connor stares off for a second, and I watch his eyes tighten in confusion. "I've been meaning to ask," he says, clearing his throat. He looks between both of them. "Did either of you fuck in the showers?"

"No way," Ryke answers first.

Oh. Shit. We couldn't have been the only ones, right?

Loren says, "Lily was too scared to take a shower naked for six whole months. Do you really think we were going to fuck in there?"

So there's no footage of Lily bathing in the nude. She must have kept her swimsuit on. Thank God. I'll take that miracle.

"Did you two do anything?" Loren asks us.

We stay silent as we both recall the blow job. I look far more suspicious than Connor.

Loren meets my gaze, and I glare. He laughs harder. "Oh, this is too rich."

"What's rich would be my foot to your balls," I retort.

"Why don't you just hit Connor?" Loren banters. "And then he can spank you for it."

"Or I can just spank you," Connor says.

Loren laughs. "Before or after you tie me up?"

"After."

Loren grins, and I cut him off as his mouth opens again, "You're both adorable. We get it." Before he can comment, I add, "How are Lily and Daisy doing?" I haven't spoken to either of them about the tapes yet. I've been avoiding, and they've been giving me space while I packed.

Loren and Ryke say nothing at first, and my eyes must widen

to saucers because Connor returns to my side, drawing me to his chest.

"You go," Ryke whispers to his brother.

Loren shakes his head and then rolls his eyes. Then he looks at me. "Lil is concerned about you. She's fine, but . . . I mean . . ." He cringes. "We're both kind of relieved." He looks guilty for saying so. "Honestly, we're just glad it's not us."

"Me too," I say.

He exhales and runs a hand through his hair. "I'm sorry. Really, Rose. If that was Lil . . ." His face breaks, and it looks like there's a physical weight that bears on his shoulders, dropping them.

"She's okay," I say with a nod. If not her, then me, right? I can handle this. If I keep repeating it, it may come true. Or I'll just believe it until it does. "And Daisy?" I ask.

Ryke stuffs his hands in his jeans. "She's been quiet. I think she's just in shock."

"She'll be okay," I say again with another nod.

"Yeah," Ryke says, his muscles tense, "she'll be fine." It's like he's trying my new tactic. Repeat it and believe it.

Connor kisses my cheek and departs from me again to help with the table.

I take a deep breath as I watch them lift the antique in the air. The last piece of furniture in this townhouse. And the last moment left before we're free from the reality show.

But I realize that I'll never be free from Scott Van Wright.

He stamped himself all over me.

And distributed it to the world.

Fifty

Connor Cobalt

'm sorry," I apologize to my mother almost immediately as I walk into her office, a city view of Philadelphia covering a whole wall. Her office is minimal. A couple black bookshelves and a clean desk. No pictures of her family. Everything personal and private is kept out of sight.

"Shut the door," she says stiffly.

I close it behind me. The blinds are already snapped shut on all the windows that peer into the hallway. We're alone.

I take a seat in the chair across from her desk. I wait for her to say something about the sex tape, but she stares at her computer, clicking her mouse for an extra minute. Leaving me to my own fucking thoughts.

I always protected my reputation. It meant everything to me. But I don't even care anymore. I have what I want: a job at Cobalt Inc. and my girlfriend. Besides Rose's well-being, the only thing I worry about is how I've hurt *this* company.

Scott can collect his cash.

I have the girl. Now I just need to secure my position here.

I wait for my mother to say, *you're fired*. To strip me of my standing as interim CEO. To hand everything I've worked for to Steve Balm. I could lose something important to me, something that I've spent *years* toiling over, in five minutes or less.

"I'm willing to make this right," I say. "Whatever you need me to do." It's a lofty statement, and I'm not sure I'm prepared to pay. But I fucking make it, and I wait for her response.

She finally swivels in her chair, facing me. And she says absolutely nothing. She just stares at me, testing me, maybe. She wears a face I can barely even read.

"Did you watch the tape?" I ask, internally cringing at the idea of my mother seeing me screw my girlfriend.

"No," she says flatly. "I've read about your situation with Rose online. You have the lawyers involved, I hope?"

"Yes."

She exhales loudly and nods a few times before leaning back in her chair. "Connor," she starts. "I don't think I've ever told you this, but . . . I'm really proud of you."

Wait. I repeat her words over again in my head. "Are we talking about the same situation . . . ?"

She smiles. She *actually* smiles. "You have a sex tape. And I'm not proud of you for that, although, I really want to talk to Rose at the wedding. To clarify. I was in a bad place when we met at the restaurant, and I was projecting. I mistook your relationship with her as somewhat distant and contrived. Really, that was what I had with your father."

"My father." She never talks of Jim. *I* never talk of Jim. He's nothing more than a name on a birth certificate.

"We were rarely intimate." Why is she telling me this? "When we were, it was to have children. And then I couldn't have any more after the twins . . ." She clears her throat, and lines wrinkle her forehead in hurt. She lets me see it.

Sweat gathers underneath my white button-down. My whole body heats at her unfamiliar sincerity. I feel like I'm on fire. It's my *only* feeling in this moment. I don't understand my reaction. I can't understand anything. I just listen and try to let my mind reconnect to my body.

414 · KRISTA RITCHIE and BECCA RITCHIE

"Hearing about you and Rose . . . I think you're going to make it for the long run."

My mother just approved of my relationship *after* a sex tape circulated online. What world do I fucking live in?

"Like I was saying," she says, "I'm proud of you." She straightens up and rests her hands on her desk, shifting papers nervously. She shows me that emotion as well. And then her dark blue eyes meet mine. "You're incredibly intelligent, and you will do *great* things in life, Richard . . . Connor . . . Cobalt." She smiles at my full name, as though she remembers when she chose it for me. "I have no doubt about this." Her eyes tighten in pain the longer she stares in my direction. I don't know how much time passes. Maybe a minute before she says, "And I'm so very *sorry* for things that I have done to you."

"What are you talking about?" I shake my head. She's put a weight on my chest that I can't release.

"I made you feel like you didn't need a father in your life—that it was so unimportant that you could live without one." She takes a sip from a glass of water. "It's taken some therapy to come to terms with this, but I have . . ." She pauses. "You didn't need Jim. And you didn't need me. I gave you necessary tools to thrive on your own, but I never gave you the ones that every child deserves." She wipes a tear before it falls. "I never showed you love. And I'm *so* sorry for that. I hope . . . I hope that Rose can do what I've neglected for so many years."

I open my mouth, but she cuts me off with a raised hand.

"Let me finish. There's something else." She grabs a tissue, sniffs, and walks around her desk.

She sits in the chair next to me.

And just by the serious, tortured look on her face—I know there's no way to prepare for her words. I can't anticipate anything she's going to say.

So I grip the armrest, I clench my teeth and I brace myself.

I don't want to fall.

I never have before.

feel blindsided.

My whole life I always made sure I knew every possible path, every probability and *what if*, so that I wasn't ever assaulted by this feeling. And today, I wake up and there it is.

The path I never saw coming.

I left Cobalt Inc. with this insane thing ripping through my chest. I thought about calling Frederick, but there's only one person I want to see. And it's not my therapist.

The Calloway Couture loft is crammed with people and boxes, bustling around with fervent urgency. A dramatic change from months ago. Her company is still in flux. She won't know how the sex tape will impact it until a few weeks pass.

I find Rose in her glass-walled office in the back. She subconsciously touches the bruise on her cheek, concealed with makeup, as she scans her computer screen. I enter quickly and shut the door.

She springs to her feet in an instant upon seeing me. "What's wrong?" Her fingers touch the corners of my eyes, as if she needs to feel my tears to know they're real. I don't blame her. I did the same fucking thing.

I don't remember the last time I cried. But it was probably over something trivial. A grade. An accomplishment I didn't fully succeed. The things that used to matter to me. I've never cried over a person until now.

"Hold on," Rose chokes, worry coating her voice. She moves swiftly, drawing cream curtains closed so that her employees can't see into her office.

I take a seat on her white couch, another breathtaking view through the window. This time New York City. And then Rose sinks down on the cushion, turning her body towards mine.

She rubs my leg. "Connor . . ."

I take her hand in mine, lacing our fingers together slowly. I try to speak, to let it out, but I shake my head and pinch my eyes as they outflow. Why is this so hard? Why do real emotions have to be so devastating? Why do they have to cripple me?

"It's okay. You don't have to say anything."

But I do. I need to fucking say it. "I hate her . . ." I start. The first thing that comes out of my mouth is impudent and juvenile. I can't take it back. I just keep going. "I hate that she has continued to blind me. No matter *how* wide I open my eyes, there's been a haze that only she could clear. And she made me believe that I was walking in the fucking clear sky." I pinch my eyes again, and I actually scream, one that burns my throat. "I am so—"

"Don't you dare say *stupid*," she snaps. "You're *not* stupid, Richard."

"I feel like an idiot," I tell her. "I was fooled by my own mother for two fucking years, Rose. Two years, and she couldn't find it in her heart to tell her *only* son that she has breast cancer? That she's *dying*?" My throat swells as the truth bears down on me. "She made me believe I'd be taking over Cobalt Inc. in five years, maybe ten. And this whole time, she knew I'd be taking it in two months."

Rose's mouth falls. "Two . . . months?"

"Two months. That's how long she has left." I extend my arms. "And she didn't think it was important to tell me."

Not until now. She was scared. I saw the fear in her eyes at her office. It's why she's been regretting and remembering the past. And yet, I can't pity her. I can't wish her farewell.

I only hate that it took *death* for her to see her mistakes.

And I hate that it's taken me the same to see mine.

I unlace my fingers from Rose, and I hold her one hand in between two of mine, just staring at them for a while. I call her stubborn, but in the past year and a half, I've been worse.

I meet those fierce yellow-green eyes. Even in the wake of my pain, she has this resilience that's more beautiful than words can describe. It's fire to my water. And I want her to burn me alive.

"You're the only one who has ever loved me," I confess, my chest heavy. "Not a mother. Not a father. Not a friend. Just you, Rose." All these years, I never thought I'd need anyone but me to survive. My mother thought the same.

I was wrong.

"I don't want to be sixty years old and wishing I'd opened myself up to the people I care about. I don't want to look back and regret that I wasn't a better friend or a better man to the woman I adore."

She's already crying. I haven't even said it yet.

Tears fall down her cheeks, matching mine.

"And I can't tell you how long I've been fighting the truth, but it's been a while," I say.

The next words come from the core of my chest. Each word is like taking on water and breathing in oxygen—a paradox that I enjoy very much.

"I am so *deeply* in love with you, Rose." I wipe her cheeks with my thumb.

She tries to smile but every time she does, more tears fall. I can tell they're from a place of joy by the way her eyes light. And then she says, "Ca vous a pris pas mal de temps." *It took you long enough.*

I said the same thing to her once. "How long do we have left?"

She finally smiles through the tears. "Forever."

I draw her to my chest and kiss her strongly, not letting go.

I realize, in this very moment, that love was the only thing missing from my life.

And it's the only thing that matters to me.

I can live with that.

As stupid as it may seem.

Fifty-one

Rose Calloway

Connor reties the halter on my bridesmaid's dress in the limo while I read an article to him off my phone. When I finish I say, "Well?"

"You shouldn't fixate on a gossip columnist."

"It's not a gossip site. This is a *news* article, Richard," I snap. "Did you not hear what they said?" I'm about to reread the part of the article where they condemn him for not being a real dominant in a dominant/submissive relationship. I didn't even know there were standards that had to be met.

"There aren't rules," he says calmly. "We do what works for us, and if no one on the internet likes it, then they're free to watch another porn that doesn't star *us*." He grins. "Although, they won't be as good . . ."

I turn around and smack his chest. "I'm serious."

"So am I," he says, staring down at me with an intense gaze, like he'd love to consume all of me.

Love.

I smile. Yes, he loves me.

That never gets old.

"You need to stop reading all of these articles that dissect the sex videos," he says in a low, husky voice. "It'll spin your mind."

"Maybe I like my mind to be spun."

"I can find a much healthier way to do that." His lips rise, and he leans close to kiss me, but the limo bumps down the cobblestone street, tearing my attention to the outside.

"We're here," I say, filled with a flurry of emotions.

Our limo ditches the rabid media behind the entry, and I roll down my window, hearing the helicopters buzzing in the air. I ignore them and focus on the palace looming ahead, taking in the stunning architecture and massive size. This really is a wedding fit for a queen.

I hope Lily is more excited than anxious today. I feel like I'm carrying nerves for the both of us. I'm not sure what to expect. Connor has taken the reins of the wedding, which means every detail is a surprise. He's already confessed to changing the venue, no longer a church in the heart of Paris.

We're a little bit outside of the city now. "I still don't know how you booked the Château de Fontainebleau," I tell him, stunned.

Connor wraps an arm over my shoulders and leans into my ear. "I have my ways."

Connor and his ways. "You mean your connections," I clarify.

"Those, yes." He smiles.

I check the time on my cell again, and he slips it right out of my hand. I ignore his tactics to calm my nerves, and I hike up my bright pink bridesmaid dress to climb to the seat closest to the driver. "Excuse me," I say in clipped words. "Could you drive just a little faster? We're running behind."

"We're thirty minutes early," Connor reminds me, his smile only widening.

"And I wanted to be an hour early," I snap at him. "But someone spent fifteen minutes just choosing cufflinks. I don't think Loren really cares that you put on your . . ." I glance at his wrists. "Are those real gold?"

His grin lifts to his eyes, which only makes me roll mine. And then I catch a peek out the window and my stomach dives. What the . . . *fuck*!

I grab at my dress again, bunching the pink fabric in my hand so that I don't rip it. I move to the window and practically stick my entire head out like a dog. Not the most unladylike thing I've done. But it's close. Connor's hands land on my hips and pull me back in.

"There are cameras in the sky," he says.

"And there are roses on the path!" I scream, my eyes bugged. "You changed the flowers to roses?!" Lily is going to kill me. This is so, so, so wrong. I chose *orchids*. Neutral flower territory.

Connor's eyebrows furrow in confusion, and he follows my frantic gaze. "That must have been a mistake." He turns back to me and cups my cheeks. "Breathe. I'm going to text the wedding coordinator and have them change it."

"*You're* the wedding coordinator," I refute.

He grins *again*.

"Hun, I'm the wedding *delegator*. I have one wedding planner and ten wedding coordinators at my disposal, which really are just glorified assistants."

Of course he would delegate all of his duties. Now I'm really nervous. He has put trust into other people, whereas I'd rather kill myself by trying to do it alone. *Check your pride, Rose.* Right, my pride is not fucking up *anything* today. I go to look at what else has been ruined, but he keeps his hands on my shoulders, forcing me to stay.

"This is going to be a long day. I want you beside me, not crawling out of a window," he tells me. "What do you say? You accept this challenge, Rose Calloway?"

I nod, willing to feed into his plans to calm my nerves.

Just this once.

Where is everyone?!" My heels clap down the empty corridor that echoes. No one is here. I don't understand. No Lily or Loren. No Ryke or Daisy. No guests or parents. I'm not stupid. It's clear that Connor changed the time of the wedding.

"What'd you push it back to?"

"Four," he says. "You wanted to be early."

"Not *three* hours early." Is he crazy?

I put my hands on my hips, but he sets his palm on the small of my back and leads me in a new direction.

"Where are we going?"

"Outside."

"I need to call Lily. I need to find her and make sure she's not hyperventilating."

"Lily's fine."

"I'm sure she's on the precipice of a mental breakdown." I ignore his comment. "It's my duty as the maid of honor to calm her."

"Has anyone ever told you to stop and smell the roses?" he asks with an edging smile.

I roll my eyes. "Ha ha," I say. "I've heard them all, believe me—" I'm distracted as soon as my heels sink into the manicured lawn. And then I look up and I become rooted to the earth. Connor waits by my side, his hand never leaving my back.

Cream, pink and red roses cascade along hedges, filling the gardens. But it's not the gorgeous flowers that have me overflowing with emotion.

In the open courtyard stand Lily, Daisy and Poppy, wearing pale pink bridesmaids' dresses, simple and light, unlike the one I'm smothered in. Almost like something I used to wear at ballet recitals.

"I don't . . ." I shake my head as I take in their bright, glowing features. Lily is crying. And smiling.

Then I see Poppy's husband and Ryke and Loren, all in tuxes, dapper and handsome. And then . . .

"Mother?"

My mom wipes a couple tears as she smiles. She has her hands to her chest, choked with emotion, her pearls gone for the day. I almost start crying at the sight. My father stands by her side with an equally heartfelt reaction towards me.

Connor gently leads me closer to them.

I add together all the pieces and I shake my head quickly. "Connor, Connor, we can't hijack my sister's wedding."

"I didn't," Connor says.

"We gave it to him a month ago," Loren explains with a growing smile.

"What?" I look between all of them, incensed that they kept a secret from me at first, but then I absorb each face, each family member and friend.

Everyone is happy.

I imagined today as a brutal one. Yelling. Screaming. Tugging Lily down the aisle, praying both her and Loren would say yes. "But . . ." I stammer as I glance at both my mother and father. I haven't processed what's happening to me yet. ". . . Lily's inheritance. You said she couldn't get it back until she married Loren."

"We're still engaged," Lily says. She sidles next to Loren and he wraps an arm around her waist. "We're just waiting to get married like we wanted to."

"And it's okay," my dad says with a nod. "We're not making their marriage a stipulation to anything. They can do that on their own time."

I look to my mother. She reaches to her collar where her pearls would sit, but without them present, she touches the hollowness of her bone. It's her only tell, her only giveaway that she may not be one hundred percent satisfied with this outcome for my sister. But her lips stay pressed in a thin line, not arguing. She's accepting it now, and that's a start. The reality show did repair more of Lily's image than this wedding could have. People were given six months of footage to fall in love with her and Loren instead of a dozen pictures.

"It's okay," Lily says again. "This day is yours."

"What?" My voice is lost to shock.

Connor takes my hand, and I face him. It's quiet. The only

noise from the fountain beside us and the birds flapping in the sky. The helicopters sound far away from the courtyard, like little insects in the distance.

"Rose," Connor breathes. And then he drops to one knee. He takes the black box from his pocket and flips it open. "Will you spend the rest of your life with me?"

I don't even look at the diamond. "Yes," I say, not hesitating, not thinking. I just say the one word that makes the most sense because my heart tells me so. I'm in such a fog that I only realize he's standing and kissing me when everyone claps around us.

I smile and hold on to his face, not wanting my lips to part from his yet.

He grins into the kiss.

I'm getting married.

Today.

Holy shit. He breaks apart, and Daisy approaches me first with a dress box. She opens it, and I see the gown I sewed folded neatly underneath plastic wrapping. "We had the bust altered so you'd fit in it and not Lily," she admits. "I stole the gown from your closet."

I run my fingers over the plastic. I designed my own wedding dress. I smile. The dress I know I'll love. The material is delicate, as thin as a ballet recital outfit. It will reach my collarbone, how I like my clothes. Connor, I realize, found better bridesmaids' gowns to match what I had created for Lily.

"It's perfect," I say. I glance back at Connor and I shake my head. "I can't believe you did all of this for me."

"I know what you love," he says, "I was happy to make this day ours."

I breathe out slowly so I don't start crying all over again. My sisters begin to trickle inside to get ready for the wedding . . . *my* wedding. Loren and Ryke follow suit. With Poppy's husband and my father in tow.

Connor and my mother are the only two who linger in the courtyard.

My mother takes my hands in hers. "Rose," she says with glassy eyes. "I love you, and I never thought you'd get married . . ."

I can't help but laugh because I never thought I would either.

"So this day is a dream for me as much as I know it is for you."

I'll take it. "Thank you," I say, kissing her cheek. She kisses mine back.

"I'll see you inside." She pats Connor's arm before she disappears into the palace.

Connor tilts his head, and he wears that arrogant, conceited smile I know so well. He edges forward and wraps his arms around my waist. "I love you," he says. *I love you.*

The words fill me more than anything else. His lips touch my forehead, and he holds me so close, and I sway with him a little, as though we're dancing at our reception. As though we've already said *I do.*

"One day," he breathes, "we're going to look back and recount all that we've done together. And we're going to think, *goddamn, we were only twenty-four.*"

My eyes well. "We're the responsible pair."

"The ones who clean everyone's messes."

"The ones everyone turns to," I add.

"The most adult, even though we're fairly new at this."

I laugh into a tearful smile. This is about to happen. We're going to be together. It feels like the start of a lifetime. Any fears I ever had, any reservations, are gone. I trust that he'll stay here, for me.

That I am more than just a chase.

"Kiss the sky with me," Connor whispers, a beautiful smile pulling his lips, "and don't ever come down."

Epilogue

Connor Cobalt

THREE MONTHS LATER

Hot, blinding spotlights bear down on me, my hands on either side of a glass podium. Three hundred faces stare back. And I can't see a single one. It's like being supine on a hospital table, gazing at white fluorescents with no recognition of what lies beyond.

I'm not nervous. My palms aren't clammy. The only sweat that beads my forehead derives from these lights.

The Cobalt Inc. logo rotates on a screen behind me, subsidiary names like *MagNetic* printed beneath. I've already talked about my mother. How she had a vision for this company, the typical things everyone would expect to hear after the CEO passed, leaving her son everything.

I step out of the podium, in a suit that embodies my confidence.

One day, I'm at Penn, sitting in the front of class and turning in assignments about managerial theories. And in a flash of time, I'm here. Twenty-four years old. Addressing men and women twice my age about Cobalt Inc.'s newest undertaking, with no one else commanding the stage but me.

I smile, not able to see a thing. And I don't even care. "Galileo said, 'All truths are easy to understand once they are discovered,'" I tell the crowd. "'The point is to discover them.'" The only one who would know how apropos that is to my life would be the girl in the very first row.

"Today, I'm going to tell you two truths."

I walk towards the edge of the stage with certainty.

"I know women," I say, which causes a wave of chuckling. The sex tapes are public knowledge by now. And instead of shying away from the publicity, both Rose and I have taken advantage of it—as business students would.

"And I know diamonds." My lips rise even higher.

The Cobalt Inc. logo fades behind me.

Cobalt Diamonds replaces it.

Everyone claps, more loudly as they read the tagline: *IF THERE'S ANYTHING WE KNOW, IT'S WOMEN AND DIAMONDS.*

The industry my mother built was always meant to interconnect with others. Magnets, paints, gemstones—we could have started a jewelry franchise years ago, but Cobalt wasn't a well-known name before the reality show, and we would have had to buy out another company, something we didn't want to do.

The sex tapes have immortalized me as something far greater than I am—a dominant god that can fulfill a woman's every fantasy—and belief has more power than anything I can ever construct myself.

It's given a face to my mother's company and a much bigger future.

I tell the crowd that our Director of Advertising will discuss marketing strategies. I thank them, and instead of heading backstage, I walk down the stairs to the convention floor.

My eyes adjust slowly to the darkness, but the cheering has suddenly escalated. And when I blink a few times, I realize that everyone is on their feet.

Rose included.

She claps with them, her yellow-green eyes narrowed with passion and fire. I approach her, and without a word, I hold my wife's hand and lead her down the aisle of businessmen and women. A few people pat my shoulder on the way out.

"Diamonds," she says with the shake of her head. I've been keeping this secret from her for months now. A smile lights up her face. "I'd say it's genius, but I'm afraid of inflating your ego. It's already hard living with Loren's and yours together."

I grin and lower my head to whisper in her ear, "Ladies and gentlemen, she called me a genius, and she didn't even glare when she said it."

She shoots me one now.

I kiss her temple and stand up straight, pushing through the double doors into the quiet hallway. Several people in suits and nametags walk around with purpose, leather binders to their chests, paying attention to us only when they recognize our faces.

I hold her by the waist and lift her hand, pointing out the large diamond on her finger, stones encased all around the band. "This was one of the first designs," I say.

"I have a Cobalt original?"

"Yes."

She appraises the ring on her finger, her lips rising again. "When someone asks me who I'm wearing, I'm going to say me and my husband."

The strangeness of that appeals to me just as much as it does to her. I lift her chin so her eyes meet mine, her lipstick dark red, bolding her features. "How much time do I have left with you?" I ask her.

"All day," she says. "I cleared my schedule."

I frown. "*You* cleared your schedule?" I almost laugh. "I saw your to-do list this morning. It was five pages long."

"I'm trying something new," she says, touching my chest with her hands and smoothing my suit.

"And what's that?"

"Delegation," she says. "I have a store manager. She's taking care of the inventory and the mindless tasks." Rose opened a boutique with her clothes in Philadelphia, no longer under the command of a department store. She could have accepted a couple offers from them. Many people were asking for a lingerie line from Rose, the demand increasing.

She's been designing one, but not for H&M or Saks. It'll all go in *her* new store. And even though she's given up millions of dollars in return for being a small business owner, she's happy. I can see it in her eyes. The pressure of success and fear of failure is finally gone.

"But we do have dinner plans," she says.

"We do?" My brows rise.

"Loren and Lily are meeting us at a restaurant a few blocks over." Rose tucks her hair behind her ear. "I think Lily is doing better." She nods to herself.

After the sex tapes, Rose's name wasn't tarnished the way Lily's was. Women praised her for her openness and many wanted to ask her questions.

Rose looks physically ill when we talk about the differences between this case and the sex addiction leak. Even now, her eyes tighten as she stares off in recollection of the past few months. Lily was quiet towards Rose for a while.

"It's not fair," I heard Lily cry to Loren one day.

She's right.

It's not really fair.

Rose hates that Lily was beaten down, especially since her sister was the one with the illness. But Rose had sex with her long-term boyfriend. Lily was with many different partners before Loren. Rose was the virgin. Lily was the slut. In the eyes of the world, one is right, one is wrong.

And changing the world—if that's in anyone's power—*time* has to be on your side. One of the few things I can't control.

Rose's eyes catch a newspaper on a nearby bench. I follow her gaze to see the headline: **NEW CONNOR AND ROSE COBALT SEX TAPE SOLD FOR $35 MILLION**. Scott just sold the rights to the footage of us in the bathroom. The one where Rose gives me head. It's a reminder that he's profiting off us even months after the reality show has ended. We dropped the lawsuit about a month ago. The time and stress to battle him in court wasn't worth what we have now.

We surrendered. And Scott Van Wright won.

But he didn't win what matters.

Though, I do take solace in the fact that he doesn't have footage of us in the Alps, the night Rose lost her virginity, the night we slept together for the very first time. He can sell as many sex tapes as he wants, but that moment is ours, and only ours, forever.

When I reroute my attention from the newspaper and back to Rose, I realize she's already left the headline in the past. She's studying me with an entranced, wistful gaze.

"What is it?" I ask. My heart lightens and soars as I keep watching her look at me this way.

She shakes her head with a smile, and tears crest her eyes as she says, "I love you more than anyone."

My mouth falls a little. I never thought I'd reach that place in her heart, above her sisters. It seemed unfathomable, for however much I wanted it to be true.

When the shock passes, I smile deeply and grip the back of her head, my fingers sliding through her silky hair. "I love you more than I could ever love myself." I whisper the words and lift Rose's chin again, raising her gaze to mine, not to say anything else, but to just smile as I watch her eyes churn with a familiar, unbridled emotion.

I love knowing I'll fall asleep and wake up to those impassioned eyes. I love that the most terrifying *what if*—the one without her—is the path that won't ever come true. My new dreams are in the faraway future, filled with children. And love.

ACKNOWLEDGMENTS

This book is about dreaming big. And we want to thank our parents for allowing us to dream the biggest dreams of all, for encouraging us to go after them and giving us support that we will never be able to repay. The most we can say is thank you, right here, for being the whisper in our ear that told us we could be anything and do anything. Thanks, Mom and Dad. We owe you big time.

Thanks to our brother. Even when you're toiling over your own work, you constantly think about ways to help us further our careers. One day, big brother, we're going to celebrate together, and we know you'll be right by our side.

And to the rest of our family and friends—the constant love is what keeps us going. And to our French translators, Violaine, Sarah and Nieku, you girls rock. Thank you, Nieku, for all those *Gossip Girl* nights in our dorm room. We miss them dearly.

To our readers, our fans, this book is for you. Like all great television, fandoms drive every scene, every word, and they are the chorus to what could be a silent play.

Thank you for giving music to our work.

You are the impassioned spirits that paint our world with color. We will never forget that. We promise.

EXTENDED EPILOGUE

Bora Bora Honeymoon

Rose Calloway

**THE MOMENTS AFTER I LOST MY MIND AND
MARRIED AN INFURIATING, NARCISSISTIC GENIUS WHO
HAS CAPTURED AND EVISCERATED MY HEART.
TRANSLATION: I LOVE HIM.**

> Rose ~~Magdala Calloway~~
> Rose ~~Cobalt~~
> Rose ~~Calloway-Cobalt~~
> Rose-what-the-fuck-are-you-doing-Calloway

"When I suggested hyphenating your last name, that's not entirely what I had in mind."

I plant a scathing glare on Connor, and his lips rise.

"Seven hyphens is rather excessive," he adds, not even attempting to amend his first statement into something more helpful.

I continue drilling a hole between his eyes, partially to hide my indecisiveness today. We sit in the county clerk's office, filling out our marriage license after the fact. He surprised me with our wedding in France, so we're working backwards and going through the proper formalities before our honeymoon.

I like following the rules, but Connor Cobalt likes guiding me between lines and through loopholes. When I'm with him, the world never seems to collapse in on itself, no matter how far out of bounds we go and which way we turn. Everything remains in our power. I hold on to that confidence, and this backwards event isn't even close to agitating—like an itch I can't scratch—as I thought it might be.

"Your problem is with the amount of hyphens?" I let out a short laugh that sounds close to a snort. *He's* the one who's lost his mind. "I wrote *fuck* as a middle name."

"I never claimed it was an eloquent choice." He pockets his cell into his black slacks, dressed in a perfectly ironed button-down, wavy brown hair styled, eyes a deep, hypnotic blue. He gives his full attention to me, and in doing so, Connor silently declares my importance in his life.

I'm his number one.

That fact, that triumph and award, settles warmly inside my heart.

But I read between his words.

Connor would still let me choose the ineloquent name, even if it's not what he would want for me. *This is your choice*, he's saying. No matter what I pick, it's my decision. He has yet to voice what *he* wants—which surname he'd like me to legally take. I never thought his unbiased participation would be so irritating, but I crave hearing his opinion.

I tuck my Chanel purse closer to my hip, straightening my back and shifting in the uncomfortable wooden chair, my ass numb by now. A notebook splays on my lap. I've begun scrawling out surname possibilities, ones that'll replace my ID, passport, email addresses and other forms of identification.

Connor stretches his arm over the back of my chair, rotated towards me, and his other hand rests on my thigh, the hem of my black dress riding up higher. I stiffen at the closeness of my . . . *husband.*

Husband.

I wonder when or if I'll ever grow used to our new relationship status, but there are no "rewind" or "reverse" warning signs flashing, no reaction that says, *you fucked up, Rose. You did something wrong.* Being together, forever, with this man feels too destined and too mighty to question.

Love and reason keep me by his side.

I whip my head to him, zoning in on his lips, which begin to rise in self-satisfaction. My eyes flash hot. "What do you prefer? Calloway or Cobalt or hyphenation?"

"They're all equally appealing," he lies. I can tell. I spot it in the lines of his forehead.

I glare. "I did not just marry a liar."

He cocks his head, very faint amusement drawing his mouth upward. "You married a genius."

"All geniuses aren't liars," I refute.

"No, but I'm smart enough to let you make this decision on your own."

My chest tightens. "It's your name, Richard," I counter.

"It is my name," he confirms, rather arrogantly.

I roll my eyes and stare at the notebook. I neatly write the words: *Rose Cobalt.*

I gauge his reaction, missing it the first time I wrote this as a choice. The more I scrutinize him, the more I realize that I can't read his poker face. He lets me see the glimmer of curiosity, the intrigue at what my decision might be, but he won't let me see what he wants.

"I know I'm handsome," he says, "but you need to look at the paper and not my face, Rose Magdala Calloway."

I bristle at the sound of my middle name. I'm most definitely changing that. "I can think properly while staring at your face."

"Then you're the only one." He grins.

Ugh—that grin. I unconsciously smooth my lips together, and

his eyes flit to them and back to me, as though saying, *you want to kiss me, Rose.*

No. *Yes.*

I can't even decide if I want to be kissed by my own husband, and I'm supposed to choose my forever last name. For twenty-three years, I've been Rose Magdala Calloway, and I've never really considered being called anything else.

"You're a narcissist," I suddenly say aloud.

His muscles begin to coil and tighten, but his face stays one hundred percent composed. "I'm that too." He never denies it.

"Just say it," I prod. "You want me to be Rose Cobalt, to claim this win as your own."

I watch any lingering humor fade, seriousness hardening his jaw. "A name is just a name."

"If you truly believed that, you'd let more people call you Richard." He likes the alliteration of Connor Cobalt and the advantage he gains by telling people, *you can call me Connor, my middle name*—as though they're on a friendlier basis. When in actuality, they aren't.

"Rose," he says at first, and then he pauses. He's unable to articulate exactly what he wants. It's not often this happens. And I realize that he's worried. He's truly worried that if I believe he wants me to be Rose Cobalt, I'll do the opposite to win the unspoken game we play. We're used to competing against each other, and sometimes there has to be a loser in order to win.

I can defeat him in one blow and write: *Rose Calloway.* It'd be a knockout punch. Or I could write: *Rose Calloway-Cobalt.* A tie, more or less. Neither of us enjoys ties, and the hyphen isn't as appealing to me as I thought it would be.

Rose Cobalt is a declaration to Connor that I rarely ever send. It's basically kneeling at his feet, shedding my clothes, bare and vulnerable and entirely his.

My body heats, and my fingers grow clammy around my pen.

It's what he wants, and the stubborn part of me refuses to give in so willingly.

Leave me out of it, I hear him in the back of my head.

Our push-and-pull relationship seeps into every moment of our lives, the fun and the serious parts.

"I want to ask you something," I say, breaking the short silence. I turn my head, and he still wears that severity, no humor or burgeoning grin. "Answer truthfully, not what you know I want to hear."

"I won't manipulate you, Rose," he assures me.

I nod, believing him. "Other than me, have you ever imagined someone taking your last name? Even for a second?"

"No," he says without missing a beat.

"Why not?"

He begins to grin.

I glare.

He laughs into a brighter smile. "Your memory needs some help, darling."

I try not to look confused, but I am.

He leads me to logic that circles his brain. "Moments ago, you reminded me that I'm a narcissist."

It clicks. "You'd never want to share your last name with someone."

"Never," he says, leaning closer, his cologne spinning my head, a masculine, intoxicating sandalwood scent. "I've never been good at sharing."

"But you would share your last name now?"

"Only with you."

I raise my chin a little, our lips closer. "Why is that?"

He tucks a piece of hair behind my ear, holding my face for a moment, and I sink into his calm gaze, a languid river. His thumb slowly traces my bottom lip. "Do you really need to ask?" he whispers.

My breath shallows. I know the answer.

If he wants me attached to his last name, in association with him, then I'd have to be his equal. He'd never deliberately attach himself to anyone he'd consider inferior. He's too egotistical to accept that avenue.

I'll be the only person linked to him this intimately. The more I toss these facts around, the more pleased I become.

I hate to bring up the subject of *children*, especially when the idea is so far off into the future. But I like planning, and I'd hate to fuck up this aspect by not mentioning it. My name affects more than just me.

"When we have children, whose name are they taking?"

His brows almost jump in surprise. He composes himself before his shock lasts long. "I thought you would've said *if* we have kids, not *when*."

"I already agreed to them," I snap. "I can revoke my earlier—"

"*When* we have children." He smiles, rubbing my thigh some to show that he's happy with my word choice. "They'll take our name." He's already agreed to hyphenate his name, if that's what I choose. I think he knows I don't like the hyphen, so he's agreeing to something that he's certain won't ever come to fruition.

"What if I remain Calloway?" I home in on his features, and his lips lower into an inexpressive line.

"Then every other kid can be Calloway and every other one can be Cobalt."

I glower. "That's absurd, Richard."

He tries not to laugh. "We can play a game of Scrabble for it. The first one to two hundred points can choose whether our children will be Calloway kids or Cobalt kids."

Even as he says it, the idea of Calloway babies sounds strange, a name synonymous with four sisters: Poppy, Lily, Daisy and me.

Connor never grew up with brothers and sisters, and the name Cobalt has largely just consisted of him—an untarnished name that deserves rowdy, belligerent and soulfully good children to mark all over it, claiming it as their own.

I challenge Connor, "What if we have a Cobalt boy who's into heavy metal and slams the bedroom door in our face—will you regret giving him your last name?"

Connor immediately shakes his head. "Not for a moment." He wears this fondness in his eyes, as though he'd hope for a future similar to that one. I know Connor well enough to understand *how much* he values unique personalities.

He even adds, "Our children are a part of you and me, Rose."

It all makes more sense, why he'd be willing to let them share his name but no one else. Why he'd *want* them to. Why he'd want *me* to.

He's not manipulating me to choose his name, but I'm uncovering how much we'd both gain from it—the power that *I* feel from this choice. To be the only person connected this closely to Connor Cobalt.

I've won something greater here.

I've won him.

Just as he's won me.

There's only one problem: I named my brand Calloway Couture. Even though I can personally step away from the name but keep the business as is—I still want to feel a connection to it.

Connor watches me intently but says nothing. He waits, his thumb stroking my cheek, and I sense his tense body, never relaxing.

I'd take very little pleasure in that knockout punch, even if it's a clear victory against him. I don't want to see a trace of *real* hurt across his face, not from my own hands or anyone else's.

I close the notebook and go straight for the marriage license, my decision set. Connor's hand drops, but he never questions my actions.

In my neatest handwriting, I scrawl my new middle and last name: *Rose Calloway Cobalt*.

When I turn to Connor, his lips touch mine, sweeping me in a powerful exchange, his hand lost in my glossy brown hair. Flushed, I unconsciously near, my fingers gripping his biceps, stiff and barely moving, wanting more despite my lack of proficiency.

All too quickly, the kiss drifts to my cheek, his breath heavy with mine, and he whispers, "Je t'aime."

I love you.

Rose Cobalt

Boredom and a head cold have taken over during the twenty-three-hour flight to our honeymoon destination. I sit across from Connor on his private plane, a table separating us with our fifth game of chess. He's beaten me all five times, which strengthens the boring part of the flight and the fact that I'm slightly ill.

If my head stopped pounding, even for a second, I'd be able to concentrate. Instead, an elephant has camped out in my brain.

Connor scrutinizes me with more concern than I want to meet. I refuse to let a common cold ruin our honeymoon. I'm stronger than this.

"It's your turn," I snap, trying not to shiver. *You have a fever, Rose.* I cross my arms and tilt my chin up. I can conquer anything. *Fuck you, fever.*

His eyes briefly flit to the board. "You've made a banal move."

"Banal?" I scowl and scrutinize the board, unsure of what move I actually made. I can't even remember which piece I shifted.

"Predictable," he says, "ordinary. Inconsequential, in this case." He doesn't flash a smile as he "educates" me on a word I understand just fine.

"Regardless of what my move was, it's still your turn."

He rests his forearms on either side of the board, leaning closer to me. His six-foot-four height makes him seem even nearer. I like being sick about as much as he does. We usually push through illnesses with medicine and water, going about our day as though nothing has changed, no one able to spot the weakness in us.

In fact, I've *never* seen him ill, not once. Besides monstrous hangovers, he's never seen *me* sick like this either. I slyly took some medicine earlier to avoid a fever, but it's not doing its job apparently.

Suddenly, Connor raises his hand to touch my forehead.

I slap it away. "Richard."

"Rose." His usual placid, calm expression has morphed into unbridled concern. "You need to sleep."

"I'm fine."

"You lost five rounds of chess," he reminds me. "I've known you haven't felt well since the first one—now you're shaking."

"I am not." I shiver. *Stop shivering. Goddammit. You're a tornado, not the person being swept beneath it.*

He's about to refute, but I speak first.

"Let's play a new game." He's bored. I'm bored, and it's my fault—or at least my cold's fault. Maybe I can concentrate better with a game that has less logic in it but higher stakes.

Connor stands.

I shoot him a boiling glare and point at him. "Sit down," I order, "or I won't talk to you the rest of the trip." It's a juvenile statement, but a hammer is crashing down on my cranium every two seconds—I just want him to be stimulated. If I sleep, I'll be worsening this already dull plane ride.

Connor sets his palms flat on the table, stretching over, towering and staring down at me. "No."

He won't listen to an ultimatum like this one. He tries to touch my forehead again, and I stubbornly smack his hand away.

"You're being obstinate," he says but never budges from his stance.

"So are you." When we both dig in our feet, *games* become the best solution to end disputes. "Trivia," I say, "first one to answer a question wrong loses."

He straightens up, not returning to his seat, most likely to make a point that I can't order him around so easily. "And the stakes?"

I don't think long about this. I say the first thing in the front of my brain. "If I win, you have to write me a *truthful* love letter, professing your love *to me*, not to yourself." I have no idea what he'd write, and that unknown intrigues me.

His lips almost tic upwards. "And if I win?"

I pause, wanting his reward to be better than simply *you can touch my forehead*. It should be grander, more pleasurable and exhilarating. This is our honeymoon after all. The words spill out before I question them more. "Anytime you're aroused . . . even a little bit, I'll sleep with you." I think sometimes he holds back around me, knowing I need rest after we've fucked harder, longer. I'm telling him he can sleep with me at any moment, any time.

Even through the start of a fever, my neck warms by this declaration. I strangely want to know how many times he becomes aroused by me, at which moments—if they're random or have some consistency behind them.

Connor scrutinizes me for a moment, and I bet he can tell his reward would partly be a reward for me too. I think he's going to renounce it and choose something else like, *I want to touch your forehead*.

Then he nods. "Okay, darling."

I can't recall the frustrating game, which I want to wipe from my memory. Five minutes after our terms, I cross my arms over my chest, losing faster than I ever have before.

Connor still towers above me. Turbulence shakes the plane a little, and he clutches my headrest.

I huff under my breath. "Most husbands would let their wives win the game." He demolished me.

"Then I'm in the more intelligent minority." He knows I would've been pissed if he *let* me win.

I roll my eyes and rub my cold arms, a chill never leaving me. My white sweater can't defeat this illness. My only symptoms have been a fever and pressure on my head, which makes me hopeful that it'll only last twenty-four hours.

Connor clasps my hand, his palm hot against my skin. My chest falls, aching at this new warmth. He guides me to my feet, and he lets go of my hand, his fingers drifting to the small of my back. My head whirls as he leads me down the aisle, towards a door where the small bedroom lies, thanks to the lavish private plane.

When he opens the door and enters with me, it clicks. "You're collecting your winnings already?" I ask. I didn't think he'd even be partially aroused during this flight.

He gives me a look that I can't decipher, his brow slightly arched. "Lie down." The forceful command almost knocks me backwards.

Without protesting, I sit on the edge of the bed, a cream comforter with gold hemmed pillows. I scoot towards the wall, my limbs sore already. I wonder if this is another symptom of my cold. When I reach the pillows, I stay upright, watching him and wondering his intent.

Sex, Rose. He's going to fuck you.

I lack the energy to be a brilliant participant, but I'd let him do what he wants. I made the terms of the game. It's my own doing.

He unbuttons his shirt, eyes dead set on me. My head is so heavy that I find myself lying down completely, my cheek on a large feather pillow.

Connor says something in deep, husky French that I struggle to translate.

"Yes," I reply softly, agreeing to his words because they sound nice.

He removes his slacks and stands only in navy boxer briefs, his body sculpted, biceps carved, abs defined—all so awfully infuriating and attractive. I plant my gaze on his so his ego doesn't mushroom by my lingering stare.

He's not amused like he'd normally be. There's no shadow of a grin. There's no humor in his deep blues. He climbs onto the bed, setting a knee on either side of my body. With one hand, he strokes my hair off my forehead, a calming caress that he repeats over and over.

My heavy eyelids begin to close.

With his other hand, he unzips my confined skirt and pulls it off my legs, a greater, larger chill snaking across my skin.

My eyes snap open and I shudder against him. He tangles his legs with mine, quickly removing my sweater and unsnapping my bra. He leaves my black panties on and tugs me against his strong body, his chest. He lies on his side with me pressed to him. I bury my head into the crook of his shoulder, basking in this sudden skin-to-skin heat that reaches deeper than my clothes could.

Connor makes sure we're both beneath the comforter, encasing us further, and I find myself scooting closer, even though there's nowhere else to go but against his chest, his legs and arms. He braces me to him, letting me soak in his body temperature.

I wait for him to slip inside of me, rock against me, but instead, he begins stroking my hair again, lulling me, and gently, my eyes close once more.

I murmur, "I don't think I'm that wet, so you might need to use something." *Lube*, my brain can't even find the technical word right now.

His lips skim my ear, his breath like dragon fire. *More*, I internally plead. I need him. And he says, "I'm not fucking you."

I'm too tired to open my eyes. I'm too tired to even process what this means exactly—other than a penis is not going into my vagina. I make a sound like *hmm?*

Every stroke of his hand creates a blazing trail of heat. "I want to hold my wife," he whispers. "I want to take care of you. How does that sound, Rose?"

It sounds better than I imagined. I only have enough energy for one word. "Perfect," I breathe so softly, falling asleep in his arms.

Connor Cobalt

Bora Bora rests northwest of Tahiti, a South Pacific island in French Polynesia. I expect Rose to stubbornly want to sunbathe with a 103-degree fever the first day we arrive. I fully plan to pick her up and set her on the bed. The minute we enter our bungalow—stilted above a body of water and overlooking Mount Otemanu—she falls asleep, curled on the couch.

I carry her to bed, gently placing her beneath the white covers. Then I unpack her clothes, knowing she'd want them folded in drawers and not sitting in her suitcase. I glance over at her every so often, less concerned than I'd been on the plane.

I have more self-control than most men, and it took all of it to remain seated while we flew. I wanted to take her temperature, to prove to her that she had a fever and stubbornness wasn't going to vanquish it. But I didn't marry someone that submits to me so easily.

Rose is a challenge. One I adore and love.

My wife.

My wife.

I repeat it over and over, and the power behind it and love never fades. If there is a loss of meaning in repetition, then that one phrase has conquered the rule, denounced its very existence.

My wife.

Never did I think I'd possess someone as much as they've possessed me. It's one of the few times I'm okay with being wrong.

But I won't make it a habit.

We've landed. Rose is content and safe, which means I can indulge in my honeymoon and indulge her. There are some moments that happen only once. Honeymoons aren't sacred that way, not for everyone.

I know this is it for me.

My one honeymoon.

With my one wife.

And so it begins.

Y ou haven't been aroused by me at all?" Rose questions the next day. Her fever broke this morning, and she had enough strength to put on her black bikini. She stands and eats a piece of watermelon out of a bowl. In the living room, the sliding doors are open to the deck, the extinct volcano and turquoise water in sight.

The atmosphere in Bora Bora is as exquisite as the view in front of me. Color has returned to Rose's cheeks and a rare flyaway hair hangs over her ear. My worry about her health has dissipated to subtle concern. I'm more preoccupied with making this week special for her.

I rub sunscreen on my bicep and abs, about ten feet separating us. "Surprised?" I ask, my confidence supporting my six-foot-four frame. I agreed to the terms of the bet because I knew she'd enjoy them as much as me, but I was also keenly aware of how I'd break them until she felt better.

Neither of us would enjoy fucking when she's sick.

She forks another piece of watermelon. "That will be your cock if you're lying to me."

Someone's feeling better. I don't hide my smile. "I'll be sure to keep the cutlery away from you for the rest of the trip."

Her glare punctures my blue gaze. "My nails will suffice." She glances down at her fork. "And don't you dare hide the silverware." I wouldn't, even if I wanted to rile her. Testing her OCD by forcing her to eat with her hands is an infantile and disgusting tactic. One I won't take part in.

"Your hands can stay away from my cock then," I reply, rubbing in the sunscreen on my neck. "All I need is your mouth." I don't hide my grin, and her glower, one of fire and brimstone, almost makes me hard.

"So I can bite you."

"If you bite off my cock, you're hurting yourself too, darling."

She purses her lips, not denying it.

I take a step towards her, just one. She inhales strongly, and I squirt some sunscreen onto my palm and work on my other bicep and lower abs.

Her eyes flit across my skin. "I hate your body."

I grin. "You love it."

She combats me with her sharp gaze. "You don't know that. I could have married you for your mind alone and not because of . . ." Her eyes lower to the muscles on my abdomen and then lower to the lines that draw downward to my erection. ". . . that." She finishes with a ragged breath.

"So you love my mind and hate my body," I say with an arch of a brow. "Do you always hate things that make you wet?"

"I'm *not* wet." She points the forked watermelon at me. "And you didn't answer me."

Have I been aroused this trip? "You want me to say it bluntly?" I question, taking one step nearer.

She nods once and then eats that watermelon to hide the flush in her cheeks.

"I'd never put my cock inside of you without your prior consent."

"I consented," she refutes.

I reach her, clasping her elbow and drawing her towards me. I hear her gasp beneath her breath. I say, "I know you took cold medicine. I know you didn't feel well. How is that consent?" It's stubbornness and I know Rose well enough that I can piece apart the two.

Her shoulders relax, and her lips seem to curve upward, despite her fiery gaze burning holes into me. "I'm no longer sick, so the terms of the bet can apply now." She's aroused and curious, which is practically like Rose squeezing my cock.

"Have you put on sunscreen yet?" I evade her comment, trapping a gruff sound in the base of my throat. I appear composed, even as my imagination runs quickly. I picture Rose spread open wide, my shaft driving into her. I'm the only one that hears the noises that breach her lips. And I'll be the *only* man ever privileged to hear them. These hard, cemented truths come from the fact that she is my wife. That I am her husband. That I have her for our entire lifetime together. It's a new realization, one I hold on to.

"No," she answers me, setting the bowl of fruit aside and extending her hand for the bottle.

I don't give it to her. Instead I squirt some on my palm and begin to rub her shoulders and arms with the sunscreen. She hesitates at first, not used to giving up this control—but as her breath shallows again, she's understanding how much she likes it.

Rose rests her hands uncertainly on my biceps while I massage her, my hand dipping between her breasts, on the tops, and then to her abdomen, leaving no exposed skin untouched. She's soft and warm and beautiful. I'm even harder than before.

"How does this feel?" I ask deeply.

She swallows. "Horrible."

I smile. "Such lies." I spin her around abruptly, and she lets out a pleasured sound. Then I lean her over the couch armrest, ass perched up. Her ass—this is a priceless view that beats the crystal blue scenery outside.

I spank her once, twice—and she writhes, clutching on to a decorative pillow. My cock throbs now, and it takes me a minute to relax, so I can prolong this for both of us.

"So you like to run your nails along the cocks of liars. Do you want to know what *I* do to liars?"

She turns her head to glare at me. "Whatever it is, it's not better than my punishment."

Just you wait, darling. I take her bathing suit bottoms and pull up, until they dig into her pussy and ass like an uncomfortable thong.

She lets out an abnormal noise that sounds like a whimper— and I study her for a second, to ensure that it was pleasure and not pain. Her toes struggle to touch the ground, but they curl, and her thighs vibrate.

Pleasure.

I smile more and rub her reddened ass, my erection in line with its perfection. I want to pound into her. Right now.

Patience.

"How does that feel, Rose?" I ask, pulling her bikini bottoms harder, the fabric digging into her wetness. She moans this time at the pressure, unmistakable arousal.

I open her legs a little more and then slide my fingers between her thighs. She's more than wet. She's soaked, and she's probably been this way most of the morning—our banter from much earlier in bed and in the bathroom enough foreplay.

I lower my bathing suit trunks, my cock springing free, and she catches a glimpse of it before I fist her hair, pulling harder.

She moans, "Connor." I haven't pushed into her yet, and she gasps loudly, close to an orgasm. I want to feel her muscles clench around my cock, so I don't waste time. I remove her bikini bottoms.

Then with one hand on my shaft, I fit deeply inside of her, moving closer and closer until I'm all the way in. It almost blinds me.

I can't even thrust before she cries, before she climaxes and contracts—I grunt but keep from coming. And I thrust, rocking against her and working her up to another orgasm.

This is your wife.

I have her completely, and I never want to leave.

Connor Cobalt

I point up to the night sky, the stars appearing in droves without any coverage to cloud them. "There's Virgo," I tell her.

When I was younger, around six, I enjoyed astronomy, the science behind the stars. When I began attending boarding school, the hobby fell far behind my other pursuits, but the knowledge never faded.

Rose has her head on my shoulder, lying with me on the edge of the dock, a blanket beneath us and our wine glasses set down. Time is slow here, and I wish it could last forever. For the days to pass by with leisurely tranquility—but we'll return home soon. Back to our lives and the busy city.

"I see it," Rose replies. "Spica is bright tonight." Spica is the brightest star in the Virgo constellation. I smile, loving that she knows these random facts like me.

"Do you know the story of Astraea?" I ask her.

"Yes," she muses. "She was a virgin—"

"Like you were," I say into a smile.

Rose glances up at me, glaring of course. "But I didn't flee to the heavens and become a constellation." Astraea is the constellation Virgo, remaining there until she returns to Earth during the next Golden Age. At least, according to mythology.

"You're in the stars, darling," I tell Rose. "We both are."

Her eyes lighten by this declaration. "Where are we?" She draws her gaze to the night again.

"We're the brightest, strongest stars in the sky, the ones that will *burn* for generations until a black hole destroys the galaxy."

"Sounds like a tragic ending."

I pull her closer to me, my hand caressing her arm. "So is the way of the universe."

She rolls onto her forearms, putting unnecessary space between us that I don't like. Her eyes remain fiercely determined. "The only tragedy is that I ruined the first day here."

"Rose," I start. I know she's upset that she was sick. She feels like she ruined my honeymoon, but it's *our* honeymoon. A twenty-four-hour cold doesn't have the power to ruin anything. Being around her—whether it's while she suffers a fever or is perfectly healthy enough to threaten my cock—is more than enough for me.

"Don't try to dissuade me," she combats. "I ruined a day here, so I've been thinking about how to make up for it."

She takes a large breath and my confusion pours through me. I don't attempt to contain this sentiment, to hide it from her, not like I once would.

"Okay," I say, unknowing which direction she's headed.

With eyes like molten lava, she says, "Skinny-dipping."

I arch a brow, my lips immediately pulling upward. "Skinny-dipping?" I glance to the ocean, illuminated by the moonlight. "Right now?"

She nods. "And then we'll come back to the dock and you can make love to me under the stars."

The plan sounds nice aloud, something Rose would construct, but it also sounds too calculated and organized, so much so that I sense her nerves behind the actions.

I'd like to make it all more comfortable for her—easier for Rose in a way. Having sex outside is a big deal for a girl who values cleanliness. Stripping in public is also a difficult task since we're at a resort. We might have a bungalow with an unobstructed view, but there are still two that sit adjacent to ours.

"What if I want to fast-forward to making love?" I ask. "What happens then?" I brush my fingers against the soft, bare skin of her arm and I watch goose bumps appear.

"You can't go out of order," she refutes.

"So be it." I rise to my feet, quickly enough that shock freezes her for an extended second. She gathers her bearings, determination straightening her back.

I outstretch a hand to help Rose to her feet. Sixty percent of the time, she stubbornly rejects my offer, but today isn't one of those days. She clasps my hand, and I help her rise. She rests on the soles of her slippers.

Her fingers graze her black silk chemise, about to lift it over her head. Before the hem even reaches her hips, I effortlessly and swiftly grab her around the waist.

"Richard!" she yells as I pick her up, slippers falling off her feet, her back pressed against my bare chest. She kicks the air. *"Richard!"*

I carry her to the ocean and, without wasting another second, I toss her into the water, Rose shrieking and cursing me in one breath. I quickly jump in after her, my drawstring pants still on.

The water is warm. Even at night, the temperature is close to bath water. My head breaches the surface a short moment after her, and she spits water from her mouth, her brown hair messy and tangled at her shoulder. We both tread in the ocean, her yellow-green eyes drilling into my skull.

"I'm going to cut out your heart and feed it to the sharks," she threatens.

"We are the sharks," I refute with a grin.

She splashes water at me with her hand. I just laugh and she lets out another growl.

She stares at her wet wardrobe and huffs. "This is *silk*."

"I'll buy you another, darling."

Rose swims closer, and I never swim away, even with her threats to kill me. When she's close enough, she hangs on to the band of my drawstring pants. For a moment, I wonder if she's going to tug them off, but instead, she uses me as a support to stay afloat. "Why?" she snaps.

"Because we're extraordinary, not for the things we do, but for who we are. You don't need to feel like you have to push boundaries for me. Simply existing will always be enough."

Her lips part at my words, and she holds tighter to my waist.

I add, "And I enjoy speeding up the process so I can fuck you beneath the stars."

She plants her hand firmly on my shoulder and pushes until I sink underneath the water. When she releases, I reach the surface and can't help but laugh.

She splashes me again. "You fail. This isn't even close to skinny-dipping." Her smile peeks as she says it, knowing it's not something she *has* to do to make our honeymoon memorable.

"If you truly want to skinny-dip, I can help with that," I tease, skimming her silk chemise beneath the water.

She grips my hand. "I've changed my mind," she replies. "I want *you* to skinny-dip, and then we can make love under the stars."

"You have very strict demands. You do know this means I'll have harsher ones later."

Her throat bobs, and I lift her thigh, skillfully guiding her legs around my waist, able to tread water and keep us both above the surface.

"Fine," she says, her voice suddenly quiet in the night. Her eyes lower to my chest, beads of water rolling down. "Strip . . ." She can't see my drawstring pants, but she can feel the fabric against her legs.

I smile as I tug off my pants. She helps me so we both don't drown, and without boxer briefs, I'm naked in seconds. Her breath deepens, nothing separating my cock from her body.

She wraps her arms around my neck, and I clutch the softness of her hips beneath the silk. The nighttime silence, with the stars overhead, creates an intimate, undying moment. I inhale every fragile second of it.

"You made a mistake," she whispers.

"I don't make mistakes," I reply softly, her lips inches from mine.

"You made one when you married me then. We're going to kill each other." I don't think she believes this, but maybe she fears that I do.

I brush her hair out of her face, and I see relief and relaxation when the strands don't settle messily on her cheeks. *We're perfect together.* To believe anything else is a lie. I lift her chin, and I breathe, "I'll die happy then."

Rare tears well in her eyes, and she lets out an angered noise. "Salt water is in my eye."

"Even the thought of my death brings her to tears."

She glowers and clutches on to my neck. "I'm not crying over your hypothetical death."

I kiss her cheek. "Then what?"

She takes a deep breath before she says, "This—what we have together—has never felt more right."

We look at each other's lips at the same time, and I kiss her forcefully, my pulse thrumming and my mind brightening. I can feel her tense against me, her hands running up my neck, to my wet hair, and in the heat of our kiss, a smile lifts my lips and one raises hers.

Memorable.

This honeymoon is already that for me.

I'll remember the passion in her eyes the most—the way she splashes me with fervor and the way she proudly raises her chin with each hostile word.

I'll remember how vulnerable she looked when she was sick, and how she let me hold her, care for her. How I can call her my wife for the first time, how she smiles in those rare seconds but breathes fire into ordinary moments.

I'll remember how limitless we feel and how vast our future will be.

I'll remember it all.

Every vivid frame of color.

Rose Cobalt

Our honeymoon goes by in a flash, and I wonder if the rest of our lives will move this quickly. I hope not, and since Connor hates "time," I know he'd wish for it to slow down too.

I pack while he showers, and I remember how we spent the morning in a private-enough pool cabana, a sliver of beach nearby. The end of the trip roused me somehow. I felt brazen and invincible, enough to try something new. I wasn't trying to please Connor this time or create the *best* honeymoon experience. I just did what felt right in the moment.

We had sex.

In a cabana.

Not very many people were around—no one could see, of course. But the public act was something I've never done. We never screwed on the bungalow deck beneath the stars. I heard laughing from the nearby one, which made me paranoid and nervous.

The cabana sex wasn't preplanned. It just happened, and I was able to block out my rambling thoughts to love the beginning, middle and end.

I unzip a flap of my suitcase and then pause.

I narrow my eyes, spotting a white envelope that wasn't there before. I retrieve it, my mind racing, and then I notice Connor's handwriting.

"Of the very instant that I saw you, Did my heart fly at your service."

I know this quote well. Shakespeare. *The Tempest.*

My chest swells. I delicately open the letter, unfolding the paper, careful not to cause more creases. I wonder when he wrote this—maybe the first day when he unpacked my clothes? I inhale once before reading.

Darling,

You asked me to be truthful. Here's the truth.

I spent tonight pressing a washcloth to your forehead, staring into yellow-green eyes that tried to devour me in their ill, weathered state. And I'd spend another hundred immeasurable years looking into those eyes without even a shadow of a complaint.

Even sick and tired and worn, you match me as I'd want to be matched. You make me happy as I'd want to be happy. You love me as I could only dream of being loved.

I will repay this back in kindness. I will match you as you need to be matched. I will make you happy as you want to be happy. And I will love you, adore you, admire you and respect you as you could only dream of being loved, adored, admired and respected.

My wedding vows remain true. (I know you remember those.)

I have to end this here. You're about to wake up and catch me writing, darling. Read slowly.

Love, your forever friend, competitor, teammate and husband.

P.S. We're both winners. Always.

Tears stream down my cheeks, and when I look up, I realize the shower is off and Connor stands in the doorway, a towel around his waist. He watches me as I'm knelt by the suitcase, reading his love letter and rendered speechless.

I've never read anything more soulful, meant just for me.

He tilts his head, his lips lifting a fraction. "Here's to us," he says, love in his eyes, "may we conquer every adversary together."

Here's to us.

I know our love will win in the end.

BONUS TEXT MESSAGE THREAD

CONNOR: Dracula, Bigfoot, the Grinch

ROSE: All the things you don't believe in.

CONNOR: You're evading.

ROSE: I'm thinking, Richard.

CONNOR: Is this one that difficult for you?

ROSE: Please. You wish you could stump me.

ROSE: You should have a talk with the devil. Maybe he'll let you swap your ego for patience this time.

CONNOR: I don't need to barter with a fictional creature for intelligence.

ROSE: Your ego isn't equivalent to brilliance.

CONNOR: I believe I'm brilliant. Is that not an ego?

ROSE: I hate you.

ROSE: and I need you to clarify whether this is Dracula from the novel.

CONNOR: Would this make a difference?

ROSE: Yes, sunlight doesn't kill the novel version of Dracula.

CONNOR: Do you know where that first originated? Vampires dying by sunlight?

ROSE: The silent film Nosferatu. Which is based on the novel Dracula by Bram Stoker.

CONNOR: Oui bien.

ROSE: Anything else you'd like to quiz me on?

CONNOR: Later. With your legs spread.

CONNOR: You need to finish the game first. Dracula here is from the film version. He can die by the sun.

ROSE: Fuck. Kill. Marry.

CONNOR: You'd marry the Grinch? Why?

ROSE: I'm not creeping in the fucking woods with bigfoot or shut away in the dark with Dracula. I'd rather marry a furry green holiday hater who ends up growing his heart rather than shrinking it.

CONNOR: Interesting.

ROSE: Tooth Fairy, Santa Claus, Mrs. Claus

ROSE: Still all things you refuse to believe in.

CONNOR: Refusal might not be the right word, darling.

ROSE: Regardless of the wordage, you have to play the game.

CONNOR: Feeling festive?

ROSE: Who's evading now?

CONNOR: Kill. Fuck. Marry.

ROSE: What's wrong with the Tooth Fairy?

CONNOR: It has wings. It's an insect.

ROSE: It's a fictional creature, Richard.

CONNOR: It collects human teeth.

ROSE: So you'd rather fuck a jolly bearded man who rides on a sleigh and delivers presents to children once a year?

CONNOR: Delusional. But fuckable.

CONNOR: And let's be clear, I'd rather fuck you.

Daisy Calloway Moves Out of Villanova

Daisy Calloway

There are spectacular, monumental moments in one's life. Core memories that are etched deeper than ink in a diary, seeded into the depths of your soul.

Moving away from home is one of those big milestones that I'm told I'll never forget, but it's hard to picture me remembering such a lonesome affair. There's no *Goodbye, Daisy* banner, no confetti tossed from the second-floor banister, and definitely no cupcakes.

That's how I know it's not a party. No cake or cupcakes in sight.

Though I don't expect my mom to whip up an elaborate spread to wish me off from my childhood home. In fact, a part of me believes she might set up a blockade at the door. Rose even said that I should lay little seeds to prepare our mother for my eventual departure from the nest.

Maybe I should have done that. It would've been the smarter decision, and of course it would be, Rose concocted it.

Instead, I'm springing this news on my mom over breakfast parfaits on our courtyard patio. I imagine I'm in a boxing ring and putting on my gloves, ready for the knock-out-drag-out fight that's about to go down.

I remember three very important things:

I'm eighteen.

I graduated from high school.

It's time to leave home.

My brain already coordinates her verbal retort. *You graduated high school yesterday, Daisy. Why the rush?*

My stomach unsettles, and I stir my spoon in the yogurt, no appetite for even a bite. Exhaustion tugs at my shoulders, but I battle the fatigue—my eyes burn. Temples throb. I imagine myself just lying in a patch of soft grass and never waking up.

It sounds nice.

It shouldn't sound nice. I know that, but sleeping isn't that easy these days. And I wish it were as simple as it used to be.

"Mom," I say so softly I barely hear my own voice.

She's busying herself by reading something on her phone, her parfait already halfway eaten.

I clear my throat, and before I can even speak again, my mom's head swings up, eyes lasered on me like I just burped in a silent auditorium. "Daisy, that's a very grotesque sound."

"Sorry," I apologize, even though I don't really mean it. "I have to tell you something. And before you say *no*, just know that this thing I have to tell you—it's something that I'm really, *really* looking forward to. More than . . . anything, ever."

She sets her phone on the table, giving me all of her attention. "Is this about Fashion Week?"

I shake my head, not letting that event enter my brain. My knees bounce, and I restrain myself from standing up from the table to pace. "No, it's about my living situation. I'm eighteen now, and since high school is over, I'm ready to move out." My pulse speeds with my words. "I found this great apartment in the city, and I signed the lease. I can move in today." Her face pinches, and I add some facts that I think she'll like. "I'll be closer to casting calls, so I thought it'd be a win-win."

My mom has been with me since the start of my modeling career, and in all that time we've spent together, I still can't figure out *exactly* what she's thinking.

But I wait for the condemnation. The yelling. The screaming. The *why did you make this choice without my involvement?* retort. The emotional bits that'll unsteady me.

Instead, she asks plainly, "On your own?"

"I thought about living with Rose," I say. "But she's living with Lily and Lo and—" *I don't want to bother them.* I can barely get the rest out before my mom waves her hand like she's swatting my words away.

I've said the wrong things.

My stomach sours. "Mom," I say in desperation. "*Please.* I want this more than you can even know. It's this exciting new chapter in my life, and what better way to start it than on my own?"

She ponders this for a second, and maybe she's realizing that I'm not telling her I'm leaving.

I'm still asking for her permission.

She picks up her glass of freshly squeezed orange juice. "Do you need me to call the movers?"

Her question blows me back for a second. It was that easy? No boxing gloves needed. She sees my shock, and she tilts her head. "I see you want this," she says. "And you said it yourself, you've graduated. You're ready."

Warmth washes over me, a kind of relief that I haven't felt in months. I want to say *thank you* a million times over, but I'm still stupefied in my chair. Did this all just happen? Am I really moving out?

Hope flickers inside me, a dimmed light reigniting.

She's picking up her phone. "The movers?" she asks me again.

"Uh, no." I shake my head. "No. No need. I'm not bringing much. I figured I could come back if I forget anything."

She smiles, knowing I won't be a total stranger. It's not like I'm moving to a different state.

Just further into the city.

In an apartment in Philadelphia.

Two floors below Ryke Meadows.

He'll be close.

He'll be right there.

I don't tell my mom this little fact, which also happens to be one of the biggest reasons I'm looking forward to this move. I don't think she'll be pleased about Ryke being that close, but I'm soaking in the fact that this is easy. Telling her.

Moving out.

Relief keeps swelling and overwhelming me.

After breakfast, I leave the patio and head upstairs. I grab a duffel full of clothes from my bed. Already packed. *Already ready.*

I walk quietly in the empty hall. I'm the last of the Calloway sisters to live in the Villanova mansion. The last one to go. I don't call Poppy, Rose or Lily to help me. I don't think I need it, and I wouldn't want to trouble anyone anyway.

At the foyer of my childhood home, I look around.

No fanfare. No noise.

It's just silence.

I wonder if I'll remember this in ten, twenty years. Or if new memories will take root.

If they do and this one is written over like an old tape, I just hope the new memories are far less lonely.

"Goodbye," I whisper, my voice hollow and quiet to my ears. It's the last thing I say before I leave.

KEEP READING FOR AN
EXCERPT FROM THE NEXT NOVEL
IN THE ADDICTED SERIES

Hothouse Flower

Ryke Meadows

I run. Not away from anything. I have a fucking destination: the end of a long suburban street lined with four colonial houses and acres of dewy grass. It's as secluded as it can be. Six in the morning. The sky is barely light enough to see my feet pound the asphalt.

I fucking love early mornings.

I love watching the sun rise more than watching it set.

I keep running. My breathing steadies in a trained pattern. Thanks to a collegiate track scholarship, and thanks to climbing rocks—a sport that I sincerely fucking crave—I don't have to *think* about inhaling and exhaling. I just *do*. I just focus on the end of the street, and I go after it. I don't fucking slow down. I don't stop. I see what I have to do, and I fucking make it happen.

I hear my brother's shoes hit the cement behind me, his legs pumping as quickly as mine. He tries to keep up with my pace. He's not running towards shit. My brother—he's always running away. I listen to the heaviness of his soles, and I want to fucking grab his wrist and pull him ahead of me. I want him to be unburdened and light, to feel that runner's high.

But he's weighed down by too much to reach anything good. I don't slow to let him catch me. I want him to push himself as far as he can go. I know he can get here.

He just has to fucking try.

One minute later, we reach the end of the street that we were shooting for, next to an oak tree. Lo breathes heavily, not in exhaustion, more like anger. His nose flares, and his cheekbones cut brutally sharp. I remember meeting him for the very first time.

It was about three years ago.

And he looked at me with those same pissed-off amber-colored eyes, and that same *I fucking hate the world* expression. He was twenty-one back then. Our relationship balances somewhere between rocky and stable, but it was never meant to be perfect.

"You can't go easy on me just once?" Lo asks, pushing the longer strands of his light brown hair off his forehead. The sides are trimmed short.

"If I slowed down, we would have been *walking*."

Lo rolls his eyes and scowls. He's been in a bad place for a few months, and this run was supposed to release some of the tension. But it's not helping.

I see the tightness in his chest, the way he can still barely fucking breathe.

He squats and rubs his eyes.

"What do you need?" I ask him seriously.

"A fucking glass of whiskey. One ice cube. Think you can do that for me, big *bro*?"

I glare. I hate the way he calls me *bro*. It's with fucking scorn. I can count on my hand the number of times he's called me "brother" with affection or admiration. But he usually acts like I don't deserve the title yet.

Maybe I don't.

I knew about Loren Hale for practically all my life, and I didn't even say *hi*. I think back often to when I was fifteen, sixteen, seventeen and my father asked every fucking week: "Do you want to meet your brother?"

I rejected the offer every single time.

When I was in college, I came to terms with the fact that I

would never know him. I thought I was at peace. I stopped hating Loren Hale for just existing. I stopped listening to my mother condemn a kid that had no say in being born. I slowly stopped talking to my father, losing contact because I didn't need him.

The trust fund, I use. I figure it's payment for all the lies I had to keep for that fucking asshole.

One day. That's all it took to change my idealistic, head-in-the-fucking-sand life. Outside at a college Halloween party, a fight started. I watched four guys on the track team—the one *I* was the captain of at Penn—go up against a lean-built guy. I recognized him from all those photos my father showed me.

He wasn't how I'd imagined. He wasn't surrounded by frat guys, crushing beers over their heads.

He was alone.

His girlfriend came into the fight later, to defend him, but it was too late. She missed the part where my teammate accused him of drinking expensive booze in a locked cabinet. She missed the part where Lo egged him on, just so the guy would swing.

He hit my brother. I stood and watched Lo get decked in the face.

It was in that fucking moment that I realized how wrong I had been. I didn't see a prick with a hundred friends and cash up to his chin. Not a jock, not an athlete like me. I saw a guy *wanting* to be punched, asking to feel that pain. I saw someone so fucking hurt and broken and sick.

Four against one.

All that time, I wanted to live the life he had. I hated playing the bastard outcast when I was really the legitimate son. But if our roles were reversed, if I had lived with my alcoholic father, I would have been there.

That would have been me: tormented, drunk, weak and alone.

My father was trying to tell me that Lo wasn't the popular kid I'd dreamed up. He was just as much of an outsider as I was. The difference: I had the strength to defend myself. I wasn't beaten down by our father like Lo had been. I didn't even contemplate the fucking horror of living with Jonathan twenty-four-seven, hearing the *why are you such a pussy?* comment every day. I had blinders on. I could only see what was wrong with *me*. I couldn't fathom Loren getting a shitty bargain too.

That night at the Halloween party, I left the false peace I'd built for myself. It wasn't a gut reaction. I stood there and watched Lo get beat on before I made a decision to intervene. And once I fucking made it, I never turned back.

"You want a glass of whiskey?" I give him a look. "Why don't I just push you in front of a fucking freight train? It's about the same."

He stands up and lets out an agitated laugh. "Do you even know what this feels like?" He extends his arms, his eyes bloodshot. "I *feel* like I'm going out of my goddamn mind, Ryke. Tell me what I should do? Huh? Nothing takes this pain away, not running, not fucking the girl I love, not *anything*."

I haven't been where he is, not to this extent.

"You relapsed a few times," I say. "But you can get back to where you were."

He shakes his head.

"So what?" I narrow my eyes. "You're going to drink a beer? You're going to chug a bottle of whiskey? Then what? You'll ruin your relationship with Lily. You'll feel like *shit* in the morning. You'll wish you were fucking dead—"

"What do you think I'm wishing now?!" he shouts, his face reddening in pain. And my lungs constrict. "I hate myself for breaking my sobriety. I *hate* that I'm at this place in my life again."

"You were under a lot of scrutiny," I backpedal, realizing he doesn't need me to be a hardass, something I revert to on instinct. I push people too much sometimes.

"You're under the same scrutiny, and I didn't see you breaking your sobriety."

"It's different." I haven't had a drink in nine years. "The media was saying some pretty awful shit, Lo. You coped the first way you knew how. No one blames you. We just want to fucking help you." We're all public spectacles, under constant gaze of cameras, because of the Calloway girls, the daughters of a soda mogul.

By proximity to the Calloways, we've been roped into the spotlight. It's not fucking fun. I wear a baseball cap just to try to disguise myself, but thankfully cameramen have better things to do than film us this early in the morning.

But they'll be out trying to get a picture of us at noon.

"You don't believe them, do you?" Lo suddenly asks, his voice still edged.

"Who?" I ask.

"The news, all those reporters . . . you don't think our dad actually did those things to me?"

I try to hold back a cringe. Someone told the press that Jonathan physically abuses Lo. The rumors just kept escalating after that. I don't know if our dad could hit him . . . or molest him. I don't want to believe it, but there's a fucking sliver of doubt that says *maybe. Maybe it could have happened.*

"It's not fucking true!" Lo shouts at me.

"Okay, okay." I raise my hands to get him to calm down.

He's been like this since the accusations, pissed and angry and looking for a way to fix things. Booze was his solution unfortunately.

Our father filed a defamation lawsuit, but no matter the outcome of the court case, it won't change the way people look at both of them. Vilifying our father, pitying Loren. There's no going back.

"You just have to move fucking forward," I tell him. "Don't worry about what people think."

Loren inhales deeply and stares at the sky like he wants to murder a flock of birds. "You say shit, Ryke, like it's the easiest

482 · KRISTA RITCHIE and BECCA RITCHIE

thing in the world. Do you know how annoying that is?" He looks back down at me, his features all sharp, like a blade.

"I'll keep saying it then, just to irritate the fuck out of you." *What else are big brothers for?*

He sighs heavily.

I rub the back of his head playfully and then guide him towards his house. I drop my hand off his shoulder, and he stops in the middle of the road, his brows scrunching.

"About your trip to California . . ." He trails off. "I know I haven't asked about it in months. I've been too self-absorbed—"

"Don't worry about it." I motion with my head to the white colonial house. "Let's go make some breakfast for the girls."

"Wait," he says, holding out his hand. "I have to say this."

But I don't want to hear it. I've made up my mind already. I'm not going to California. Not when he's in a bad place with his recovery. I'm his sponsor. I have to be here.

"I need you to go," he says. I open my mouth and he cuts me off. "I can already hear your stupid fucking rebuttal. And I'm telling you to *go*. Climb your mountains. Do whatever you need to do. You've had this planned for a long time, and I'm not going to ruin it for you."

"I can always reschedule. Those mountains aren't fucking moving, Lo." I've wanted to free-solo climb three rock formations, back-to-back, in Yosemite since I turned eighteen. I've been working up to the challenge for years. I can wait a little longer.

"I will feel like *shit* if you don't go," he says. "And I'll drink. I can promise you that."

I glare.

"I don't need you," he says with malice. "I don't fucking need *you* to hold my hand. I need you to be goddamn selfish like me for once in your life so I don't feel like utter shit compared to you, alright?"

I internally cringe. I was selfish for so many fucking years. I didn't give a fuck about him. I don't want to be that guy again.

But I hear him begging me. I hear *please fucking go. I'm losing my mind.*

"Okay," I say on instinct. "I'll go."

His shoulders instantly relax, and he lets out another deep breath. He nods to himself. I wonder how long he's been carrying that weight on his chest.

I can't explain why I love him so much. Maybe because he's the only person who understands what it's like to be manipulated by Jonathan for his gain. Or maybe because I know deep down there's a soul that needs love more than anyone else, and I can't help but reciprocate to the fullest degree.

I put my arm around his shoulder again and say, "Maybe one day you'll be able to outrun me."

He lets out a dry, bitter laugh. "Maybe if I break both your legs."

I grin. "Would you even be fucking fast enough to do that?"

"Give me a lacrosse stick and we'll see."

"Not fucking happening, little brother."

I don't say it with scorn.

I never do. And I never will.

Krista **and Becca Ritchie** are *New York Times* and *USA Today* bestselling authors and identical twins—one a science nerd, the other a comic book geek—but with their shared passion for writing, they combined their mental powers as kids and have never stopped telling stories. They love superheroes, flawed characters and soul mate love.

CONNECT ONLINE

KBRitchie.com
KBMRitchie

Ready to find
your next great read?

Let us help.

Visit prh.com/nextread

Penguin
Random
House